THE
UnDelightened

Bentz Deyo

FOR UPDATES ON BOOK TWO AND THE REST OF THE
UNDELIGHTENED SERIES, CHECK THE AUTHOR'S
WEBSITE AT WWW.BENTZDEYO.COM

THE UNDELIGHTENED

BENTZ DEYO

THIRD FLOOR PUBLISHING, LLC

Third Floor Publishing, LLC
121 Hawkins Place, #120, Boonton, NJ 07005
First paperback edition: February 2014

Deyo, Bentz
The Undelightened: a novel / by Bentz Deyo – 1st ed.
ISBN 978-0-9911551-0-1

Cover Design Lisa Marie Pompilio
Author Headshot by Elaine Zelker Photography

Visit the website at www.bentzdeyo.com

Printed in the United States of America

For Jennifer.
I couldn't quite get there until I had you.

"*Light thinks it travels faster than anything but it is wrong.* No *matter how fast light travels, it finds the darkness has always got there first, and is waiting for it.*"

—T. Pratchett

CHAPTER 1

So what are you gonna do to her?" the young man with the blue eyes asked, looking across the center console of the Range Rover into the black eyes of his brother.

"That's exactly the point, Leam," the black-eyed brother laughed, a shrill, almost mechanical laugh, unbecoming of a handsome seventeen year-old boy who had been sixteen last night. "I'm not sure what I'll do to her. That's the beauty of this whole thing. Once the ceremony is over, I'll know what my new self will be capable of, and then I'll just know what to do...like instinct."

The silver SUV exited off the highway and cruised its way down the one lane Boulevard toward the plush suburbs of Harbing, New Jersey. The rain was lightening a bit, and a thick hazy mist seemed to be emitting from the wet leaves of the many oaks that lined both sides of the street. The mist was so dense, the tree branches looked to be spewing clouds of smoke.

Sitting with his feet up near the dash, Leam stared at his brother, studying his face. Zach had the look of someone who had been waiting for something for a very long time and could now see it coming to fruition, like children staring at presents under the tree on Christmas morning, waiting for permission to start opening.

"And Mother is sure that when it's over," the younger brother continued—younger by a year less one day, "I will go on to accomplish tremendous acts of Darkness. In her exact words, she said, 'Zach, my child, you will have it all! You will be capable of the unspeakable. You will be more beautiful than you are now!'"

"Beautiful? Who's she kidding, you're disgusting."

"Really?" Zach said, sliding a cell phone out of his pocket with surprising speed.

"Yeah, you're a monster."

"Care to see how many girls text me a day, begging for me to come over? And it's not to study, Leam. They don't text me to study."

Leam shrugged, glancing over his shoulder. Muffled thumping sounded from the cargo area in the back.

"I'll give you a couple of their numbers," Zach went on. "Might do you some good to have a little fun instead of moping around all the time like some loser crybaby. You gotta snap out of this, Leam, I'm serious, you've been like a zombie for a year now. No one can stand to be around you for more than a second. And because you stink, too. Take a shower and cheer up."

Leam turned back around, peering out past the raindrops that were sliding down the front windshield. His eyes adjusted focus, catching a distorted glimpse of himself reflecting off the glass. It was the same woeful face that always looked back at him, whether it be off a windowpane, his bathroom mirror, or the giant stainless steel refrigerator in the kitchen. The reflection he had grown to expect never smiled.

The Range Rover turned right onto Whitewax Way, its headlights illuminating only a few feet ahead, unable to penetrate the thick fog that had lowered over the town. Zach didn't slow down, accustomed to the heavy fog at dusk near their home.

"But enough about you and your misery," Zach said, with a handsome, toothy grin. "Tonight is all about me. I've waited forever for the 18th of July and now it's here."

"You're under the assumption that the ceremony will automatically be a success." Leam looked down at his hands: identical, pure white, C-shaped markings on both, stretching from the inside tip of the index finger to the inside tip of the thumb. He looked over at his brother's unblemished hands gripping the steering wheel. "Nothing that should or shouldn't happen is ever a certainty."

"I don't really feel like figuring out what you're trying to say," Zach said, "but this is definitely happening, whether I get the fat-ass who did yours or not. You're just pissed that yours was a massive failure. Mine won't be. And then…"

He stopped speaking. Zach seemed to be struggling to suppress his emotions, and sure enough, a second later, he burst out laughing, shrill and mechanical. "And then tonight I become an immortal!" Zach shouted. "I'll finally be able to leave this nagging humanity behind me, ready to serve the Cause in any capacity."

"Watch the road," Leam said as the passenger-side tires scraped up against the curb. "Why do you get so excited? It's weird."

"God, you're jealous of me." Zach veered the SUV back onto the even pavement. "It's so pathetic."

"See, I think it's pathetic that you think you'll become immortal," Leam scoffed. "You don't have a clue, do you? Have you ever taken the time out of your stupid day to read any of the books in Father's library, or do you spend all that time trying to keep your hair looking so luscious and chasing around slutty Unknowing girls? He's got about twenty on delightenment alone up there—what it is and how to prepare and stuff. You ever taken the time to glance at any of them? Hmmm?"

"Read all the books you want." Zach's eyes were shiny with defiance. "Father's always gonna like me more."

"You won't be immortal," Leam said. "Gideon only *delays* your natural progression of aging. This is one of the many powers he has over you once you delighten. When you upset him, which you will, you age. You make a mistake—BOOM— he scorges you and you're a year older. You have no idea what you're in for because you haven't even—"

"I DO KNOW!" The back of Zach's neck was a bright shade of pink. "I know what's in store for me and I know how it works! And it's *my* turn now! Get that through your head.

Come midnight is *my* time! You had your chance last year. It's over, Leam, for you it's over, so come to grips with it, all right?"

"You think I care?" The Range Rover approached the end of Whitewax Way. "Do you think any of it matters to me?"

"I know it does," Zach answered, pulling into the only driveway that branched off the cul-de-sac, the SUV coming to a stop in front of a black, wrought iron gate. The gate was laced with intricate, metal ivy leaves, and the posts on each side of the gate were capped with dull, slightly-rusted silver statues. On the left post, a crow perched, with a drooping flower hanging from its beak; on the right post stood what looked like a cloaked monk, hood lowered, eyes hidden.

Zach inhaled a large breath and blew toward the crow. A few seconds passed and the weathered crow started gleaming with such intensity that its now freshly-polished silver was almost white. The crow's mouth opened and the flower fell from its beak. Its petals separated away from the stem and began to dance with the fog as if a swirly wind had arisen from the cobblestoned driveway. The bright petals made their way along the length of the gate, one of them brushing the cloaked monk, settling on its shoulder. The inanimate monk now sparked to life, also gleaming as brightly as the bird. The monk's stubby hands pulled the hood away from its face, revealing red eyes, like lasers, and they penetrated through the windshield, scanning both faces.

"Proceed," the monk whispered, then pulled his hood back over his eyes, causing the flower petal to blow off his shoulder. The gleaming petal was blown back toward the crow, along with the others, reforming into a flower. When it found its way back into the waiting crow's beak, the flower began to lose its luster, as did the monk. In the blink of an eye, the two gateposts were again muted, rusty and still.

"Say what you want, Leam, but we all know it crushed you," Zach said, as the gate began to creak open. "Regardless, you should know that Mother believes you'll never delighten, *if* you even get another chance. She said the cursed spark inside you will never fully extinguish."

"I don't take stock in anything your mother says."

"She's your mother, too."

"Not by blood," Leam said.

"Oh, that's right, your mother's dead," Zach sneered, his foot back on the gas.

Leam said nothing as the Range Rover crept up the cobbled driveway that snaked its way toward Whitewax Manor. Protected by tall stone walls that surrounded the estate, the Manor resembled something that might be described as half country club half medieval castle. But from this distance the fog was masking most of the vast structure—only the very tip of the tallest chimney was cleanly visible.

Zach parked up front and cut the engine, a wild expression on his face. He took his hands off the wheel, running his fingers through brown hair that fell almost to his shoulders. "You want to bring the Unknowing through the back for me? I need a shower. And I need to prepare."

"She was your idea. Do it yourself."

"Just do it, I'll owe you one."

Zach flashed Leam his striking grin, hopped out of the car with a casual ease, and walked toward the front door like a proud naked man strutting across a nude beach, passing the plush trees and tall statues that lined the Manor's approach. Reaching the threshold, he pressed the palm of his hand against the center of the huge, iron door, which creaked open upon contact.

Squinting through the fog, Leam watched Zach disappear as the door closed behind him. It was a big night for his brother. Life changing. Leam thought back to the night of his own seventeenth birthday, the night he had failed *his* delightenment. Something his father had said to the fat man who'd overseen the ceremony had stuck in Leam's mind. Something his father had said like it was a matter of life and death.

"Are you not aware of what he qualifies to be? That he has the potential to become..."

And that was all Leam had heard. He thought about that snippet of conversation often, though, and had spent countless hours in the second-floor library searching for anything his father could have been alluding to. Over a period of months, he had immersed himself in every pertinent volume, but had found only one reference—one person of Darkness—that could be as important as the tone his father's voice had suggested. Leam dismissed it, though; there was no way he could be the one mentioned in that book. Not a chance. He was way too ordinary. Plus, he was a failure. He couldn't even delighten.

It nagged him, though, what his father had said to the fat man, and a couple of months later he asked his dad about it. The reply was gruff, and upsetting.

"Only the questions of the delightened get answered. Out of the thousands of Dark families around the world, the Holts have remained one of the most distinguished and honorable. We have had, and will continue to have, a strong influence over the war against the Light. We live to serve Gideon, and do anything he asks of us, play any role he chooses for us, so that we may carry out his orders to aid in the fulfillment of the Cause.

"But you, Leam, you aren't one of us anymore. You will not be taught our secrets. You will never be welcomed into Darkness Headquarters. As of now, you are not meant to know our ways. Most likely you will never know. But do know this, Leam. You have stained our honor."

That was the last thing the man had said to him, ten months ago, and it was this conversation that shoved Leam into the deep hole of depression he had been trapped in since that day; and to make things worse, he had no friends who could lower a rope and try to pull him out. At school, every so often, some of the normal, non-magical kids would invite him to join their lunch table or to go get stoned behind the janitor's van, but Leam always declined. If any of them were to find out about him and his family, it meant their death. He had been taught at a young age that regular humans were dirty and weak, and—like the caged mice in old man Scotterson's AP Biology class—they deserved no respite from the experimentation that Darkness administered on them in its quest to rid them of the Light's protection. Put simply, Unknowings couldn't know. It had always been that way. But the Unks at school that made an effort with Leam didn't really seem too terrible.

Another thump, accompanied this time by frightened whimpering, pulled Leam's thoughts away from his sad, sorry little life. He got out and walked to the back of the Range Rover. With a heavy sigh he opened the hatch, and a stench of sweat and urine wafted out at him.

The unlucky woman Zach had grabbed behind a supermarket a few towns over was still tied up, but had somehow bitten through the strip of duct tape covering her mouth. She looked almost comical with two giant, silver lips. Her eyes were watering and bleary; she reminded Leam of a frightened house cat. Her purse was on its side in the corner, its content sprawled out around her feet.

"Please!" the woman pleaded. "Please let me go! I have children, two children! My twin boys! Please!"

"It's not about that." Leam noticed his tone was eerily flat, which was probably freaking out the lady even more.

"Please let me go, please, I beg you! I didn't hear anything, I don't know anything! Digeon or whoever...delightenment...I didn't hear it. I won't say a word, I promise, you can just let me go!"

Leam stared at the pitiful woman. A lump rose in his throat that he had difficulty swallowing back down. He closed his eyes, opened them, and then struck the woman's head with the heel of his right hand, knocking her out cold. He lifted her out, hoisting her onto his upper back and started walking through the fog around the mansion toward the back of the estate.

"It's best this way," he said to the unconscious woman draped over his shoulder.

Other than his words, the only sound was the crunching of wet gravel beneath his sneakers.

"You don't want to be conscious any longer than you have to be. Not for what's in store for you tonight."

CHAPTER 2

Eloa parked next to her father's white pickup at the top of the steep driveway, grabbing her dance shoes as she got out of her car, and headed to the narrow pathway that twisted through the hedges and heavy brush all the way to the back door.

Excited to see her dad's truck home, she started up the path. It was well after 10 P.M.—she had stayed several hours after class to work one-on-one with her instructor, Miss Chetwidth—but she doubted her dad would care that it was so late, or even notice. He had been so busy with work things lately that they had spent next to no time together since her graduation from high school a couple months ago. Still, it'd be nice to give him a hug and say hi. She pictured him and couldn't keep a smile off her face. He looked just like one of those corny dudes with long, flowing blond hair on the cover of cheesy, paperback romance novels.

She pulled out her hair elastic with a moan, shaking her long black hair out of a ponytail. It had been stretched back for so long it ached. She started around the corner of the one-story ranch, her finger absently rubbing the dove-shaped birthmark on the back of her neck. It barely showed, even when her hair was up for dance class, because she was so pale, although her dad always said that a soft light radiating inside of her gave her skin a glow.

Her iPhone buzzed against her hip and she pulled it from her bag. A text from Bridgette, a friend she had met at dance class a few years back:

Party! RIGHT NOW! My house! Cute boys everywhere! Get over here now!

Eloa's cheeks flushed. That sounded like it could be fun—once all the awkward introductions to the Harbing High guys were out of the way, of course—but the pull to see her dad was a bit stronger than the allure of a party. Besides, unlike all those lucky Unknowing teenagers getting ready to drink and flirt with each other, school was not yet over for Eloa. Tonight she had to study and prepare for her upcoming purification: the ceremony that would endow her with magical abilities—if she passed—which would be amazing. But a part of her longed to switch lives with Bridgette or any of the other girls from class. What it would be like to have no idea about the existence of Darkness and Light, and live an ignorant, blissful, normal life. She sighed, coming up on the back door.

After a quick text back to Bridgette—*Can't–Next time for sure...let me know if ur precious Flower Boy shows up*—she looked up and froze midstep. The screen door was popped out askew, the top hinge busted, and fresh blood was smeared on the door frame. She immediately backed into a thin break in the hedges, pulled up her Favorites, and tapped Dad.

"Pick up, Dad, pick up," she whispered, her hand shaking, struggling to keep the phone pressed tightly to her ear. Five rings. Voice mail.

She tried again, listening for sounds of approaching footsteps or chainsaws cranking to life.

"C'mon, Dad, c'mon, c'mon, answer the phone!" Five rings. Voice mail.

Crap. Okay. What were her options? She had nobody else to call—no one of the Light lived anywhere near here, not that she knew of. In fact, other than her father the only person of magic she'd ever met was Sebastian, and why would a man so skilled in magic need a cell phone? She only had one option:

to go in. But not through the screen door into the living room, that'd be too reckless. A roundabout route would be safer and give her a chance to find her nerve. There'd be no avoiding the living room altogether, though—not if she was to adhere to her father's protocol for in-house emergencies.

She squeezed through the hedges, shimmying alongside the house to the nearest window. She slid it up and hoisted herself into her dad's office, her leg scraping against a fire poker that had for some reason been wedged in the window sill, tearing a run in her tights. She gritted her teeth and yanked out the poker.

The room was trashed, papers strewn on the desk and all over the floor, overturned chairs, her father's peace lily lying sadly on its side. Even his magnificent, white-marble bust of a stallion was broken, cracked in two.

Behind the shattered closet door, Eloa could see the safe where her dad stored all sorts of charts, graphs and faded leather journals. She had never seen it open, and the fact that it was empty spiked her anxiety with sharp jagged peaks—her dad was obsessed with keeping it locked with defensive enchantments. So if *he* hadn't emptied the safe, someone with formidable magical powers had. She placed her hand over her heart, struggling to push down the terrible thoughts and gruesome images popping up in her head.

She crossed to the door and pushed it open, tiptoeing down a hallway that stretched to the living room. It was in there that her dad had installed a threat indicator up in the corner of the ceiling above the piano: a simple device with a small bulb that—if all was safe—flashed with white light every five seconds. A blink of blue light, however, if followed directly by a white, meant that she was to stay home and wait for his word. Two winks of blue in a row, and she was to arm herself with the gun duck taped underneath the coffee table and hide behind the basement refrigerator. And if she saw three consecutive blue flashes: haul ass to her dad's bedroom bathroom and hide in the secret compartment beneath the tub.

With silent breaths she kept moving, clutching the fire poker with an iron grip. If she could manage it, anyone without a wild mane of blond hair who jumped out at her was getting stabbed in the face. Reaching the hallway's end, she slowed a step before the living room, and with trembling breath, turned the corner.

At first look, it appeared there had been no struggle at all until her feet sunk an inch into wet carpet—warm, red liquid bubbling up between her toes—and her eyes found a blood-drenched trail extending all the way to the broken screen door. And there was something odd stuck in the trail...what was that? Eloa took a few weak-kneed steps and bent down, tossing the fire poker aside. She peeled whatever it was off the carpet with her right hand, then smacked her left over her mouth to silence a scream.

A lock of long blond hair, caked in blood, lay shivering atop her fingers.

"No..."

She yanked her head to the side, just catching the flash of white above the piano before it dimmed cold.

Eyes trained on the tiny bulb, it flashed again, five seconds later.

BLUE.

With sweaty palms and eyes unwavering, she waited for the next flash.

BLUE.

Hands shaking, she dropped the lock of hair, ready to either grab the gun under the coffee table or dart to the bathtub. The bulb blinked once more.

RED.

"Oh God no..."

Red. Red. How could she have forgotten red? Fear crippled her body as her father's measured voice sounded in her head.

"And blue, blue, red, Lo, if you ever see blue, blue, red...get out of the house and drive away as fast as you can."

CHAPTER 3

I t was an hour shy of midnight.

Leam was walking the short distance down the candlelit hallway from his bedroom on the fourth floor of the Holt Manor to the giant circular staircase that wound its way down the core of the mansion, spiraling to the corridor on the first floor that led to the front door. He stopped in front of an old mirror that was bookended by two paintings: one of Benjamin Franklin hanging from a rope above a pit of fire, the other a portrait of Leam's great-grandparents. The painting was of his father's grandparents, of course. There were no paintings or pictures or statues of anyone from his birth mother's family on the premises. Leam didn't even know what his mom had looked like—he knew only her name. Aggie.

He stared into the mirror and despondence peeked back at him. His hair was brown and thick, above grayish-blue eyes. He had a good nose, and like most good noses, there wasn't really a way to describe it. His face was handsome and strong, the exact opposite of how he felt.

He took a deep breath, hands a jitter. *Why am I nervous? Because of the torture sure to befall the woman tied up in the pantry? Is it about Zach's delightenment? The pain he should be expecting?*

you to disobey any order he may give you. Never, ever, betray him or the Cause. His punishment will come swiftly, be fierce, and the safety of your family will be in jeopardy, as well."

Bram, standing near the door, glanced at the empty fireplace across the room, and then looked into the torturous flames of its twin, picking at the handle of his knife. Leam wondered if his dad was nervous for him.

"Finally," the fat man went on, "as I'm sure you are well aware, if the delightenment is a success, you will no longer be completely human. A good thing, as it separates you from the Unknowings. There will be, for lack of a better word, magic inside of you. Beautiful, Dark magic coursing through your veins. The most immediate difference regarding your new self is that you will cease to age. Your body will remain as it is right now, for as long as you please Gideon and stay in his good graces. But if and when you err, that is to say, do something that displeases him, you will be scorged, which believe me, is a most…" the fat man shivered, wiping pellets of sweat off his forehead, "…a most excruciating experience, if I do say so myself."

Bram grunted in agreement. Leam remained outwardly calm, but his insides were churning and his thoughts were moving a million miles a minute. This was all very real now.

"And directly after being scorged, you will have physically aged one full year, just like that…as quickly as you can say 'Nippity-tippity.' You will then remain—" he bent his fat fingers into air quotes, "—eighteen years old until your next misstep, and so on and so on. Yes?"

Leam nodded.

"Good." The fat man took off his glasses and stuffed them back into his pocket. "Good, good. Well, with the preliminaries out of the way, let's begin, shall we?"

Leam caught his father's eye. Bram gave him the smallest of winks, then shifted his weight and stared into the depths of the fire. The clock in the corner began to chime.

The fat man leaned forward in his chair and spoke one final word.

"Drink."

CHAPTER 4

"ZACH!"

Leam snapped out of the memory, and was glad to do so. What happened after that drink would be with him for the rest of his life and he didn't need to relive it right now.

"ZACH!" the foulest woman in the world screeched again, her nasal voice carrying upward three stories from the base of the main staircase that corkscrewed through the center of the Manor. "IT'S TIME!"

A door opened down the hallway opposite the staircase—the door just before the side steps that ascended to the natatorium on the top floor. Zach strode out of his bedroom in a white robe, his head high, passing the game room and art studio, his brown hair swaying across his shoulders with each step. He had the looks of a soccer star or boy-band singer that millions of teenage girls would swoon over as they taped up posters of his image inside their lockers and on their bedroom walls.

"You've never looked more like a woman than you do right now," Leam said as Zach sauntered up to him.

"Quiet, mutt," Zach growled. "Where's *yours*? Still hanging in your closet, white as the day you last wore it?"

"Yours could have a similar fate."

"You wish." Zach laughed. The smell of his Old Spice was strong beneath Leam's nose. "How's the Unknowing?"

"Unconscious. Lying on the floor in the pantry."

"Perfect." Zach clapped his hand on his brother's shoulder and began to spiral his way down the main staircase. Leam followed. They passed the third floor—with its dark hallway they were forbidden to ever walk down—and then the second, forty steps remaining.

"You nervous, Zach?"

"Nope. Got no reason to be."

"That's a bit naive," Leam said. "However it goes down tonight, though, you'll be changed forever."

Zach stopped a dozen or so winding steps from the polished wooden panels of the spacious first-floor corridor.

"Anything I should know? Anything you can tell me from your books?" he asked, his face that of a fresh-eyed soldier asking a grizzled veteran for advice before battle.

"You don't want any tips from me. My robe's still white, remember?"

Zach's eyebrows climbed. "You won't give me anything?"

"It's different for everybody," Leam said. "That's all anybody really knows."

Zach blinked a few times and descended the last few steps where his mother, Sara, waited for him, flustered.

"There you are, my child," the skinny woman gushed, her long, straight blond hair shimmering as she fidgeted with her son's robe, creasing a wrinkle or two out of the collar. "You look so handsome."

Zach nodded, grinning at his brother.

"And you look ready," she sighed.

"I am, Mother. I've waited for this a long time."

"I know you have, darling, I know you have. And so have your father and I. He especially, after the, uhh, *embarrassing* disappointment of last year."

Hand on the rail, Leam took the insult—the most recent of a thousand demeaning comments his stepmother had fired his way throughout his childhood and adolescence. He looked at the woman, his face blank, jaw clenched. Above a short red skirt, she sported a formfitting black sweater. Until recently, Leam had wondered why Sara wore sweaters year round, and his theory had been that her soul was so cold she needed to be ensconced in winter clothing, even during summer months like these. A month ago, though, he had escaped to the top floor in search of solace—Zach had grown keen to tossing smoke bombs into Leam's bedroom every ten minutes—and he had seen Sara naked, getting out of the pool. Small, black scars were speckled all over her upper body; a more likely reason she continually remained covered up. Passing her on the street, you might think she was quite beautiful, but if you scrutinized her for a few minutes you would find her oddly unappealing. She was very thin, very pale, with a constant sneer on her face that, in Leam's opinion, made her look like a sewer rat. And he knew she was even uglier on the inside, beneath her skin—a slightly blemished apple rotting from the inside out.

"Now Zach, you haven't eaten any dairy today, have you?" Sara asked, eyes wide and unblinking. "Milk, cheese, those fat-free Yoplaits you like…they can impair your mind as the delightening transformation takes place."

"No, Mother, only some bread."

"Wait, what?" Leam stared at his stepmother. "You never told me that."

"Oops," she said, adjusting her sweater. "A slip of the mind."

"Yeah, I bet."

"Leam, it's a family tradition, you're not family, so we'll leave it that."

"Whatever."

"Exactly, Leam, with you it's always whatever."

"Mother, I have prepared exactly as instructed," Zach chimed in. "I know how momentous tonight is for me *and* our family."

Sara smiled as broadly as her tiny lips would allow, her eyes still fixed on her stepson.

"Do you see, Leam? Do you see how a young man born into a distinguished family should act?"

"Oh, yes, Sara, golly, he's perfect."

"Tsk, tsk, tsk. Mocking your superiors as always, lurching around with poor posture, getting in everybody's way... Don't you get bored with it? Is it not tiring being such a pest? The day we're rid of you, oooooh that'll be a splendid one. But right now that's a dream that will have to wait.

"Zach," she said, putting her hands around the back of his head, "there's been a development and there's next to no time for you to hear it. Gideon has business with your father to attend to tonight, and thusly has informed us that he...*personally*...will be performing your delightenment."

Zach's eyes grew as big as the Range Rover's headlamps—a scared doe scampering across a freshly paved road. Even Leam felt his heart pounding, and he was nothing but a spectator.

"Do not fret, my child," Sara whispered, holding her son's eyes, "for this is a blessing, not a curse. An honor of the highest, you will be envied by all of Darkness who share your age, and you and Gideon will form a bond that can never be destroyed. Do you understand? Nod your head if you understand, this is no time for fear. I mean it, Zach. Good. Now compose yourself and await his arrival at the front door, he is never late. Leam, get back upstairs. I'm sure Gideon would be disgusted by the sight of you, and besides—"

The doorbell chimed, a long, soothing, majestic tone.

"It's time," Sara whispered, eyes smoldering. She took Zach's hand and strode to the front door, Leam lagging behind with hesitancy. His panicked mind thought to bolt up to his room and climb under the covers, and he would have, too, if it hadn't been Sara who suggested it.

So he went to the door out of stubborn spite, despite the danger. Leam had never met the leader of Darkness, and though there were tens of thousands of followers, it was possible Gideon had been told that Leam Holt had not successfully delightened. So how was Leam going to be treated? Would he be ignored? Would he be mocked to the point of tear-shedding? Berated until he crapped himself? Would Gideon walk right up to him and break his face in half? Whatever was to happen, though, was seconds away. With the sound of a sharp gust of wind, Bram appeared out of nowhere and, without a word to his family, opened the front door.

There stood a man of exceedingly slim proportions dressed completely in black, from his polished shoes to the collar of his trench coat. His face was terrifying, like a deranged clown, and seemed almost thinner than the rest of his body if that was possible. His eyes were cloudy, the pupils opaque, and his thin nose was perched above huge fish-balloon lips.

He entered the house and removed his bowler hat, unburdening a thicket of bright orange hair. Handing his hat and cane to Bram, he threw a lippy smile at Sara, who stumbled backward as if the wind had been knocked out of her.

"Hello," Gideon said, his voice faint and slippery, the accent unlike any Leam had ever heard, in real life or on TV. "Sara, you look good enough to eat. Bram. Young Zach."

"Welcome, sir," Bram said, shutting the door and hanging Gideon's hat and cane on an ornate silver coat hanger, each hanging post shaped like the beak of a large bird.

"And young Leam," Gideon continued, tilting his head to the side. "My, my, my. After hearing of your unfortunate night many moons ago, I've been...concerned."

Leam bowed his head. "It's an honor to meet you, sir. I've been worried you'd be angry with me. I'm not sure what went wrong."

Gideon glared at him, his upper lip pulling back from his teeth; Leam could do nothing but shudder despite his best efforts not to. He felt an iron lump of terror clunk into his chest, and Gideon's eyes bulged from their sockets as if pulled by some sort of fear-tasting magnetism.

"What can I get you, Gideon?" Sara breathed. "Anything? Is there anything you desire?"

Gideon looked away from Leam as if a binding-spell had been broken. "No. I will speak with Bram privately. Then the ceremony."

"We're honored it will be you," Bram said. "Terribly honored. I hope it isn't an inconvenience."

"I haven't performed a delightenment in over a hundred years. Curiously," he turned to the boys with a wispy finger pointed at Bram, "it was the delightenment of this man's father."

Bram shifted his weight, his thumb incessantly flicking the gilded-bronze handle of his sheathed knife.

"That's a weird coincidence," Zach stated.

"It is. And we must always be wary of coincidences," Gideon said, cracking his neck, once to the left, once to the right. "The two of you go to the sitting room and wait for me."

"Both of us?" Zach blurted out, unable to suppress the shock in his voice.

"Zach!" Bram shouted. "How dare you! Never question—"

"I'm sorry," Zach interrupted. "I'm sorry, sir, but...both of us?"

"Gideon, please," Sara said, her face twisted in horror. "He's nervous, he knows not what he says. He's still very young. He hasn't learned yet, he's still very young."

Gideon's expression was unreadable—a poker face fit for the gods. Sara looked ready to cry, Zach looked ready to pee his pants. The seconds of silence that ticked by seemed like minutes, until Gideon began to laugh. Leam noticed there was something off about it, like a shouted whisper.

"I want Leam there to see it," Gideon said. "So that means you do, too."

"Yes, sir," Zach said in a hurry.

"A rare occurrence for someone not yet bound to the Cause," Gideon said, eyes flicking to Leam, the rest of him perfectly still—a mummy wrapped in black toilet paper. "But before that, Zach, you will be taught not to cast doubt on anything I ever say again."

Zach was frozen stiff, like the giant statues just outside the front door. A horrifying smile stretched the skin of Gideon's face taut, highlighting the already pronounced bones of his face.

"Go," he said.

Leam and Zach turned in unison, walking past the enormous living room to their right, making their way toward the fire-lit sitting room where an empty stemless wineglass was perched on a dark wooden table, waiting to be filled.

CHAPTER 5

Skidding to a stop outside an old, small, gray-stucco house, Eloa jumped out of her car and slammed the door, darting over the damp lawn and up the porch steps. With hands clenched stiff like frozen claws, she banged on the weathered screen door, peering through the pane of glass on the front door behind it and listening hard for anyone coming up behind her.

A lamp flickered on upstairs, the top steps illuminated with a soft, orange glow. A pair of tattered slippers descended into view, and then the old man wearing them. He was fumbling with a set of eyeglasses that had gotten snagged to the sleeve of his brown bathrobe. He had a bend to him as he sloped down to the foyer, like he couldn't straighten up even if he stood still.

"Who's making that racket?"

"Larry, it's me! It's Eloa!"

"I'm coming... I'm coming."

A click of the lock, a creak of a door and a squeak of another, and Eloa was inside a small foyer cramped with hats and umbrellas on pegs, shoes and boots on either side of the cast iron radiator. Her heartbeat hadn't slowed a pulse on the frantic drive over from her house in Cliff Edge.

"Everything all right?" called a woman's voice from upstairs.

"I can't," Eloa whispered, eyes longingly on the staircase and thoughts on the guestroom she always slept in at the end of the hall on the second floor.

"Why not, dear?"

"I don't know, I just can't."

"Sweetheart, listen to me." Mary tucked a stray hair behind Eloa's ear before clasping her hands together on her lap. "You're well aware that Larry and I know very little about who you and your father are, and the strange...*circumstances* of your lives. The less we know the better. Your father has reminded me of that many times, which we accept because we love you. However, if something has happened, something terrible, dear...I want you to know I feel prepared enough to hear it."

"I'm just a little spooked, I promise. It's nothing, I promise. I thought I saw a giant bear on my way up to the porch... It's nothing, everything is fine, I promise."

"Sweetheart, what in the world has happened to your feet?"

Eloa felt a quick jolt in her chest. "Nothing, that's not it...it's from dancing...we did this artistic piece in class today with...paints...so the floor would have different colored footprints on it."

Before Mary had time to say anything, Larry came back in, groaning, favoring his left side, the straps of Eloa's giant, white duffel bag clenched in his hand.

"Larry, my God!" Eloa said, rushing forward. "Give me that!"

"Honestly, Larry, your back," Mary said, shuffling in her yellow slippers right behind Eloa. "Why throw money at Dr. Schnippner if you aren't going to do what he says?"

"I'm fine, I'm fine," Larry muttered, giving Eloa the bag. He hunched over next to the coat pegs, dabbing at his hairline with a handkerchief.

As Mary tended to her husband, Eloa rushed up the stairs. Hurrying across the hallway carpet, she heard Larry—"I'm not in a wheelchair, Mare Bear, I can carry a suitcase"—and a moment later—"Poor girl's scared to death"—then it was Mary's gentle voice—"I'm worried this time. She says she was running from a bear, of all things"—then Larry once more, as Eloa, lips quivering, pushed open the guestroom door—"There's no way to help, not if she won't let us."

Eloa closed the guestroom door, dropping her bag to the floor, and flung herself onto a fluffy white bed. Her chest felt like it was contracting into a knot of pain. The tears were pouring out, accompanied by a deep, occasional sob that cut sharp against her throat.

What should I do? What should I do? What do I do?

She buried her face in the top pillow to muffle her sobbing. Squeezing her eyes shut, though, only made things worse. All she could picture was that bloody lock of long, blond hair matted to the carpet in her living room.

What should I do? What should I—

The answer came to her in a beacon of clear, sharp light.

"The poem..." she breathed.

How could she have forgotten? When she was child, her father had taught her four verses to recite in times of great peril that would summon help to those of Light who needed it. Lifting her head off the pillow, she sat up, swinging her legs over the edge of the bed.

"Help or hinder, not the latter, I'm— Wait... Help or hinder, not the— No! Not it! Eloa, *think!*" But her concentration was weak; the bloody lock of hair was at the forefront of her mind. "Think! Help or hinder, not the latter, I'm—"

A dog barked right next to her and she fell off the bed.

"BARRY! You scared me!"

The beagle hopped down on the carpet, rubbing his wet nose in Eloa's face. For the moment she did nothing to stop him. It felt sort of nice. "Okay, okay. Scoot," she said, shooing him away. She tried to control her breathing—maybe it would help her remember—using techniques dancers apply to calm nerves before a recital. She couldn't get her body to stop shaking, nor could she loosen the knot in her chest.

Then, with the suddenness of the flash of red light above her dad's piano, she felt a pinch of hope. "Help or hinder, not the latter, I'm lost as to what to do. Genuinely urgent, is the… Genuinely urgent, is—"

The doorbell chimed.

Eloa sprung to her feet, standing Marine upright. The poem she couldn't seem to remember quite right, now completely forgotten. Unless it was a couple of drunk kids ding-dong-ditching as they stumbled home from Bridgette's party, Eloa knew that whoever rang that doorbell did so because she was inside. Was Darkness at the door? Had the psychos who trashed her house and snatched up her father come for *her* now?

She pressed her ear against the door, straining for sounds below. She could make out two muffled voices: one was Larry's, the other—smooth and relaxed—she didn't recognize. There was a break in the discussion, followed by the sound of deadened footsteps. Eloa opened the door a hair.

"Loey?" Larry called up. "Come back down, please. You have a visitor."

"Weapon," she whispered, her eyes tracing the room, landing on a paperweight atop the desk. *Good enough*, she thought, but stopped herself before she took a step. Would arming herself really matter? Seriously? What chance did an unpurified teenager have against men and women who wielded Dark, powerful magic and had no qualms about using it to maim or kill?

"You cannot hide from this," she mouthed to herself and was out the door, passing the half bathroom on her right and gliding down the stairs, Barry the beagle, yipping, close on her heels.

She froze when she reached the landing and instantly felt the fear that had been weighing her down thin. Larry, a goofy smile on his face, was conversing with the most intriguing man Eloa had ever laid eyes on. She saw that the palm of the man's hand faced her, fingers outstretched, but it fell to his side before she could give it a second thought. Though he wore a simple, gray T-shirt and blue jeans, he exuded an aura of…majesty, would be the only way she would describe it. He wasn't the most handsome man she had ever seen, but there was something fascinating about him, something curious. He was tall, well over six feet, and as he was speaking to Larry, only his lips moved, the rest of his body a polished marble statue. She couldn't look away. The dog growled; Barry hated all strangers.

"Eloa," the man said, a statement not a question.

Eloa mouthed an inaudible *yes*.

"I am a friend of your father. My name is Porlo."

Eloa smiled at his name. The man smiled back.

"It's a strange one, I know," he said. "I've always wondered where the name came from but my parents died when I was much younger, so...I'm afraid I'll never know."

Eloa blinked a few times before finding her voice. "It's a lovely name, and no stranger than my own."

"Kind of you to lie," Porlo said. His eyes flicked to Barry, who stopped growling and sat on his haunches. The sound of porcelain cups tinkling together could be heard coming from the kitchen.

"And if you wouldn't mind," the man said to her, "I'd like to talk with you for a few minutes? Larry, would it be possible for your granddaughter to speak with me out on your front porch? It won't take long."

"Oh, yes, that would be fine." Larry's eyes looked a little sleepy, and Eloa felt bad for having disturbed his night. "That would be fine, right, Loey?"

She nodded and the man named Porlo smiled at her.

"How hospitable. Thank you," Porlo said. "I know it's late but this cannot wait for morning."

"Sure. Sure," Larry said, wincing as he made a move toward the kitchen.

"Your back is bothering you," Porlo said, another statement.

"How'd you know?"

"I used to work for my older brother, Mathias. He's a chiropractor." Porlo threw a quick wink at Eloa, his hand on the center of Larry's back. "That should do it."

Làrry took a slow step forward, then smiled as he stood up straight and tall. "Incredible...absolutely incredible. Not an ounce of pain! How can I—?"

"All I ask is a few moments of privacy with your grand-daughter," Porlo said.

Larry nodded and headed for the kitchen, a fresh bounce in his step.

Porlo held the weathered screen door open. Eloa stepped outside and sat down on one of the two wicker chairs at the far end of the porch. Porlo closed the door and took the empty seat, pulling a smoking pipe from one of the pouches of his carrying bag.

"Do you mind?" he asked.

"No."

Without lighting it, he took a deep pull, exhaling a cloud of bluish-white smoke that puffed away from the house, dispersing out into the night. The scentless air now smelled of fresh apples. Porlo took another drag, closing his eyes as the smoke bellowed from his nostrils. Eloa watched him—a moment later looking away, nervous he might catch her staring. She looked past the front yard, across Stoneladen Lane to the heavy woodlands beyond it. The fog had all but disappeared. Out of the corner of her eye, she saw him raise his palm toward her, fingers separated like before. Her worry and fear resurfaced.

"You're here about my dad, right?"

"I am." Porlo lowered his hand.

"How did you know to find me here?"

"I know a lot about you."

"And how is that?"

"I'm a friend of your father…as I said. We've worked together, many times. Before and after you were born. You'd be surprised how much—"

"Please, okay!" Eloa interrupted. "Tell me what's happened to him. I'm losing it, I really am."

"He's fine."

"*He's fine?* How can that be? His hair, I found it, it was soaked in blood. Blood-soaked! He's my dad but I'm not a child. Tell me what's really going on!"

"I am. He's fine, Eloa. I'd bet my life on it."

"So you'd bet your life on it... I don't even know you! You didn't see the blood! It was a horror movie!"

"A moment before I was here, Eloa, I was there. The blood's fake. Like in the movies...as you said."

Eloa shot him a look. "That blood was real. I help out at the vet twice a week. I've aced every practical biology exam I've ever taken. I know it when I see it."

"Of course it was real, but the blood isn't his."

"Whose was it?" she asked incredulously, searching for cracks in the very authentic expression on his face. As she searched, the skin—the skin on his face—began to bubble. Eloa's legs went numb. She inched closer to see thick drops of blood seeping out of the pores, out of his eyes, out of his nose, his ears. "Porlo! Your face!"

"My face?" Porlo said. It was like someone had dumped a vat of steaming marinara sauce all over him, all over his skin, clothes, everywhere.

"YOUR FACE!"

"Relax." Porlo grinned. "I'm illustrating a point. Don't forget what a powerful man of Light Jace is. Decades ago I saw him take out four of Darkness with brute force alone, sans any magic. You can imagine what he's capable of doing *with* magic. At your house, the rooms that were ransacked, the blood...he created it, and he did so for a reason. I've worked alongside him many times, I know the man's style. I know his moves."

"Done for a reason? What's the reason?"

"*That* I don't know."

"Will you stop it with the blood already!" Eloa cried, turning away. "It's dripping in your mouth, it's making me sick!"

"It's gone," Porlo said. Eloa turned back to see the man as he was a minute ago. "A bit tactless on my part, I apologize," he added with a grin.

"But why wouldn't he tell me first," Eloa said, a break in her voice. "My father...before he destroyed the house. That's what makes no sense."

"Again, I'm sure he had his reasons. Between us—and I mean that, all right?—he was working on something big.

Something involving Gideon's specific plans. You've noticed how busy he's been. My guess is that they probably caught wind of it so Jace needs to lie low, and he had to make it look like he didn't just disappear."

Eloa was staring out across the lawn.

"What is it?" Porlo asked.

"You know I think you might be right. Mary and Larry said that he told them I would be coming to stay here for a while. He told them that weeks ago."

"And I'm sure he had good reason to. But I know if he could've told you, he would have, so don't be upset about that. He loves you. His eyes spark like firewood when he speaks of you."

At this, Eloa hid her face from Porlo. She focused on her breathing.

"Whatever he's been working on," she said after a minute, "whatever that *something big* is…he took it with him. The safe was emptied."

"I can't tell you anything else, Eloa. If he didn't confide in you, it's not my place to say."

"But I don't know *anything!* The house was trashed and the alarm was triggered! That's it, that's all I know!"

"Mine went off, too," Porlo said, digging around for something in his carrying bag. "Your father installed an alarm at my place three days after you were born. If it was ever to go off, I was to bring you—" he pulled out a small red box, "—this."

He handed it to her. As she took hold of the package, their fingers touched.

"You are to open this tonight, but only once you are back in your bedroom with the door closed. Is that understood?"

"Yes," she whispered.

"You say you know nothing…that you've been left in the dark. Perhaps the contents of that box will shed some light."

She nodded. Porlo stood up and threw the strap of his bag over his shoulder.

"Porlo?"

"Yes?"

"You truly believe my dad's okay?"

"Jace is as strong as they come. I've seen him do *incredible* things. Whatever this is, he can handle it. You know that." Porlo held out his pipe. "You want some? It helps calm the nerves."

"I can't. It's one of the things on my Purifying list. It can hurt your chances."

"Shame." Porlo wet his lips and inhaled from the pipe deeply. "We didn't have that rule back in my day."

Eloa picked at a corner of the package in her lap, her eyes glued to the pipe. The smell was intoxicating.

"What's wrong now?" Porlo asked.

"Nothing."

"There's something else," Porlo prodded. "What is it?"

"I told you, it's nothing."

"Eloa, your dad saved my life once. I would be dead if it wasn't for him, so if there's anything I can do to help *you*, I owe that to him, please."

"It's nothing serious." Eloa looked up at him. "It's just...it's this." She held up the red box. "It's you. My dad's office torn to shreds... It's these sorts of things that gets me tensed up about my purification. It's like a tightness inside of me, if that makes any sense."

"Sort of." Porlo stepped closer.

"I...what I mean is..."

"Out with it."

"I don't know whether or not I want to be a part of this life."

Porlo stopped in front of her chair. She looked up and held his eyes, apple-scented smoke hovering in the small space between them.

"You're very beautiful when you're vulnerable," he said, and Eloa felt her face heat up in a flash. "I understand how you feel. I do. I get that this is a scary time. The only thing I would say to that, though, is this. If during the last year of *my* training, every yet-to-be-purified felt the way you do, and then chose to live simpler, *normal* lives...the forces of Darkness would've swept in like hawks and claimed victory inside of a year. We'd have all been slaughtered. And without us, the Unknowings don't stand a chance."

"No, I know," Eloa said. "I get that."

"Your grandmother will be coming out in a few moments with a tray of tea. Please give her my most sincere apologies that I was unable to stay and enjoy a cup."

"But—"

"I'm sure our paths will cross again, Miss Eloa Frost, and when they do, I hope to have the time to answer any questions you would like to ask me."

She could do nothing but gaze at him, this tall, mysterious man, her face still flush. She felt a little squirm beneath her navel.

"I like your outfit, by the way," he said. "Flattering. Very flattering."

Eloa looked down at her leotard and dance tights; she had completely forgotten what she was wearing. When she looked back up—feeling more vulnerable than before—he was gone.

CHAPTER 6

I'm dead. It's over," Zach said, head jerking every which way, wide-pupiled eyes focusing on anything and everything. "You heard him, Leam, what did he say? That I'll learn to never question him again?"

"That's right."

"Jesus Christ."

"Maybe it was a just a scare tactic," Leam said, standing by the wall in the back of the sitting room of the Manor, watching his brother pace wobbly-kneed from fireplace to fireplace. "I mean I bet Gideon can get to you worse psychologically than he can by...you know...torturing you."

"Oh great, that's great, Leam, that's really good news," Zach said, pacing, his long white robe swooshing across the royal blue, gold-trimmed Oriental rug. "And what the hell does he want you in here for anyway? *That* is absurd!"

"Hey, it's not like I want to be here," Leam said, thinking about his room, his bed and being left alone.

"Right. Sure. Right. You're telling me you're not a little curious why Gideon told you to come in here for this?"

"Not really."

"You've read all the books, Copernicus. How can it be normal to have your failure of a brother sitting in on the most important event of your life? Seriously?"

"Be quiet, you idiot!" Leam urged, peeking at the door. "You want Gideon to overhear you questioning him again? How stupid are you?"

"Shut up, Leam, now's not the time." Zach's side-to-sides had quickened, somewhere between speed-walking and a jog. "Don't call me stupid. I'm already boiling. I'm fired up as is."

"Gideon is pissed at you. *Gideon!* I feel like you're overlooking that."

Zach stopped. He shook out his entire body like a dog getting out of the water, and took a few long, deep breaths. Leam watched him go to an armchair and sit down—the same chair, Leam noticed, that he himself had occupied one year ago.

"I just don't get it," Zach said, sinking into the cushion, legs crossed, hands behind his head. "This isn't about you—it's supposed to be all about me."

"It will be," Leam said, leaning up against one of the windows that bookended the cold and empty of the two fireplaces; the other—across the room—roared with fire. "The ceremony'll begin before you know it and then you won't even remember I'm here. It's insane, though, that you're more worried about that than Gideon's punishment."

"This is my night. Why would he punish me?"

"Are you insane? He told you he was going to."

"Well whatever." Zach picked at the belt of his robe. "Pain is only temporary, right?"

"No," Leam said, "no, it's not. You think the jackass who came up with that saying had just been tortured by the Darkest man in existence? The guy had probably just stubbed his toe. Gideon can do things to you to keep you suffering forever. I heard he cast a spell on some guy Father used to know, and now the guy's skin melts off his face, grows back just as painfully, and then melts off again and again, and it never stops."

"That cannot be true." Zach shook his head, grinding his knuckles together. "And even if it were, the guy would have killed himself by now."

"Not if Gideon salt and peppered the curse with an anti-suicidal enchantment."

"WHY ARE YOU SAYING THESE THINGS TO ME!"

"Because your life is real now, Zach! High school—mommy watching over you, catering to your every need—sex with every Unknowing girl you can get your hands on—watching DVDs all day sucking down Fritos like a trough pig. Those are all things of your past. That all ends for you tonight, right now. Gideon... joining the war...spreading Darkness. That's your future. Kiss all the other crap goodbye."

"Whatever. What the hell do you know?"

"Zach, he's going to hurt you."

Zach gazed vacantly at the burning logs in the fireplace, tucking his brown hair behind his ears over and over and over. "Whatever Gideon does to me," he said, after a particularly loud crack from the flames, "it won't be that bad. He's all about the war against the Light, right? And after I delighten, I'll be helping him win it, won't I? He *needs* me, that's what you don't understand. He's not gonna be melting *my* face off."

"Zach—"

"Whatever the punishment is, I'll handle it. It's all a part of leaving that other stuff behind. What counts tonight is the delightenment."

Leam shrugged and put his hands in his pockets.

"And let me be clear on one thing..."

"What's that?" Leam asked.

"Do not interfere. No matter what."

"What am I gonna do?"

"I mean it, Leam."

Footsteps approached the door.

"It will all be over soon... It will all be over soon," Zach whispered, spinning around to see the gold door handle turn. "Wish me luck."

Leam couldn't bring himself to say the words, and then the door opened and in walked Bram, scratching at his beard. He looked right through Leam.

"Tonight, my son becomes a man," he said, beaming at Zach, a closed fist over the center of his chest. From behind him, a second voice spoke, sending a cold shiver cutting through the toasty heat radiating from the fire.

"Tell me. Did you say the same thing last year, I wonder?" Gideon asked, stepping into the room, his teeth bared, his skin like sallow candle wax. This was not the man who had said his hellos near the front door earlier. No, this man had become someone else entirely. At first glance, he looked to be wearing a clown mask, the type frequenting young children's nightmares. His mouth was wide open, as if tasting the air, and his eyes, my God, those eyes. Dead dull, but sparking crazy at the same time. The eyes of a rabid bobcat, or those of a manic-depressive man years removed from his last patch of sanity. One look at him—eerily still, standing beneath the door frame—and it was boldly apparent that anything horrible or bizarre that a creative mind could possibly imagine *could* actually happen in this room, anything at all. Leam felt terrified just looking at him. Gideon was—*Jesus Christ, was he really?*—literally foaming at the mouth, saliva bubbles dribbling out of the corners of that clown mask grin. He approached Zach, and Leam thought he saw his brother mouth the word *Mommy.*

Gideon snapped his fingers and a black throne appeared in front of Zach's armchair. He sat down, eyes bulging, and leaned forward. Zach shuddered as Gideon inhaled his scent as if Zach's face was a platter of cupcakes.

"Some believe," Gideon began, in that creepy, unfamiliar accent of his, running his pale fingers through Zach's hair, "that physical pain should not be a requisite before the ritual of de-lightenment. They are mistaken. It is the pain that stays with you so that you remember."

Thank the sweet Lord I didn't get Gideon, Leam thought, grateful that the fat man who'd done his had gone straight into the delightenment. The pain that night had been so unbearable once the ceremony had started, Leam couldn't fathom the notion of being tortured beforehand, as well.

"But, *Zach,* what level of pain?" Gideon snarled, continuing to sniff at Zach's face. Their lips were a hair away from touching; Leam was impressed Zach didn't recoil. "More severe than usual I think."

Zach scrunched his eyes closed, his face as stark white and glossy as cream cheese.

"*Both of us?*" Gideon whined, in a sardonic, baby-talk kind of voice that startled Leam, and seemed to catch Bram off guard, too.

"I didn't mean to say that!" Zach said. "I wasn't thinki—"

"*Both of us?*" Gideon mocked. "*I'm sorry, sir, but both of us?*"

Leam watched Gideon's mouth go open, as if stuck in a yawn, and again, those crazy bobcat eyes, glinting at their prey.

"Do you not know anything about me, Zach? Can you not guess how I run my ship? How I operate? How I wage this war? How I control everyone beneath me? No. How could you? If you dared to question one single word that comes from my mouth, how could you? Because you know what that does?"

Before Zach could shake his head or utter 'no', Gideon's clown mask face twisted into a grotesque, angry knot, and in a wretched blare, Gideon screamed, "THAT INSULTS ME, YOU STUPID BOY!"

From the sheer force of the words, Zach's hair rippled backward as flecks of spittle speckled his face like he was trudging head on into the gales of a sand storm.

"THAT INSULTS ME, *you speck of dust!*" Gideon bellowed, savagely smacking Zach's face over and over for emphasis. "You're lucky I don't claw your teeth out, *you speck of dust!*" His eyes bulged with such severity that the stringy red roots holding them in their sockets looked to be close to snapping off. "A pawn offending the soon-to-be Cronos Maxima! Tsk tsk tsk tsk tsk tsk...tsk."

Leam's eyes skipped back and forth from his father and Gideon. The latter was wheezing, whether with rage or excitement Leam couldn't tell. The former looked like he had swallowed some rank meat.

"I am the future," Gideon spat at Zach, a spider considering a fly, "and you either join me or I put you in the ground."

Leam shifted his weight, suddenly very conscious of the markings on his hands.

And then, like an anvil out the window, Gideon's frightening intensity dropped off, his enthusiastic fury gone, just like that. It scared Leam how swiftly the leader of Darkness could flip the switch.

"Delightenment is the most important occurrence of your life because it binds you to the Cause." Gideon's eyes narrowed. Or were they closed? "That's something you want, right Zach, to be loyal and obedient in your service to the Cause?"

"Yes," Zach stammered. "Yes, sir."

"Then now," Gideon said, a quick peek at the grandfather clock, ten minutes away from twelve chimes, "you will prove it." He held up Zach's face by the chin, then spoke in the baby-talk voice, "You're a sweet boy, aren't you?"

The throne vanished and Gideon was now floating toward the thirty-foot high ceiling. Leam noticed his father rising upward, too, before realizing that his own feet had left the ground. It was as if the gravity had been sucked out of the room, each curly strand of Gideon's orange hair swimming in the thick vacuum of air. Leam hit the ceiling flat-bodied, and watched from a bird's eye view as a pair of coarse brambly ropes fastened Zach's body to the chair, burning through his robe. The burning spread over the fabric quickly yet controlled, and the robe soon disintegrated, leaving Zach naked, the hot rope sizzling into his skin.

Leam was sure Zach was in agony—How could he not be?—but his brother's screams were muffled by a loud swooshing sound, like everyone was inside a giant hourglass that had just been flipped over. Sand was shooting into the room out of the cold and inactive fireplace, grains of sand, pouring and pouring into the room, the floor of which was soon covered in seconds. The swooshing sound was then eaten up by a howling wind, and sand clouds whipped around, a desert storm indoors. The beach beneath them kept rising, slowly burying the oak shelving—home to books, artifacts, gizmos—that lined the edges of the room. Up and up it rose, past Zach's shins, and rising toward his lap. Up and up, past his chest, up and up and up, until it stopped, leveling out an inch above the base of his neck.

Leam looked at Bram—red-faced and covered in sweat—and then at Gideon, who was dancing, hovering fifteen feet above the sand, laughing, extending out his arms, swaying his hands like he was performing some sort of sick puppet show. Pinned to the ceiling, all Leam could do was watch as the spectacle below him grew more terrible and perverse.

A rat, a *big* greasy rat—like the ones Leam had seen scurrying in and out of NYC subway tracks when he used to explore the city—was poking its twitchy, whiskered snout out of the sand. Baring slimy, yellow teeth, it pulled itself out and started to wobble toward the exposed flesh of Zach's face. Gideon kept laughing, and more and more rats surfaced from the blanket of sand beneath him—a rat emerging for every flick of his finger.

Leam wanted to cover his eyes, as his father was doing, but he needed to take it all in. Zach had grown into a real asshole, but still, it'd be a disservice to his brother if he didn't watch. If he chose to turn away and hide from it, to be blind of Gideon's wrath. The wind continued to wail, as did Zach as the first rat reached him and began gnawing on one of his eyes.

The small bud of pity that had sprouted inside of Leam the moment magical rope had rendered Zach immobile had been growing larger and larger, nourished by the revolting freak show glistening below; the torturous symphony Gideon was conducting from above. Leam clenched his upper and lower teeth together and pushed downward with all his strength, only to get about five feet away before being sucked back to the ceiling like a stray paperclip firing back into a magnet's grasp. His brother's face was being eaten off his skull, and all Leam could do was watch.

Gideon watched Leam struggle, roaring with laughter. More rats, dozens of them, were now taking turns ripping off skin and cartilage from Zach's mutilated face, gnawing through cheekbone like beavers would a log. Spread out like a starfish high above, Leam, for a second time, put all his might into freeing himself from the spell pasting him and Bram to the ceiling, but his efforts only thickened the glue. He had nothing to give, no way to help; a frozen snow angel, paralyzed and useless.

"STOP!" Leam screamed, and Gideon was a foot in front of him in an instant, straight-faced, bobbing up and down.

"Would you rather it be you?" he shouted, pushing his palm close to Leam's face. It stunk like nothing Leam had ever smelled before. Bile rose in his throat.

"I stop this now," Gideon yelled over the wind, "and the delightenment crashes and burns before the glass touches his lips! It goes belly up! Is that what you want, Leam? Another Holt failure? One less man beside me, one less man to join the ranks? *Tell me that's what you want*, if that's how it is! Say it to me if you've got the stones, Leam, go on and *say it to me if you've got the stones!*"

Looking past Gideon's stinking fingers—Zach's face unrecognizable, little more than a bloody squirrel carcass flattened into the asphalt—Leam violently shook his head.

"Use your words!" Gideon withdrew his hand. "*Say it!*"

"LET HIM SUFFER!" Leam screamed. "THE CAUSE NEEDS HIM, SIR! HE MUST DELIGHTEN, SIR, NO MATTER HOW LONG IT TAKES!"

"There it is," Gideon said.

And, belly down, like a skydiver, Gideon glided across the room to Bram, who was biting his lip so hard, blood was dripping into his beard. The stemless wine glass that had been buried along with everything else fired out of the sand into Gideon's hand, filling up with the same purple viscous liquid the fat man had put in Leam's glass a year ago. Bram was shouting something Leam couldn't make out, spitting blood into the glass held in front of him. He took out a vial from his pocket with trembling hands and dumped what could only have been Sara's blood in with his own.

Gideon drifted down to sand level—the rats sunk underneath in unison—and dropped a pill into the contents of the glass, turning it foamy white at once. Stretching to what was left of Zach's head, Gideon emptied the glass into Zach's lopsided half-mouth.

And then—the very moment the last drop dripped from the rim—the room fell quiet, the wind no more. The beach eroded, every particle of sand spilling into the fireplace, gone. Bram and

Leam plummeted to the floor as Gideon touched down in the center of the room.

"It's over, young Zach," he said, a mirror the size of a dinner plate in his hand. A chalk-white Zach braved a look at his reflection, a soft moan escaping his lips.

On his hands and knees, breathing hard, Leam couldn't believe Zach was exactly as he had been five minutes ago, though the robe draped around him now was as black as the piano in the music room on the other side of the Manor. The only other difference was the thick white tattoos snaked around his forearms and biceps where the rope coils had fried into his skin.

Zach looked up at Gideon, not with fear or hatred, but with gratification.

"Are they permanent?" he whispered.

"Yes."

"What are they? Scars? Tattoos?"

"A combination of both."

Zach traced his fingers over his scars, mouth hanging open like a sweaty dog left out in the heat.

"Young Zach..." Gideon waited for the boy to look up. "Welcome."

"YES!" Bram shouted, an ear-to-ear grin, slapping his hands together so forcefully it sounded like a clap of thunder. "Well done, son! Well done!"

That was it? Leam thought to himself. *It can't be. How the hell was his actual delightenment so quick, that couldn't have been longer than a few seconds? He drinks, and like that, he's delightened?* The minutes—or had it been hours—after Leam had drank from *his* glass last year had been the most excruciating of his life. Why had it been so different? He looked at Zach, and then his father. It was difficult to gauge who looked more pleased. Had they forgotten the rat-sand horror show already?

"Your powers, up to this point in your life," Gideon was saying to Zach, "as is true of all children of Darkness before their delightenment, have been inactive. Not so for you anymore. Forget about your scars for now, you have a lifetime to admire them. I want you to stare at your brother and keep your focus. Do not let your concentration waver. When your mind is clear, that is to say void of external distractions, think...*fire*."

Zach stood up, squinting across the room at Leam. After a few seconds, Leam cursed as his shirt began to smoke, the collar and the edges of his sleeves burning. Gideon laughed, flicking his fingers. Droplets of water sprung from the tips, pelting into Leam's T-shirt, extinguishing the little fizzes.

"Ohhhhhhh, baby," Zach said, a crooked grin on his face.

"You'll be a quick learner," Gideon said, rubbing his hands together beneath his nose. "I can sense there is a dirty little Unk in our company tonight. Feel free to use her for practice."

"I can't wait," Zach whispered.

Leam had forgotten about the woman tied up in the pantry, undoubtedly terrified out of her mind, if she had regained consciousness. His empty stomach ached as he thought of the role he played in getting her inside the Manor. It seemed she was soon to be tortured at the hands of a boy who had just been tortured himself.

"But before you have your fun, we mustn't neglect tradition," Gideon continued. "Read the Creed of Delightenment aloud so that each word will seep into your darkened soul. You're a part of the war now, don't you ever try to hide from it."

An image of a timeworn piece of paper about the size of a door appeared out of thin air and rippled into the middle of the room, hovering above the rug as if it had been projected on an invisible screen. Its edges were burned and frayed in places, and the old Gothic calligraphy was of a font that might be seen chiseled into ancient tombstones.

Zach smoothed the front of his black robe and recited:

The Creed of Delightenment —

Newly delightened, be excited.

You have left your profane human existence behind you and have become a part of something much larger than your mind, as it is right now, can fully conceive.

You are a member of Darkness, and a combatant of the war.

The affiliates of Light are a worthy adversary and cannot be underestimated. They are strong and knowledgeable, and we must extinguish their Light before they can break through the blanket of Darkness, and discover the secrets that it protects.

Once the war is won, it has been prophesized that all Light will be smothered, the earth—and the Unknowings that inhabit it—left cloaked in nothing but Darkness.

You are now a part of that Prophecy, which means you were destined to be where you are, right now, to help the Cause.

You will do everything in your power, and everything asked of you, to see that the Prophecy comes to fruition.

You. The Cause. The Prophecy.

The image evaporated into the air. Gideon's bony hands latched onto Zach's arms, and the snake-like tattoos brightened for a moment, a cold light, whitish-blue. "You. The Cause. The Prophecy," Gideon echoed.

"They're beautiful," Zach said, gawking at his arms like they were naked women. "So very beautiful."

"No one, including myself," Gideon said, "knows what the purpose of your delightenment scars will be. They might come to your aid in battle, be linked to an alternate being, or be nothing more than skin decoration. You're not meant to know until it reveals itself, if it ever does. It is my belief, however, that the Word—whenever it is destined to exist—will shed some light on the matter."

"The Word, sir?" Zach asked.

"Bram, have you taught this child nothing?" Gideon asked, laughing. "Shall I ask him to recite his ABCs?"

"I believe I told him about the Word, sir, but perhaps I'm mistaken."

Gideon's laughter died. He straightened his fingers and boiling hot tar shot from the tips, plastering Bram's face. Bram shrieked with pain, retreating into a corner. Gideon closed his fingers into a fist, and the black tar evaporated; red, pustule sores left behind in its stead.

"You're either mistaken or you're not, Bram. There is no perhaps."

"I didn't explain it to him, sir," Bram panted. "I ask forgiveness."

"Legend has it that the Word will appear shortly before the fulfillment of our Prophecy," Leam intervened, stepping a little closer to the thin man with the orange hair. "The physical form it'll take is unknown, as are the instructions it'll provide to win the war. It is said that it will speak to those of Light, as well, although they refer to the phenomenon as the Spirit of the Coming. According to legend, the instructions won't be cut and dry. They will retain a more mystical element, as it often is with things of a magical nature, so it is believed the Word will offer clues. In essence, the Word is helpful and necessitous, but it won't be handing over secrets to victory in a gift-wrapped box with a pretty little bow on it."

An ugly grin spread across Gideon's face. "It appears you have taught this one well."

Bram shook his head, still shuddering in the corner, beeswax-like goo leaking out of his sores. "Not a day goes by where Leam isn't in that library."

Leam resisted the urge to shout to his father that the reason he spent so much damn time reading all those books was because he wanted to be knowledgeable enough to discuss any topic in case his dad ever felt like spending time with him.

"So, you have read about the Word." Gideon stepped up to Leam, leaning his head in slowly, whether to smell or intimidate, Leam couldn't be sure. "Tell me. What do you know about the Prophecy?"

"Not much, sir," Leam said, his breath wafting straight into Gideon's skull of a face; the man didn't seem to mind. "Only that there will be a prophet or messiah or something. Someone essential to winning our war with the Light. From what I gather, the Prophecy is often alluded to, but there is very little written about what it specifically entails. At least that's what I can gather from the books in my father's library, sir."

"You must be pleased to have graduated school. No more worthless tests of academia aside those wretched Skunks?"

"I am, sir."

"That's good, for I have some news for you, young Leam Holt." Hidden behind his upper lip, Gideon's tongue slid across his top set of teeth. "High school is finished, but for you, class is not yet over. You will meet with an associate of mine tomorrow morning. Think of it as your first real day of school."

"Yes, sir." Leam's palms began to sweat. He hid them behind his back as the last year of his life flashed before his eyes. Struggling to fill the long, sad days. Feelings of disgrace and worthlessness. Meandering aimlessly about the Manor, wandering in gloom, asking himself what the world held for an undelightened outcast. His family ignoring him as if he didn't exist, each of them certain that he would never amount to anything, both in Darkness and the world as it is in the eyes of the Unknowings. The last twelve months had been a thick cloud of depression and shame, and yet...

"Think of it as your first real day of school."

"My associate will be at the south side of Black Patch Park at 8:30 tomorrow morning," Gideon said to Leam. "You will listen to him and answer any questions that he asks. I am fond of him so anything other than politeness and compliance will be taken as a personal insult to me. The aftermath of the last time I was insulted..." he gestured to Zach, "...you've just witnessed. Have I made myself clear?"

"Quite clear, sir."

Gideon turned away, the door popped open and he walked out, his fire-orange hair brushing the top of the doorframe, the grandfather clock saying goodbye with twelve chimes. Bram, with pustule juice smeared all over his face like raspberry jelly, was close on Gideon's heels, Zach a few steps behind his father. Before leaving the room, Zach spun around.

"You should have wished me good luck, hotshot." Leam's shirt began to smolder again. "Next time you'll do what I say."

Leam patted down the wispy upstarts of smoke, watching his brother strut toward the front door with his head held so high he was almost staring at the ceiling. Leam closed his eyes and, again, Gideon's voice rang out inside the walls of his mind.

"Think of it as your first real day of school."

Perhaps he *was* meant for something. Maybe he was going to be schooled in the ways of Darkness because he did *actually* matter. But for now he had to keep a level head and not daydream of what might be. It was a meeting with some guy that worked for Gideon, that's all. Still, though, a spark had been lit, and tomorrow morning suddenly seemed very far away.

Leam left the sitting room, reaching the corridor just in time to see Sara holding her son's forearms, her face a mess of giddy madness.

"They are beyond lovely, Gideon. There are no words to describe their beauty."

"I have high hopes for him," Gideon uttered, eyes on Sara's sweater, then her legs. "He's in. One of us. Teach him well."

"Of course." Sara opened her mouth, wet strings of cherry-red lipstick pulling apart. "Anything you need of me will be yours."

Gideon fixed his stare on her as Leam looked at his father, who seemed to be occupied with something in the nearby dining room, his hand gripped around the bronze handle of his knife.

"Take care of your face, Bram" Gideon said, stepping to the front door, "and keep Zach focused."

"Sir," Bram grunted.

"And also be reminded that some of the most power-ful men of Darkness were—" Gideon stopped, eyes darting to Leam, "—slow starters. It is as if their souls need to be darkened at a snail's pace in order for them to achieve their potential. Potential for great things."

Bram nodded, noticeably flustered. "Of course, sir. Thank you."

Zach cleared his throat, his fingers jittery at his sides.

"The Unknowing, sir. Will you stay and watch? I've been dying to prove myself to you."

"Ah, now that is something I would quite enjoy," Gideon said, nostrils twitching, eyes, again, beginning to swell. "A young warrior, the blood in his veins electric with fresh magic, inflicting his sickest desires upon a peasant weakling. The beautiful dance of predator versus prey...*us* versus them. But you will celebrate on your own, Zach, because the night, for me, is not yet ready to shut its eyes."

Flattening down his mane of orange hair with one hand, Gideon plucked his bowler hat from the bird-beak coat hanger with the other and placed it delicately on his head.

"'Til we meet again," he said, and though Leam couldn't quite tell who Gideon was looking at, he was sure those words were meant for him.

CHAPTER 7

Bright fluorescent lights beamed down from the narrow ceiling as Miller walked down the longest hallway inside the Light's Center of Operations, a glass door waiting at its end, beyond which was the Room of the River. There were other glass doors to his sides that he glanced through as he passed...

A room filled with huge snakes and brave men dressed in white coats holding iPads or notebooks and pens. A room, with walls that were gushing out purple water, that was rotating—the ceiling becoming the floor, and vice versa, every half revolution—with boys and girls in their late teens trying to stay upright as they concentrated on keeping objects hovering in front of their faces—coins, apples, toasters. A room with walls that looked like giant pizza ovens, a table in the center with three or four women typing away on the keyboards of large orange computers.

Farther down, a glass door on his right swung open and Miller's reflection bounced twenty or so yards back at him: a youngish-looking man with normal-guy brown hair in jeans and a sea-green long-sleeve T-shirt, *SKI VAIL* in bold red across the chest. A young woman with red hair tied back into a ponytail stuck her head out. She smiled when she saw him and came out into the hall, adjusting her sky blue scrubs.

"Miller."

"Hey, Sam."

"What are you doing in these parts of the COO? I could sense someone out here who shouldn't be."

"I go where I go," Miller said with a grin as he neared.

"That's profound."

"Got a telemast just now." Miller tapped the side of his head. "Message from Mr. Tso, DOU."

"Department of Urgency. You better get to it."

"He's coming in from somewhere," Miller said, gesturing all the way down the hallway to the Room of the River. "Not due in there for…" Miller held out a fist and opened it. Hanging in the air just above his palm was a set of digital numbers—laser red—counting down from 2:41, 2:40, 2:39. "…another two to three minutes."

"Inside the Room of the River? Moving up I see," she said. "I've heard you've been working directly for Sebastian."

"Twice now," Miller said, stopping a few feet away from her. He could smell baby powder. She always smelled like baby powder. He liked it. "How've you been, Sam? You look good."

"That's because I just started my shift. It's messy in there. Each month's worse than the last."

Miller peered into a room filled with hospital beds occupied by patients caked with blood, missing appendages, bandaged up in casts. All of them had the same, foggy look in their eyes.

"Unknowings?" he asked.

"Yes. All injuries inflicted by Darkness. They're bewitched into believing they're in a hospital of their own. The Department of Unknowing Protection is bringing them in five at a time at a pace where only two are ready to be taken back out."

"Darkness," Miller muttered, looking in at a Japanese girl of about five, both eyes swollen shut, a breathing tube jutting out of a bloody, toothless mouth.

"It's starting to feel like we're slipping behind," Sam said. She looked up at Miller, who could sense that she yearned for him to say something, *anything*, that would help put her at ease. He didn't have those words.

"Well, I got my orders," he said. "Better get going."

"Find me afterward if you want to get a coffee." Sam put her hand gently on his hip. Again he smelled fresh baby powder.

"Or a drink," Miller said, as he turned away, heading down the hallway.

"Or a drink," Sam echoed, ducking back into the infirmary.

Miller opened his hand—1:15, 1:14—as he came upon the end door. Through the glass he could see nothing but a dark, cavernous space. When he was three steps from the door, the glass began to shimmer like rain, the entire plane of the door now a thin waterfall. He walked through it and looked around. It was no cave.

The Room of the River was an enormous rainforest, and rumored to be much more than that, in the confines of a massive, greenhouse-esque structure. Huge plush trees, trickling streams running every which way, exotic birds perched on leafy branches, weird little monkeys slinking around, and—as the room's name suggested—a giant, flowing river dissecting the jungle. The air smelled fresh, felt damp and sang with sounds of wildlife. Squinting through a blind of leaves, Miller could see a huge tube poking out of the middle of the river, like a giant version of those chutes that Unknowings fired canisters of money and checks through outside a bank. The tube extended up and out of sight.

"Through here, Mr. Miller. You're one and half seconds late."

Miller followed the trail of the voice, curving around tree trunks, passing sloths and tree slugs clinging to vines, stepping over giant insects and poison-arrow frogs, until he reached the bank of the river where an old Chinese man sat holding a swirly crystal ball, which Miller recognized as a Moon Flux.

"It's good to meet you, Mr. Tso," Miller said. "How are you doing?"

"Fine, fine. Take a seat."

Miller obliged, sitting down on the edge of the riverbank, his purple Nikes dangling a foot or two above the streaming water. "Mr. Tso, why does this place appear to be a cave from the outside?"

"We've no time for irrelevance," Tso said. "You know my name, but do you know what I do?"

Miller rubbed his earlobe between his thumb and finger—a habit of his when excited. "You handle urgent matters."

"Precisely. You arrived here at a leisurely pace and stopped to say 'hi-hello' to an attractive woman. From this point on there will be no leisure and no stopping."

Miller nodded once. "Absolutely."

"You need to find Jace Frost of Cliff Edge, New Jersey. This man is a major player. When you find him, you contact me immediately via telemast."

"Yes, sir."

"Do you know him?"

"Frost? No."

"Do you know of him?"

"I've heard a few things."

"Do you know what he's working on?"

"No."

"He's working on a mission named Break Lock."

"What is that?"

"That's classified is what that is. The mere fact that this has been directed to Urgency should suffice for your purposes."

"Yes, sir," Miller said, rubbing his earlobe again. Above the river noise, a Macaw squawked in the distance.

"This comes from the top. Sebastian has just been informed that Frost's house has been ransacked and Frost has disappeared," Tso said. "'If this man is missing,' Sebastian said to me directly, 'he needs to be found. Jace Frost possesses information that cannot be lost.'"

"So then Sebastian knows he's alive?" Miller asked.

"Yes."

"How?"

"Does it matter? Sebastian leads the Light. If he says so, it's so."

"Sorry, sir, it's my nature to be thorough."

"No need to dig any deeper, Mr. Miller, as that's the extent of what I know."

Miller stood up. Tso's gaze remained on the river.

"I give you his words once more," Tso said, his gnarled, grayish fingers wrapped around the swirly crystal ball. "'If this man is missing, he needs to be found.'"

Miller nodded and took off, sprinting through the rainforest back the way he came. He could feel the eyes of the birds and monkeys on him before he shot through the Water Glass into the hallway, squinting under the glare of the fluorescent lights. Sam stuck her head out with a smile that fell flat a half second later.

"What's wrong?" she asked.

"Rain check on that drink, Sam," Miller said, flying by her. Again he caught the scent of baby powder, but this time wasted not a second to relish it. As his legs took him toward the nearest of the COO's exits, his mind was set on one thing only, and nothing else.

Jace Frost of Cliff Edge, New Jersey.

CHAPTER 8

Eloa was back upstairs in the guestroom—her new bedroom—the lid of the red box Porlo had given her lying next to an empty teacup on the bedside table. Perched on the edge of the fluffy bed, Eloa had been still for several minutes, the box resting on her lap, her eyes lost in the clouds of white tissue paper inside. Clamped between her thumb and forefinger was a sky-blue envelope; on the back, a stallion head stamp of crimson wax broken over the opening. Barry barked, a hollow yap from somewhere downstairs, and Eloa blinked. Slipping the note carefully out of the envelope, she recognized her father's handwriting.

> *Eloa,*
>
> *Keep this on you always. It will ensure your safety.*
> *Keep it hidden.*
> *Do not mention it to anyone.*
> *I will explain when I can.*
>
> *I love you,*
> *Dad*

She reread the note once and coaxed it back inside the envelope, which she slid between the mattress and the box spring. Whatever this object was beneath the tissue clouds, it had to be of extreme importance because her father had addressed her by her full name. She couldn't remember the last time he hadn't called her Lo. She counted from ten to one inside her head, releasing a breath on the even numbers, then peeled away the topmost sheet of tissue paper. An icy shiver slid up her spine; whatever was inside was chilled. That, or the box was a tiny refrigerator. She put her hand in deeper, fingers tingling.

Another yelp—compact, and less distant—this time right outside the room. She got off the bed and opened the door. Barry stood in the hallway, thick clear strands of drool dangling from his mouth like melting icicles. Eloa leaned over to scratch behind his ears but he nipped her hand away playfully and tore between her long legs, hopping over the giant, white duffel bag that she'd dropped on the carpet earlier—back before Porlo had existed in her world—and combed the edges of the room, nose sniffing, tail wagging.

Eventually the quirky beagle settled himself in the exact center point of the room, his brown eyes twinkling at Eloa, who heaved her bag atop the old wooden dresser and got back on the bed, the red box again in her hands. She pulled away the last of the tissues and a sharp breath of air escaped her lips. Barry's ears perked up as she removed the most beautiful trinket she had ever seen.

It was a small medallion, made of a dense, cold, silvery metal, and shaped like a starfish but with seven arms instead of five. Each arm looked to be made of tiny metal strings that wove around each other, patterning into an intricate sort of metal lace. The base of each arm connected to the base of its neighbors, forming a seven-sided hole in the center.

Eloa went back to the dresser, opening the top drawer and removing the jewelry box she had kept there since she was a little girl. She pulled out an ordinary silver necklace and ran one of the ends through the middle of the medallion. Clasping the ends of the necklace together behind her neck, she shivered, the pale skin hidden under her leotard stung by the medallion's wintry bite.

Eloa leaned back against the wall—lavender-papered, patterned with white ducks—forcing herself to release the tension in her body, shoulders lowering, eyelids grateful for the prospect to become heavy. The thought of examining every single thing that had happened tonight—reliving it inside her head—seemed more exhausting than studying purification manuals or listening to Bridgette talk about boys for fifty hours nonstop. Right now, accepting what Porlo had said, and having faith that her dad knew what he was doing, felt right and now that her skin had adjusted to it, the frigid touch of the starfish arms over her breastbone came with a warm, calming sense of security.

She looked around the room, now that her mind was relaxed enough to take it in, noticing how it differed from the way she had remembered it. The room had new yellow curtains, a TV and a desk from IKEA.

It was all quite inconsistent with the rest of the house, which was filled with old furniture and second-hand appliances. It was obvious that Mary and Larry knew they were getting a houseguest for an indeterminate amount of time. She smiled at their generosity. It hurt that she couldn't fill them in on the little she knew.

"There's no way to help, not if she won't let us."

Eloa closed the dresser drawer, the jewelry box back in its cave for another hibernation. She dug through her bag, sifting through socks and shirts, pushing aside her jogging sneakers and a couple of books (*Catch 22*, *It's Time to Purify*, *An Unquiet Mind*), and removed a framed photo of three people standing on a perfectly green lawn, a small, pretty cottage out of focus in the background. The girl in the photograph was wearing a white sundress, laughing, reaching up on tippy toes to play with the long blond hair of a muscled man in beige swim trunks: Eloa, around the age of eleven, and her dad at their summer home in Cape Cod. The third person, a man who looked to be in his early forties—clean and tan, with glaring white teeth—wore a red faded V-neck T-shirt and blue jeans. His hair was silver, nothing like gray, and he was beautiful.

"Sebastian," Eloa said—Barry's ears twitched. If anyone was to know where her father had gone, or where he was *laying low*, as Porlo had put it, it would be Sebastian. That day—the day of the photo, before it had been taken—Eloa had hidden in the bushes around the side of the cottage, eavesdropping on a hushed discussion between Sebastian and her dad. That was over six years ago, and although the inflections of both voices exposed the conversation as one of grim urgency, she could only recall snippets.

"*...is being delegated to the Department of Unknowing Protection, leaving us shorthanded elsewhere at the COO. Purification and Youth Development, Prophecy Intel...*"

"*...problem because Unknowing-on-Unknowing crime is dangerously rising to a...*"

"*...know it isn't easy being the leader of the Light, Sebastian, but if Gideon is...*"

"*...sheet of Light is tiring, Jace, and evil is not. It's energized. Look at Lebanon, look at 9/11, the gangs in...*"

Later that day in the front yard, when expressions of ease and comfort had settled onto both men's faces, Eloa recalled thinking, with the naivety of having lived a mere eleven years and all of them happy, that she had wanted to remember this day always, sensing that she might never again see this man who she had just met; this man that she was inexplicably drawn to, like she was too cold and he was the sun; this man with silver hair brighter than polished gun metal.

When it had happened, there had been no photographer a few steps away, no friendly neighbor bearing a tray of cold lemonade, a camera strap over his neck. It'd just been the three of them—she stretching to touch the tips of her dad's hair—when the sky and all that was beneath it lit up with a stunning flash for the briefest of moments. She would have missed it if she had blinked—and to her shock, or rather her *amazement*, a photograph had seesawed down from the sky, dancing like crisp leaves do when blown away from their branches.

Barry growled, or maybe he was snoring, his eyes closed. Eloa popped the frame open and peeled the picture away from the backside of the glass. She had never seen magic before, and what Sebastian had told her when the photo drifted into her eleven-year-old hands, she had written on the back with a Sharpie as green as the grass on the front.

"*Question everything you can. Remain steadfastly curious about how things come to be. But never, ever, let go of your willingness to believe.*"

She squeezed out of her leotard and tights, slipped on her nightgown and slid socks over her blood-stained feet so as not to stain the fresh linens. She'd scrub the soles of her feet clean in the shower when she got up tomorrow, or maybe later in the morning if she decided on a jog. She climbed into bed, eyes lost in the ceiling, her right hand placed over the silver medallion. Barry jumped up and nestled between her legs, resting his chin on her feet. After a few minutes, his rhythmic breathing calmed the rest of her mind, the part that wasn't completely convinced that her dad was unharmed, and soon her eyes fell shut, her hand quiet atop the medallion that would remain hanging from her neck until she heard otherwise.

She would not remember anything from her dream the following morning. A dream of two men walking away from a dark-haired baby across a vast meadow toward the tree line a mile or two away. The baby was crying, perched in an abandoned crib made of gold, lying on a layer of blue apples. The backs of the two men became smaller and smaller as they neared the woods. The baby continued to cry, and when the men had disappeared into the forest, a million shiny starfish fell from the sky like glittery hail, thumping onto the ground, melting through the grass, and dissolving into the dirt below.

CHAPTER 9

L eam beeped the Range Rover locked and started trudging up a caked-dirt trail scant of the foliage that surrounded it but ribbed with hundreds of ancient, bone-hard roots yawing every which way. He climbed upward, cutting through this heavily wooded area of Harbing known as Cricket Tourne.

His measured pace wasn't a product of unfamiliarity—Leam had frequented the Cricket ever since he had learned to ride a bike, often as an escape from Manor life, less often to dispose of things that needed to be disposed—nor was it a result of navigating over pesky roots, for Leam had been surefooted since the day he took his first steps, back when Zach was still dependent on Sara's teat. He moved slowly simply because he had no cause to hurry. After his revitalizing chat with Gideon—*"Think of it as your first real day of school."*—Leam knew he had no shot at sleep. Not tonight. Not with the looming meeting with Gideon's "associate" tomorrow morning in the very heart of Harbing at Black Patch Park. Nervous? A little bit, yeah. Excited? Sure. Worried/scared? Oh definitely. So if he wasn't to sleep, he wasn't to hurry.

His neck was stiff, though, his upper back growing sore. Leam figured these were results of two factors: one, falling from the ceiling like a sack of bones and slamming onto the floor mid-Zach's delightenment; and two, the dead weight of the unconscious, middle-aged woman draped over his shoulders.

Half hour ago at the Manor's front door, Zach—the Zach who Leam was growing to despise—had been upset.

"Screw it. I have no taste for it anymore. Not with him gone."

The *him* was Gideon, of course; the *it*, what was sure to have been a fantastic spectacle of torture and cruelty starring *Zach the Magic-Virgin Himself* (and don't forget his fancy-fresh serpentine arm tattoos!) and *Pamela*—Leam had caught the name on her driver's license while stuffing what had fallen out of her purse back into it—*the Unwilling Unknowing!*

And next had come the four words that led Leam here, trudging up this trail, weaving through the Cricket's maze of oaks.

"Get rid of her."

Zach had said it in the off-handish way a smug person might tell a waiter, "And sparkling water for the table" after ordering everyone's meals.

"Get rid of her."

And before Leam could even *think* of objecting, Sara had rushed over. Bram, who Leam had hoped would want to talk to him again now that Gideon had shown an interest, was nowhere to be seen—probably off to the kitchen to get a big fat *Congratulations!* cake for Zach. There wasn't a chance in hell Leam was going to stand around and watch Sara and Zach ooh and ah over the stupid arm tattoos, so he left them to it and went to the pantry to scoop up Pamela.

As if the Range Rover was on autopilot, he had driven to the Cricket with only a vague idea of where he was going. His mind had been occupied, churning out dozens of make-believe scenarios of how things might unfold at Black Patch Park in the morning, the oddest of which ended with him and the female associate of Leam's imagination making out in the large fountain.

Here, now, up through the Cricket, closing in on the cavernous hole he had discovered long ago—the perfect place to dispose of things that needed to be disposed—Leam's earlier hesitancy to kill the woman was weakening with each step, yet he couldn't put his finger on why. He shifted his load, and Pamela's flaccid hand wiped across the back of his head. The forearm that had been snuggled against her side flopped forward, the hand drooping into Leam's line of vision. All of a sudden, both of his pinkies began to prickle, and Leam stopped dead in his tracks.

Whoa, whoa, whoa.

His pinkies were definitely prickling. He hadn't felt it in over a year, but he *knew* that prickle.

"It will all be over soon," he whispered, an echo of what Zach had said a minute before those giant rats had eaten off his face. Leam had whispered it without thinking, a reflex, just like he had driven here without really thinking. He found himself uncertain whether his words were for himself or the woman, who had begun to stir.

Pamela began to moan—groggy, fearful moaning—but Leam paid her no heed. Trees and a few boulders passed them by in the night, leaves whispering to them in soft wind. The soles of his feet were beginning to burn, not scalding, just uncomfortable. He clenched his teeth...he knew that *burn*, too.

"Please," Pamela shuddered, "whoever you are—"

"Be quiet, I'm thinking."

And he was. He was trying to piece it all together before it took over him. *Why now? Why are you here now?* The bull, as the voice in Leam's mind referred to it—a muscular horned beast, its coat the darkest of blacks—had been sleeping for at least a year, he was sure of it, a deep sleep, hidden and forgotten. And now it was awakening...his pinkies, the soles of his feet...oh, it was definitely stirring, with its short forceful snorts and diamond-hard hooves digging into the deepest and darkest within him.

He knew what came next—

"Let me go, please let me go." Pamela, again. Crying.

"Shut your mouth," Leam said flatly. He dropped her to the ground with a terrible thud, bent down and latched his hands around her ankles. He started up again, dragging her behind him up the trail like a sleigh, her shoulder blades the runners.

Yes, he knew what came next, and sure enough, his eyelids were blinking, rapidly they blinked, to the point where Leam felt like they were hummingbird wings or tiny pages shuffling in a flipbook. The heat in his feet was rising and good thing, too, because Leam and his sleigh were close to the cavernous hole, and once the burn started to rise he had little chance to stop it; he'd be handing the reins over to the bull, forfeiting control.

Leam and Pamela, plus the annoying shrieks and wails that accompanied Pamela on their travels, came up upon the hole—its mouth concealed by a thick cluster of oaks—her head jostling up and down as it skidded over small rocks and the bone-hard roots. Leam felt the bull pushing up through his chest as he let go of Pamela's ankles, her legs flopping against the nubby trunk of one of the cluster trees.

The burn surged up Leam's neck—he staggered backward—a slow mighty surge that swelled into his head, pumping it full with black heat. Pamela's pleads of "*Please!*" grabbed his attention; he looked down at her as if she was a television set and he was mildly interested in the program. He noticed that the bottom hem of her green blouse must have snagged onto a root knuckle: it was bunched up to her breast line, her pale, loose stomach exposed. Leam thought of pancake batter.

"Please," she moaned, "you don't have to do this. My sons, they need me. Can't you…"

Leam's mind-voice tuned her out.

I bet it woke up because of Gideon. Yes, because of the meeting coming up in the park! That's the difference—that's gotta be it—that's the only change there's been. I failed to delighten, the worst thing that could ever happen, and I turned into this depressed, weakling loser, so the bull must have trotted off into hiding, with any passion or purpose I once had strapped to its back…

"The delightenment," Leam muttered, faintly and distantly conscious of Pamela's tiresome sobbing.

That's when it happened, it had to have been. The fat man failed me and then the bull ambled off to sleep. How did I miss that? I didn't realize it had left me. I didn't even know it had

*gone. But it's back now. I'm hot and it's back! Can you be-
lieve it!?*

Pamela sat up, coughing, dry dirt smudges and faint smears
of blood on her forehead and at the corner of her mouth. Leam
looked pleasantly startled, as if he was noticing her for the
first time.

"Hi there!" He bent down for a closer look at that whiny
face and those tear-stained eyes. "You know, Pam, you could get
me in a lot of trouble. Did you know that, kiddo? I shouldn't be
saying these sorts of things in front of an Unk like yourself...
Gideon...Delightenment...what-have-you...but what's the difference? I mean, *really*, you're dead anyway, right?"

"No, no, no, no," Pamela urged, eyes bulging like those of
a constipated toad. He had to lean in—a quick, smooth movement so unlike the Leam of the last twelve months—to hear her
urgent whispering. "You can't kill me! My sons! They need a
mother!"

"Yeah, that'd be nice." Leam laughed.

"I DON'T WANT TO DIE!"

"*If you only knew.*" Leam rounded on her. "You'd be *begging* me to snap your neck and toss you in the hole. I'd be doing
you a favor, there's nothing but a rotting future for you and your
darling boys. You know what life is gonna be like for you people? *Do you?* You have no idea how bad it's gonna get, and how
quickly it's gonna get here."

There was a change in the woman, Leam saw it immediately. Her eyes were soaked but the tears had stopped, her
face flush, the ragged breathing beneath her bosom somewhat
more controlled. The scaredy-cat was gone, no question. Perhaps chased off by the bull.

"Listen to me," Pamela said, as if talking to colleagues
around a business table. Leam furrowed his brow, smiling. Her
abrupt change of tactic, if that's what this was, had come around
quicker than the metamorphosis burning under his skin.

"You're young, aren't you?" Pamela asked. Her words
were dispassionate, direct. "You're in high school?"

"I guess you could say I'm still in school, kiddo."

"That's good. Then I'm offering something I know you want." Turning her head from him, she pulled off her jeans, a process that took more time than it should have, and lay back, the runners of the sleigh easing onto the trail roots.

Leam looked down at her like she was in a zoo exhibition. Was she...yes, she was *writhing*, writhing around on the hard dirt in her bunched-up blouse and giant white panties...a blank, dead smile...bleary, watery eyes. By the look of her, it seemed she was no longer the scaredy-cat or the business woman, but a combination of both. Was that possible? To be both at the same time? The top of Leam's head—the very highest point at the tip of his skull—tingled, a cooling sensation, like jumping into the pool.

"You think I've never been with a woman?" Leam lied. "You think this'll spare your life?"

"Take me," she said quivering. "It's what you want. It's what *all* boys want."

"Embarrassing," Leam said, dismissing the cold trickle under his scalp.

"But it's what all boys want, isn't it? It's what all boys want..."

"*You're embarrassing yourself.*"

"THEN WHAT DO YOU WANT FROM ME?" Pamela snapped, pushing herself up on her elbows. The business woman had just kicked the scaredy-cat out the window. "Out with it! Tell me what you want! There must be something! You haven't killed me yet so what do you want?"

"Have it your way." Leam crouched down, the pool heater cranking up. "Time to die. But don't fret, I'll make sure to check in on the twins."

Pamela—scaredy-cat Pamela—screamed, (*man, this lady can turn on a dime!*) swatting Leam away and scurrying off down the trail like a giant squirrel, scuffing up her hands and knees as she distanced herself from her captor and his cluster of oaks.

Leam went to grab her, to drag her back to the cavernous hole and finish the job, but this attempt at escape, this sad, scampering woman fleeing from him in those huge white panties reminded him of something from very long ago. The heater knocked off with a jolt, and the cool tingly pool water was dripping again, fueled by the resurrection of this one memory.

Sharp and blazingly vivid, it was of Zach—the Zach he'd once loved—on the floor of the music room, crawling away from Leam on hands and knees after getting spooked by a beetle, half screaming, half giggling, his diaper swaying left and right as he scuttled off to a safer, *non*-beetle area of the room. Leam was no more than three at the time, but the memory was bright—those cloud-white Huggies swaying—void of the usual haze that attaches itself to distant memories, fogging them up and blurring their edges.

Cool water continued dripping down from the tip of his skull, yet this time a flow, the constant stream of a faucet, spilling through his head with a fierce chill, raining now, spitting down with force, the power of the memory behind it, pouring down in buckets, gushing down, filling into his body like ocean water flooding a sand castle's moat, to the tips of his fingers and the soles of his feet; glowing water balloons, cold, and bright with color, splattering into dark spaces, filling the shadowy nooks and cozy-warm crannies.

Leam put his hand on the nearest oak, the bark's rough texture a comfort, and breathed in the forest air. It had a freshness to it found only in the depths of the Cricket. Inside of him— somewhere deep, in a cavernous hole—the horned bull shook out its muscular body, water spraying from its sleek black coat in thick drops. It was quieting, and with one last snort, the bull lay down and was still.

In the dark distance, Leam watched Pamela and those big white panties scamper off down the wooded hill and vanish over the trail drop. He did nothing to stop her.

CHAPTER 10

Everything was black, and Leam couldn't move.

He opened his eyes to find himself fastened to a bright green plastic chair, the kind that usually made its home in a middle school cafeteria. His hands were tied to his sides, his legs fastened securely to those of the chair, all with taut, pink rope. He couldn't budge anything below his neck, not a bit. The earlier trickle of pleasant bemusement had been swapped out for a widening stream of justifiable panic.

He jerked his head to the right, then the left. Everything was white, yes, but in varying shades, he noticed, lending the space depth and the appearance of motion. The shades of white began to morph into identifiable shapes. Before he knew it, he and the green chair were no longer swimming in a colorless void. A room was forming around them that could have passed as a normal, brightly-lit office conference room, if it hadn't been the size of a football field or even bigger. An off-white Formica table that had to be two hundred feet long stretched down the center of the room, diminishing to a tiny point in the distance. Surrounding him, Leam could make out the faint form of walls and ceiling, both white of course. A dreadful sensation of imprisonment collapsed over him, making him feel like he had been buried alive.

His mouth shot open to scream but instantly became stuffed full with a rubbery, sponge-like matter that he was unable to spit out or swallow. His anxiety spiked with throbbing pulses. Had his tongue engorged like a water balloon expanding with blood?

He thrashed his body against the rope—violently and with everything he had—expending all reserves of energy, hell-bent on escape. He sucked in harsh pockets of breath through his nostrils as fear pumped through his body, reaching places inside him that had never tasted it before. Only his head could move, though, shifting with spastic jolts at first, then—as gloom set it—transitioning to movements more feeble and pathetic. Beads of perspiration slid off his forehead leaving behind itchy tracks of wetness. Any moment now he would break down crying. He could feel it coming on.

But then he heard something. A flickity-clickity noise grew louder and louder, becoming more distinct.

Steps, Leam thought, and sure enough, faintly at first, a man in a yellow suit emerged out of the white abyss, his hard-soled shoes clicking against the tabletop as he walked toward Leam, stopping at the very edge. In one of his hands was a canister, a steel-gray cylinder with dark red vapor spewing from its top. The other hand held three crystal-clear ice cubes. A gasp caught in Leam's throat when his eyes flicked up to the man's face.

The yellow man didn't have a face, not really. No mouth, no nose, no ears; just a set of eyes that considered the immobile Leam for a moment, then closed. The eyelids began to bubble as if they were roasting over a pit of fire, and then they melted through the skin of his featureless face. The split second that the eyes completely disappeared, a new substance seeped through, three inches below where the eyes had been, forming into a mouth. The lips separated.

"Why are you here?"

The voice wasn't familiar. Yellow man's lips started to bubble, trickling back into the skin. The fizzy substance reappeared, this time on the sides of his head, forming into ears. The sponge in Leam's mouth evaporated; it hadn't been his tongue after all.

"I don't know where I am," Leam wheezed, gulping in breaths of air. "I don't know how I got here, I was sent by Gideon, though. You're his associate, right? Gideon sent me here."

Yellow man's ears were gone, replaced by the mouth again. "If you got here...I have something you need to see." He held up the steel-gray cylinder, casually dropping what Leam had thought were ice cubes. They didn't shatter against the table top, they stuck to it—like clear wads of gooey chewing gum—and began to melt into three tiny glistening pools of water.

Yellow man—the lone feature, ears—held out the cylinder as wisps of red vapor steamed out, collectively materializing into the head of a giant horse for a moment before evaporating. Leam only saw it peripherally, his focus trained on the little puddles next to the yellow man's hard-soled shoes, all three beginning to crystallize into three-dimensional matter. It was as if miniature ice sculptures were growing out of tiny, frozen lakes.

As each crystal figure was transforming, its clearness began to speckle with color. The first—the biggest of the set—turning black, the next becoming pale brown, the last clouding into white, and to Leam's amazement, each tiny sculpture took the form of a bird. The black bird flew onto his shoulder and began snapping at his ear; the brown bird flapped back and forth in no particular pattern whatsoever; and the white bird hovered in front of Leam's face for a moment, as if to say hello, and then took off into the sky, through the invisibly white ceiling, and all Leam could see now was white, nothing else, just white, consuming him, the white, white, white...

"Time to get up, human."

The dream lingered, wings still flapping in that fuzzy place between sleeping and waking. Leam's eyes opened, adjusting to a blurry face high above him. He went to sit up but Zach's knees were pinning his arms to the bed. Leam tried to wriggle and nudge his way out of the hold, as he had while tied up in pink rope, but nothing doing. His brother was simply much stronger now than he'd been the day before.

"Keep struggling, dummy, and I'll set you on fire." Zach's bagel and cream cheese breath wafted into Leam's face. "I've been practicing straight through the night." He stared at the pillow next to Leam's head and—PHWOOSH—it burst into a blaze of flames. Zach let it burn, reveling in Leam's profanity-laden objections, then spit out a giant slop of water as if his mouth was the open end of a fire hose, splashing the flames dead and leaving the pillow soaked and charred.

"Say mercy, Leam, and I'll let you up."

Leam knew he had no shot at breaking free. Zach was made out of iron. He forced his muscles to relax, breath after breath after breath, and with painstaking effort, coaxed his body limp so that it oozed back into the maroon comforter that spread over his king-size mattress.

"That's a *good* boy, Kibbles, good *boy*." Zach said, patting Leam on the head. He hopped off the bed, giddy with himself, and pushed up the sleeves of his black Adidas track suit. "Father wants you up. Naturally he questions your dependability so he sent me up here. 'One of the reasons that boy didn't delighten,' he said. I told him no problem, I'd go light your pillow on fire."

"You could've just said, 'wake up'." Leam wiped his eyes with the heels of his hands, the smell of charred fabric thick and damp beneath his nose.

"Mother said to burn the one beneath your head, but then...she..." Zach blinked stupidly a couple times as if he had forgotten something he had wanted to say. "Anyway, this associate—Gideon's associate, btw—the meeting's this morning."

"Hey, idiot, you don't think I know that?" Leam was off the bed now and moving to the dresser. "You think I would forget to do something that the leader of Darkness wants me to do? Look at you with your fancy new magic tricks, Zach, but you're still so freaking stupid."

"Look at *me?* You couldn't even delighten. Read all those books about it and for what? Mother's cousin's kid out in Utah, the one with three teeth and the snot dripping out of his nose... even *he* pulled it off. First try, too! Father's right, you're an embarrassment."

"When'd he say that?" Leam asked, pulling a black Ramones T-shirt over his head.

"I don't know, a couple days ago. He says it all the time."

"If I'm such an embarrassment, why did Gideon set up Black Patch Park?"

Zach swept his hair away from his face and let his fingers brush over the scar tissue on his arms. "Cutting through the crap, Leam, I don't see that as a good thing." His iPhone buzzed. He checked the message—something that made him smile and adjust himself—then the phone was back in his pocket. "So what did you do with the woman? The Unknowing?"

"I took care of it."

"I know that, but how?"

"If you cared so much about it, you should have done it yourself." Leam buttoned his jeans, stuffed his feet into his sneakers and sat down on the side of the bed to tie the laces. He flicked off a leaf stem stuck behind the tongue of his left sneaker, and his mind stabbed hold of last night at the Cricket, how that powerful black bull had stirred inside of him. But the stretch of time when the bull had taken the reins was as fuzzy as the space between sleeping and waking—that tender fog between dream and reality—and just as difficult to recall. Whatever had happened, the end result had been Pamela's escape from the cavernous hole and the cluster of oaks that protected it.

"I can't have her linked to me, Leam. You know more than anyone how much of a nuisance Unk cops can be with their constant—"

"It's taken care of." Leam looked down to find his left thumb tracing over the marking on his right hand. "I guess your big plans to prove yourself to Gideon fell through the cracks," he said.

"It wasn't a total loss. After you left *to take care of it*, Father got some wine from the cellar and we all got a little toasty."

"The loving family of three."

"Father got pretty sauced up and said something... It slipped out of his mouth, he didn't mean to say it. Something Gideon must have discussed with him when we were waiting in the sitting room."

"What was it?"

Zach hesitated. Leam could tell by his brother's face that Zach didn't really want to tell *him*, but he absolutely had to tell somebody.

"You brought it up, Zach. What slipped out?"

"Fine." Zach peeked out the door before turning to Leam with a smile. "Somewhere between bottle two and three, we clinked glasses and he said the celebration was a two-for-one. My delightenment, obviously, and how Jergen Seventeen was almost ready."

"*What* seventeen?"

"Jergen, I think he said. Or maybe Goojin."

"What is that?"

"That's what I asked him. He shook his head. I could see it in his eyes he had said too much. But *celebration*, Leam. Something big's going down, and celebration means it's good for Darkness. Remember afterward how Gideon said he had somewhere to go?"

"Who could forget, it pulled the curtain over your precious magic show."

"He said his night wasn't ready to sleep yet or something. I bet you anything it had something to do with the Goojin thing, whatever that is or does, and if Father's been entrusted with it, then there's a chance I might be a part of it at some point, too."

Leam flung the crispy-wet pillow into the corner. It slid against the crack of his bathroom door. "If it's important, then they're not gonna let Zach Holt be a part of it."

Lines of disdain erased the excitement written all over Zach's face, clearing the path for another expression Leam had never seen before. Zach looked haunted, almost dead.

"Leam, Leam, jealous little Leam," Zach sighed, strutting around the room, touching Leam's things at random with his finger as he spoke. "Did you hear how Gideon was speaking about me to Mother and Father? I know you did. Must have been tough for you to go wait in the corner like an unwanted child and hear your little brother being praised like that. And doubly-tough 'cause they're praises you yourself will never hear…obviously. You're the family joke, big brother. The failure—"

"That might be changing soon."

"—the court jester. So on and so on, you get the idea."

Leam felt hot and shot a look at his pinkies. "Get out of my room."

"So be it, m'lord," Zach said with a bow and a laugh. A second buzz hummed from his pocket, and out came the phone again. His pupils danced across the text, widening with glee. "How easily Unknowing girls are trained, my god! It's like taking carrots from a fat guy."

"Just go, Zach."

Zach crossed to the door as he texted a reply back to an easily-trained Unknowing girl. "You know, Leam, Mother tried to convince Father to let you sleep in so you'd miss the whole damn thing. 'Then maybe,' she said, 'just maybe, Gideon would get clued in on what a waste you are, and we'd be rid of you for good.'"

"I don't care what your mommy thinks of me," Leam said, red-faced.

"Sure you don't." Zach turned around in the door frame. "Oh, and I almost forgot…happy birthday, you old turd." He snickered, brimming with a meadow-fresh air of confidence, another side effect, undoubtedly, of awakened magic. His face was alive now, without a trace of death. "Try not to crap yourself at the park."

Zach sauntered off toward the spiral staircase, most likely off to defile some poor Harbing High girl.

"Court jester," Leam mumbled under his breath, and as he racked his brain for any possible circumstance that would allow for him to beat the living piss out of his brother—not an easy solution considering the prick's new powers—the alarm clock on his bedside blared out in short loud honks. A rubbery spool of nerves bounced inside Leam's belly as he was stricken with the reality that his meeting with Gideon's associate was going down soon, real soon, in less than an hour.

Gideon! his inside voice screamed out.

Leam silenced the alarm.

This ain't some no-name slug off the streets, no, no, no, we're talking about GIDEON!

Leam's legs suddenly felt like they were made of linguini; he sat down at the base of his king-size bed. A peculiar, hollow feeling stole over him, and from somewhere inside—a dwelling unknown—Leam heard, *Find it, find it, find it.* But what was the it?

Without conscious thought, Leam's eyes snapped to the top shelf of his desk, centering on a little old object an inch back from the edge, still wobbling a bit from Zach's swaggering touch. Leam moved to it and picked it up, eyeing the small piece of wood—similar to an acorn. Wrapping his fingers around it, a memory played like a black-and-white video just behind his eyes.

He and his brother were sharing a peanut butter and jelly sandwich, sitting on the island countertop in the middle of the kitchen, hundreds of knives and cleavers of varying sizes hanging ominously overhead, glinting in the shafts of dusty sunlight piercing through the windows. From somewhere far off, Leam could faintly hear the shouting of an argument between his stepmother and father, the volume escalating with each bite, and—

BANG!

—Sara burst through the wooden swinging door, her arms clutched around a large cardboard box, Bram close on her heels. The argument they brought saturated the kitchen with a thick uneasiness Leam could almost taste.

"I don't care that your disgusting ex-girlfriend is dead!" Sara screamed, her pale face grotesque in her fury. Leam got the impression she had no idea he and Zach were in the room. "Her trash is getting burned in the pit, and don't you dare *try to stop me."*

"Relax," Bram said gruffly. "I had no clue it was in the closet. Aggie must have—"

"And don't you dare *say that name in this house!"*

"My house. And if she put it in there before I… It's news to me, that's what I'm saying, I had no clue it was hidden up there."

"Uh huh," she said, nodding her head like a psychopath with weird fast little jerks.

"But even if I did, SO WHAT?" Bram shouted, and pride nipped at Leam—his dad wasn't laying down for this one. "It was seven years ago! Leam had just been born!"

"I think you knew all along, asshole, that's what I think."

Zach's eyes widened—a reflex, Leam figured, at the word asshole—but remained focused on his lap.

"Relax, Sara." Bram looked over at his boys, narrowing his eyes as he turned back to his wife. "Calm down, all right?"

"I will not," Sara said softly. An eerie hush fell over the kitchen; they all knew this woman was much more dangerous speaking quietly than when shouting. "She was a disease. You want proof? Look at her shifty, snot-nosed son." She pointed at Leam, who was giving the last bite of the sandwich to Zach. "The box and everything in it is getting burned to ashes. I will not have this refuse in my home. I will not have my child stumble across any of that slut's things. Have I made myself clear?"

"You have no reason to be this upset," Bram reasoned. "How can something this trivial make—"

"Trivial?" she said quietly.

"It is a box with some stuff in it. That's all."

"Don't you patronize me, don't you dare. Trivial? Really? Trivial? Perhaps we should consult Gideon on the matter. We both know how he felt about you and her."

"I've paid severely for that already, have you forgotten?" The words were motoring out and almost sounded like one fifteen-syllable word. "You want proof?" he said, eyes rabid as he started to unbutton his dark brown flannel. "It always seems to slip your mind, doesn't it?"

"What I think—keep your shirt on!—is that I'll extend a little invitation to Gideon to come chat about—"

"ARE YOU DERANGED?" Bram howled, the hanging knives and cleavers trembling.

Leam grabbed Zach's hand and slid off the counter, four bare feet smacking onto the shiny, black-tiled floor. Leam led Zach toward the door that opened out to the Manor's massive backyard, peeking back at his father, who was pacing back and forth like he was an angry bull and Sara was wearing red.

"Froggy!" Zach exclaimed after spotting a small frog awk-wardly flopping around in the space between the pantry and basement door. He crept over to it, bending down for a better look. "It's hurt."

Sara dropped the box on the countertop and took a few steps toward Zach, leaving Bram holding the edges of his shirt together. "Frog, Zach," Sara said. "Not froggy. And they're as weak and unsanitary as the tramp whose belongings are about to be engulfed in flames. Kill it."

Leam could tell by the look registering on Zach's face that he understood his mom was dead serious. Zach looked back down at the injured little frog, tears welling in his eyes.

"Kill it, Zach," Sara said, looking briefly back at Bram.

Zach's back was to Sara; only Leam could see how upset he was.

"Kill it," she said again.

Leam glided over, pushed his brother aside, and squashed the frog as hard as he could with his foot. Slimy green pieces of dead frog pelted against the walls, some of its guts sticking to Zach's face as he gazed up at his brother wearing a mixed ex-pression of confusion and relief. Leam smiled at him.

"You see what I mean?" Sara squealed at Bram. "Always interfering, always begging for attention." And as she proceeded to reprimand her husband, Leam slid back to the island, stretch-ing his arm into the box on tippy toes, eager to grasp hold of something, anything, that had belonged to his mother. Again and again his snatching fingers grabbed nothing but air. If he could just reach his hand in a little farther...

Sara was bound to turn back for the box at any second, that Leam knew, and he was a blink away from giving up, when something small and rigid shot up into his hand. He pocketed it, heart pounding, just as Sara swung back around to the counter and snatched up the box. As she stepped to the backdoor, she squinted at the puddle of green gunk on the floor and—POOF—the frog was intact again, alive, favoring one leg as it had before.

"Zach," she commanded, "you kill this one." And she threw open the door, briskly walking across the lawn, splitting *the two rows of black rose bushes toward the pit that had recently been built at the edge of the property.*

Leam's vice-like grip on the small and rigid object loosened, blood inking color back into his bone-white fingers. He pocketed the acorn. After a shaky sigh and a few sharp slaps on his own cheeks, Leam left the room.

CHAPTER 11

Leam parked the silver Range Rover between a mail truck and a maroon Cadillac convertible, hopped out and slammed the door behind him. His legs set a brisk pace up the asphalt ramp that led to the redbrick pathways that curved around the common of Black Patch Park. He didn't really know why he was moving so hurriedly—Gideon had specified 8:30 in the morning, and the silver face of Leam's leather-banded watch read 8:19—but the reason why his hands were shaking and his empty stomach was jumpy, that he knew. This was hands down the most significant day of his life, and it had nothing to do with turning eighteen years-old.

Entering at the south side of the park as Gideon had instructed, Leam took off his Ray Bans—the early morning sun had yielded to the persistent clouds that were now cast overhead—and looked around.

A stretch of benches toed the line separating the pathway from the trees and plush foliage. A grubby old man with a mop of white hair sat on the first bench, chewing graham crackers and spitting them onto the path where, mobbed around his filthy sneakers, twenty or so hungry pigeons were scrapping over the brown globs of wet crumb.

That is a gross, gross man, Leam thought. *What kind of sicko* encourages *interaction with pigeons?*

The next bench was unoccupied. A homeless guy was sleeping or dead beneath dirty newspapers on the third. Number four hosted a Chinese woman jabbering on her blue tooth and, standing in front of the last, where the pathway bended eastward to the right, two girls were laughing together looking at something on one of their smart phones.

"Nice shirt," some kid said, strolling by, decked out in black with a skateboard dangling from his hip, one of its wheels harnessed into a belt loop. He looked familiar...possibly had sat behind Leam in geometry or maybe worked the pizza place cattycorner from Bram's flower shop. "Vintage."

Leam just nodded and took a seat on the empty bench. His nerves had flared up again, permitting dry and uneasy thoughts to ignite. What was the real reason Gideon wanted him here? To kill him? Get rid of him because he hadn't delightened? It was plausible. But why here then, in a place swarming with Unknowings? That made no sense. So then what? Did Leam have something to prove so that he might *possibly* be accepted back into Darkness?

While his brain churned out these possibilities, the sound of trickling water seeped through to his conscience. Leam took notice of the ornate marble fountain that lived in the center of the park. He knew it well, having sat on these benches many times throughout his youth. A massive mythological sculpture of intertwined gods, goddesses and beasts, the fountain's cold water gushed from spouts creatively disguised as gaping mouths, tips of spears, valves of horns. A satyr's face was twisted up in a scrunch familiar to Leam, and he made the connection almost instantly. Pamela had worn the exact same look as Leam had bent down to grab her. That was another thing—he didn't really know what to think of his night at the Cricket apart from the fact that it would never have taken place if it weren't for his brother.

Zach...Zach...

Leam couldn't quite put his finger on how he felt about Zach at the moment, and was disheartened to find that, if he had to label it with one word, it would be envy. Zach had *magic* now. He could set objects on fire—Leam's shirt and pillow, for example—and do all sorts of other things if he wanted to, including shutting the yapping mouth of the Chinese woman two benches over with the snap of his finger. Yes, Zach had powers, which gave him a chance to be in on that Goojin project, or anything else just as exciting that Gideon might enlist him to do—and to be sent to some exotic locale to do it. And Leam, the magicless older brother, was sitting on a park bench in New Jersey between a disgusting old man regurgitating graham crackers and a dead hobo.

How had he convinced himself in eight short hours— *"Think of it as your first real day of school."*—that he was meant for bigger things? Had the resurrection of the bull figured into that mindset? Before leaving his room yesterday evening to see Zach off to his delightenment, he had fleetingly considered suicide as a means of escape from his lonesome, miserable life. Why now had Leam thought that, all of a sudden, he was going to be some snazzy big shot in the throes of Darkness?

He shook his head with tiny back-and-forths and, poetically, put his hand smack down onto a sloppy puddle of bird shit.

Most significant day of my life? he thought, looking indifferently at the whitish-brown slop dribbling off his fingers. *Get real, loser.*

As he took a tissue out of his pocket with his clean hand and wiped the bird crap off the other, the white tattoo-like markings on both caught his eye. It was their birthday, too. He studied them, as he did on occasion, to see if they had changed in any way. He thought back to what Gideon had said last night, when Zach had asked about the snake tattoos.

"No one, including myself, knows what the purpose of your delightenment scars will be. You're not meant to know until it reveals itself, if it ever does."

Leam wondered if he would ever discover the purpose of his own tattoos, or if they even had a purpose. His gut told him that they did, and he grinned at the thought of it until he was struck over the head with a blunt realization. He had failed. He didn't delighten. How had that slipped his mind? Zach pointed this out to him fifty times a day. So it stood to reason that Leam's markings were not delightenment scars, not technically. So if that was the case…what the hell were they?

Frenzied slapping noises smacked Leam away from his daydreams. The score of pigeons—furious, now, by the look of them—were attacking Old-man Graham Cracker, some grabbing hold of the gnarled, moth-eaten clothes with the grips of their feet, not letting go yet still flapping wings, while others zipped around and pecked bloody, pin-prick dots into his wrinkled old-man skin. Leam jumped up to help. Yeah, the guy was disgusting—as gross as they come, and had probably Hershey-squirted his Depends already—but he was, after all, a helpless old person. But the moment Leam's butt was off the bench, the crazed pigeons deserted their original prey and swarmed toward Leam in an angry cloud of beaks and feathers.

Before he could blink, the cloud knocked him back onto the bench, and he was left with only swinging arms and kicking feet to defend himself. It felt like more pigeons were joining the battle, possibly hundreds, attacking from all sides, and his attempts to swat them away became more and more futile. Leam closed his eyes, his intuition persuading his pride to give in—as he had when Zach had him pinned to the bed this morning—and the moment it did, a comfy peacefulness snuggled into him. His body went still. All pigeon and park sounds were muffled, and no longer could he feel the smacking and scratching. In fact, he couldn't feel a thing.

Leam opened his eyes.

"Whoa…"

He was still seated on the bench, but inside a hazy protective bubble, the pigeons hovering close by, their images blurred by the wavy material billowing around him. He pushed out at the bubble with his fists. It felt cold and rubbery, as well as impenetrable. The moment his mind registered he was safe—DING—a bell sounded, and a touch screen popped out of thin air in front of his face. The screen lit up with separately colored words. Leam read the first one, color pink:

Remove

The second, green, below the pink:

Attack

But before he could read any of the other words—his eyes had managed just a swift unfocused swoop down the tier of colors: red, purple, orange, yellow—a boom like thunder bellowed in the distance. The touch screen melted into air, gone.

A dark, blurry image of a man was seated on the bench to Leam's left, outside the bubble's wavy haze. The man leaned in, his mouth open wide into an O, his lips nearly pressed against the bubble. A foggy puff of breath clouded a small circular patch of the bubble's skin. The circle expanded rapidly—the fog freezing into ice—until Leam was left shivering inside a smoggy igloo. Outside, in the warmth of the park, a dark blurry finger tapped the frozen globe and thin icy cracks fissured over its surface like a spider web until it shattered, shards of ice crumbling down onto Leam, the seat of the bench and the redbrick pathway beneath his feet. He laughed, conscious of how insane this all was, but at the same time not really caring. It beat lying under the covers all day like a mope, that was for sure. Leam looked to his left.

The bubble breaker was a black man, wearing black jeans and a black leather jacket over a black T-shirt. His kinky white hair was divided into thirds, as if he had shaved inch-wide streaks over the left and right sides of his skull, leaving two bald bands of skin, from front to back. Above his eyes, thick white tattoos replaced eyebrows, if the man had ever had them.

"Well, looky what we have here," the man said, extending out a hand. His mouth was smiling, but his dark eyes didn't share the sentiment. "You are intriguing, sport, I'll say that about you."

Leam stared blankly at the man and his three white Mohawks, still processing the pigeon attack turned weird-human-sized-bubble-thing. It had been exhilarating, and part of him was saddened it had ended.

"It's rude not to shake an offered hand, Mr. Holt."

"Sorry." Leam quickly shook the man's hand. He couldn't decide which was more unpleasant: being called Mr. Holt, or the contact with the associate's hand, which had the distasteful feel of wet paper. "You're Gideon's associate, right?"

"I'm afraid I don't need you to tell me who I am."

"Sorry," Leam said again. He didn't have to be a brain surgeon to figure out that this was going about as well as a donkey trying to do the hibbity-dibbity with a field mouse. "I don't have my wits about me right now, sir. It's been a crazy couple of minutes."

"Oh, I quite agree. So let us move past introductions and ignore any inclinations to engage in small talk. I'm a busy man and I'm sure you have other things to do—"

You're wrong about that one, Eyebrows.

"—as well, so let's jump right into the fat of it, shall we? I want to know what was going through your mind when the birds fled from my friend, Thomas, right there next to us, and came straight for you?"

Leam looked over. Old-man Graham Cracker flashed him a sleazy grin, his teeth like solid capsules of brown mustard. "Who? That old guy right there?"

"Thomas."

"That's your *friend?*"

Gideon's associate leaned in, putting his palm on Leam's thigh. "Do we have a problem here?"

Leam shook his head. He could have sworn the man's eyebrow markings had pulsed white light for a second. *Keep it up, Leam, you're doing great. You're doing real real good.*

"The pigeons, Mr. Holt. What went through your mind?"

"Right, let me think for a second…"

"Think quickly, Mr. Holt. It was only a moment ago."

Though he had known him for about fifteen seconds, this guy gave Leam the heebie-jeebies and he wasn't sure whether he wanted to fill him in on everything. In Leam's opinion, what had happened inside the bubble was between him and the bubble…*his* bubble. So he'd lie to the guy, make something up, and in a hurry, too. But the echo of Gideon's words last night were blocking access to the creative, make-stuff-up compartment of his brain. *"I want you to listen to him and answer any questions that he asks. I am quite fond of this man, so anything other than politeness and compliance will be taken as a personal insult to me."* The never-would-he-forget memory of what happened to Zach when Zach had inadvertently insulted Gideon was still vivid and fresh. This made it a no-brainer; Leam decided on the truth. So he recounted every detail he could remember for the associate.

"Pink and green," the associate said a few minutes later after Leam had finished. "How wonderfully perplexing! Well, Leam, thank you for sharing, you are indeed a sweetheart."

Leam faked a smile.

"So...*Mr.* Holt...you've obviously come to the conclusion that this has all been a test. It'd have been a disappointment, and one that came with consequences, if you hadn't. But what was its purpose? That is to say, *what* was being tested?"

Leam shrugged, and before he could stop himself said, "How would I know? It's your test."

And there it was again—that bright flash of light above the associate's eyes.

"Sir," Leam added in haste, setting his sights down at the bubble's puddled remains. The silence that ensued—the break of conversation that seemed to stretch on for hours—pricked at Leam's nerves like sharp tiny pins. When it got to be too much, Leam braved a look up, a gesture the associate seemed to be waiting for.

"Your protective instincts were being tested, Leam." A cup of coffee magically popped into his large hand, and he took a long sip. "It's your reaction to what would happen, innately, under the distress of an attack. Even one as unusual as...pigeons." A smile fell onto his face. Like its predecessor, it wasn't a good one—something was off about it, like a bride in a flamingo-pink gown.

"But I'm not delighted," Leam said. "I didn't make any of that happen. It just happened on its own. I don't have powers."

"Yes, but you are *mature* enough to have powers now, even if they're still keeping warm inside that soul of yours. If you wanted to move a penny across a table with your mind, you wouldn't be able to budge it no matter how many hours you tried. But if your body senses danger, or that something around you is amiss—something threatening—then your magic is *capable* of responding on its own. Adrenaline levels, microsympnotic activity in your brain, what have you, they can trigger your magical defensive abilities to aid you away from harm. Now, I should say that many who fail delightenment do not have powers that are responsive to danger. Some do, though, and you are one of them. And from the looks of things, your powers are quite sophisticated."

"How so?"

"I didn't create the bubble, Mr. Holt, you did, and what you created was quite rare. I've overseen many of these tests over the years and most of those who are gifted with undelightened defensive powers have been elementary. A firecracker, a small puff of toxic gas, steam shooting out of an orifice—things of that nature."

Eyes wide, Leam listened, listened *hard* to every word. This was all very fascinating...the bubble, the associate, even that filthy geezer, Thomas, who was somehow in on it all. End result: Leam had created magic and it felt fantastic.

"Your protective orb, when it was ready, took form instantly," the associate continued, the white eyebrow tattoos rising high on his forehead, "and the computer screen is exceptionally advanced when you consider that you were given the option to retreat, yes, but the choice to attack, also. Defense and offense. Quite extraordinary."

"Great." Leam smacked his palms together in one firm clap. "So what's next?"

The associate laughed, a loud snapping bark. "I had a feeling about you!" He barked again, everything smiling but his eyes. Then, like lightning, he jabbed his finger into Leam's neck, pushing firmly into the jugular. "You don't get to ask me questions like that, my big buddy. You want to know what's next? You wait for me to tell you. You try your luck again, I'll slit your throat."

"Yes, sir," Leam said quietly. There was a rustling to his left that Leam recognized as the shuffling of the hobo's newspapers/blanket. Why didn't the hobo, or the parkgoers around who were more alive, seem to care that a leather-clad man with three white Mohawks was ramming his finger into a teenager's neck? Had none of them noticed?

"But," the associate said cheerfully, withdrawing his hand. "I'm optimistic that things will work out for you, Mr. Holt, and thus, for us."

"Thank you, sir." Leam felt a droplet of blood slide down his neck from where that purplish, razor-sharp fingernail had pierced his skin. He made no move to wipe it up.

"It's all up to Gideon, though, as I'm sure you've assumed. It's very rare that he makes himself present for someone's delightenment, and even more so for someone's second shot, but if I was a betting man, I'd wager that he'll be at your next effort. Between us—" he jabbed his finger forward again and Leam flinched, "—Gideon finds you to be *intriguing* so it would be unwise of you to give up on your aspirations to join the Cause. I have a friend, I suppose you could call him, who took two tries to delighten, and he's now as powerful as Gideon will allow a member of Darkness to be. So keep your eyes on the prize."

"I will, sir."

"Shakey, shakey, shakey...bakey, bakey, bakey. Yes?"

"Absolutely," Leam responded, wondering what the hell that could have meant.

"Good." The associate stared off in the direction of the fountain, sipping at his coffee every now and again. Leam waited, foot tapping, his butt on the edge of the bench, unsure of whether he was supposed to stay or allowed to leave. He didn't want his throat slit, though a few days ago that might have sounded like a fine idea, so he didn't dare ask. Just kept waiting, watching the faint up-and-down of the newspaper sheet curled over the hobo's ribcage.

"I have fond memories of this place, Mr. Holt. Killed my first Unknowing here, as a matter of fact. Teenage little twerp with a butt-cut. Dumb-looking kid. Crybaby. That's the only problem coming to a place like this. The Unknowings. Their stench. I don't know how you can stand it." He scratched one of his non-eyebrows and then spat an enormous coffee-tainted wad of mucus onto the ground. "They'll all be under our control soon, right where we want them. They certainly will...the ones that survive. They certainly will."

"How'd you do it?" Leam asked. "The butt-cut kid. How'd you kill him?"

"It doesn't matter," the associate said with a lazy wave of that big, blackish-purple hand. "They're cattle, Leam."

Leam nodded. His eyes found the nasty glob of phlegm, shining next to his sneaker.

"The Light," the associate mused, "they've done an admirable job protecting them for so long, that's no secret. It's quite astonishing, really. But Gideon, well...well, there's never been one like him before. Never. And besides, common sense will tell you that in the long run it's easier to harm your enemies than protect your own. September eleven, an appropriate example."

"Can I ask you one thing, if that's all right?"

"Fire away," the associate said, scratching the left of the two bald streaks on his head.

"How did all these Unknowings..." Leam gestured down the path in the direction of the homeless guy, the blue-tooth yapping Chinese lady, a few walkers and joggers, "...how'd none of them freak out with the pigeons and the bubble and everything? I mean, how could they miss it?"

"Simply put, I walled a barrier of invisibility around you."

"Oh."

"I'd just have rather slaughtered them, though, all these Unks. Like this little stinkfart here," the associate said as the "Nice shirt" kid swooshed by on his skateboard. "But that'd be a mess, and an inconvenient one to clean up, at that. I can tell you this, though, I'd start with that Chinese lady screaming into her phone."

Leam had to agree with him there. He leaned back on the bench and felt the associate sizing him up. *Don't let him intimidate you,* Leam thought. The sound of his inner voice came as a surprising comfort to him. He pursed his lips, exhaling as if blowing out a tasty mouthful of cigarette smoke. *Today's not yesterday. Do not let this creep bully you, Leam, it'll only start an ugly pattern.*

He turned to the associate with a half-smile on his face, looking him dead in the eye. He thought he saw the associate's pupils double in size for a second but he couldn't be sure. The associate returned the look, a *long* look, then leaned back, crossing his legs.

"You may go," he said.

"Okay," Leam said. "Well, thank y—"

"Go, Leam."

Leam nodded, standing up, and was only two strides from the bench when a bird streaked by in a blur of beige—one last pigeon straggler, Leam's split-second instinct reasoned—and he ducked down with an awkward hop into the path to dodge it and—SLAM—crashed right into a passing jogger, both falling to the ground.

"Sorry!" Leam blurted out, quick to his feet. "Are you okay?"

"I think so," the dark-haired girl said, inspecting her long legs and then her elbow for scratches and cuts.

Leam looked down at her. His insides felt like he had been thrown from a plane into the clouds. The pigeons, the associate, the fountain, Old-man Graham Cracker...they had all stayed aboard. The colors and shapes of the park had been erased, as if he was back in the white nothingness of his dream, except the faceless yellow man and his orange, vapor-spewing canister had wondrously been replaced by this beautiful dark-haired girl.

Leam shook the clouds from his head and reached down to help her up, his arm brushing against something cold and silver hanging from her neck, and—ZAP—a jolt of energy surged through his veins like lightning. The lingering whiteness flipped itself over to black, and Leam fell over, the left side of his face smacking onto the path with a sickening *thwap*.

CHAPTER 12

Leam was piloting a small sailboat, the clouds above him a deep bluish-gray with a cigarette smoke swirl. The water was choppy, the wind battered the sail heavy, and the boat moved with speed. There was no land in sight. Seated near the bow to his left, windward-side, was a woman, her white top flapping behind her like seagull's wings, her long hair bristling in the gale. A book lay in her lap, her hands resting on its faded yellow cover. He couldn't quite make out her face; with every tilt of his head in aim for a clearer angle, hers tilted with it. Two puppet heads being maneuvered by the same set of strings.

The woman twisted away from him, peering down through the whitecaps, his eyes followed suit. Something just below the surface was keeping pace, something odd, something clearly foreign to these waters, waters Leam had never experienced. It was all new: the boat, what he could see of the woman, the water, the something odd and foreign keeping pace. Yet a whiff of intuition was whispering to him over and over, "You've been here before, you've been here before," which tied his stomach into a knot.

Conditions were harshening, the sky now as dark as the water, and the thing—whatever it was—disappeared under the juddering boat. With his left hand clasped over the rudder like an iron claw, Leam slid to the right in pursuit. For a quick fleeting *second—that for Leam nearly slowed to a stop—the something odd and foreign pierced up through the water, mean black eyes bulging out of a brown and furry face. Leam shot a look at the woman—her head slanted up carefree at the tempest above— then back to the thing, its razor-sharp teeth bared, black eyes glinting something fierce and fiendish as it dipped back below the surface. Leam stabbed his hand through the water to grab it the very moment that the untended boom swung around like an angry two-by-four, knocking him overboard into the freezing cold water...*

"Are you all right?"

The water wrapped around him like a cocoon of black ice, and his mind fled from his body in panic.

CHAPTER 13

"Are you all right?" Eloa said again, standing over a boy in a Ramones T-shirt, the one who had sent her flailing to the ground right when Katy Perry had nailed that last high note. She yanked off her earphones. "Hello! Can you hear me?"

Something was disturbingly wrong with the Ramones boy, who flipped over from stomach to back a few times, his feet kicking wildly as if the redbrick pathway was a shark-infested moat guarding Black Patch Park's fountain. His head spasmed to and fro, blood leaking thickly from a nasty gash that spread from his left ear to the top of the nearest cheekbone.

"Oh, Jesus, he's dying," Eloa muttered, sliding her iPhone out of its sleeve on her armband. She closed out the playlist, tapped *Home*, *Keypad*, *9* and the first *1*, when the Ramones boy gasped, curled into a fetal position for a brief moment, and then sprung uncoiled, sucking in sharp lungfuls of air. Eloa bent down as she resleeved her phone, careful to keep distance between herself and the fat drops of blood dripping off his face. "Are you all right?" she asked a third time.

"Yeah, I…" He hunched up on his elbows, eyes glossy and dream-like, as if he had found himself in a place where he hadn't expected to be.

"I've never seen anything like that," she said. "Are you sure you're okay? You were swimming on a walking path."

"Was I? I…"

"Ooh, careful. Don't get up too quickly. You smacked your head on the ground. It looks pretty bad."

"No, it's not that," he said, gathering himself. "My head's fine. I…" He sat up, feeling the sleeve of his T-shirt, then the thighs of his jeans. "My pants…they're dry."

"I should hope so," Eloa said, before she could stop herself.

He laughed into a smile; it was very becoming. "I ran into you, didn't I?" He hopped to his feet. "Are you hurt?"

"No, not at all." He was cute, and she was unsure whether the muddy trail of blood sliding down his face was a contributing factor to that or not. "You look familiar."

"I do?" the Ramones boy asked, lifting up his shirt, using the inside to wipe clean the cut on his face. Eloa nearly chanced a peek at his bare stomach but chickened out half way.

"I've seen you before," she said, twisting and untwisting the hem of her green Under Armour tank-top around her finger.

"No, I'd have remembered."

"Did you go to Crystal Prep, by any chance?"

"I didn't. I just graduated from Harbing High, actually," he answered. "Here in Harbing."

"So Harbing High's in Harbing, is it?"

"Hard to believe." He smiled again—his deep blue eyes glued on hers—and it was just as becoming as the first. She could feel her face go very warm, very quickly.

An abrasive, phlegmy throat-clearing sounded to her left. She turned to the source: a smiling dirty old man seated on a bench, shifting from one butt cheek to the other. She turned back to the Ramones boy to find those blue eyes waiting for her. She felt blood rush to her cheeks. It felt too hot for nine o'clock in the morning. She racked her mind for something to break the awkward silence and if she was lucky, that penetrating stare, too.

"That is a *really* gross old man," she said with a side head nod. The Ramones boy's eyes looked over, and this time she waited for their return. It took longer than she would have thought.

"So gross," he said to her with that same, becoming smile, his voice much softer now, nearly a whisper.

Eloa looked away, pretending to fiddle with the Velcro strap of her armband.

"I feel like I'm acting like such a creep," he said. "It's just... what I'm trying to say is that I'm not a creep...not at all, okay..." He raised his arms, palms upward as if to say *Can anyone help me out here?* His eyebrows were jumping around, his breaths were short and sharp, and he seemed to be preoccupied with the sky. All of it made Eloa wonder if this boy had ever spoken to a human being before. But he graduated from Harbing High. It wasn't like he was homeschooled by a robot. So maybe *she* was the culprit for the mindless blabber tumbling from his mouth. She smiled.

"It's just," he continued, "it's been a crazy morning and... pigeons...pigeons... My mind's full of all different sorts of... stuff here, okay...bubble...I was in this bub... Wow...okay... What a creep. I should just shut my mouth, okay, just...lock my lips tight and just...Pop! Close them up, right? Shut *up*, Leam... Stop *talking*, why won't you...*stop...talking? Stop—*"

"You're odd," she cut in, a life preserver for his drowning words.

"And I'm sorry about that," he said.

"It's not a bad thing."

He was close now. The uneasy stream of nerves breathing from his mouth felt warm against her cheek.

"It isn't?" He looked both highly confused and deep in thought at the same time, like an old man looking at a menu in a diner. "I've never met anyone who likes creeps before."

She smiled, shoulders dropping. "Actually I think I said odd, didn't I? But if you'd like to stick with creep, stick with creep."

He laughed. "Did you ever—?" He stopped himself after another anxious look in the gross old man's direction.

"What were you going to say?" she asked, as something peculiar on the skin of one of his hands snagged her attention. He pocketed both into his jeans. "I mean, if you'd like to, please finish what you were saying."

"I don't really know what I was gonna say." He toed the compact groove of dirt between two pathway bricks. "I'm all over the place right now."

"I know that feeling."

He smiled, though not like before, and kept on kicking at the path. She seized the chance to study his face and, strangely, Bridgette's gossipy voice vaulted into her head and struck up a conversation.

"He's really cute, Eloa. Hello!"

"I know that, go away!"

"Hot, even. But a major weirdo."

"We're all weird."

"A creep, I meant. He said so himself."

"What are you doing here? Can I help you with something?"

"Look at him, though. Wow. Reach your hand out and take a squeeze of that cute little butt!"

"Bridgette!"

"What? I would."

"Shocking."

"Maybe I'll go find Flower Boy and we'll do a nice double date."

"Yes. Please. Go."

"Eloa, stop being such a prude and squeeze his—"

"You said you go to Prep school, right?" The Ramones boy had found his nerve again in a big way, his eyes wide, zeroed in right on her. "Crystal Prep?"

"I did, yes. I just finished, too."

"Oh, watch out." He took a step to the side. "Stroller."

Eloa followed suit, peeking down at a little girl as the mother pushed the stroller past them. Like a silverfish to a lure, Eloa's eyes darted to the blood-red ribbon twisted through the little girl's blond braid of hair. She gasped.

"You okay?"

Eloa said nothing, maybe nodding, maybe not.

"So why are you jogging around here?" he asked. "Crystal Prep's in Cliff Edge, right? That's like an hour away."

"It is," she said with a false smile. Since lacing up her jogging sneakers on the steps of Mary and Larry's front porch, her mind had been occupied with her dad and where he could be—though not whether or not he was alive; it wouldn't dare go there. But after banging into this boy, she hadn't thought about her dad for at least a minute until prompted by the red-ribbon braid. "Umm, my grandparents live here, so..."

The Ramones boy went to say something, but another man—his voice velvety smooth—beat him to the punch.

"That's a beautiful necklace. Quite unusual."

Eloa clamped her hand over the silver starfish hanging between the inner curves of her breasts. She felt her face go red as she dropped it beneath her tank top; the medallion swung back and forth until the fabric snuffed it still.

A black man, dressed from head to toe in leather, eyeballed her up and down. Strange tattoos where his eyebrows should have been seemed to light up against the stark contrast of the sunless park.

"Watch yourself," the man said to no one in particular, popping on some shades. "There's no wall of invisibility around you now." Strutting away down the path, the man couldn't have been more out of place, yet seemed to draw no attention from the handful of park goers in the vicinity.

"Who was that guy?" Eloa asked.

"That's nobody." Leam's eyes poured in on hers in a flood of blue. "Just some mental patient from St Francis's probably. He's right, though, about your necklace. Why were you so quick to hide it?"

"It's...special to me. I don't know, I don't like talking about it. Why'd you hide your hands before?"

He stared at her and she hadn't a clue as to what was running through his head. His poker face was a good one; he might step up and plant a kiss on her lips, he might step up and plant a right hook into the side of her face. He did neither. A *galunk* of his Adam's apple tipped off a dry swallow and he pulled out his hands, odd white markings stamped on the sides of the index fingers and thumbs. Eloa noticed that the pinkies were twitching. *Nerves,* she thought.

"Birthmarks," he said. "But like you, don't like talking about it much." His response was void of the acidic edge the words might imply. In fact, he seemed more at ease than he had been a moment ago—even with the twitchy pinkies—and that blue that lived in his eyes almost, *almost,* pushed Eloa's dad from her mind.

"Any chance you want to go somewhere?" he asked. "Get some breakfast or something? Taylor ham, egg and cheese over at Zippies? Over at the diner? Did you eat? You probably ate."

"I did. I should probably be getting back anyway." She offered a smile and bent over to tighten her laces, her ponytail falling down over her head, baring the back of her neck. She came back up and felt her stomach drop. His eyebrows had narrowed, casting a dark shadow over his eyes. Before she knew what to make of it, his face brightened with the return of that becoming smile.

"I'm sorry I knocked you up," he said, followed quickly by, "Down! I'm sorry I knocked you *down.*"

"Well if it had to happen—" she began to jog away from him, back the way she had come, "—it was nice that it was you."

"I'm Leam, by the way," he called after her, and she turned, twenty yards away now, jogging backward to answer him before curving around a bend.

"Eloa. I'm Eloa."

CHAPTER 14

The room was dark and Gideon was naked, save for a tattered pair of briefs, the yellowy withered band clinging around his emaciated waistline. He sat on a chair fit for a skeleton, its spongy cushion—sweat-stained and smelly—conformed perfectly to his body. The usually-springy curls atop his head fell loosely over his half-closed eyes like a fraying orange curtain. The little light there was in the room—Gideon's private quarters located on the second-story of Darkness Headquarters—was eerie, and emanated from two sources. The first was natural light, filtering through a small high window in the upper-left junction of wall and ceiling. The second: the glow of the warm, bluish water of a large aquarium filled with tiny floating diamonds, its surface laden with dead goldfish.

Gideon's slender, willowy fingers tickled the wide back of an animal resting on a dirty bath mat at his side, cooing and licking its paws...or perhaps its hooves. The pony-size creature had the body of an armadillo, and a half turkey, half lizard face. Its nostrils—a lizard-like feature, this, not the turkey—twitched in unison with the stink rising from its anus.

Gideon dug his yellow nails into the animal's hide more firmly and pulled back, unearthing a cloud of yolk-colored dandruff flakes. He sniffed his fingers. The pupils of his eyes rolled back until the sockets held nothing but two little cloudy fish bowls.

"So goooooooooooooooooooooooooooooooood, my sweet Li Li…"

As the black-dot pupils reemerged, Gideon held out a fist and flicked his fingers open. A squawking chicken appeared out of thin air, suspended in front of the large armadillian creature, which snorted, licking its leathery lips. In one monstrous chomp, the chicken was swallowed whole, down into the mercy of Li Li's perpetually stormy bowels.

"Good, Li Li," Gideon purred, stroking the animal's gizzard. Then, like a sheet of wind, Gideon was on his feet. His dark clothing, cast into a corner earlier that morning, swarmed angrily across the floor like a black nest of scorpions, climbing onto his white blotchy body not a moment before a small sandy-colored bird landed in the small window up in the corner, the tip of the Washington Monument behind it, far in the distance.

"Come," Gideon declared, his voice, though, lacking its usual command. His hollow cheeks, most always sallow, blushed like rose blooms. His hands dropped to his waist, quick bony fingers double checking that the black button-down was securely tucked into the pants with no midriff flesh exposed. The bird—a small, ordinary looking breed of bird named the Whiplap—stayed put, its head, from the looks of it, shuddering with minor spasms. "I said…*come*."

The whiplap winged into the dark room and the bar of late-afternoon sunlight streaming through the small window captured its descent like a dusty spotlight. Curly strings of brown smoke puffed from Gideon's fingertips, weaving together and solidifying into a thin piece of pinewood the size of a bar-stool seat. The whiplap, as it had done countless times before, landed on the floating pinewood which swayed back and forth as it always did between Gideon, who had retaken his seat, and his stink-a-fied pet.

The bird began to shiver—not because of temperature or its proximity to Li Li—and the shiver turned into a shake and the shake turned into a convulsion so violent that the whiplap became a tannish, milk-chocolaty blur until—POOF—in its stead stood a diminutive man clutching at his side, gasping as if he had just finished a tiny man marathon. No taller than four inches, his color was as sandy as it was in whiplap form, his greasy body coated in sweat. His little lips opened but it was Gideon who spoke first.

"Reflecting on last night's news had become so delightfully satisfying and then...*you* show up. I presume it wasn't your aim to fly in here and rape me of that mounting pleasure?"

"So sorry, sir, ya know, sorry, so sorry," the tiny man chirped, speaking as rapidly as he had the day Gideon had discovered him. "I know, oh boy do I know, that you are *not* to be disturbed in here, ya know, not without an appointment, sir, no sir—" he gasped for air, "—and that, let me tell you, will—"

"We both know you're not to be here, so tell me why you are." The hot blotchy patches of skin beneath Gideon's clothes had begun to cool. The whiplap had seen nothing, Gideon would have coaxed it out of its beady little eyes if he had. "And quickly, before these angry fingers wrap around you and squeeze feathers out of your ears."

"Yes, sir, absolutely," the tiny man spoke, his arms beating up and down as if they had remained wings. "Okay, okay, okay, okay, *so*...I was tailing the mark, ya know, which took me to the town park—"

"This morning? You were on Leam Holt *this* morning?"

"Oh, yes, sir, I was, yes, yes, *absolutely*, yes, sir, I was."

"Three states south in ten hours," Gideon said, the dimming bar of sunlight in his periphery, "with those tiny breakable wings. You must have something to say."

"Oh, yes, sir, what I saw I thought I better tell you lickety-split," the whiplap squeaked. "Because it was a *coincidence,* ya know?" Gideon's ears perked up. "A coincidence, sir, and, sir, we must always be wary of coincidences."

"How very right you are." Gideon leaned in. "So tell me."

"Yes, sir. So I'm tailing him from Whitewax Manor to Black Patch P—"

"I know about the park."

"Yes yes of course you do," the whiplap chirped, though his cautious, fearful eyes screamed confusion. "So then there's these pigeons, and *boy* do I hate a flippin' pigeon, ya know, but that's for another, for another, *time*, obviously, okay, okay, *so*... so then there's this black guy, and then the mark's in this giant bubble, ya know, then—"

"I will be told all of this later, from a much more capable mind," Gideon said, his flat ears twitching in small, anticipatory movements. "Get to why you flew this entire way without rest, stupid bird. Why you almost burst your lungs into rubbery little pieces while doing it. Get to *that!* Get to the *coincidence!*"

The whiplap's head bopped north and south in speedy little convulsions. His beady eyes engorged—his words seemed to have gotten themselves snared at the back of his tongue—at the sight of an advancing bony hand chock-full of angry fingers.

"The the the...*coincidence*," the whiplap finally sputtered out, "is that th-the mark bumped right into this girl..." His arm fluttering stopped for a moment and a small warble escaped his lips, a warble that Gideon was certain the whiplap had tried to catch before it was set free. "Bumped right into a girl, sir, a girl that, that...we know."

Li Li nudged its half-turkey half-lizard head under Gideon's twig-thin arm, perhaps hungry or flatulent. Gideon humanely shooed it away with a snapping jolt of electricity from one hand, the other reaching closer and closer to grab the whiplap. Li-Li bellowed like a harpooned whale, then flopped and waddled away into a corner near a large, perpetually spinning globe.

"What girl?" Gideon asked, though he knew exactly what girl. Yes, he knew exactly what girl because it was just too damn perfect. He made no attempt to disguise the excitement in his voice.

"The daughter of my...my last mark," the whiplap squeaked, eyes locked on those angry, approaching fingers. "The one before the Holt boy, sir."

Gideon's hand withdrew.

"The daughter," the whiplap repeated, weakly flapping his arms.

Gideon leaned back, closing his eyes, closing them into darkness, shutting them away from the eerie, aquarium-blue light, sealing them closed into the black canvas of his mind, and—

BANG!

—the canvas burst to life. Bright neon wires of dazzling colors sizzled against the backdrop of that darkness, the ends of some snatching hold onto the beginnings of others, sparks showering as they did so amidst thunderous bangs and booms. He was gazing up at his own personal fireworks show, and the spacious black sky, so suddenly vivid with connecting cables of color…Gideon knew what that was, too. He let the colors, dominantly yellows and blues, wash over him for a short, indeterminate amount of time.

"So," he said, eyelids separating the canvas as they opened. "Strong connection?"

"Oh, yes, sir, ya know, very much so," the whiplap chirped merrily.

"Good."

"Him more than her," the whiplap added with a smile. The first ever inside this room, and, as it would turn out to be, the last.

"Tell me what they did."

"Just talked, ya know, nothin' lovey dovey, sir. Afterward, ya know, she jogged home."

"The girl jogged home?" Gideon rose to his feet. The eyes below his furrowed brow saw the whiplap go white as paper. Li Li cowered farther into the corner. "What did *he* do?"

Fear had crippled the whiplap's tiny face, now veiled in a dusky grayishness; the faint shaft of light through the small high window had vanished, just as the sun outside had behind the horizon. He took a timid, mousy step backward and said not a word, quivering away from the gaunt face moving closer, pushing its way through semi-darkness like the mask of a bodiless, wide-eyed clown.

Gideon needn't speak—the watery-yellow trickle dribbling down the whiplap's leg spoke for itself—yet upon arrival, this whiplap had just about caught the leader of Darkness in a compromising position and as to that, a tinkle of nervous pee fell well short of atonement.

Gideon held his hand high over the whiplap like a dangling metal claw inside one of those booths children punch quarters into to try to grab a stuffed animal or cheap glittery watch. The greasy whiplap was bone dry in seconds, as if held under a restroom hand dryer. Two things then happened in succession. First, the whiplap peeked up at Gideon, whose teeth were bared, breaths jagged. Next, the whiplap looked down with a shriek to see the pinewood was now a tray of glowing hot coals. He tried to jump off but his feet were glued on the deep-red embers, blackening with pain. He tried again, same result.

"Cry if you must, weakling," Gideon whispered, his swirly-white eyes bulging out of their sockets, his flat orange hair bright against the dark. "But you did this to yourself, *didn't you?*"

"*YES!*" the whiplap screamed. His feet were ablaze, a lick of fire at each ankle had begun to climb up his feather-light legs.

"I told you your mark, *didn't I?*"

"YES! YES! Leam Holt!"

"Then how would you know the daughter jogged home? You didn't assume, *did you?*"

"NO! NO!" the whiplap screamed, as fire scaled from thighs to waist.

"Then—"

"I FOLLOWED HER! YOU KNOW I DID! I FOLLOWED HER, I FOLLOWED HER, I FOLLOWED HER!"

"And we've talked about you and her once before," Gideon sneered, inhaling the scent of burning flesh, "*haven't we?*"

"YES! I'm SORRY! I'm so so sorry!" the tiny man cried, skin melting off his chin, his lower body as black and charred as a midnight yule log.

"So so sorry," Gideon echoed, his upper lip peeling back from his teeth as the flames engulfing his servant danced before his eyes. A second later, a thick stream of water gushed from his eyes, dousing the crispy whiplap with the sizzling sound of an egg hitting the pan. "Oh are you hurt, precious little darling?

Are you in pain, you grubby little maggot? Cut and dry, the next time you say sorry will be the last."

The whiplap chirped a faint '*Yes*', dropping his head like a battered housewife to find himself exactly as he had been before the pinewood—which, complete with the pee puddle, had reappeared beneath his feet—had transformed into a flat slab of fiery coals.

"You will continue to trail *him*. If he and the girl shall meet, you stay with *him* when they part. There are a thousand skimpy trollops like her. *Say it!*"

"W-wh-wh-what?"

"THERE ARE A THOUSAND SKIMPY TRAMPS LIKE HER. *SAY IT!*"

"Th-there are a th-thousand skimp—"

"But there is only one Leam Holt."

"There is only one Leam Holt," the whiplap repeated, flinching as Gideon's pinky darted forward. His yellow nail dipped into the shallow pool of urine and brought a drip up to his mouth. A pink, reptilian-like tongue flicked out for a taste.

"It confuses me, this crush of yours," Gideon whispered, smacking his lips together, taking his time with his words. "Tell me. How would you bed her? Hmmm? How would you steal her innocence? Tell me how that would work. You're the size of a salt shaker and more times than not, you're a bird."

"Yes, but you said, you said you could help me, you said you could grow me—"

"Of course I can, stupid bird, but you're more useful to me as you are. Once I've won the war—" he paused, and with a snap of magic, his impotent curls of hair stiffened, springing out like the follicles of an orange-grassed Chia Pet, "—then grow you we will."

"W-w-won—won—won—won the war?" the whiplap stuttered. "But you told me you'd grow me when—"

"I've changed my mind," Gideon laughed. With the suddenness of a cashier's drawer, his arm shot forward, the hand snatching and squeezing until the Whiplap's face went blue. "*Stay...on...the boy.*"

The whiplap nodded, his eyes sparkly with tears.

"No snack." Gideon released his grip. "Pop and go."

The whiplap flapped his greasy arms with all his might, becoming a blurry ball of brown until—POP—he was again the small, sandy-colored bird who had flown in before. Bird legs bending, the whiplap bowed before Gideon with a wing pressed across its breast. The pinewood vanished and, through the stink, the bird darted out of the small high window, scraping the edges with the tips of its wings.

Gideon watched it go, thinking he might need to keep an eye on his little winged friend, harmless as he may be. Infatuations were for the weak; Gideon had never cared for a single soul, an attribution of his rise to power. But an innocent schoolgirl crush could fester and cloud judgment, and thus, as weak-willed as he knew the whiplap to be, the bird had to be monitored. But that could wait. One doesn't get set on fire, then instantly head out to cause problems for the person who lit the match. For now, Gideon needed the whiplap on Leam Holt.

Floating back to his chair, Gideon licked his lips, shirt and pants peeling off as he went.

"Li Li." His voice was feathery soft, eyes bluey with aquarium light. As the chair sponged him in, he could hear Li Li behind him, plodding back over with fat, hesitant steps...plodding back over to her master...to the master of them all.

"So the boy likes the girl," the thin man said to either Li Li or himself, and his lips peeled back into a taut, wicked smile.

CHAPTER 15

The last of dusk bid adieu to the Manor's trees, bushes, ponds and gardens, as full night sunk over the Holt estate in blacks and dark grays. Leam lay atop his comforter, eyes lost in the chalky white sky of his bedroom ceiling.

From the hallway came a weird noise, like the shuffling of a worn deck of cards. Leam propped himself up on his elbow, eyes on the door he had closed after coming home from the park around noon and—*there it was again!*—the shuffling, this time followed by a strange two-legged shadow crossing past the split between door and floor.

Leam jumped off the bed and yanked the door open, bursting into the candlelit hallway. His head swung to the right in pursuit of the shuffling shadow and there, for a split second, all the way down at the end atop the seldom-used-by-anyone-but-Leam back staircase—the shortest route to his father's library—he spotted a glittery, reddish-brown *something* before it descended down the stairs. It was gone, but Leam rubbed his eyes and looked again.

What was that thing? Possibilities sprouted in his mind like enlarging heads of cauliflower. Could it be another of Gideon's tests? Anything and everything could be now. Was it an animal wearing a cloak? A midget in theatrical costume? A small child with an unlucky face and a really broad back? The possibilities kept churning out, each more bizarre than its predecessor, then finally, the inevitable question, in one form or another, that one asks one self at moments like these, even those aware of the existence of magic: *It had looked so real, but maybe my imagination had—?*

"Leam."

The blend of his name and the low, gruff voice that spoke it startled Leam in a way that the *F*-word from a priest's mouth would turn heads. He twisted around to see his father—chomping on something gray and greasy—standing straight and formidable on the landing in front the spiral staircase, specks of candlelight glinting off the ends of a knife blade in his hand. He tossed aside a chicken bone which disappeared with a *pop!* before it hit the floor. He looked angry, but he always looked angry.

"Hi," Leam said, grinning. "Hi, Father."

"Bram."

"Right." Leam's grin weakened. "Did you see that?" he asked, thumb pointed toward the back staircase.

"Follow me." Bram spun on the heel of his black Ultra Force Combat boot and stepped down the stairs.

With a last look down the hall, Leam closed his bedroom door, closed off his thoughts regarding the costume midget and set off after his father. Anxiety invaded his mind like a swarm of yellow jackets, and each thought as to why Bram had come for him blossomed from a sting of nervy dread.

Was Bram, who was swinging around the handrail post between the fourth and third floor, leading his son somewhere to jam that knife blade into one of Leam's ears and yank it out the other, all red and sticky with brain pulp?

Had the Unknowing Pamela summoned the courage to go to the Unk cops, several of whom might be standing fifty-five… fifty…forty-five feet now below, stinking of bacon and Taylor ham, guns at their sides, ready to slap handcuff's on Leam and drag him to the Harbing PD station?

Or was it possible that the fat man had returned, seated comfortably in the sitting room with his delightenment kit, waiting patiently to torture the crap out of Leam again just for kicks?

One thing was for sure, affirmed by his morning at the park: anything was possible, magic or otherwise.

As Leam's left foot hit the corridor floor—no doughnut squad by the door, he was glad to see—Bram punched through the swinging door on his right into the kitchen. Leam came in a second or two after, spotting his brother on his left. Zach, donned head to toe in royal-blue exercise sweats, seemed to be practicing debonair looks into a mirror hung beneath the wineglass/tumbler cabinet opposite the kitchen's island. His face registered surprise that tightened into confusion.

"Whoa, what are you doing with *him?*" Zach yelled at his father, who was past the giant stainless steel fridge, striding in the direction of the back door.

"Come, Leam."

"But Father?"

"Shut up, Zach," Bram said.

Zach turned to Leam, his face going pink. "Why can't I come?" he shouted, but Bram had already thrown the basement door open, the hard-rubber soles of his boots pattering down wood-planked stairs.

"Tell me where you're going, Leam?" Zach's voice was trembling.

"Don't worry about that, Zachy," Leam said as brightly as he could muster, wanting to know the very same thing. He put his sweaty hand on the basement bannister. "Worry if the tides have turned."

"Did the tides turn on that brand new Jeep Grand Cherokee sitting in the driveway with a red bow on it?" Zach dangled a set of car keys at Leam.

"Get back to your mirror." Leam shut the door behind him, closing the basement stairwell off from both Zach and the kitchen's cold white luminescence. The snow-colored toes of Leam's Nikes blushed in an ominous red glow rising from the bottommost of the Manor. It had an acrid smell he couldn't place and the feel of Mr. Praffist's darkroom, where Leam and his classmates developed photographs for their senior year portfolios.

Leam had been down here more times than he could count, but the lighting had always been as bright and clean as a doctor's office examining room. He couldn't see or hear Bram as he descended.

He thought to call out but restrained himself, uncertain whether he could isolate the panic hammering his heart from his voice. Besides, Bram had said "Come, Leam," which was a long way from "Lag behind, then cry out for Daddy." Reaching the cement floor—smoothly painted gray, Leam recalled, unless that had changed, too—his eyes beamed forward through a multitude of thick, dust-free bars of red light, pointed in all directions, from above, from the sides, from below.

"Come, Leam." Bram's deep tones reached him with echo-like hollowness. Leam could see nothing but red. "To the shop."

Confused, Leam chased after Bram's words amidst the red sea of light, perplexed as to how one would get from here to his father's shop located across town at the far end of Capnick Street next to the old video store turned new-age art gallery. Despite being blinded by scarlet, he charged forward, really running now, really running, and then—WHOOSH—he felt the floor beneath him vanish.

With stomach-clenching shock, Leam screamed—a short one, for he willed himself quiet—free-falling through clouds of inky, blood-colored smoke. He thrashed and grasped for things that weren't there, dropping, falling, falling deep below the foundation, deep, deep, deep until his body was thrown upward with the trajectory of a boomerang, and up he shot, up, up, up, and up, arms and legs flailing in slow fluid motions as if floating inside a giant Petri dish. With a relieved *ha-ha!* of a laugh, he felt his momentum slow and with a great *thwoop* sound, he stopped, feet touching down on the thick forest-green carpeting of his father's office, located in the back of *Bram's Florist*.

"Whoa…"

"Here we are." Bram stood in front of a polished-cedar desk, sheathing the blade into the scabbard aside his hip, his dark eyes planted on Leam all the while. "Quicker way here than you're used to, boy."

Leam wiped sweat away from his eyebrows with the underside of his T-shirt. He composed himself and came right out with it. "Why are you speaking to me again, Father?"

"Bram," Bram corrected him again, eyes glinting with a hawk-like shine.

"Why now? Why all of a sudden?" Leam's voice had broken and he looked away, pretending to scrutinize the gas lamp-lit office for anything new, any addition since he had stopped helping out around the shop a little over a year ago. The office was small, in a comfy way, and had no door. Shelving covered all four walls upon which sat random items, some of which Leam recognized. Books, for instance, glassware, framed black-and-white photos of northeastern American flowers, an oversized bone-white skeleton key, a leafy plant similar to holly twisted into a headdress. The epitome of randomness.

"You can figure that out," Bram said. "Zach is who he is, but let's not pretend he's the smart one, boy."

"The night I didn't delighten..." Leam held Bram's eyes best he could before casting a vague gaze in the area of a yellow orb clasped in a ruby-red claw sitting atop a shelf. "...that was when everything ended for me. It was like I didn't exist."

"You didn't." Bram scratched the stubble on the underside of his chin. "Fathers of Darkness aren't fathers for life, boy. You don't learn *that*, you'll learn my boot up your ass. The day you hit seventeen, as it is, you were no longer my son; I, no longer your father. We were to be colleagues, Leam. Understand? You were to join me...*us*...to fight the Light. *That's* what was to happen, *that's* what was to begin." Bram paused, opening his mouth like a hungry baby bird. He cleared his throat. "But *you* failed it, boy. You failed me. You *shamed* me. Colleague, no. Son, no. You, Leam, were nothing."

Leam pulled his wet eyes from the yellow orb and centered in on his father. "Am I still nothing?" His fingers were trembling—pinkies, specifically. "You bring me down here to tell me I was nothing, am I still nothing, Bram, am I nothing?"

"That I don't know. But until I hear otherwise, you are."

"So what am I here for?" Leam's tone was hot. "To be disciplined?"

"No."

"You gonna stab my face with that blade of yours?"

"I am not."

"So it has to do with the park, then."

Bram nodded. Once. And his eyes glimmered something fierce between the down and the up.

"So it's Gideon," Leam said. "He wants you to what? He wants you to—"

"He doesn't know you're here, boy." Bram raised his hand in front of his bearded face, both the middle and little finger pointed at the ceiling. The gas lamps in the corners extinguished, the room shining over with a silver quality.

Leam felt a mist he couldn't see touch his face and arms, and then...

Knock, knock, knock.

Silver shine, gone; gas lamps ablaze like before.

The wall behind Leam began to rise, shelving and all, like an elevator, up through a rectangular abyss in the ceiling. While the shelving rose, the *knock knock knocker* was exposed, her black suede high-heeled boots first, then the white fishnet stockings that climbed under the skirt of a tight white dress and, lastly, when the ceiling had swallowed the wall whole, her hideous face, ancient and ghost-white, with mushy features that seemed to shrivel inward. Her glistening scalp, however, was immaculate, like a flesh-colored balloon.

"What is it, Helen?" Bram grumbled, his fingers tapping the surface of his desk as if practicing piano chords unworthy of his time.

"That high school girl was here again. Sniffing around," Helen said, a black-stoned hallway behind her. "Sniffing around like the rodent she is."

"Who?"

"The petite little thing who skips in here on occasion, popping bubbles with the chewing gum. Asks if *the hot guy* has started work again." Helen threw Leam a look that said, *That'd be you. Spoiled little Zach's never set foot in the store.*

"Why do I care about this?" Bram asked.

"No matter." Helen double-ticked her tongue off the roof of her mouth as if summoning a horse. "Hello, Leam."

"Hi." Leam noted a disturbing flicker of lust on Helen's wrinkly face, which would most certainly haunt his dreams for weeks. Goose pimples sprouted on the backs of his arms and neck.

"A man who calls himself Borle came in," Helen said, her attention back on her boss. Bram's eyebrows rose. Helen clasped her old-woman hands together into a hollow ball, then opened them. A thin black plate—its dimensions those of an index card—was now suspended in the air with what appeared to be a human head the size of a ping pong ball, pulsating and bleeding, atop. It shot through the air into Bram's hand, shedding specks of blood that evaporated in its wake. "Said to give you this. I'll leave you to it." Helen backed out of the office, the wall sliding back down from the ceiling with a bang. The shelf stuff hummed like plucked guitar strings.

"What is that?" Leam asked, eyes on whatever the throbbing and red thing was that Bram was placing on the desk.

"That's not for you to know, boy." Bram turned to Leam with his middle finger and pinky pointing north once more. "But I say you're old enough to know one or two other things."

Again the lamps snuffed out and the room became coated with that damp, silver shine. The mist Leam had felt before returned, thickening into rain that did not fall, into droplets that did not move. It was beautiful, like a sheet of dew, and in the beauty Leam saw three grayish images in succession, nearly invisible in the silver shine. The first and the second—clouds and waves—melted together to form the third. The girl from the park.

Leam blinked and Eloa was gone. The weightless rain, as well. The room still had a silvery tint to it, but now with a hardened, metallic sharpness. Leam paced the edges, gaping at what, at some point mid-rain, had replaced the bone-white key, the yellow orb, and all of the random stuff. Weapons. They could be nothing else.

"Everything you see but will not touch," Bram said, "has been specifically designed, some of my own creation, to harm or to kill our enemy."

Leam soaked up the weaponry—knifed contraptions, bottles filled with what he assumed to be poison, small boxes with blinking lights—hardly daring to breathe lest it make a sound that *out*-sounded anything his father was saying.

"Sophisticated works of magic, all of them. Some attack their eyes, some their hearts, their genitals, their innards…but the *they*, as I said, are the enemy. *The Light*. There are twenty-seven shops like mine that serve the tens of thousands of Darkness scattered around the world. And as necessary as it is to smash out as many Lights as we can, it doesn't boil down to Darkness and Light killing each other off, Leam. Not really. It's about the Unknowings. It's been about them the whole time. We fight for control over the Unknowings, to turn them evil…and the Light protects them from our poison as best they can. This war, of which the Unks are unaware, came to be *because* of them. We could kill all seven billion if we wanted to, easy, and weapons as high-level as these wouldn't be necessary—they have no magic to fight us off with. Sitting ducks, stupid and clueless. Weak. But under a perpetually Dark sky, they would *thrive*."

Leam nodded. He had read about most of this anyway.

"The Cause's mission, you know," Bram went on. "To influence Unknowings until all *they* know is wrath, murder, torture, rape, hate. But more importantly, that they know not love. For love is weakness. The ultimate weakness, Leam, but a weakness the Light considers to be their greatest strength. Love is a venom of vulnerability. It makes man do things he wouldn't do if he stood outside the orbit of its influence."

"Got it." Leam squinted through a cloudy glass cube that contained what appeared to be a metal rose submersed in thick, brownish syrup. "But everything I see appears to harm the body." His eyes flicked to a pickaxe wrapped in coarse twine. "You say they're meant specifically for the Light. So for the Unks, then— wouldn't you need weapons that attack the mind?"

"Been eavesdropping on me and Gideon last night, boy?" Bram ran a hand through his beard. "I said you're old enough to know a few things, but not all things, and not that." Bram gestured to the shelving. His arm seemed to float in slow motion through the silver shine. "I'll teach you how to use these. Once you delighten, I'll show you much. Take it as incentive. To get through whatever's coming next."

"I don't need your incentives. I'm not going back to how I used to be, not a shot in the world."

Bram grunted, either in approval or he had something in his throat. He flicked his eyes at a bowl lined with black-velvet atop the highest shelf of the opposite wall. From it, a small diamond rose from a pile of many, floating over to Bram under Leam's watchful eye.

"I want you to take this." Bram caught the diamond between the pads of his index finger and thumb. "Go through every book in the library for any mention of what it may be or represent."

"What it may be? It's a diamond."

"Yes. But it might be more than that. Gideon is to know nothing of this 'til you delighten and if you *don't*, it dies with you, understand? Your lessons, if you want to call them that, come first. But only your lessons."

Bram dropped the diamond into Leam's cupped palm and two things happened at once. A white light blinked from Leam's tattoos and the soles of his feet *burned*, the burn of the bull. It came on quicker than it had at the Cricket.

"Ah-ha," Bram said, and although both the blink and the burn were brief, an element of *knowing* shone from his eyes. Understanding.

"You're different, boy," he whispered, staring in hard. "You're not like the rest of us. If you are to survive it all, you'll find out why. Your *difference* is the most important part of you. It's our family's chance to be rewarded beyond any other. It must thrive, yet be under your control. You're not a child. The last year of your life, at the very least, has taught you that."

"Yet—" Leam's face flushed with warmth as he strained to get the words out, "—you...keep...calling...me...*boy!*"

Bram darted his palm forward, knocking Leam backward, throwing his body into the shelves, some of which snapped in half, upending the black-velvet bowl, diamonds scattering through the air. Bram's fingers curled as if he were holding an invisible grapefruit; the diamonds froze midflight, sticking to the air, an echo of the unmoving water droplets that had preceded the items-into-weapons transformation. Leam thudded to the ground as a series of Light-fight tools rained down upon him.

"You mouth off to Gideon, you'll get a lot worse, boy! Get up!"

Leam rose, tossing the weapons aside, feet scorching, eyelids shuffling like a flip book, the black bull digging its hooves in, kicking up dust that clouded Leam's ability to reason.

"No, no you don't." Bram rushed forward like a leopard, the sparkly plane of diamonds bending out of his way. "Control it, Leam. Feel it, yes, but exercise control. It will do you no good to slip away against me."

Noses nearly touching, Leam could smell the remnants of chicken on Bram's breath. Leam squeezed his eyes shut, willing himself tranquil with painful concentration, focusing on the chicken smell and only on that. There was no hot, there was no cold; only smell. Then it happened. The trickle of pool water against his scalp—same as the drip at the Cricket, cooling the fire, slowing his mind into a chilly daze as the heat scrubbed itself clean.

"There you are, boy," Bram said. "I can see you now."

For a second time Leam saw it, the fierce glimmer in his father's eyes, a flash that could have been, *just* could have been, maybe, *maybe,* just could have been...pride.

"Yeah, you see me now," Leam echoed, wishing—if it *had* been a glimpse of pride—that he had never seen it. The gas lamps of the office were on again. The weapons and the silver shine gone, as if they never had existed. "You see me now, Bram, but how easy was it to throw me away like I was trash? For me not to *exist* as anything but garbage for twelve months?"

"A kiddie question, boy, not a man's. It's not about that anymore. *He's* giving you a second chance. You will leave the past where it was, and you will take that chance, hear me?"

"Yeah, but—"

Leam felt the green carpet pull out from beneath him, dropping him into red inky smoke, falling again, like before, falling, falling down and down, dropping down, then up around a U-bend with centrifugal speed, rising, rising like a man shot through a cannon pointed skyward, rising up, up through the clouds of red, up and up, until his heart was squeezed as gravity took back its stubborn hold, spitting Leam onto the Manor's basement floor. He landed in a fetal position and stayed in it for several wheezy breaths before sitting himself up against the wall. There were no red bars of light slanting every which way like before. The basement was bright and clear, back to how it always had been.

He could feel the small mass of the diamond, its pin-pricked points pressing into the flesh inside his fist. He leaned his head back against the wall, smiled and broke down crying.

CHAPTER 16

A far cry south of suburban New Jersey, a man in black leather took two very deep breaths before pressing the hidden doorbell outside of a large, two-story brick building. Fifty yards behind him extended a road without streetlamps, the double-yellow lines stretching westward to American University, eastward to Rock Creek Park.

A slight whirring sound purred above him as a blue laser-line scanned over his triple Mohawk hairstyle. The door popped away from the jamb an inch or two and the associate heaved it open. A triangular patch of gleaming light spilled onto the concrete courtyard, contracting into nothing as the door swung shut. From the inside pocket of his jacket, he pulled out his shades and popped them on, shielding his eyes from the magnificent luminosity of Darkness Headquarters' massive front room. Despite the sweltering heat that punched him in the face every time he entered, the sheer size of the place gave the associate goose pimples.

"You always come prepared, don't you?"

Gideon's voice sprang forward, cutting through the stink of rotting deli meat that sat heavy in the air. The associate would have bet all the bondage gear in his bedroom closet that the stench emanated from his boss, who stood behind a three hundred foot long table inside a raised colonnade at the center of the room. The thin man was also clad in black—heavy cotton, not leather, with several metal zippers running horizontal down his legs.

"I learned from the best," the associate responded with a little bow. An unsettling noise, like that of wasps inside a cram-packed hive, dwarfed the clacking of his shoes against the maroon tiling, as if invisible speakers had been hung from the junctions of where the gold-plated walls met the corners of the black-glassed ceiling.

"Tell me. Do you hide your eyes to hinder my ability to read you?" Gideon asked, his tone icy in the heat.

"We both know, sir, that you possess other means to thread the humble thoughts from my mind," he responded, moving past *Dressing of the Unk*, a bronze-gilded statue of a pair of tall men in trench coats lowering a rippled cloth over a third man, shorter than the other two, and naked, with dead-black circles for eyes.

"Get upstairs, girls," Gideon said.

The associate—whose attention had been diverted by a deathly-thin mutt caged in the far left corner, trembling atop a urine-stained sheet of the *Washington Post*—just now noticed that three women were seated near Gideon. All three were squeezed inside form-fitting mini dresses, candy red. The taller of the two black women reminded the associate of an Unk he had bedded and killed during his stay in Paris back when Charles de Gaulle was overseeing the development of French atomic weapons. *Maybe it's her granddaughter*, he thought. *Maybe he'll share her with me if he likes what I have to say.*

Up the colonnade steps, the associate stopped in front the giant table. Gideon's face looked more mask-like than ever, his bulging eyes swelling up tight against the sockets.

The associate smiled. "We may have something."

"Get upstairs, you *disgusting* beasts," Gideon spat out. The women rose—the same dead smile coated on each face—stepping past Gideon toward the ivory staircase at the other end of the room, the toes and heels of their white stilettos crossing the floor with staccato-like taps and pings. The associate watched the women ascend to whatever chambers and passages lay above. The best he could do was guess; he knew only this room and the adjacent cells.

"Unknowings?" the associate asked Gideon, making little effort to hide his contempt.

"Bewitched into believing they're with George Clooney."

"Who's that, may I ask?"

Gideon scratched his scalp, his fingers deep in the fire-orange forest rooted in his skull. "Just one of the many." He smelled his hand.

"Quite striking. The women, sir. All three."

"No." Gideon was as still as a tree, his cloudy, red-veined eyes locked on the associate as if nothing else around them existed. "But easy and willing."

"Two qualities for females that are of far more importance than beauty, sir," the associate said. He looked down and cleared his throat, the noise swallowed up by the waspish drone. "But a man should do whatever he wants to whomever he wants."

"You loathe women." Gideon smiled, pulling his stare away from the associate. It settled in the direction of the starving mutt.

"I'll say it again, sir, I learned from the best."

"So," Gideon said. "Tell me."

"Yes. The prospect Leam Hol—"

The associate was interrupted by a metallic *clunk* followed by the hollow-sounding steps of two men walking through a door frame that had just appeared in the back wall, the collars of their black trench coats flapped up to their jaws.

"Tell me, men," Gideon said with his back to the men as they crossed the room. The shorter man—his stubby fingers clamped around an empty test tube—scrunched his face up, nostrils twitching. The other man, with the sharp-edged goatee whom the associate recognized as Flint, gave no signs of affliction from the flesh-stink or the unsettling buzzing overhead.

"The shooter himself," Flint said, without slowing his pace, "Unknowing 45G17, was the final victim. Twenty-six dead, sixty-one wounded, twenty-one in critical condition. The fear has spread nationally." He grinned. "Kavitch and I are on route to the university to collect the mind serum before 45G17 is transported to the morgue."

"They always kill themselves afterward," Gideon said. "I don't like that."

"I know, sir, the boys at Sick Keep are working on that." Flint and Kavitch had nearly reached a transient door that opened opposite where they'd come in. "Several of my guys are replenishing stock back in Weaponry. They'll be shooting through intermittently. Ignore them."

"Shall we speak elsewhere?" the associate asked Gideon, his dark eyes finding the ivory staircase, gateway to the wonders above. "Or is Leam Ho—" The associate clapped his hand over his mouth; his lips had cemented together. Gideon leaned in, eyes wild, and without moving his mouth, his voice hissed inside the associate's head.

"Leam Holt is not for all ears, fool!"

Under the doorframe Flint had turned back, eyes squinted at the colonnade.

"Problem?" Gideon asked. Flint shook his head, and with Kavitch on his heels, disappeared inside the vanishing door, the gold wall smooth and whole again.

From the surface of the table—a giant mirror reflecting the ceiling's black glass—grew something gold and circular, as if an inner tube was pushing through. Gideon turned it like a steering wheel and he, the associate and the table started to spin. The colonnade and the walls beyond it blurred into paintbrush-like streaks of white and gold. Before slowing to a stop, the giant table shrunk to the size of a teacher's desk, behind which Gideon was seated in a black marble throne.

He brought his hands together as if in prayer, then threw them back open into the position that accompanies the words *Don't shoot!* Sheets of dark, translucent glass filled the spaces between the columns, as a blaring silence pounded the associate's ears, the air becoming frigid. The associate broke the lip-cementation curse—or, more likely, Gideon had lifted it himself—gulping down oxygen that shivered into breath clouds on the way back out.

"Take them off your face," Gideon said, and the associate peeled off his sunglasses. "What have you of our young Leam Holt?"

With a quick look for a chair that wasn't there, the associate straightened, shutting his eyes, the white markings above them flickering with hot light. As the gaps between flickers lengthened, his eyelids popped open, and the associate accounted the events exactly as they had transpired at Black Patch Park.

"And how honest was he?" Gideon asked several minutes later, opening a drawer and removing an empty jar, setting it on the desktop.

"Very. He paused, though, after I asked him about the bubble, during which, I assume, he was contemplating whether or not to be truthful."

"A propensity for reckless spontaneity is a weakness. The boy's cynicism is encouraging."

"The Cause cannot be left in the hands of the irrationally impulsive," the associate agreed.

"And what of the bubble?"

"I've never seen anything like it before. Not from an undelightened."

The jar lifted off the desk, floating under Gideon's nose as the tin lid unscrewed itself. Whatever odor festered inside seemed to satisfy him. "How do you explain the computer screen?"

"Before a person's delightenment, defensive magic...it just happens. The boy or girl is under distress, and the magic reacts. For Leam, it brought forth several options. Remove and Attack were the two he could recall."

A group of five men who looked to be in their twenties—brawny, meat-stick type guys, all in black trench coats—rushed in from the wall-door through which Flint and Kavitch had appeared, their images hazy beyond the translucent glass as they disappeared through wall-door number two.

"Both seem standard," Gideon said, "considering the circumstances."

"Remove is natural," the associate went on. "Mind senses danger, body gets away from danger. It's quite rare, though, that his innate mechanisms of defense have a yearning to attack."

"How do you know that?"

"The colors. When interpreting pre-delightened magic, or unpurified for that matter, color is believed to have meaning. It's subjective, yes, but worth the speculation. The boy saw two options, one pink, one green. What's odd is which option paired with which color. In Leam's psyche, *Remove* is pink, which rarely showcases itself in pre-delightened magic. Therefore one could conclude that the boy would *rarely* submit to an assault."

Gideon's eyes narrowed. Gray breath streamed through the thin crack between his lips.

"The color green," the associate continued, "represents normalcy—a raw baseness inside him. A foundation. So it is very *uncommon* that the normal, run-of-the-mill green that resides within him requested an attack. His instinct is not to run or retreat. It's the exact opposite."

"He passes Test One, I take it?"

"Yes."

"Then make the second round deathly. If young Leam Holt is a true possibility, he'll find a way to survive. If he doesn't, we know more quickly that the search goes on."

"Smart."

The faint clank of the entrance door opening sounded behind him. Gideon rose to his feet at once. Everything inside the colonnade started to spin again.

"Test his physical ability," Gideon yelled over the whirling howl, his thicket of fiery hair flattening backward as the rotation speed increased, "his courage, his discipline under pressure. And test his patience. Get him angry. Open up the Darkness inside him and see what comes out."

The associate nodded, his back stuck to some curving, invisible force. He felt like he was spinning inside one of those twirling teacups that Unks ride at Disney World, and other horrid places as such. The glass walls shattered into tiny pieces that melted into the air, and the electric brightness of DHQ, the heat and the incessant buzzing attacked his senses. By the time he had acclimated, Gideon was thirty feet to the front door already, met by a large, bulky man in a black trench coat who had entered moments ago with a gas mask pulled over his face. As the associate scurried over to them, he honed in on the metal container in the man's hardened hands. The size of a thirty-pack of beer, it looked like it held something of precious value.

"Tell me, Raxton," Gideon said.

"We're nearly there, sir," the man said. He pulled off the gas mask, exposing a toughened face, a thick, blue-veined scar slicing down from the corner of his right eye to the corner of his mouth. There was little white around the large black pupils of his eyes, similar to those of the naked bronzed man in the *Dressing of the Unk* statue next to him. "Experiment, tinker, experiment, tinker. But we're close. A week. Two at the most, and *Gujin7B* will be ready to meet the world."

The associate watched Gideon lean in closer to the hardened man and heard the soft edges of a whisper that sounded like "sugar cookies." The buzzing masked everything else, though, like a fist of wasps trapped between the walls of his brain. The smell of rotting flesh was worse than ever.

Near the dog cage, a tall man with an unusually long neck ducked under a forming doorframe, his legs so thin and lengthy it looked like he was walking on stilts. His neck was so long, the associate wasn't sure whether or not the man was human. He was *part* human, for sure, but one of his parents could easily have been half of a giraffe.

"What is it, Garrick?" Gideon asked.

"Goldilocks is asking for you." Garrick spoke like he was deaf or had a wad of mashed potatoes stuffed in his mouth.

Gideon rubbed his eyes with his fists, then smoothed back his hair. "Is that your pet name for the one with gold teeth or the one with gold hair?"

"Gold hair."

"Tell him I'll be in shortly." Gideon's big lips twisted into a grin. "He should hear the news, too, right, Raxton?"

Raxton nodded, a bark of laughter snapping out of his mouth. With one hand he pulled the gas mask back over his scarred face—the container of *Gujin7B* secure in the other—and followed the giraffe man, who was retreating to deliver Gideon's message.

"I'll start preparations right away," the associate said, eyeing the entrance door. The room's blistery-hot air was wrapped around him like an electric blanket. "The second round of tests, sir."

"You'll do something for me first." Gideon stepped closer. The potency of the rotting-flesh odor doubled if not tripled. The associate fought off an impulse to gag, but just barely. He could feel the odor staining his skin. "I need you to find the fat man."

"Your fat man, sir?"

"A year ago he told me that the prospect wasn't ready. That he wouldn't be an asset to the Cause. He suggested the prospect be given another shot in a few years. Recent events prove there's more to young Leam Holt than that. Either, *A*, the fat man didn't notice the uniqueness of the boy and is therefore inept, or *B*, he discovered something and chose to keep it from me. Either way, he has to be found. Track him down. Find out the truth. He hasn't been seen in a year and if he doesn't want to be found, he's not going to make it easy."

"Consider it done." The associate nodded, wiping his brow. "If the fat man's caused an issue, it'll be a personal honor to rectify it."

Gideon said nothing, his bulging eyes ablaze inside that clown-mask face. The associate went for the door, halted, then went for the door again.

"What is it?" Gideon said.

The associate turned back. "Who's Goldilocks, sir?"

In a blazing second, Gideon had slid across the floor, screeching to a stop not a foot away from the associate. A horrible smile curled upward with madness, Gideon's face nothing but lips, teeth and enormous red-veined eyes. "The prospect met a girl at the park," he said, "yet you're set to leave me without disclosing it. Why?"

The associate could feel his heart peppering his ribs, fearing the worst, and the worst for anyone of Darkness meant being scorged, which went beyond the worst pain has to offer. Scorging changed a man, and not just the instantaneous physical aging. It messed with the mind, more often than not. It rattled the brain.

"No reason," the associate forced out. "Didn't think to." He had shot for a casual tone and feared he had missed. His and Gideon's breaths were puffing into each other's faces. If the associate stuck out his tongue, the tip might touch Gideon's chin. "It didn't seem important."

"How very wrong you were."

All at once the associate was terrified, repulsed and captivated.

"How so?"

"You ask me who Goldilocks is," Gideon said, his pupils engorging to a frightening size, dry spittle caking at the corners of his mouth. What he said next was barely audible over the buzzing of invisible wasps.

"He's the girl's father."

CHAPTER 17

...Mary and Larry have been so understanding, but that doesn't make any of it easier. I climbed through the window in his office! I saw his hair on the carpet! I'm entitled to be upset, and for as long as I want. But all I really want is Dad to come get me, bring me home, tell me all about the wild adventure he's been on. But that's a dream. He's in trouble, I can just feel it and it's hard for me to justify sitting up here and waiting. But that poem, that stupid poem! I can't get past those first two verses. I've been up here all day but I can't piece it together, so how am I supposed to summon help? I recited it to him every night while he fixed dinner until I was 12! Now I need it and it's gone.

But maybe that's a sign. Maybe that's the proof that...

A scratch at the bedroom door.

Eloa put her pen down and got up to let Barry in, smoothing the hemline of her T-shirt over the waist of her jeans.

"Barry," she sighed after opening the door. The beagle licked one of her bare feet and darted to the bed, hopping on and settling in, his head resting just over the edge. A strong, midnight wind whirled outside, rattling a loose pane of the middle window behind him. His fuzzy ears perked up. Eloa kissed him on his nose, grabbing the photo off the bedside table on her way back to the desk.

Frozen inside the frame, they looked out at her. She in her white dress, her dad in his beige bathing suit, and the mystical Sebastian, dressed as Eloa was presently, his shirt red, though, not violet. She frowned, placing the photo face down on the white Formica, and sat back in her swivel chair. She grabbed her pen, picking up where she had left off midsentence. Strings of letters inked onto the crinkly-new pages of her journal.

> *...I'm not meant for this life. And if he was home safe, I'd tell him. I'd tell him I don't want anything to do with the magical world, even if Porlo thinks I'd be endangering the world to leave the Light. But is that even allowed? Can somebody leave if that's what they want? If they want to escape? My purification is in a few months, or was supposed to be...*

She gasped, covering her mouth. She shook her head several times and with extreme hesitancy, she resumed.

> *I'm horrible, horrible! I just had the most awful thought I've ever had in my whole life. I'll write it down completely, only so I can SEE how horrible it is and never think it again.*
>
> *A parent needs to be present for a son or daughter to purify. I don't have a mother, so if Dad never came back, I'd never be able to purify. I could stay here or live with Bridgette and never again hear the words Darkness and Light unless they meant darkness and light.*
>
> *THIS IS WHAT GOES THROUGH MY HEAD! It sickens me. Twisted! Selfish!*

Another sound at the door, this time a knock. Eloa grabbed a black Sharpie from a cup of pens and markers and scribbled out her last few lines before sliding the latest edition of Cosmo—courtesy of Bridgette—over her journal, a smiling Blake Lively beaming up at her next to a caption that read "How To Know if Your Man Is Into Other Men."

"It's open."

Mary came in carrying a tray—warm turkey sandwich, three homemade chocolate peanut butter cookies, cold glass of milk—setting it down in front of Eloa.

"Thought you might be hungry, dear. It's after midnight. You've been up here a long time."

"Oh, thank you. You didn't have to do all this for me."

"It's no trouble, dear. Can't seem to fall asleep, neither one of us. Larry's back is feeling much better, though, which is lovely."

"That's good."

"If I were you I might eat those cookies first, before Larry finds out you have some up here. He's already eaten the rest of the batch."

"I will. They smell fantastic."

"You sure you don't want to come downstairs for a little while? Larry's watching some show about a man who tried to build a Starbucks in the middle of Afghanistan. I'm sure we might be able to convince him to switch to a different program if you'd like."

"No, he can watch his show. If it's all the same, I'd rather stay up here."

"That's why I brought up the tray. Sleep well, dear."

"Night."

Eloa picked up a triangular half of sandwich, peeling the crusts off. She heard the bottom of the door scrubbing over the carpet and set the sandwich down.

"Mary?"

The scrubbing stopped. "Shall I take Barry out of the room, dear?"

"No, he's fine." The wind continued to howl outside, a lonely continuous gust. "I wanted to say thank you, Mary."

"You've already thanked me."

Eloa turned—she felt her top lip trembling—and looked into the sweet old woman's eyes. "I need you to hear it again."

"Oh, dear, my sweet, sweet dear," Mary said, clasping her hands over her heart. "You never have to thank me like that. Never."

"I just…"

"Just what, dear? What is it?" Mary took a step back inside the room. "I won't judge you."

"I'm scared." Eloa dropped her eyes. "I don't know if I'll ever get to see him again. He could be hurt, he could be—" Her voice broke. Hot, stinging tears prickled down both cheeks. She lifted the milk glass and wiped her eyes with the napkin underneath. Mary took another step in but Eloa waved her off, swiveling back around to face the front window, focusing on a paint-chipped section of the sill. "I'm fine, I'm fine. I really am."

A loud stillness hung in the room, broken by Mary's tender voice. "Do you believe in God, Eloa?"

The question frightened Eloa, coming at her from behind like a visit from a ghost. She couldn't imagine a more loaded question. A peculiar sensation of discomfort came over her, similar to how it felt when one finds out that he or she's in trouble.

"Well, even if you don't, dear, it can never hurt to pray," Mary said. "I love you, sweetheart."

Eloa heard the door scrub closed. She dried her eyes best she could and crumpled the napkin in her hand. The sandwich in front of her looked good and she took a bite of it. She realized she hadn't eaten all day. Three minutes later, she had finished most of the sandwich, two of the cookies and all of the milk, which had seemed to wash away much of her anxiety. She saw her running sneakers strewn in the corner, and her mind captured the image of the boy she had knocked into while jogging through the park.

He was handsome, she thought, though shy and socially awkward. What had he said? "*I'm sorry I knocked you up.*" She snorted in her hand. The laugh had come out of nowhere, startling her. She picked up the third cookie but decided against it, placing it back down next to the shreds of bread crust.

But there were other moments, she remembered, that the boy—Leam, he had said his name was—seemed perfectly calm, apart from the restless blue living in his eyes. He was kind of a mystery, which she liked, but the best thing about him was that he was normal. Not "normal" as in "un-strange"—he was clearly odd—but normal in the sense that he hadn't a clue about the magical world around him. He didn't have to read *It's Time to Purify*. He would never be taught to hone his magic in order to destroy Darker beings. *That* world didn't exist in his world, the world of Unknowings, where people believed in "God" and feared "Satan." She could go to Bridgette's parties with this Leam, fit in, experience a life where strange men don't show up on the porch late at night and bleed through every pore of their face to prove that magical people like her dad are just fine and dandy even though the house was trashed, the office safe emptied, the highest alert triggered, and a pleasant memento left behind, caked into the carpet fibers.

She banged the bottom of her fist onto the desk—the food tray, pens and pencils shook—and got up, striding to the dresser. Barry's eyes followed her, his wagging tail falling limp. She leaned against the wall, slowing down her breathing. A minute or so later, she took off all her clothes and slipped on the nightgown that had been laid over her large white duffel bag.

She went to the window, rubbing her neck just above the shoulders. The skin beneath her necklace chain was tender; the weight of the hanging silver starfish had left a pink, shallow indentation running across the back of her neck. The white wings of her dove-like birthmark seemed to flap as the skin slid back and forth beneath the pressure of her fingers.

That stupid poem she couldn't remember had seemed like the only gateway to discover the reason behind her father's disappearance. But now she thought of something else that might help her, or better yet...*someone* else.

"I need to talk to you," she whispered, opening the dusty window, letting the wind feel her skin.

She closed her eyes, picturing his face—as if he would be able to hear her if she concentrated on it hard enough.

"Porlo, come back to me."

CHAPTER 18

A thinning cloud of blue climbed the warm Tennessee air, his eyes tracking it until the night sky swallowed the pipe smoke whole. Two faint stars blinked down at him from a moonless stretch of black.

From somewhere deep inside his carrying bag—strapped over his shoulder and snug against the hip of his jeans—he felt a weak vibration, which he dismissed, peering through a broken panel of the drawn wooden shutters that stretched across the front window of the establishment: The Ship Pile. It looked gloomy inside, like dusk indoors. Fastened to rusty metal bindings that were secured to the tavern's brick walls, small torches smoldered, flickering dim, soft-orange light over grimy wooden tables, stools, a few booths in the back, while casting the undersides and shadows into further darkness. Porlo exhaled one last drag, pocketing the pipe back in his bag, and went in. The heavy oak door groaned closed behind him.

He moved straight to the bar—tall legs, long strides—his eyes aimed at the line of booths alongside a skinny red-vinyl walkway, a step above the main floor. He could see the back of large-headed, wide-bodied individual seated at the only occupied of the four booths, the farthest back. A smell of stale beer and potato chips hung in the air as the flashing shine of the television set—a rerun of tonight's Braves game, 4-2 Mets in the sixth—competed with the dull torch flames. Porlo could feel the probing eyes of the smattering of biker dudes and country drunks follow him. He made two fists and unclenched them; the eyes of the locals closed and opened in unison. He stepped up to the counter. The Unknowings gave the stranger no further notice.

Porlo laid his pleasant smile on the bartender. She blushed, and through gapped, cigarette-stained teeth, a soft moan escaped a mouth painted thick with black lipstick. Porlo saw a once youthful appearance stolen by two packs a day and a steady diet of cheap vodka. She started to sweat, staring at his gray T-shirt as if hoping to see through it.

"What can I get ya, sweetie?" she said, her ugly southern twang piercing at him like tiny needles. She planted her hands on the stained bar top, slouching over a touch so he couldn't miss the tremendous cleavage bursting above the scooped neckline of her sequined shirt. "Name's Chasty, if ya carin' to know."

"Chasty, I was hoping you could tell me what the gentleman in the back is drinking tonight."

An old man—three ashtrays and two small sticky beer puddles down the counter—looked over at Porlo, then rolled his head back to the Braves game.

"Ya talkin' 'bout Chubbs, sweetie?" Chasty asked.

"Is that his name?"

"Maybe. S'what I call him anyways."

"He's in here a lot, I take it?"

"Every night." She bit her lower lip: two yellow tombstones sinking into wet, dark soil. He smiled. "And every night's a pitcher of Bud, a shaker of Jack."

"I'll take one of each, please."

Chasty pulled down the tap, smiling. A foamy stream of beer poured into a soap-stained plastic pitcher. Tiny suds sprayed from the spout, misting onto her neck and chest like glitter. When the pitcher was full and the head had settled, she placed it in front of him.

"I hope ya don't mind me askin' what ya carry in that fancy lil' bag, would ya, doll face?"

"Can you keep a secret?"

She nodded. Porlo leaned in and whispered into her ear. When he pulled away, her eyes looked a little drowsy, glazed over like a Christmas ham. She pulled out a bottle of Jack Daniels from under the bar top and pushed it up next to the Budweiser.

"You have a very pleasant way about you," Porlo said while she continued to gaze at him. He placed the tip of his trigger finger onto the bar and—WHOOSH—an Unknowing hundred dollar bill appeared beneath it. Chasty took it without much fuss, tucking it inside her bra. Porlo noted that the paper eyes of Benjamin Franklin had more life to them than hers.

Pitcher in one hand, bottle in the other, Porlo made a smooth beeline toward the booths; a line that a moment ago had been impeded with scattered chairs and unclean tables; a line to the man he had been sent here to see. None of the bargoers seemed to notice him pass.

Porlo went over the plan in his head as he treaded past booths one, two and three, well aware of the circumstances that had been laid out for him. He knew the man in the fourth booth hadn't been seen by Darkness in some time. He knew the man would be aware he was in danger. He knew the man had information about some boy named Leam Holt.

"Mind if I sit?" Porlo said, sliding in opposite the man, who resembled an obese, human-sized chicken. Porlo's eyes flicked to the groaning door, to the old man at the counter, to Chasty, then back to the fat man.

The fat man lifted his head away from the beef stew he had been slurping into his mouth. A smooshy piece of carrot stuck to the middle of his three chins.

"Not looking for company," he said, wiping his mouth with the sleeve of his white turtleneck. His red eyebrows furrowed together like the joining of two burning forests as Porlo set the booze and beer down next to a crude engraving on the scratched-up wooden tabletop that read, *Don da Long Jon*, a phone number, then *Satisfastion Garenteed*.

"Let me pour you a drink, at least," Porlo said, leaning back against the black cushion—a few puffs of the cotton stuffing poked through like clouds hanging in dark skies. "While you finish your meal."

A stream of beer spurted from the center of the plastic pitcher like water from a drinking fountain, spilling into the empty pint glass next the fat man's hand, which darted forward with surprising speed. Porlo was ready for it. His right palm was aimed square at the fat man's chest, and the invisible line of a paralysis curse jetted under the arc of flowing beer. The fat man's face strained into a deep maroon, his forearms and trembling hands fixed to the table.

"Calm it down, il grasso," Porlo said, as the pitcher, pint, shaker, whiskey bottle and bowl of stew slid across the table, nestling against the wall to his right. "I've got you beat."

The fat man struggled and tensed for minutes. Porlo waited for the impending surrender, keeping his hand flat, dead-set at the fat man's chest. The unnatural, eggplant color in the fat man's face began to dilute, and he opened his mouth, the only area of his body that he seemed able to move.

"I know why you're here," he spat out. "You'll never get it out of me."

"As to the first, I can't really say, but I assure you I will not leave this bar without extracting the knowledge I was sent for."

"Sent on a little errand by Sebastian, are we? If that's what you Light mongers are still calling him these days."

"Listen to me." Porlo leaned in. "I'll get it out of you, friend. I can promise you that. So it would serve you well to answer my questions through normal forms of communication that won't cause you any lasting side effects. You're not daft. You understand what I mean."

"There's nothing up there to extract," the fat man clucked, eyes trained on Porlo's steady hand.

"Then why have you been hiding from Gideon in this dirt hole for so long? If that's what Dark mongers still refer to him as."

"I'm not telling you a single thing, chappy."

"Then you've forced my hand," Porlo said. After another quick, triple eye-flick—closed, watching baseball, scrubbing out pint glasses with a dirty washcloth—Porlo quieted his nerves. Things were about to get very painful, and more so for him than the fat man, who would experience minor discomfort at most.

"I know what you are," the fat man whispered, no longer attempting to break free.

"I thought you would."

"You're a *threader*. But I've been trained to break the spell you wish to cast."

"Have you?"

"You thought you'd stroll in here, flash a grin at Chasty, sit down at *my* booth, interrupt *my* meal and start pulling thoughts, opinions, secrets, from *my* mind—"

"As if unraveling a spool of thread. Exactly right."

"I won't let you."

"Yet, you have such trouble with a simple paralysis curse."

"This is far from simple."

Porlo shrugged.

"But look around you!" Sweat blots were soaking through the fat man's turtleneck in symmetrical patterns. "We're not alone. The bar patrons, they'll—"

"They'll hear not a peep, fat man, not even if you scream. They don't even know I'm here and they don't see you anymore. Besides, extracted strings of thought are invis—"

"Invisible to Unknowing eyes, yes, I know many things." The fat man stuck his tongue out as if to lick the bottommost of his chins. "It's a dangerous game you're playing, chappy. It can go horribly wrong for you."

"This ain't my first rodeo, partner. I'm in and I'm out. You've never crossed paths with anyone close to my strength of mind and ability."

"But I'm not one of your shiny-assed test dummies."

"You're ready to play, then?" Porlo flashed him a mischievous, school-boy grin.

The fat man shrugged. "I've got nothing to lose. If you found me, soon so will he. But I'm not giving you what you want."

"Being aware of what's about to happen to you doesn't mean you have a chance to stop it. I'll get what I came for."

"Care to share the specifics?"

"The would-be delightenment of Leam Holt, son of Bram Holt, Harbing, New Jersey."

The fat man smiled. Porlo heard an almost imperceptible cracking of stew broth that had crusted over in the corners of the man's mouth.

"See, now that's a blunder, chappy. I'm burying what I have on the boy right now."

"I never blunder, fat man." Porlo checked his watch. "It's the challenge I chase."

With difficulty, the fat man leaned his head forward maybe an inch, but below the neck he was still. The nearest torch flame cast a wavering crack of light across his eyes. "Then get on with it."

Porlo dropped his chin, eyes boring into the center of the fat man's forehead, just above his eyes.

And it began.

The tentacles of Porlo's mind energy sprung forward and whittled into the fat man's skull. Porlo felt his legs and arms go numb at once, a testament to the command the fat man had over his own cerebral defenses. Porlo honed in, gritting his teeth, and a grin lit up the fat man's sweat-coated face. For a moment, all Porlo could see was the grin, the bone-chilling grin, frozen in front of him, stuck in time. With a suffocating pressure inside his own head, Porlo willed his threads into the fat man's brain deep enough to sift through the strings of thought in search of the one he needed—the one woven together with every thought relating to the Holt boy. The fat man's lips dropped to neutral, as if the corners of his mouth were weighed down by tiny anvils. His eyes went blank, vacant of the spit-fire glimmer that had been burning in them a moment ago.

For the time being, Porlo had him and he jumped right in.

"What did you know about Leam Holt before presiding over his delightenment?"

"Only that the father was a devoted man of Darkness," the fat man said, words zipping out of his mouth like angry sparrows from a birdhouse. His face, though, was void of emotion. "But the mother, she was one of you."

"Your impressions after you met him?" Porlo asked, wishing, as he always did at this point, that he could yank out the string before the onset of true pain, take it home, and decipher it there. But threading only freed the thoughts from the areas of the brain where the fat man had hid them. The information inside the thoughts had to be transferred through spoken word.

"My impression was that he was different. That he was very sure of himself."

"And once you had begun?" An aching manifested behind Porlo's temples, and some of his facial muscles began to twitch. "What did you see?"

"I've performed delightenments for over two centuries," the fat man fired out, his pudgy face still a blank canvas. "During every ceremony I've done, I can see into the subject's mind clear as water and assess the Dark potential of his or her magical capabilities. Every ceremony, that is, until his."

"What was different?" Porlo winced, sharp points of pressure clawing through his head. He suctioned onto the thought and started extricating it. Eye contact was the key at this stage but the fat man was putting up a fight. *Guy's tougher than a pit bull.*

"Two things struck me."

Porlo swallowed hard. "The first?"

"How he handled pain."

"You sought to test how—"

"WE'RE NOT RUNNING A COUNTRY CLUB, CHAPPY!" the fat man shouted, eyes ablaze, his doughy face contorted in a sweaty mask of rage and fury.

Physical relief flooded through Porlo's body—albeit temporary, he well knew. He stole a look at the tavern's diners and drunks; not one set of eyes was aimed his way so he brought his gaze back to the fat man, who was all sorts of fired up.

"I GOT YOU NOW, DON'T I, CHAPPY? I'LL BREAK YOU, I TOLD YOU I WOULD! I'LL KI—"

With a lip-sealed scream, Porlo threaded the fat man back into a state of half-consciousness, repairing the severed connection. The severity of the pain was double what it had been a second ago, as if two giant hands had pulled the top of Porlo's skull off and were digging into his brain, stabbing it with long pointy fingernails.

"His pain threshold is high," Porlo choked out. "What's the second?"

The fat man squirmed, his body jiggling beneath his cherry-red face. Porlo strengthened the paralysis curse, his hand steady yet tiring. Life fled the fat man's face again, a mere shell with dead eyes.

"What was it?" Porlo sharpened his focus further. "The other thing that made him different from all the rest?"

"When performing the ritual we are taught to assess three components of the subject before the actual *delightening* takes place: the mind, the body, the soul—"

"Hurry it up!"

"The mind and body are secondary; the soul being the entity that delightens. The mind cannot be changed and the body remains untouched, apart from personal markings that form on the skin. It's the soul that is altered. I extinguish any Light from the subject's soul."

"*Get to it*, fat man! Get to it quickly!"

"When I secured my mind's eye to the window of his soul, my heart just about leaped from my chest. I never knew such a thing could exist."

Porlo could see that his eyes were still dead and his body lifeless, but the words the fat man spoke no longer fired out like terse bullets. Instead they were delivered with unparalleled beauty. He became a gifted storyteller telling his very best story.

"It was a perfectly round globe. A planet, if you will, churning in space, though not the infinite blackness of the universe that exists outside of earth, no. No, far from it. This space was bright, as difficult to look at as the sun, and within it spun his soul, a breathtaking sphere, comprised of two opposing swirls of mass. One dark and slippery, like ink swirling around in the clear water of a fish bowl. The other was wavy and had a reddish tint to it, like rose petals still secured to the stem, gently billowing in a soft breeze. And these two amazing entities were splashing into each other, sticking to one another, pushing together and pulling apart. Pools of red and black swimming inside each other, coexisting, yes, but both seemingly fighting to conquer the other. If it was all there was, it'd be all we ever needed."

Porlo bent, but didn't give in to a compulsion begging him to slash through the string and end it. A panicked voice screamed through his brain, "*It's taking too long, end it now, end it now! He's fried! Save yourself! Get out! Get out!*" Porlo silenced it best he could.

"What else?" he demanded, nauseous from the throbbing in his head. He could feel his neck muscles go limp. "There's something more, I can feel it, fat man, do you hear me in there?"

"I don't believe anyone has suffered like that. I was crueler to this boy than any other before him."

"*Focus*, fat man! There's something more! Something else!"

"It was yellow—"

"What was?"

"—as yellow as the sun. Who is this boy, I ask you? Who is this Leam Holt?"

"Wait!" Porlo's eyes felt like they were being yanked out of his sockets. He broke eye contact, he had to, yet with every remaining drop of mind energy he threaded on, reeling the thought in, praying he had hooked on tight enough. "Stay with me! What was—?"

"His potential is staggering, my fair-magic friend. It's why I failed him. It's the reason I fled. What would Gideon do to me if I was the one who had delighted a boy with the potential to be more powerful than he? What would happ—?"

And that was the last thing the fat man said. Porlo—doused in sweat and shivers—had no choice but to pull away. In all his years of threading, he had never needed so much time to needle a thought-string loose. He didn't need to look over at the drooling, comatose face to know that the fat man was a goner; nothing now but a vegetable. Porlo eased back onto the cushion, twitching and trembling while he caught his breath. Twitching and trembling were two side effects he could handle, but would that be the extent of it?

He checked his watch and then covered his face with his hands. The threading had lasted over four minutes, twice as long as he should have allowed. A hundred and twenty extra seconds was an eternity.

Four minutes, it had been. *Four minutes.*

"Now you can rest," he said, looking at a man who'd allowed his brain to be sautéed in an effort to protect Dark secrets. "This war was not for you."

Porlo grabbed his carrying bag as he slid out of the booth, quickly left the tavern and lit his pipe. He pulled deeply as the door creaked closed and watched the curls of blue smoke rise. A small sandy-colored bird crossed his line of sight, flapping away from its perch atop the tattered canopy of the Ship Pile.

I'll be fine, Porlo thought. *I'm strong.*

As he put the pipe away, his eyes found something black and shiny at the bottom of his bag.

I'll be fine. I'm no longer responsible for just myself. I'll be fine because I'm needed.

Tasting his lips, he looked up at the night. No moon, no stars. He took a peek through a broken panel of the window shutter—Chasty was heading to the restroom, or more likely, to the fat man—and then Porlo vanished, leaving only thinning palls of sweet-smelling smoke behind.

CHAPTER 19

Leam awoke. His face felt like it was about to melt off, his eyes blinded by beams of sunlight streaking through the windows. At first, he thought he might've fallen asleep in a random guestroom because his bed always stayed hidden in shadows in the morning. Then he turned over and looked at the clock, *his* clock. 3:33 P.M. *What the…!*

He sat up against the headboard, his stomach rumbling, upset at being neglected. Leam had been so frazzled last night after falling through the red clouds of smoke en route from his father's shop to the Manor's basement, that he hadn't grabbed anything to eat from the kitchen on the way back to his room. Yesterday had been the most bizarre day of his life, yet somehow he had been able to quiet the chatter in his mind enough to zonk out by nine o'clock, maybe even earlier.

So why had he slept for so long? Zach could have drugged him, could've poured magical sleeping juice down his throat in the early hours of the night. Or maybe it was only 7 A.M. and Sara had tricked the sunlight to pour through the west-facing bedroom windows. Leam's best guess, though, was that the magic he'd done for the first time had tired him out like a chubby little warthog running up a hill. Now, it hadn't been necessarily *real*, the magic; Gideon's associate had said it was strictly defensive, but it had happened nonetheless, exhausting him into sixteen hours of deep sleep. A dreamless sleep, he figured, because all he could recall was one image burning on the inside of his eyelids the whole time: a tall, long-haired beauty in a green Under Armour tank top. Oh, baby. Maybe that was why he'd hibernated…he hadn't wanted to let that image slip away.

But as for laying eyes on the real thing, how was he going to get in touch with her? He had no idea where she lived, didn't know her number, email, nothing. She'd said she'd gone to Crystal Prep and that she was staying with her grandparents somewhere, but…

Is that all I know?

Leam pondered for a minute, deciding to wait for her in the park tomorrow morning. It wasn't much of a shot but it seemed to be the best option. It wasn't so outlandish to think that she might jog through there every morning. She was in great shape. From what he saw, oh yeah, she was definitely in great shape.

That would be for tomorrow, so what about today? Gideon hadn't set up another meeting or given Leam any instructions, so…

Leam's eyes found the vertical, inch-wide strip of darkness between his closet door and the frame. He got out of bed and went to it, nudging the door open wider. From the hip pocket of his delightenment robe, still as white as it was the day he had last worn it, he took out a small metal cylinder that had a keychain ring attachment on one end and a screw cap on the other. An engraving read, "Leam I. Holt ~ HH Class of 2013." He unscrewed the cap, shaking out the tiny diamond his father had given him last night. He rolled it around his open palm, studying it as sunlight glinted off into a thousand directions. He dropped the diamond back into the cylinder—he had stuffed a cotton ball into the bottom last night to keep the gem safe—and slipped the cylinder back into the hip pocket of the robe.

After throwing on his clothes, same ones as yesterday, Leam left his room to head to his father's library.

Only a couple steps into the hall, though, Leam found Zach seated on the landing. His back was to Leam as he purred into his iPhone like Romeo beneath the balcony.

"But, baby, I'm not like Billy Criggins and those guys....It's jibber-jabber....Yeah well of course Kate and Zoey are gonna say that about me, they're jealous of you, and besides, they're skanks...but you know me the *real* me, baby. I got it. I got it all....Of course....Good girl. I'm gonna have some soup and then I'm coming over....I don't care about your damn mother.... Good....Good, cuz nobody talks to me like that or bad things happen....Yes....Well you'll make it up to me when I get there."

Zach stood up, and as Leam started for the library again, he heard his brother say, "Billy freaking Criggins. You gotta be kidding me," followed by footsteps bumping down stairs.

The stretch of hallway that ran from the spiraling center staircase near Leam's room down to the back stairs that descended to Bram's library was the same length as the stretch running the opposite way, down to Zach's bedroom at the far end, but as for similarities that was about it. Between Zach's and Leam's rooms were a bunch of other rooms: a game room with a billiard table, a few guestrooms, an art studio, a den area with a comfy couch and a flat screen where Leam hung out sometimes, and several bathrooms sprinkled in between. The hallway Leam was walking down—a small smile on his face, his father's diamond on his mind—had no doors on either side, no rooms at all, just a windowless, uncarpeted, wooden-walled corridor. Statues and weird artifacts lined the walls, upon which hung various portraits of various sizes from various eras.

Snuggled against a section of wall on the left was a huge armoire—the size of a garage door—made of brown wicker that wove into floral patterning with leaves interlaced throughout. He traced his fingers over the wicker bumps and grooves as he went by, thinking about Zach, wondering what he was doing for the Cause in these early stages of his delightened life. How much had he been entrusted with? Did Zach know anything about Goojin 70, or whatever the hell he had called it yesterday morning? Leam didn't think so. Not if the two bullet points on Zach's agenda for the day were to have his kind of fun with a high school Unknowing girl, and to eat soup.

His brother still had his entire senior year to finish, Leam thought as he passed an old silver sword pinned to the wall by a thick metal stake thrust through its elaborate hilt. But after that Zach would be assigned an Occu-Wait: a job that doesn't cause suspicion in the eyes of the Unknowings. Leam knew the importance of keeping up appearances—as would anyone who had read *Eyes and Ears Everywhere*—making it seem like the many homes of Darkness scattered across the country were normal households with normal families. Placing Dark men and women into Unknowing jobs that benefitted Cause strategies was just as important. Bram's was the flower shop—a perfect cover for his weapon trafficking, Leam was proud to now know. Plus, Leam had overheard once that Sara had Occu-waited at a day spa somewhere ritzy up in Connecticut before Bram had wooed her on down to Harbing.

But what will yours be, Zach? Leam wondered, halfway along now, a few paces from a glass showcase that housed a collection of polished trumpets, which Sara, for some reason, had removed from the music room, which was down on the first floor beneath the library. He made a silent wish, walking by a series of rusted daggers bolted to the wall, that Zach's first Occu-wait would have something to do with cleaning up feces, or being the guy responsible for oiling up bodybuilders before they took the stage.

Nearing the back staircase, Leam came upon a curious painting he had never seen before, its frame void of the dust that overspread the neighboring portraits. The setting was the interior of a train from what looked like the late 1800s, the seats of which were occupied by sheep dressed in old-fashioned business suits, talking to each other, drinking tea, reading newspapers and doing other miscellaneous tasks that sheep dressed in business suits might do on a train.

Leam focused on something far off in the background in the very last row of the cabin: a smudge of yellow paint, the only yellow in the entire painting. To him it looked like a book being held in one of the sheep's hands or whatever it was that sheep had at the end of their arm-legs. It looked familiar, but Leam couldn't place it. He strode the last twenty or so feet to the landing, his stomach making sounds that suggested it had started eating itself.

The back staircase looked like something out of the future—entirely chrome plated; steps, ceiling and walls. As Leam descended to the second floor, he ducked under the hundreds of inanimate birds that hovered in the stairwell, eerily lifelike, apart from their silver coloring.

Leam opened the glass-paned door at the bottom of the stairs and stepped onto the cushy, deep maroon carpeting of Bram's library, where a score of candles always burned, even during daytime hours.

Shelving covered every inch of every wall, as it did in his father's office at *Bram's Florist*, stacked full of books, though, not weapons. Leam gazed up at the ceiling. Hundreds of book spines stared down at him, each volume held into position by his father's anti-gravitational enchantment. Leam closed his eyes with a pleasant sigh. He loved the smell of the room.

Ignoring the hunger pangs in his belly, Leam grabbed ten or so books off of the top shelf on his immediate right and stepped over to his father's Find-a-Thought: a large ivory contraption cosmetically similar to a washing machine. He placed the stack of books on the nearest polished-oak table—one of many in the room, with leather chairs and ottomans and reading lamps scattered about—and dropped the top one (*Myths of the Dark*, by Crank Teeters) inside the contraption. He closed the lid and kept his palm down on the cold ivory while concentrating on the word *diamond*, repeating it over and over in his mind. The Find-a-Thought's lid shook beneath his hand as if caught in an aftershock, glowing like a light bulb. Leam lifted the top. *Myths of the Dark* soared out like a murky comet, rocketing into its proper slot on the proper shelf.

Leam went through the same procedure with the second book, then the third, the fourth, the fifth—but when the lid opened, each one flung back to the slot from which it had been removed, the pages empty of anything associated with diamonds. Leam grabbed another stack from a shelf, and five minutes later, grabbed another, waiting for one of the books to rise out of the Find-a-Thought and float into his hands.

Twenty minutes later the growling in his stomach had gone from a pug protecting its favorite toy to a starving wolf guarding a kill. He pointed at the half-stack on the table—books seventy-five through eighty—as if gesturing to a toddler to stay put, then moved to the French doors that opened out into a spacious area that led to second floor access to the main spiral staircase. On his way out, candlelight flickered off something on a desk at the far end of the library—something bronze, small, glittery—but Leam's belly called the shots right now; curiosity would have to wait its turn.

He stepped out and headed to the stairs, swallowing down little pools of hunger saliva. He went down to the first floor and turned right, pausing outside the entranceway to the kitchen. A pair of voices had found his ear, which, after a few tender steps, he pressed against the swinging door.

"Do what I say, all right, my child? Has Mommy ever let you down?"

"This is cold."

Leam heard a *clink*, followed by the *click click click* of a stove burner turning over.

"Why don't you just let me heat it up with my mind."

"I think you know the reason for that by now, my lovely."

"It's so stupid. Saving the strength of my powers by doing common tasks just how the Unknowings do them? How much magical energy could I possibly waste heating up a bowl of tomato soup?"

"It matters. You'd be surprised. Gideon himself practices conservation."

"Yeah right. No chance *Gideon* puts a pot of soup on the stove."

"Well, maybe not Gideon, but others certainly do. Your father does. It's a smart habit and it's a good idea for you to start getting used to it."

"But I need the practice! Besides, I'd rather follow in Gideon's footsteps than Father's. No offense."

"Do not disrespect your father in his own home."

"It's not disrespect. I'm just saying that I want to be a *substantial* part of the Cause. I want to prove to Gideon that

I'm worthy of taking on a bigger role than Father. I want to be important."

"I did not raise you to be ignorant, my child. You have no idea what your father has done for the good of the Cause. What we both have. But I do see big things for you, Zach Holt. You may very well play a role that exceeds that of any other Holt or Bishop."

"I'm gonna have to just to keep our name out of the garbage. Leam soils our reputation, he wasn't even delighted. He doesn't do anything. He's a bum."

"Thankfully, you are nothing like your half-brother. You will go on to great things. He will go on to the Burger King night shift."

"But what great things, Mother? Yesterday I was staking out a house owned by Unks. What is *that*? Nothing—that's what that is. Pointless."

"That will change soon, I promise you. You forget your situation is different from other children of Darkness."

"How so?"

"Gideon and your mother are very close."

"He listens to you?"

"More than you would imagine. Mommy won't let you down. You concentrate on controlling your...leisurely habits, as you've promised, and leave the rest to me."

"Fine."

"Now tell me, sweetheart, is that rash on the inside of your leg still bothering you? I don't know why you won't let me treat it. After you eat, I want you up to the fifth floor to dip that leg in the pool, and I don't want to hear any—"

"What was that?" Zach interrupted.

"What was what?" Another *clink*. "Here, your soup's ready."

"I could've sworn I heard—"

Leam pushed the door open, heading for what Sara referred to as the "Carb Cabinet" on the other side of the island in the far corner.

"Speak of the devil," Zach said. He was seated on stool at the island. "We were just talking about you."

"*Speak of the devil*," Sara laughed. "Honestly! The sayings Unknowings come up with."

"Wow, Leam," Zach sneered, as Leam surveyed the contents of the snack cupboard. "You got up before nightfall. Good for you. A real go-getter today."

"Yes, Leam. It's so nice to see you," Sara said. "Can we get you anything?"

"Any soup left?" Leam asked, his palms firm on the countertop. Sara was in his periphery, standing near the swinging door opposite the one through which Leam had entered.

"No," Sara said.

The soup in the pot vanished as Leam looked over at the stove. He wanted to point out that she should've exercised magical conservation, but thought better of it and grabbed a box of Ritz.

"So, what were you guys talking about?" he asked, chomping down on crackers three at a time.

"Don't worry about that," Zach said. "It's got nothing to do with you."

"You just said 'speak of the devil' four seconds ago," Leam said, looking at Zach the way a person looks at the TV right when the power goes off. Zach blinked a couple of times, picked up his spoon and went to town on his soup.

"Something's different about you," Sara said, stepping closer to Leam as he shoved an eight-stack of Ritz in his mouth. "What happened yesterday, Leam?"

Leam shrugged.

"Tell me right now, Leam. This very instant."

Leam attempted to say "Mind your business" but all that came out was undecipherable mumbo-jumbo and cracker crumbs that shot from his mouth like an angry dust cloud right into Sara's pointy face. She was fire-engine red in seconds, as if a child had colored over her paleness with a crayon. A laugh slipped out of Zach's mouth before he could catch it.

"Sowwy, Sawa," Leam said, trying to swallow down the remains.

"BRAM!" she screamed.

"He's not here, Mother, remember?" Zach said.

"You're a smug little rodent, aren't you, Leam?" Sara spat, snatching the sleeve of Ritz out of Leam's hand and smashing them down on the counter. She held up her hand a foot from her face as if studying an invisible grapefruit: the face-full of crumbs shot into her palm like tiny metal shards firing into the pull of a magnet.

"Careful bringing rodents up in front of Zachy-poo," Leam said. Zach shivered, goose pimples budding up his tattooed arms.

"Tell me what happened yesterday, Leam," Sara said. She was still near him, but he could barely hear her over the soft hum of the refrigerator.

"I'm not taking your crap anymore, Sara. The days where I drop my head and crawl back to my room are gone."

"That's not your room anymore."

"Say again?"

"I know something happened yesterday." Sara smoothed back her already tightly-stretched hair, hand over hand like a clairvoyant clearing away unwanted mental energy. "I have a sixth sense about these things."

"What things?"

"Things that simpleminded boys try to conceal."

"I'm not a boy."

"Oh yes you are. A lazy, friendless, gutless, *boy.*"

Her red-lipstick mouth twisted into a satisfied smile, which Leam reciprocated with a grin of his own. Zach slurped his soup.

"You're gonna be very sorry how you treated me, Sara."

"I am? Why is that?"

"Because sometime soon I'm gonna be a guy who can do something about it."

Leam turned away, reaching into the Carb Cabinet and pulling out a box of frosted blueberry Pop Tarts. When he turned back, he felt his heart plummet to the bottom of his belly. Sara's expression was beyond animalistic. Her face, that of an infuriated wild bird. Her eyes narrowed into slits and—BOOM—Leam was lifted up and thrown backward rump first into the kitchen sink. Pop Tarts jumped out of the box like fireworks, thudding into the glass windows behind him, the late afternoon sun glinting off the foil packaging as they fell scattered. Water sprung out of the faucet and turned sludgy and brown, covering Leam's clothes and skin. Before he could think to do anything, the mudwater hardened, cementing him to the sink.

Gently over the shiny black tiles of the floor, Sara stepped toward the sink. Leam's legs stuck out of the brown cement from the shins down; arms from the biceps out; shoulders up to the tip of his head.

"Do you have any concept of how this all works when someone like you threatens someone like me? This is a little lesson in manners. It's been too long," she said. "Listen to me, Leam. I don't like you. I don't like anything—*anything*—about you. To be honest I despise you so much I often find myself daydreaming about your death and how you'll be more alone than you are now."

Leam struggled against the cement's hold, his face getting hot. Sara faced her palm at him and he felt the cement tighten.

"Despite your immaturity and obvious lack of social skills, you are an adult now, technically. Your entrance to the threshold of manhood carries good news to my hands. Do you know why?"

Leam started to speak but Sara held up a finger. Nothing audible came out of his mouth.

"It's good news because Bram and I no longer view your stay here as obligatory. You're out on your own, Mr. Big Shot. Starting the first of next month, you'll no longer be granted entry here. The Manor, alas, no longer your home. You'll never walk its halls again. It's time for you to go away."

Leam went to open his mouth in protest, but Sara narrowed her eyes and Leam's jaw clamped shut and locked. Blood was flooding his face as he kicked his feet and lamely wiggled his arms. He felt like an insect that had been flipped on its back.

Over Sara's shoulder he could see his brother, half amused, still spooning in that red soup.

"Do not speak, Leam. I thought I had made that clear, but like a little child it seems you're unable to understand things the first go around. Do you find that true, my love?"

"Yeah, he's an idiot," Zach chimed in.

"He *is* an idiot, isn't he? You're so confused, Leam, it's pathetic. If I *could* I'd feel sorry for you, the peasant that you are, but feeling pity for the inferior is pitiful in and of itself.

"Now, Leam, let me stress that any sentimental mementos, silly gizmos, or any of the other trash you have lying around in the room that we have permitted you to sleep in for eighteen years must be cleared out by midnight on the thirtieth."

"And don't let me catch you in *my* room stuffing my things in your suitcase," Zach said.

"Anything left behind will get cooked out back in the pit," Sara said. "Have you heard me?"

Leam felt his jaw release. He took a few seconds to catch his breath, feeling his pinkies prickle, the soles of his feet heating up. "Father won't kick me out. Things have changed. Things you don't know about. He won't put me out on the street, not anymore."

"Who do you think runs this house?" Sara laughed. "If I want something to happen, it happens. End of story."

"He's my *father*," Leam growled, his fists clenched so tightly they shook atop the cement, while the bull began kicking up some serious clouds of sand and dust inside him. "Now, let me up!"

"No," Sara said with another laugh.

"He's not going to abandon me, you stupid woman! I know he won't, so don't stand there and tell me he will!"

"Your mother abandoned you, did she not? So why wouldn't Bram?"

"You don't know anything!" Leam shouted, his eyelids flapping up and down at an alarming speed. "Nothing! Nothing! Nothing! Nothing!"

"What are you doing?" Sara asked, taking a half-step back. "It's happening to you, isn't it?"

Leam registered true concern in her voice before the burn rising from his soles lassoed his attention away. Everything surrounding him—the cabinets, the windows, the appliances lining the counters—went a little fuzzy. A powerful desire to rise filled his chest like gun powder and—BANG—the mud-brown cement split apart in great clumps that crumbled into the sink and onto the floor.

Upright in less than a second, Leam bellowed. Zach looked to his mother for direction. Leam, covered in chalky, dirt-like residue, stepped toward Sara, heat rising up his calves, heat that was keen to take over, keen to reach the top.

"Watch it," Sara said, holding her ground, her open palm faced at the center of Leam's chest, fingertips bent down at the top knuckles. "I've known you your whole life—I know what this is. Get yourself under control or I will unleash on you."

Leam threw her a manic grin.

"I will unleash on you, Leam."

It was then, while the burn was climbing his thighs, that Leam heard a distant voice from last night—his father's—echoing between his ears.

It must thrive, yet be under your control. You're not a child.

Leam squeezed his eyes closed, muttering, "Down, down, down, down..." and soon after, he felt a ping of cool water coast down his spine beneath the skin. He had stopped the rising burn at the waist. He opened his eyes as more drops of cool water—first tens, then hundreds—cascaded down his back, sides, and torso, showering the heat downward, caging the bull.

"Wise move," Sara said.

"You can't kick me out." Leam's skin still tingled with fire. "I have a job to do here. Bram authorized it."

"Best to get it done by the end of the month, then. After that, it's over. You'll be out and you won't be able to get back in. If you try, my magic will keep you out. Do everyone a favor...stay gone once you go. You're not wanted. You never were. What kills me is that you know all this already, you dumb, *stupid little child*. Get a clue. Come to grips with it."

Leam dusted off his clothes, peeking over at Zach, searching for something, *anything*, in his brother's eyes, but Leam might as well have been looking at a pair of empty pits. He turned away, looking out at the backyard as the sky started to cloud over, out at the bushy pine tree near the shed under which he and Zach had hidden Sara's sister's giant bras—her panties, too, the size of tablecloths—when Aunt Gertie had visited over a decade ago. Leam blinked the memory away and snatched up all the Pop Tarts, cradling them against his chest. He crossed the kitchen and reached for the door, when Sara said his name. He paused but did not turn.

"You cannot win," she said. Leam could hear in her voice that she was savoring every word. "Losers never win."

Leam pushed outward and headed for the stairs. As the swinging door wobbled back and forth to a stop, Leam heard Sara's and Zach's laughter chime around the kitchen walls in a series of ringing echoes.

CHAPTER 20

Across town, Bram Holt was walking along a path of damp gravel, indifferent to the light rain that was falling onto his head and the shoulders of his black trench coat. He passed the same grave markers and tombs that he always did when he came to Gaddiel's Graveyard, one of Harbing's two cemeteries.

He wasn't a frequent visitor and never stayed particularly long, but some days he liked the idea of staying permanently, his body at rest beneath the comfort of the rich soil, his darkened soul releasing and traveling somewhere unknown.

He slowed as he went by the plot of the long-deceased Duncan family. From left to right, their grave markers read, *GRAHAM, MADELINE, ABIGAIL, CHRISTIAN.*

The Duncans' deaths were still a mystery in these parts. After their bodies were discovered in the woods off Sidwitch Lane, the cops and local detectives were mystified to learn—a few days into the investigation—that no one in Harbing or any of the neighboring towns had any idea as to where the family had lived or even who they were. The bodies were naked, apart from an old, black, faceless watch fastened around the right wrist of the nineteen-year-old boy, who would later be informally identified as Christian. Weeks later, investigators hadn't uncovered a single clue, and the results of the autopsies only added to the quandary: every body part, internal and external, of all five corpses was intact and unharmed, apart from one. Each victim's heart was missing, with no scarring or skin mutilation of any kind over the chest, or elsewhere.

Bram continued past the Duncan's plot without an inkling of remorse, despite being one of the three men responsible for the murders. He remembered how the itinerary he had been given indicated that the killings must take place immediately, and so they were.

The Cause is always above the individual, he thought, veering off the main path onto a familiar side trail of worn down grass until he had reached his destination. Aggie's final resting place. Her tombstone, wedged into the ground to the left of a low hanging Cyprus tree, was worn and dirty. Bram stopped about three yards away from it, smeared the rain beads collecting on his face away with his forearm, and pushed his fists inside the pockets of his coat. Without scanning his surroundings, he spoke.

"The hair—" Bram's lips tightened, "—after the hair I took for Leam's ceremony, I'm sure you were relieved I haven't come back until now, so... And I'm not here to disturb you this time, Aggie. I don't imagine you want to hear it, what I have to say, but I'm going to talk anyway... Sara never listens, so..."

He shifted his weight. His boots sunk a quarter of inch into the dirt beneath the wet grass.

"It's been busy. I've been caught up in a few things, often two places at once. We've created a serum for Unknowing children that increases their tendency to bully weaker peers. Suicides, grades seven through twelve, have tripled, so... And we're very close to finishing—and this one is big, Aggie—we've almost created a tasteless gaseous substance that Unks can't see that keeps some of them alive yet corrupts their..." Bram wiped rainwater off his face with the underside of his right forearm, "...but I know you don't want to hear about that kind of thing."

Bram stared at the tombstone, his eyes getting lost in the letters of her name. He was quiet for some time.

"I know who I am, Aggie. We would have never worked out—when our worlds intertwine it's always out of war. Nothing positive can come out of it. I remember the day you told me, but what was I supposed to do? I was Darkness. Gideon was noticing me, he had plans for me. What could I have done?"

He looked at the Duncan plot, then took a step closer to Aggie's tombstone. A simple one. Her name and nothing else.

"My father had just been killed, remember? The very first day the Manor was bequeathed to me. You told me in the side garden. I asked if it was mine and you slapped my face."

A small smile twitched on lips. His eyes softened with sorrow. When he next spoke, it was hard for him to hear his own words.

"I was a coward. Too soft to grab you and run away. But he would've tracked us down in a flat second... And what he did to me, I...I couldn't have that happen to you."

Bram looked away, staring off at the woods a few tombstones to his right. His eyes got lost in the swirly green of the leaves hanging from the damp oak tree branches, little drops of moisture clinging onto the edges before letting go. He closed his eyes and the memory pulled him in.

Spread eagle and naked, he was fastened by invisible chains to a dungeon wall. The ceiling, the floor and the walls were as orange as the coils atop his torturer's head.

"What did you expect, Bram? No consequence for disobedience?" Gideon extended his left arm, hand open, fingers stacked vertically. For a quick moment Bram felt a tingly bubbling in his chest and head as if a hot plate had been slid beneath his heart and another under his brain. Helpless and panic-stricken, he became conscious that the onset of scorging was underway. He screamed for help. Gideon grinned.

From the inside out, a searing red dot of fire burned into Bram's skin a few inches above his navel. It began to enlarge and the hot plates were cranking up to scalding. Again he screamed, this time the long, earsplitting shriek of a housewife who spots a large snake slithering across the kitchen floor.

"Yes, some of us have bedded Light females," Gideon said. He was twelve feet away—the dungeon was small, the size of

a city-corner bodega—his opaque eyes red-veined and bulging. "But marriage, Bram? To consider it? Tsk, tsk, tsk."

Gideon tilted his head as if watching a child doing something cute. Bram howled, his eyes shocked wide with the terror of escalating pain, as well as Gideon's nightmarish approach. Because the clothes draped around Gideon's stick-thin body matched the walls and the wild mane atop his head, Bram's eyes were tricked into the illusion that both body and hair had disappeared into the backdrop. All that was left was a crazed, grinning clown mask swimming closer and closer through an orange sea.

The circular stain was spreading amorphously across Bram's torso like thick, skin-blistering blood. "I can't, I can't," he whimpered, praying for the stain to expand more quickly, praying for it all to end.

"Did you conceive for a purpose, Bram? Tell me, did you?"

Bram shook his head. The stain had spread across most of his body. Blood—just dripping at first—was now trickling from his eyes in thin crimson waterfalls.

"Bram, did you conceive for the purpose?" Gideon asked, with a sort of gleeful lunacy.

Shaking his head violently, Bram tried to shy away from the grinning clown mask, so very near, getting so very near. He could smell the fumes of his own blood. He felt the skin on his face crinkle like aged paper.

"The mother-to-be must die, Bram." Each word vomiting from the clown mask's mouth slapped Bram across the face with a putrid, egg-like stench. "Have you heard me, you insignificant piece of scum? She dies after the birth. Nod your head if you understand. Good. But the infant lives. Nod again. Good."

Bram wept soundlessly. Thick streams of drool spilled from his mouth like gooey icicles. He could feel the stain's fire stretching over his brow, up to his scalp. The wide-smile clown face bobbed closer and closer, mere feet from his own.

"Look at you," Gideon whispered, and the expanding, bloody stain of pain that was devouring Bram fled with the swiftness of flicking down a light switch. "You've aged ten years, Bram. A decade gone that shouldn't have."

Bram nodded, tears slipping down into his beard, his limp naked body pasted to the dungeon wall like a flattened bug against a car windshield.

Gideon wiped the sweat off of Bram's brow with his fingers, which he then brought under his nose. Bram closed his eyes, closed them away from the orange, as Gideon's cracker-dry lips pressed against his ear.

"And you will be the one to kill her."

Bram swiped at the rain dripping in his ear. He could feel the touch of his trench coat, soft and comforting, carrying him away from the memory and back to the wet and the green and the graves.

"He was right to punish me, Aggie, and sometimes I force myself to revisit the pain. Me and you..." His voice trailed off, eyes floating up to the canopy of the Cyprus tree that sheltered her tombstone from the steady drizzle of the warm rain. "We hang from different branches, you and me."

Bram inched a little closer, his eyes getting as moist as the grass beneath his boots. He cleared his throat.

"And Leam. Last year...my blood, your hair...the door of Darkness was right in front of him and he couldn't push it open... I avoid him. I've stayed away because when I see him, I see you. I see you and I hate him for it. He's an unceasing reminder. But..."

Bram looked to his left then his right. When he came back, centering on the tombstone, his eyes were alive with a fire undiminished by tears or rain.

"But he's *back*, Aggie. Undelightened, but clawing back, fighting away from his failures, and if he could just grab firm hold of...of the *rope* Gideon's thrown at his feet, it could pull him back into the realm of Darkness where he belongs. He has it *in* him, Aggie. He's special, I see you in him. Anyway, if he can stabilize his mind, he...he...he's got a chance. It's early, but he's still alive so Gideon...so Gideon..."

For a while all was silent, apart from the delicate pitter-patter of rain sprinkling on leaves.

"Gideon, I sense now more than ever—" Bram's jaw muscles clenched, "—isn't solely interested in my sons' contributions to the Cause. He's after something else of mine, and if he wants her, who am I to stop him? But if I could, would I? She wants nothing to do with me, but she drools from the mouth from anything and everything about her son. Even her birds are given more time than me—*her birds!*—whether in the confines of their cage or not, and I…"

Bram reached inside his coat and pulled a knife blade from the scabbard, wrapping his hand around the sharp, cool metal, thinking about all the blood it had shed. Sometimes his own. He looked at the canopy of clouds above, as even and gray as an Englishman's suit. He looked up for a long time.

"It was foolish, me and you," he said, coming back down to earth. "We were fools."

He thought to turn and walk away. Instead, he knelt down, his knees squelching into the wet dirt and grass. He closed his eyes and placed his hand over the etched engraving of her name, the mother of his firstborn. The instant his fingers touched the stone, a flash of white light filled the sky and flooded Gaddiel's Graveyard. The burst of fluorescence lasted less than a second, gray clouds once again visible overhead.

The graveyard looked exactly as it had before the sky blazed with light, but Bram lay motionless, face down next to the grave. Occasional drops of rain seeped through the thick awning of the Cyprus tree, collecting on the back of his trench coat.

CHAPTER 21

After watching Thomas get swept up by the night, Gideon's associate closed his front door, went through the modest, uncarpeted living room—one black couch, one black loveseat, one coffee table, one lamp and a wall covered with whips, paddles, hoods and blindfolds that hung from glass pegs—and came back into the kitchen, sitting down at a circular table covered by a eggplant-colored tablecloth.

The soft amber glow of the lamp hanging overhead illuminated the items spread out on the table similar to how the morning's sunrise had thrown its first dim taste of dawn over the mountain tips and treetops of El Jabel, Colorado. The table held a mug of cold coffee, a set of car keys connected to a swab of leather bearing a stitching of the Cadillac crown emblem, a milk-stained spoon in an empty cereal bowl, a leather jacket half-hanging over the table edge, and a slew of loose-leaf papers blemished by scribbles and scratched-out notes.

Under the careful control of his mind, the mug, spoon and cereal bowl floated over the sea-green linoleum floor, dropping into the sink basin with a clatter. He closed his weary eyes, pampering them with a gentle rub. After the white eyebrow markings had received similar treatment, the associate's eyes peeked open, the pupils landing on two bowls—one for food, the other water—that lay on a red mat in the corner near the refrigerator. This didn't strike the associate as odd despite that he didn't own a pet. Not really.

The associate had gotten up early and spent all day at the table planning Leam Holt's second round of prospect testing—he worked freehand from home until the time came to actually create—when Thomas had interrupted his musing a couple minutes ago to deliver the fat man report. Like Thomas, the associate was a tracker in the Seek Department, but around the time of Christian Duncan, Operations had enlisted him for sensitive side work inside the core of Prophecy Intel. The associate loved it for two reasons: it meant face-to-face interaction with Gideon, one, and two, he was good at it. Far better than he was at tracking.

He turned in his seat to gaze out through a picture box window at the shifting blacks and greys that was the woods beyond the back of his house, leaves and branches swimming in the summer wind. His eyes went fuzzy and his focus came inward, where a blank sheet of paper awaited him inside his mind's eye, an ink bottle and a swan-feathered quill at its side. His mental energy lifted the quill, ink-dipped the tip, and began to craft a letter to be sent to his superior using the art of *telemastery*: an advanced form of communication originally developed and mastered by the Light Elite in the early nineteenth century, where a message is sent directly from one mind to another without a paper trail, evidence, or anything for the enemy to intercept. Measured against the weighty, combined population of Darkness and Light, the number of capable telemasters was small—fifty or less—and those fifty or less were chiefly men and women of power, for to learn and hone telemastic ability, one must possess an acute mental focus and near-brilliant to brilliant magical prowess, both necessitous qualities of those with aspirations to climb the ranks.

In his mind, the associate read through what he had written in order to ensure the note covered all bases.

> I sent Thomas to track down your fat man with instructions to obtain him and contact me once he had done so. Still one of the best trackers in

*the department, Thomas found him yesterday, the
night after our meeting at DHQ, at a tavern down
south. As was reported to me minutes ago, Thomas
waited at the bar of the establishment for the best
opportunity to detain the fat man, however there
was a complication and the fat man is now in a
coma. Thomas informed me that he moved the
body to a Lightless location. Anything that can be
done to revive the fat man will be. When Thomas
contacts me next, so will I contact you.*

*As to the second task, I've nearly finalized my
preparations. Once I have done so, I'll be off to
administer the next round of tests for the prospect
Leam Holt.*

*For trusting me with this mission, I am for-
ever grateful. If he is Him, then He we'll have.*

The associate's eyebrow tattoos shot crisp white light
through the window glass like a pair of oddly-shaped strobe
lights, brightening the woods in flickering patches, and then—
POOF—the note sent off, and his focus came back to the task
laid out in front him. The boy.

And he indeed had a feeling about this boy that had stuck
to him since Black Patch Park. About twenty years ago, on the
very day he had started work at P.I., the associate had devoured
all the prospect-info documentation, pre-Christian Duncan, that
Prophecy Intel had been accumulating since the very beginning.
Stacked up against all previous prospects, it was clear to the associate that Leam Holt had an originality and a flair to him that
raised warning flags—*welcome* warning flags—that Darkness
just might have something going here.

So what do you do with a prospect like this? the associate
thought, as he scanned through his notes and ideas, collecting
the sheets of paper that hadn't been crumpled into creasy wads,
and stacking them into a neat pile. *You go all out*, that's what
you do. You strip all previous work—no matter how successful
it may have been—down to its bones and rebuild it anew. You
create your masterpiece so that if the boy survives your best,

you'll know full well that Gideon will reward you. But beyond even *that*, you will be present when the miracle of prospect-into-prophet transformation actualizes. Of all the millions of Darkness that have fought and died in the last several millennia to weaken the sheet of Light and corrupt the Unknowings, *you* will be there for the victory parade.

With a healthy smile, the associate picked up his pen before another thought occurred to him, a terrifying thought, a thought that flat-lined his smile fire quick and pounded away at his heart.

What if the boy is to be the one, but the testing goes horribly wrong?

The associate grew queasy with angst by just the thought it.

He tried to free his mind of that notion, he tried to focus on the task at hand, but over the next half hour at a minimum, his ideas were repeatedly interrupted by a mad-happy clown face underneath a thicket of bright orange hair, hovering over the ink-blotted pages of his mind's eye.

CHAPTER 22

He left without telling anyone—not like anybody in the house would care—grabbing the car keys off the kitchen counter as he went out the back door. It was the morning after his stepmother had told him he had to clear out of the Manor by the end of the month. He knew Sara had been dead serious—she was the worst person to have ever lived—but he hadn't yet been able to confront Bram about it. In fact, last he saw his father was the moment before Leam had fallen through the flower shop's office carpet into the red clouds of smoke. As Leam maneuvered the Range Rover down the cobblestoned driveway onto the smooth asphalt of Whitewax Way, he realized his father had been gone all of yesterday and had yet to return home. Taking a right onto the Boulevard at the stop sign, Leam headed for the park.

Pushing the SUV up to forty, a low-pitched rattle stirred from the driver's side cup holder. Leam reached down, picking up the round piece of wood—his mother's acorn—that he must have left in the Rover a couple days ago. He rolled it around in his hand, thinking how as a child the acorn had been a comfort to him, Aggie's only possession that Sara hadn't burned in the pit, and the only tangible link between him and his dead mother. He squeezed his fingers around the coarse wood—which sometimes made him feel like he had once been loved—until a mean yet reasonable voice inside his head called out, as it always did whenever Leam felt hope from the acorn's touch, *Maybe it's just a normal piece of wood that slipped into a box of her things at some point, you stupid dumbass!*

"Shut up," Leam muttered.

Between the double yellow stripes and the sidewalk, the Rover moved swiftly down Blaff Street, cutting through the clear July air, nothing but blue spread out high above. Leam glanced out the driver side window as he was passing Harbing High, grateful that that portion of his life was over, and slammed on the brakes, the Rover screeching to a stop smack in the middle of the street. A tan Corolla swerved around him and the guy behind the wheel gave Leam the finger as he whizzed by.

Leam paid him no attention, he was too busy looking at the school, his mouth wide open, eyes glued on the left most part of the building where a bunch of ivy vines clung to the brick wall. Usually vertical, the strands of ivy had somehow repositioned themselves, strung together and unmistakably formed into ten words:

Be Brave.
Help will come when you need it most.

The blaring honk of an approaching eighteen-wheeler snapped Leam's attention back to the road. He stepped on the gas, stealing one last look at the school, but the ivy had crawled back to how he had always remembered it being.

Leam approached a crossed-walk intersection and took a right onto Falcon Avenue, peering out the windshield as the Range Rover hummed along beside the parking spots that ran parallel to Black Patch Park. Then, like out of the movies, there she was—her tank top blue this time, not green—jogging around the corner of the park and moving straight at him. Leam jerked into a space, took a breath, glanced at his face in the rearview real quick and pressed down the top right button on the door.

"Hi," he said, as the passenger window slid down. "Hey, Eloa!"

She slowed. Her eyes registered recognition but they didn't soften, nor did she offer a smile. As she came over, Leam could read from her face that she did so reluctantly.

"Hey there," Leam said, thinking this might have been a big fat juicy whopper of a mistake.

"What's that?" she asked, peeling the headphone out of her right ear.

"Nothing. I saw you and thought I'd say hi."

"Oh." She looked both ways down the street, flicked her eyes at him and looked out at the street again. Her cheeks deepened in color.

"Don't worry," Leam offered, "I'm in the car. You're safe, I can't knock you to the ground this time."

"Sure you could."

"Well....yeah, I guess." Leam sunk back into the seat.

Amidst the ensuing awkward silence, Leam felt a little envious of his brother. Sure, Zach was a first-rate jackass, but he was smooth with girls, and had probably never told one that he could run her over in his car, then sit back and stare at her like a goon.

"Is this yours? It's nice," Eloa said.

"Family car."

"Where you going?" she asked, no longer occupied by anything else around her.

"Coffee shop." A believable lie, Leam thought. How would she know that he thought coffee tasted like sludge?

Her shoulders dropped an inch. "Oh."

"Do you wanna come have a coffee? I'm not sure how often you're around here but it's just up that way and over a couple blocks."

"Ummmm. I should finish my run."

"Okay. Well if you feel like a coffee I'm gonna be there all day."

"All day?" Her eyebrows jumped up her forehead.

"All day. Literally, the entire day."

She laughed, then immediately looked unhappy about it.

"And not because I'll be waiting for you or anything creepy like that," Leam went on. "I just happen to love that place. You know what, I might actually stay there a few weeks, that's how great the place is, and again, it has nothing to do with you, or hoping you'll come in, or wanting to see you again."

"I would think they'd kick you out after a day or two."

Leam grinned. "Everybody's kicking me out these days. But I bet if I buy a hundred of those café-lattes they'll let me stay."

"Well, don't go too crazy."

"I can't promise you that."

She put the headphone back in her ear, bouncing on her toes. Leam laid a small smile on her, hoping it didn't make him look like a loser, or worse, a pervert. His arms felt squirmy as he became conscious that the way they were positioned gave off the effect that he was one of those guys who flexed his muscles while talking to girls.

"All day?" she asked again.

"Yup."

She looked in at him, smiling—maybe—and jogged off up Falcon in the direction of the high school. Leam pulled out of his spot, smiling—definitely—and drove past the park, through a few cross streets and took a left onto Capnick, slowing down as Tippy's Tattoos, PNC Bank, and the post office went by him on the right. Across the street from the Coffee Sip, Leam parallel parked between a pink Beetle and a maroon Cadillac, both convertibles. He cut the engine and got out, squinting hard all the way down to the end of the street at Bram's Florist. Twenty paces beyond it ran the Amtrak railroad that extended eastbound to New York City and westbound out past Dover.

Leam stopped himself before he started for the flower shop, spotting Helen's all-white Mercedes in its usual spot next to the tracks. He needed to talk to his father about a couple of things—his residency at the Manor, and how he hadn't had any luck researching the diamond—but not if it meant dealing with the hundred-year-old Helen and her lustful eyes. If she looked like Eloa, though, he would skip down to the shop in a little pink dress and not care who saw him.

Instead, he went into the Coffee Sip for the first time ever, and three minutes later he was seated at the third table over from the HIS and HERS, eyes on the door, a latte set on the tabletop's varnished black wood. The door opened and closed seventeen times before she came in. After that he lost count.

Seated in the corner near a shelf of espresso machines for sale and the counter where Unknowings got their straws and Splendas and napkins and cinnamon powders, Porlo looked straight through an open sheet of the Star Ledger. He saw Eloa Frost come into the Coffee Sip, gleaming with sweat and looking around. He nearly choked on a sip of his berry-blend smoothie when she sat down across the table from the boy—*the* boy, the boy the fat man said had the potential to be more powerful than arguably the most powerful leader in Darkness's history. Sinking back into the cushion of the leather armchair, Porlo's eyes narrowed into slits as he reinforced the strength of the newspaper-peek-through enchantment he had conjured up when Leam Holt walked in.

Sauntering out of Bram's Florist with a gooey-white lipstick smack on his black cheek—courtesy of Helen, of course, who had informed him that the proprietor wasn't yet in—the associate strolled up the sidewalk in no particular hurry. Beams of sunlight pierced down from the cloudless sky, glinting off the shiny buttons, buckles and zippers of his black leather jacket and pants. He leaned his butt against the hood of the boy's Range Rover and crossed his arms, waiting, watching the Coffee Sip's door fling open, swing closed.

"So how many is that for you?" Eloa said, breathing in stitches. She had sat down opposite him, both hands resting on the table next to her iPhone and headphones. "Just the one?"

"I'm seven deep. Just taking a breather. Do you want something? They've got a whole menu over there, all sorts of stuff."

"A water would be good if you don't mind. I don't have any money with me."

"A water, sure." Leam almost toppled over his chair as he stood. "Sit tight, don't move." He got in line at the counter, watching Eloa scroll through her phone as he waited for a pair of women to get their iced coffees. A minute later, Leam was back, placing three bottles of Sippy-H-2-O, the Coffee Sip's personal brand of water, on the table in front of Eloa. She put her phone down and gave him a look that was part confused, part amused.

"Didn't know how thirsty you were," he said, sitting down, pulling his seat in closer.

"Thank you." She untwisted the cap of the middle bottle. "Three should do it."

"You found the place," he said, watching her take a long sip.

"Yeah... I guess I wanted to see if you would really be here." She reached across the table and lifted Leam's coffee cup up an inch. "You don't even like coffee, do you?"

"What are you some sort of mind reader?"

She smiled and looked around the shop, fiddling with her hair elastic. Leam did the best he could to keep his eyes from straying anywhere besides her brown eyes. "It's nice in here," she said. "This whole street's cute."

"You're staying with your grandparents, I think you said, right?"

"Mmm-hmm." She adjusted the silver chain around her neck. "Over on...Stoneladen."

"Stoneladen Lane. I know right where you are."

"And what about you? Where's your parents' house?"

"My father's house. Manor, actually. I live with him and my stepmother, but it's not her house. She thinks it is, but it isn't."

"Manor?"

"Yeah, on Whitewax Way, up on past the high school."

"Sounds pretty swanky. What does your dad do?"

"He owns the flower shop down the street."

"*Flower shop...*" She stared in at him hard, as if trying to connect him to somebody or some place from her past. "Do you...work there, too?"

"Yeah, sometimes. Why, is that weird?"

"Oh, no. No, not at all. I have a friend who goes to Harbing. She mentioned something about a flower shop once. I was just trying to remember what she said."

"And what about your parents?" Leam asked. "They live in Cliff Edge, you said, right? That's what you said at the park, I think."

"My dad and I. It's just us. I've never known my mom. Don't know if she left us when I was really young or if she died. I don't know anything, really. He won't talk about it."

"So you don't have a mom?"

Eloa shook her head.

"I don't either," Leam said, leaning in close after a quick survey of the nearest Unknowings. He lowered his voice. "She died when I was a baby."

"That's terrible," Eloa whispered.

Leam nodded. "And my dad remarried, pretty much right away. The woman...his wife, the one who thinks she runs the house...she's the worst person in the entire world."

Eloa smiled. "Is she?"

"I'm dead serious." Leam could feel the bottoms of his feet begin to warm. "She's the worst person in the world. I hate her."

"Oh, please."

"And I'm not one of those jilted kids who never gave their stepparent a chance. I'm telling you that I honestly dream about pushing her face into the garbage disposal. No joke."

"Leam!" Eloa's eyes were owl-wide. It made him notice how big they were.

"I mean, not really," he lied. "It's just a figure of speech. 'I wanna push someone's face into a garbage disposal'. People say it all the time."

"Stop it," she said.

"You've never heard that one?"

"Nobody has ever heard that one."

"I'm not kidding, though. The woman is pure evil."

"Well, I'm sure you have plenty of rooms to hide from her at your *Manor*, don't you? With your servants and your giant ice cream making machines and your weirdly groomed poodles prancing around the estate."

"It's not like that," Leam said. "We don't have poodles or ice cream machines."

"You don't?" Her eyes were playful. "That's too bad."

"I mean it's huge, the place is enormous, but there's no warmth to it. I'm sort of like an outcast there."

"Are you an only child?"

"No, I have a brother."

"You do? That's nice."

"He's a jerk and an idiot."

"Oh."

"What about you? Any siblings?"

Eloa shook her head. "That's why I'm so worried about my da…" Her words fell off as her hand covered the tiny protuberance beneath the neckline of her tank top.

"What?" Leam asked, but Eloa kept shaking her head. "What are you worried about?"

"It's nothing, just…it's nothing you need to hear."

"No, sure. Sorry. You're right, I mean, I get it, you just met me, I shouldn't ask personal stuff. I'm sorry I pushed. I mean, believe me, there's a whole slew of things I won't be telling you."

"That's kind of the scariest thing anyone's ever said."

"Right, I mean I didn't mean it like that, but how 'bout this? I say we tell each other something that we would never tell each other unless we *had* to tell each other because we both *agreed* to tell each other?"

She stared at him and he felt embarrassment color his face.

What the hell was that, Leam? How many times can you say each other *in one sentence, you loser? Say it again, why don't you, and then just keep saying it.*

Leam touched his hand to his mouth—his lips felt incredibly dry—waiting for her to come up with an excuse to scurry off and get away from the awkward guy who can't speak and buys three waters, like that's real cute. Three waters. Holy crow.

"Fine, I'll go first," she said.

"Great." A laugh slipped out of his mouth, his hands grasped together on his lap. "Sure, you go first."

"The reason I said I was worried is because my dad has sort of...well, he's disappeared."

"Are you serious?"

"Yeah, it's why I'm at Mary and Larry's."

"Mary and Larry?"

"My grandparents. They have a dog named Barry if you want to make a joke."

"I would never make fun of a dog," Leam said. "But I don't get it, you have no idea where he went, your dad?"

"Not really. His friend...coworker—" she blushed, "—told me that he went off on business."

"So, what are y—"

"Your turn."

"Wait a sec..." But Leam shut his mouth, reading her face, which said, *Don't push it, buster. It was your game, now it's your turn.* He went quiet for three or four breaths, closed his eyes and brought his hands out from underneath the table. He rested them on the edge; they were a little shaky. "I told you in the park that these were birthmarks. They're not."

"What are they?"

"They're scars."

"Can I see them?" she asked. He moved them closer. "They're incredible. How does somebody get identical scars on separate hands?"

Leam didn't answer, and he could see that she didn't mind.

"They're sort of beautiful." She pushed the water bottles aside. "Can I feel them?"

Before Leam could utter no, she reached forward, taking his hands in hers. The instant she did, a bright pop of light flashed in his mind, pulling him away from her, away from the coffee shop.

It was raining. He was on a small rowboat, no land in sight. The water was choppy, the boat wildly rocking back and forth. He tried to steady it, slapping the old wooden oars against the powerful, white-topped, churning water. In front of him, he could see the back of a woman seated at the bow, gripping a taut rope that was fastened securely to both sides of the boat. Squinting through the fat raindrops pummeling down from the charcoal sky, he thought the woman's hands, tightly grasped around the soaking wet rope, were inhumanly white and scaly.

The rain was pounding harder, and the woman turned her head slowly toward the stern, toward him. He rubbed the rain from his dripping face, letting go of one of the oars, which clipped a crashing wave and shot up into the air, carried by the gusting wind into the beyond. He caught only a sliver of the woman's face before his vision was, again, impaired by the rainfall; it was like wipers sloshing water away from a windshield only once during a torrential downpour. What he saw of the woman's face was scaly, too, like her hands, and her eye was unnaturally blue. He screamed, closing his eyes, and the other oar was pulled from his hand, piercing into the dark thrashing water and disappearing below.

His eyes opened. Coffee shop. Clothes dry, rainstorm gone. Across from him, Eloa looked concerned.

"Are you okay?" she said quietly.

"Yeah, fine." Leam's hands, which he had apparently pulled away from hers, were shaking worse than before. "A little lightheaded." Beads of sweat trickled down his forehead, moistening his eyebrows like dew slipping down grass blades. "Can I ask you…" he began.

She nodded, her eyes glued to his face.

"Did you feel anything by any chance just now?"

"What do you mean?" she said.

"When you grabbed my hands, you didn't feel anything?"

"I felt your hands."

"But nothing strange, is what I'm asking."

"No. Why, what did you feel?"

"Nothing." His eyes flicked around the Coffee Sip. "Just a little shock, I guess."

"Oh." She looked off at something for a moment, then her pointer finger started in on her iPhone, tapping, tracing, tapping, tapping.

Leam wondered what was going on in her head. Despite politely pretending that nothing had happened, she had to be freaked out. Something must've happened here while he was... wherever he had gone. *How long was I on that boat? How long were my eyes closed? What should I tell her?*

He looked at her face. The awkwardness hovering between them was so thick he could feel it dampening his skin—a dark uncomfortable fog. He took a deep breath and blew his indecision into the awkwardness, hoping to disperse it through the power of words.

"I want to tell you something more," he said.

Eloa looked up at him as if he had sprang forward and kissed her mouth.

"It was more than just a shock," he said.

"I knew it," she breathed, sitting as upright as a post.

"I can be honest with you, right?"

"Of course."

"I can, right?"

"Yes! Tell me what happened."

Leam's head went up and down in short quick nods and kept on that way as he spoke. "It was weird. When you touched my hands, something happened inside me, like lightning, or a camera flash, and for a second or two it was like I was brought to another place and time. It happened at the park, too." He tried to read her face but she gave him nothing. "I'm not freaking you out, am I? I'm gonna just shut my mouth."

"What are you crazy? It's fascinating! Keep going!"

"You mean, you believe me? What I'm saying?"

"Yes!"

He smiled.

"So keep going, dummy," she pressed.

"Okay. So this flash went off and all of a sudden I'm on a boat..."

"A boat?"

"A boat I've never seen before. There's nothing around me, just water and sky and rain. But in the boat there's somebody else with me. I think it was you."

"Me?"

"Yeah. Pretty sure."

"Wait, what do you mean? So what happened?" She gawked at her hands. The expression on her face jumped back and forth in extremes consistent with that of an art lover torn between two paintings mounted side to side on a museum wall, one of which instills an odd sense of beauty, the other disgust.

"Nothing, really. This oar I was holding slipped out of my hand and before I knew it, I was back here sitting across from you." Leam hunched down slightly and lowered his voice. "But it was so real, Eloa, like I had already experienced it. But how can that be, right? So maybe it was a taste of the future or something. I have no idea."

"Well, why did you say that you were pretty sure that it was me who was with you? You couldn't tell for sure?"

"They were your hands that were holding mine when I had it, when I had this...vision, if that's what it was, so I figured it was you."

"You didn't see my face, then?"

"Not really."

"What do you mean, not really? You did or you didn't."

"It was just a glimpse," Leam said. "Just the side of your face—it was real quick." He was astounded that she was so engrossed. "I can't believe you don't think I'm insane."

"No, you're insane."

He smiled. "You're probably right."

"Touch them again."

"What?"

"C'mon." She held out her hands, a wild spark in the pupil of each eye. "Don't you want to see if you'll go back there? Back to the boat? Maybe you'll be able to stay there longer, I'll hold onto your hands real tight. Maybe you'll see more!"

"You're serious?" he asked, taking a quick inventory of the people in the room: Unks conversing at some of the tables, a few more in line by the register, a guy and his small daughter coming back from the bathroom, somebody in the corner behind a sheet of newspaper.

"Definitely," Eloa said, smacking her fingers into her palms quickly three or four times.

Leam calmed himself, like he had right before the bubble had formed around him in the park. He saw that her eyes were locked dead straight on his, said, "Here we go," and reached forward, snatching her hands out of the air.

He was standing in a massive white room. An oddly familiar white room. Everything was white—white everywhere except for the ceiling, which he sensed was a touch darker. He looked up to find that the ceiling was made of glass, and beyond the glass, clear water. He felt like he was looking up at the bottom of a freshly-cleaned fish tank. Then, in the tank, out of nowhere, a dirty wooden oar clinked against the glass and settled onto the outside of the ceiling.

Leam had only a second to correlate that his first vision from a few minutes ago was somehow above him now.

His gaze dropped down from the glass ceiling and he took in the table that stretched so far down the middle of the room that he couldn't see the end of it. The long white table, floating in the all-white room, triggered a déjà vu in his mind, and he jerked around to see if there was the lime-green chair in the corner that he had been strapped to during his abnormal dream from a few nights ago. It was—a smiling, youngish-looking man reading a yellow book was sitting in it, his legs crossed, purple Nikes on his feet. The man had his index finger over his lips and was nodding toward the table.

Something large, about the size of a grown man, was squirming on the table underneath a black, silk sheet. Close by, a tray with what looked like dentist tools hovered in the air. The sheet was raising and lowering slightly, consistent with what had to be the heavy breathing of whoever was beneath it. Leam looked beyond it.

The far end of the table disappeared into the white nothingness of the space, but some of the white was turning creamy, egg shell, and opaque. These off-white shadings were forming together into what looked like the massive head of a beautiful stallion, but the moment Leam registered it, a small, white bird flew from its mouth, and the stallion head vanished.

The bird flew toward Leam, landing on top of the black sheet and the lump of a person beneath it, stretching its wings. Behind it, Leam saw another something emerging from the nothingness, but this thing didn't blend in with the background as the stallion and the bird had. Its form contrasted with the white, and as it slinked forward, its shape became clearer. It was about the size of a beagle, only lankier with a bushy tail. Leam peered into its eyes—black and mean—as it neared the body and the bird.

Leam heard another tap against the glass ceiling, and thought he saw someone swimming above him for a second, but on closer inspection there was nothing but water. The seated man in the purple Nikes cleared his throat and, again, gestured toward the table with his head. Leam turned to see the foxlike animal leap forward and snap at the bird, its razor-sharp teeth clamping down on one of the wings. The bird screeched an awful sort of pain and...

"LEAM!"

Leam's eyes opened under the soft lighting of the coffee shop, no longer floating in the ivory void. He could hear startled whispering from surrounding tables. Eloa was staring at him, her hands red and welted.

"I had to let go," she said. "You were crushing them."

"Sorry, I—"

"I'm not hurt. What happened? Tell me everything. What did you see? Was it definitely me with you on the boat?"

"How long was I gone?" Leam asked, grabbing at his head. His eyes felt wobbly.

"I don't know. Twenty seconds."

"My body stays here, though, right?"

"Yes, of course! Tell me what you saw."

"My head feels weird. Like my brain's been all jostled."

"Leam, tell me!"

"I didn't see you, okay. I didn't go back to the boat."

The manic excitement in her eyes deflated. "Oh, so what did—"

"I didn't see anything," he said. "Everything was white. There was nothing around me."

"Nothing?" she said. "Because you were panting something. I couldn't make it out. Sounded like 'noburd thox.' And you were squeezing my hands so tightly I figured something horrible was happening to you."

"That makes no sense. There was nothing. It was just me."

"Okay. But even so, how are you so calm?"

"I'm not. Not on the inside."

"Go again," she said, her hands back in front of him on the table, a gleam in her eye that could cut clean through metal.

"No way! I'm not gonna crush your hands again. Another go and I might break your fingers."

"I told you, I'm not hurt. Take them."

"Fancy seeing you here," a velvety voice slithered down at them.

Leam tore his eyes away from Eloa's, staring up at a man decked out in black leather standing over them, the white markings above his eyes bright against his black skin tone. Gideon's associate.

"Aren't you going to introduce me to your friend, Leam?" the associate said. "I don't believe I caught her name last we met."

"Sorry," Leam said, "Eloa, this is—"

"Michael," the associate cut in.

"Michael, this is Eloa."

"You're the man from the park," Eloa said. The associate shot her a look that Leam thought rivaled one of Sara's infamous leers, and it made his ears go hot. Eloa looked down at the table as if she had been scolded in class.

"I'm going to have to break up this little powwow," the associate said. "Leam's presence is requested *elsewhere.*"

Eloa was dead still, besides for tiny mouth movements like her teeth were nibbling the inside of her bottom lip. Her face was blank, the total opposite of the riveted curiosity that had shone there like sunlight off chrome during the hand-holding hallucinations a minute ago.

"Sorry, Eloa. Michael's a friend of the family. If he's tracked me down, it's important. Are you gonna be all right?"

"But you said he... No, I'll be fine," she finished meekly.

"I would tell you that you're welcome to come with us," the associate said to Eloa, "but you're not welcome to come with us. Leam. Outside. Two minutes." The associate turned and left.

Leam's pinkies had begun to prickle. "Eloa, don't let him get to you. He's not a nice guy."

"I said I'm fine." She pushed her chair out and stood up.

"You're leaving?"

"I needed to go anyway," she said. "It's no big deal. Seriously." She hurried out of the shop, and Leam yelled his cellphone number at her as the door swung closed, and felt like a pathetic, absolute loser because of it. He started mindlessly tapping his fingers on the table as thoughts churned through his mind like pictures on a revolving scroll: Eloa's abrupt exit, the associate's return, the visions...*my God*, how real they were. He started to get up, but a warm, firm hand found the upper curl of his shoulder, pressing him back into his seat.

"You'd be wise to never see her again."

Leam twisted his head to see a man in a gray T-shirt standing next to the table, a furled up newspaper clutched in the hand that wasn't clamped down behind Leam's neck like an iron claw.

"Get *off* me," Leam said. The man obliged, and as quick as a clap of thunder, a pipe from the bag at his side shot into his hand. He pulled deeply, blue clouds of smoke billowing from his nostrils. Leam was shocked to see that none of the customers seemed to mind.

"I know who you are, Leam Holt. I know about your family. Believe it or not, I am sparing you distress when I tell you that Eloa Frost is not an Unknowing."

"What? Who are *you?*"

"She is of the Light," the man said, after another pull. "You are not. You are the furthest thing there is from the Light."

Leam suddenly felt nauseous. "She... No, she—"

"Allow me to say what I bet you already know. Someone like you cannot be with someone like her. You're not stupid. A man of Darkness can never be with a woman of Light, or vice versa. It is magical law. Put her out of your mind and don't bother her again. If you do—" the iron claw clamped around his neck again, squeezing it until Leam's temples throbbed, "—I'll find you again. It won't be pleasant." There was a sinking feeling in Leam's stomach that he knew had nothing to do with the mounting pain in his head. "I believe a man in black awaits you outside."

"How can—?" Leam started, but he was speaking to air. The man in the gray T-shirt was gone. The Coffee Sip's door hadn't opened or closed, but the man in the gray T-shirt was gone.

A gust of hollowness blew through Leam's body. What the man of Light, or whoever he was, had said flattened Leam for one simple reason: he knew it was the truth. Long ago, he had found his father staring into the pit of fire at the back edge of the Manor estate. Leam had asked him what he was doing, and had never forgotten the answer.

"Who are they, Leam? The scum of the earth? Worse than the Unknowings?"

"The Light, Father."

"Then never view them as anything but. Never sympathize with them. Never let your guard down. And heed me when I tell you that above all else, never make the deep mistake of falling for one. Flicking aside how sick and perverse that'd be, it is an impossibility. It can never happen."

A miserable smile crept onto Leam's face. What kind of sick, ironic punch in the nuts was it that the one girl he had ever liked, had ever *talked* to for longer than six seconds, was of the Light?

"It is magical law."

Bram was a disagreeable man, but he wasn't a liar. Leam knew he had only just met Eloa, but even so, they *had* something, a connection, and knowing nothing could ever come of it felt like some ogre had knocked Leam on his back and had begun laying heavy stones on his chest. Had the visions occurred because he was Dark and she was Light? Was that partly why magical law forbade these sorts of mixed relationships?

Leam shut his eyes. He could feel the upstarts of the bull—the prickling pinkies, the burn beneath his feet—but he squashed it then and there, before the eyelid shuttering, before the powerful black bull could start snorting hot air from its dusty snout. There was no time for that, and now there was no time for her, either. All his focus would go to Gideon's associate and this courtship of Darkness. He couldn't be with her? Fine. Whatever. He had other things to do. *Great things*, possibly. There'd be time for girls later. Girls who weren't prohibited by magical law.

As Leam walked to the door, some guy called out, "Hey, buddy, what was your phone number again?" and his table full of friends burst out laughing. Leam went outside and spotted the associate across the street, sitting behind the wheel of the gleaming maroon Cadillac convertible. Stepping across the sidewalk, Leam heard a whispery shriek from behind—*"That's him!"*—but was too angry, too forwardly-determined, to turn around and see who had said it. He crossed Capnick Street, eyes narrowed, chest propelling the way, and popped the passenger door open, sliding into the Caddy next to the associate.

"Beautiful, Leam. Quite attractive, indeed."

"She's nobody." Leam shut the door, sitting back into the plush, beige leather. "Just a friend."

"Just a friend, hmm? Then I'm sure you wouldn't mind if I paid her a visit every now and then." The associate raised his eyebrow tattoos in a frat boy sort of way and wiggled his tongue.

Leam looked at him without a trace of emotion, uncertain whether the associate was being serious or not. Either way, Leam wanted to kick him in the face.

"Where are we going?" Leam asked.

"This show, punk, you're not running," the associate said. He tossed a white winter hat onto Leam's lap. "Put it on." He punched the accelerator and peeled away from the curb, pulling a screeching U-turn before they hit the tracks—Leam didn't so much as peek at Bram's Florist—and zipped back up Capnick to Falcon.

"Is your name really Michael, sir?" Leam asked.

"Put the hat on."

Leam nodded once and did so. The moment he pulled the hat down over his ears, everything went black. It all went quiet. He saw nothing. He heard nothing, not the engine humming or the car whirring down the road. But worst of all—and the main reason his heart was now pounding against the walls of his chest like a jackknife into concrete—was that he couldn't even *feel* the car moving. He waved his hands around like a blind person trying to grab hold of something in an unfamiliar environment. They found nothing.

What's happening? he asked himself, kicking his feet against empty air that should've been the leg pit near the Cadillac's floorboards. He could hear the panic rising in his inner voice as it repeated over and over, *Where am I? Where am I?*

Had the associate transported him into outer space or maybe some deep black hole, like how he had always imagined the oak tree-protected abyss at the Cricket to be? How had this happened? A minute ago—the Coffee Sip, Eloa, her hands, their connection—he had never been happier, *and now this?* The flighty panic that had overtaken him was lowering itself into a sticky pit of anger, black as tar, until an unnerving thought that Leam felt had a lot of validity to it spilt over him like an egg cracked over the head.

Maybe I'm dead.

CHAPTER 23

That's him!" she said again, pointing at the boy sitting shot-gun in the Cadillac convertible that was hauling ass past them, smoke jetting out of the exhaust pipe as it screeched through a stop sign, hugged the corner and flew off down Falcon Avenue. "Flower Boy, Eloa! Did you see him? Flower Boy, Flower Boy, Flower Boy!"

"That was him? I didn't see."

Bridgette stopped chomping on the giant purple wad of gum in her mouth mid-chew. Her blue eyes—piercing and as clear as cold water—scrutinized Eloa's face. "You didn't notice him in the Sip? He's *gorgeous*. How could you miss him?"

"I don't know," Eloa said. Bridgette shrugged and the gum chewing carried on. Eloa could smell the sugary grape of it. She couldn't recall ever seeing Bridgette—who was thin, like Eloa and most of the girls in their dance class, albeit the short-est of the group—without a chunk of gum in her mouth, even while smoking a cigarette. Eloa watched her friend chomp away, thinking how Bridgette was so striking, with her petite stature and dirty blond hair, which worked for her because she was one of those annoying people who seemed to have a nice healthy tan year round.

"What are you doing here, anyway?" Bridgette said, standing as she most always did, with her hand on her right hip, which supported the meager weight of her upper body, right leg slightly bent, the left on a diagonal thirty degrees to the side, straight as a beam, ankle locked, toes pointed through her aqua-blue sandals. "Don't get me wrong, it's great to see you, but I've never seen you around here outside of the studio unless you're with me."

"Staying with some family."

"In Harbing? Gosh! Look at *you*! I don't even know who you are!"

Eloa leaned in, her eyes smiling. "But you know Flower Boy," she whispered.

"*Yes*," Bridgette said. "As much as anyone can know him, but it's just been so long since there's been a *sighting*. Wow. I needed that," she said with a dazzling smile. "It's been since graduation. Actually, I'm not even sure if I saw him at that. I'll get my hands on him at some point, though, in case you were about to ask. Gosh! I forgot how *adorable* he is! You look great in that, btw, I never look right in that kinda stuff."

"Yes, you do." Eloa smoothed down her tank top with hands that still felt tingly from the coffee shop. "How was your party the other night? Did you—?"

"Oh...m'God...*so* much fun. Billy Criggins, if you can believe it, took me out back."

"I don't know who that is, Bridge."

Bridgette stretched out the gum clamped between her teeth into a long, tacky string and wrapped it around her finger over and over, as a bored lifeguard would with the lanyard attached to his whistle. "He's no Flower Boy, but he could like be a *professional* kisser, and his hands move fast and slow at all the right times. Don't worry, I'm having another party tonight or tomorrow. Maybe both. Mom and her darling Ralph are at some retreat or expo in Phoenix 'til the end of the month, so you're coming. Don't even try to get out of it. I won't let you. You're sleeping over."

"Okay."

"*Really?*"

"Sure, that sounds pretty good."

"*Who ARE you?*" Bridgette squealed. "And what have you done with my *Lo Lo?*"

"So lemme ask you…"

"Come. Walk with me. That's me right behind that silver Range Rover. Ralph surprised me with it before they left so I have something to scoot around in at Rutgers. Isn't it *cute?* Convertible…shiny pink….perfect."

"So cute," Eloa said as Bridgette linked their arms and started to lead her across the street. "So, Bridge, about Leam—"

"Hands off, slut, he's mine."

"No, I know." Eloa blushed. "I'm just curious about this crush of yours—"

"Wait." Bridgette stopped in the middle of the street, eyelids squinting over her clear, piercing eyes. Eloa felt her face go hot; she had felt the mistake as it slipped from her lips. "How do you know his name?"

"Because," Eloa said, "because in the Coffee Gulp—"

"Sip."

"They called out the name *Liam,* the coffee people. I guess I kind of half-noticed that he went up to the counter. I wanna say he had a black shirt on, did he?"

Bridgette might have nodded. An uncomfortable moment later, any and all inquisitiveness that had flooded her face had drained. "*Always* a black T-shirt. Super hot."

"I don't know why I'm remembering that just now."

"Because," Bridgette said, her eyes shining like a gleaming pane of glass, "Leam Holt stays with you after he's gone."

The driver of a navy blue Hyundai sedan that was slowing to a stop at the intersection gave the horn a light friendly double-honk. Eloa reciprocated with an apologetic wave, taking Bridgette's hand and continuing along the crosswalk, noting that *this* hand contact hadn't sent her friend off into some cryptic dream world.

"So what's the problem, then?" Eloa asked conversationally.

"What problem? What are you talking about?"

"You told me he's never been over to one of your parties. You're so aggressive—" Bridgette spun her head around with a face that said *Excuse me?* "—in a good way," Eloa quickly added, "so there must be a reason you guys haven't gotten together?"

"Leam's weird," Bridgette said, walking over the pavement one foot in front of the other, as if on a balance beam. "He keeps to himself. I've never even seen him talk to his own brother—*he's* a grade or two younger than us, good looking, *obviously*, but a total girl-hound loser. But Leam...Leam doesn't have any friends. That's why I never approached him there. I tried not to look at him if I could help it. He's never been to my parties because I don't invite him."

"Bridgette! You're horrible!"

"His family owns the florist shop right there," Bridgette said, unfazed, as they stepped up onto the sidewalk. "See it? *That's* where I try to get him to notice me. Kind of a gloomy place, even with the flowers. He used to be there sometimes when I go in. Not for a while though, and never gave me a second glance, no matter *what* I'm wearing."

"I don't believe that," Eloa offered.

"You're probably right." Bridgette brightened, standing again with one leg on a diagonal to the side. "He *must* notice me, I mean, *hello?* Anybody call a *doctor!*" As Bridgette's voice faded, so did her smile, her eyes glued on the flower shop as if stuck in a daze. When next she spoke the tone of her voice was even, but Eloa noticed it had an airy, mystical quality to it, like the sound of wind through a forest thick with trees.

"Leam's either a blank wall or angry. He's almost always blank. Detached. But he has this haunted, angry look about him sometimes, like he's ready to kill somebody, and no one goes anywhere near him when he gets like that. That's why Billy and all the guys don't make fun of him, I think. They don't bully him around, not Leam. No one knows if he's gonna snap. I think that's so sexy."

Eloa became conscious of her hands. She clasped them together, tight over her navel.

"There are rumors," Bridgette said, like she didn't know she was speaking, her eyes still lost somewhere in the vicinity of

Bram's Florist. A second or two later, Eloa heard a gum bubble pop, and Bridgette turned to Eloa, back to her clear-eyed self. If she had been under some sort of Leam-trance, it had lifted.

"You know I didn't move here 'til freshman year," Bridgette said, pushing on sunglasses pulled from the belly of her purse. "Right after Mom married Ralph. *But,* Billy told me that in fourth or fifth grade Leam threw some kid in their class off one of the high parts on the jungle gym and the kid broke his collarbone, but the next day, the kid was like *perfectly* fine. Billy swears by it, but anything Billy Criggins says could be dead red-on-red serious or a stupid little joke. There was another one, too, though, where apparently somebody saw Leam out their window running down the road, *naked*—" her eyes widened, "—and supposedly he had blood all over him..."

"What?" Eloa said, cringing.

"The cops picked him up, I think this was in eighth grade. Next day, though, the woman who saw it—who, fyi, moved away a month later—she went down to the station asking about it and apparently the cops had no idea what she was talking about."

"Crazy," Eloa said. She was now looking down toward Leam's dad's shop. Two tall men came out of it, one husky, the other stick-thin, both wrapped in black trench coats in spite of the summer heat. "Even if it's just a bunch of talk," Eloa added, watching the men cross over the train tracks.

"Basically, the consensus around town is that he's *severely* bipolar," Bridgette said, digging through her purse. "Like I'll-paint-you-a-picture-then-cut-off-my-ear bipolar. *Ahh!*" She took out her iPhone. "Rumors are rumors, right? But the four years I've lived in Harbing, I know two things for sure. A, he was depressed all of senior year, every single day, no question about it. And B, he missed a semester and a half our junior year, and I overheard the vice principal one day telling Mrs. Fudderhum, *that witch,* that Leam had been at a *mental* hospital the whole time, somewhere close by. St. Francis's, I think he said. And you can call me a freak, but I think *that's* sexy, too."

"What is, exactly?" Eloa asked, shaking her head. "Why is that hot to you?"

"Look," Bridgette said and exhaled a breath. "I know all the guys around here. So do you, so does everybody. When you're looking at them, you know exactly who you're looking at. But Leam," Bridgette paused, closing her eyes and smiling, "he could be anybody."

"But you think he's harmless."

"Absolutely not," Bridgette said. "Have you not been listening? Anyway, if I wanted harmless I'd borrow *your* calculator and hang out with the science nerds." She started in on her phone.

Eloa interlocked her fingers. She couldn't tell for sure, but it felt like a soft, supernatural energy was stirring beneath the skin of her palms. What had happened at the Gulp had been a lightning bolt of strangeness and fascination, but she wondered if it had been the touch of her unpurified magic that had caused poor, friendless Leam to experience the supernatural, or could his mental disease have been the culprit, causing him to see things that weren't really there? Eloa didn't know. If she were Bridgette, she'd know. It would simply be the latter, a manifestation of his manic-depressive condition, because, for Bridgette, magic was something performed on stage and written about in Harry Potter books. It didn't really exist. Even four year-olds could see that the weirdo in the top hat and white gloves sawing the bikini chick in half was a fraud.

Tightening the elastic around her ponytail, Eloa watched Bridgette, who was leaning against her car, texting someone with such blinding speed that her finger nails—coated with aqua-blue polish to match her sandals—blurred into a tiny, restless Caribbean sea. Eloa thought about how she'd trade lives with Bridgette in instant. What a simple, happy life it would be *to not know*. Bridgette's stepdad Ralph had chosen to buy his stepdaughter a VW Beetle instead of trashing his home office and staging his own, bloody-haired death.

Eloa became mindful of the weight hanging from her necklace as Bridgette slipped her iPhone into her purse and dropped the purse into the back of the bug.

"What's the deal with all the Flower Boy questions anyway?" Bridgette asked.

"All I asked you was why you guys haven't hooked up."

Bridgette plucked the wad of gum off her tongue. "*Tell* me about it."

"But," Eloa said, "now I have to worry that you're fantasizing about a guy who might be planning to hack you to pieces in his basement."

"*Morbid!*" Bridgette said and giggled. She unwrapped a fresh piece of gum, wadding the old piece in the wrapper of the new. "Come on, get in. I'll give you a ride back to your *family.*"

CHAPTER 24

M r. Frost," Gideon said, stepping in through a temporary door from a flood of blazing gold light. The door vanished, and with it the light, restoring the constant darkness that fed the small, windowless dungeon, a room dissected by Gothic-style wrought-iron bars that hummed like high voltage electric cables. Dull, green-flamed torches—one in each corner—cast sickly light over Gideon and the two inmates on the other side of the bars, both sprawled on the stone floor. Between the inmates stood a second row of bars that separated Cell A from Cell B. An occasional drop of black syrupy water fell from the sticky ceiling not too high overhead. "Our fading Light bulb in the Dark," Gideon added with a grin, peering into Cell A.

An enormous, muscular man looked back at him, blinking several times. His long shags of blond hair were strewed over the ground like tangles of hay. His cheek peeled off the floor-grime as he lifted his massive head.

"That's right. Get up," Gideon said, disgusted by the sight of his large, pathetic prisoner. Gideon was also repulsed by the stench of Light that still clung to the man, and he chose to breathe through his mouth not his nose, a rare occurrence.

With a mighty groan, Frost struggled to his feet. "Water," he croaked.

"This is the reason you requested to see me? A glass of water?"

"That was days ago." Frost looked around at nothing but walls. "Felt like days…"

"It was," Gideon said. "We've been busy. You more than most could have guessed as much."

Frost—shrouded in nothing but a small loincloth—began to shake, veins and muscles pulsing and convulsing. "Have you released it?"

Gideon stepped over to Cell B as if he didn't hear the question. On the floor lying on his back was a skinny man so badly beaten that his nose and cheek bones were pounded an inch into his skull. He seemed to be trying to speak, but his lips could only open and close around a mouthful of shiny, gold teeth.

"Not yet, Jace, but the time is near," Gideon said, stepping from B back to A. "I don't know how significant you were to your most *handsome* leader and his schemes, but as to how much he knew about the work you were doing, my guess would be that you revealed very little."

"Sebastian knows more than you," Jace panted, trudging closer to Gideon as if being drawn by the hum of the wrought-iron bars. "If you see everything, he sees the same and more."

"Tell me, then," Gideon said, "why hasn't there been an attempt to free you? If he knew the ramifications of what you've stumbled upon, why has he left his little horsey to rot inside the barn?"

"Stumbled?"

"YES!" Gideon roared, and in one flat second he and Jace had slid across the floor toward each other, smacking together like a single clap of two giant hands. Jace howled, his skin sizzling against the spitting electricity of the iron bars between them—now as green as the torch flames in the corners. The men were forehead to forehead. Gideon had Jace's mitts in his hands and he bulged out his eyes in a blaze of gleaming white fire. "YES, YOU STUMBLED, YOU IGNORANT APE! FOR IF YOU TRULY KNEW ITS POWER, YOU WOULD HAVE SCREAMED IT TO ALL YOUR BRETHREN WITHIN EARSHOT!"

Jace's eyes went completely white, his upper teeth clattering against the lowers in quick hollow chops. Gideon grinned—his big stretching clown's grin—releasing Jace, who fell to the ground like a gigantic sack of meat. Jace sat himself up quickly, though, presumably with pride, but scooted away from the horrid clown mask until his back hit the wall. Gideon—now hovering above the floor as if seated in an invisible floating chair—tilted his head to one side.

"You're tired and malnourished. Rest while I speak," he said, crossing his legs. "While analyzing the journals taken from your safe, which have made for excellent reading, it became evident that you were able to gnaw a hole through our blanket of Darkness and uncover much of the chemical and magical elements used to molecularly *comprise* a certain gaseous poison we're developing. There was little else. I may assume, then, that *you* were developing its antidote without the knowledge of what the poison actually does once exposed. Tell me," he said. "Would you care to be enlightened?"

Jace's chest heaved up and down, up and down, bending the vertical fire-scars on his body, still sizzling from the iron bars. He nodded his head and closed his eyes.

"It kills the Unknowings whose hearts are too *pure*, whose souls can't be tainted enough to be of any use in the world as I envision it soon to be. The Skunks whose internal makeup will allow for an outside force to alter their souls and hearts, Gujin7B does just that. Once tainted, they will be much more *inclined* to inflict and spread evil to their fellow man, and the population will darken and darken and darken, gradually at first, but then exponentially, until there is them and us...but no you."

"No," Jace sighed. Since Gideon had seen him last, the man's healthy glowing skin had faded to an unnatural shade of gray. "We'll stop it. We always find a way."

The distractive wheezing of Cell B's occupant had become faint, garbled words. "...have to tell him...can't fail him because...can't fail him..." Gideon shot a jet of silver liquid from his palm, splashing it into the beaten man's face, silencing him as it solidified into a metal mask that covered his gold-toothed mouth and what was left of his nose.

"You're too late," Gideon told Jace. "It'll be ready before those flowing locks of yours can grow another half inch." Floating comfortably, Gideon leaned his head back, far back, inhaling deeply. He caught his ghostly reflection in the wet shine of the ceiling; the thicket of hair was brown under the nauseous light. "The gas smells like sugar cookies so I've been told. The Skunks will be drawn to it like mindless geese flocking to toxic grasslands."

"But have you overlooked anything?" Jace asked, his huge forearms resting on his knees. "Or has something not crossed that incredible mind of yours?"

"Everything crosses my mind, that's why I am who I am."

Jace's giant hand pushed the hair away from his face. "*The Prophecy*," he said.

"What about the Prophecy?"

"I'm no fool—you take stock in it. The Gujin, all your other tricks...they may cause devastation, you'll hear no argument from me. But without *a prophet,* you can't break us or poison all of those without magic who walk the earth."

"How you underestimate me," Gideon said, with a disturbing laugh that shivered Jace farther back against the wall. "I am the most feared and capable leader of Darkness that ever was. Surely you know this."

Jace spat on the floor. "I was born during Attamon's reign. I know only the pair of you."

"What you *know* is that none before me have *sniffed* the immortality of Cronos Maxima. *I* will sniff it. *I* will smell it. *I* will inhale it and I will *become* it. I am not waiting for the birth of the prophet, Jace Frost, the prophet will be born because I await him."

"You await nothing."

"Perhaps. Perhaps you're right. Perhaps he's already here."

"Delusions!" Jace shouted.

Gideon smiled at the silly beast. "Tell me. Would you care to hear about your daughter?"

At her mention, Jace rose to his feet, snorting, ready to charge. Yet he restrained himself.

"Wise of you," Gideon said. "Your magic is useless in the confines of these cells. Not that that will matter soon enough."

"You stay away from my daughter," Jace growled.

"She's been left alone," Gideon said, ignoring the muffled squealing from Cell B. Gideon's invisible throne tipped him forward until the rubber soles of his black shoes padded the floor. "*However,* unprovoked by me, she's been spending time with a young man of Darkness."

"LIES!" Jace shrieked, his features twisting into a mask of wild fury.

"I never lie, Frost, you'll be taught that soon enough—"

Jace roared, lunging forward, but a loud snap from Gideon's open palm shot him backward into the wall. Jace stuck to it spread-eagle. Gideon slipped between two of the bars and approached Jace as he would a soon-to-be-scorged member of Darkness in need of punishment.

"My, my, my," Gideon said as Jace strained, red-faced, against the immobilization curse. "This *fight* in you, it's misguided. Your raw emotion is to be your ruin, can you not see that? The Light's downfall is the concern it has over the welfare of its fellow man and the Unknowings. *Tsk, tsk, tsk.* You will lose this war because your ideals of love and compassion bind you together like leashed dogs.

"Casualties are inevitable in this war of ours, but unlike you, they cause me no worry. I enjoy the death of my men, for their role was, is and will be...to serve. Victory comes to the man who is willing to sacrifice everyone in his wake." Gideon's clown-lips curled into a smile. "Look at me. I find myself unable to utter the word *sacrifice* with a straight face. Sacrifice implies loss, but those beneath me are nothing but faceless pawns. They're my puppets. My bait."

"Because you have no heart," Jace said, his head hanging limply.

"Oh yes, I do, it's just different from yours." Gideon was now ten steps away and closing. "The dream of mankind's eternal suffering is what fries my eggs. I'm disgusted by the human species. I tolerate some to fulfill a cause, but I despise them all. *Hate* is what separates me from you. Hate is the strongest force that can drive a man, not love, and I'll tell you why. You experience fluctuating levels of love, do you not? The love you feel for your luscious young daughter varies from your love for Dick Smith or the neighbor's pet ferret. Love has faults. It's hazy and vulnerable to guile. It takes effort, and the loss of it pollutes the mind. It is a weakness, Jace. The very core of your ideology is one fat, hairy weakness. Hate is beauty—it is simple, it is direct. Everything my mind commands my body to do is fueled by hate in its purest form. Evil. And unlike love, evil doesn't blur a man's vision."

Gideon, deep into Cell A, stopped a foot from Jace and released the wall-shackle curse. Jace's feet found the floor. The breath of both men wafted together into one foul cloud. Off the whites of Jace's eyes, Gideon saw the reflection of his own, bulging out farther than ever, the veins like thin red snakes snapping around in soapy bathtub water. Neither man moved. Gold Teeth, too, was still. Asleep or dead.

A black drop of ceiling tar smacked onto Jace's nose and Gideon flashed another manic smile. The very next moment he was across the room on the free side of the bars.

"I have something for you, Jace, but it's not a cup of water." The door rematerialized in the wall, flooding the shadows and misery of the dungeon with gleeful, scorching light. The dead black silhouette of a large man stood under the frame.

"This is Raxton," Gideon said.

The silhouette approached Cell A, and as it did so, the man filling it out became more distinct. His bulk was slow-moving and quiet. A thick scar ran from one of his eyes to the mouth of his hardened face. Held in his scabbed hands were a metal container the size of a tool box and a high-tech gas mask.

"We talked about its effects on the Skunks," Gideon said, "but I would imagine you've been wondering what exposure to Gujin7B will have on persons of Light."

Gideon stepped underneath the temporary door, his skeletal body and wild hair now shaping the form of the black silhouette.

"Wonder no longer, because you, Frost, are guinea pig number one."

CHAPTER 25

Taking an occasional small sip of soda-fountain lemonade from his large plastic cup, Sebastian, wearing jeans and a white V-neck T-shirt, drifted around a crowded Illinois shopping mall, observing the habits and idiosyncrasies of the wide variety of mall walkers and would-be buyers. Sunlight—streaking down from the roof windows high overhead—blended with the store fronts' crisp modern lighting, creating an ambience that one associates with large scale commerce. Despite his striking appearance—clean, tan, handsome and alarmingly peaceful—the Unknowings seemed to pay Sebastian, who looked to be in his late thirties, no attention as he sat down on a bench between a small fountain and a kiosk crammed with cheap sunglasses.

A pretty brunette carrying several stuffed bags came out of the Baby Gap, walking past Sebastian. She had a pleasing and confident air about her, reminding him of someone he had known long ago: a happy, good-looking young woman of petite stature with mid-length auburn hair. Setting his lemonade down on the bench arm, he closed his eyes, thinking back to when he had heard the news of her death.

He was adding a cup of tap water to a bowl of pancake mix in the tiny kitchen nook of his new trailer, looking out the window at the sands of a barren desert. He had been alone here for almost two calendar months. As he had been expecting—he always knew, well before things like this happened—three quick knocks rapped on the trailer door. Dropping the wooden ladle into the batter, he turned off the burner with a wave of his hand, walked to the door and pushed it open.

Before him stood a burly man dressed in a black suit, the jacket hiding most of his black dress shirt, the top three buttons unhooked, revealing a chest covered with thick dark hair.

"One of these days, I'll be bearing good news, sir," the man said gruffly, taking off his black sunglasses.

"Come on in," Sebastian said, and the man stepped up into the trailer. He removed his jacket and sat down on a brown reclining chair in the main room as Sebastian went back to the stove and relit one of the front burners with his mind.

"I know how miserable it is to find me at your door," the man said, stroking his brambly goatee. "It must be awful to see a man who only delivers bad news."

"I had a feeling you might be coming around, Harlow. That's why you find me cooking."

"Come to think of it, I don't ever recall seeing you eat anything, sir," Harlow said.

"Only when I have a bad feeling about something."

"You've been out here a while, sir."

"I needed some time." Sebastian looked across the small counter at Harlow. "The Oklahoma City bombing... That one really got to me."

"You can't stop 'em all," Harlow said. "A tragedy, though. Hundred and sixty-eight dead, nineteen children under the age of six—"

"I know the numbers, Harlow."

"The report from the Department of After Search says it remains unclear if the bomber, one Timothy McVeigh, had been influenced by Dark forces. Unknowingly, of course."

"Unknowings are always unknowing," Sebastian said, whisking clumps of hardened powder apart into the goopy

batter. He poured a circle onto the skillet and it began to bubble. "Let's have it, then."

"Aggie Sterling's dead."

"No," Sebastian breathed. He was quiet for several moments before walking over and sitting down on the edge of a small couch across from Harlow's chair, his forearms resting on his knees. "I saw her this winter. She was hiding it from me but she was with child."

"She was, sir."

Sebastian ran his hands through his silver hair, then closed them in front of his face. "And what of the child?"

"Born a day before she died. As far as we can tell the baby's healthy, under the care of the father."

"How did she die, Harlow?" A watery shine softened Sebastian's eyes.

"We don't know, but not natural causes. She was healthy. Young."

"Give me the details, please."

"We've uncovered very little. Her body is completely intact. My guy S.P. Wiggington saw the naked corpse before it was clothed and placed in the casket. No cuts, scrapes or bruises. Nothing. Whatever may have happened, the consensus is that it was deliberate. Especially if you take the baby's father into consideration."

"What's to consider?" Sebastian asked, ignoring the burning pancake crisping over on the stove.

The corners of Harlow's mouth twitched. "He's not one of us."

"Darkness?"

Harlow nodded. "A quick riser, too."

"I didn't see it on her last we met," Sebastian said, shaking his head. "How is that possible?" He clasped his hands together, both forearms horizontal straight to the elbows, and closed his eyes, reopening them a second later. "She was three years post-Purification, but it's indicated that she possessed, at a minimum, a moderate level of magical ability."

"Precisely why the suspected murderer is the father."

"*His name?*"

"*Bram Holt.*" Harlow leaned in. "*With she who she is, sir, and he who he is, well…that's why you find me here so soon after.*"

"*When did this happen?*"

"*Nine hours ago.*"

"*And she's already in a coffin?*" Sebastian asked, the volume of his voice betraying his steady demeanor.

"*Already in the ground,*" Harlow answered. "*An Unknowing graveyard by the name of Gaddiel's. It's in the town of Harbing, sir. New Jersey.*"

"*What more do we know?*"

"*Besides that the baby was taken back to Holt's estate… nothing.*"

Sebastian sat back, flicking his hand in the direction of the kitchen nook. The burner shut off, the pan and the smoking pancake disappeared and the bowl of batter transformed into a plate hoisting a stack of fifteen perfectly cooked pancakes. "*Girl or boy?*" he asked. His eyes had found a painting of a fish swimming in murky water that hung from the opposite wall. In the background was a small dot emerging from the water.

"*Boy.*"

"*Knowing what he represents, this's got Gideon's prints stamped all over it.*"

"*What do you want to do?*" Harlow asked.

Sebastian breathed into his fist for a few moments. "*We wait. Gideon doesn't know that we know and we have to keep that advantage. Notify Prophecy Control that they shall not interfere until the boy is grown. We wait for eighteen years.*"

Harlow nodded and stood up, stuffing his arms into the sleeves of his jacket.

"*Have a safe trip back,*" Sebastian said, crossing his legs and resting his chin in the heel of his hand. Harlow shuffled to the door, turning back as he opened it.

"*Like I said, sir, one of these days I'll be bearing good news.*"

"*That would be a lovely thing, would it not?*"

"It would," Harlow said. "It would."

And down the steps and into the heat of the desert sun he went, the trailer door snapping shut behind him.

The *snap* jarred Sebastian's eyes open back into present day, not a second before a young woman of about twenty popped out of thin air right in front of Izzy's Ice Cream Parlor across the way. A white sundress with purple floral patterning fell to her knees. Sebastian recognized her—an administrative assistant at the Light's Center of Operations, aka the COO—by the magnificent white lily pinned into her glossy, golden hair. Several awkward, pimple-faced teenage boys gawked at her as they licked their ice cream cones and sipped their milkshakes.

"Mirabella," Sebastian said, and she was seated beside him before he finished articulating the last syllable of her name. The teenage boys didn't bat an eye, as if they had all simultaneously forgotten what they had been goggling at.

"Mr. Tso sent me." Mirabella's southern accent twanged above the fountain trickle, crying babies in strollers and a variety of other mall noises.

"And?"

"He says Mr. Miller, to whom he assigned the case, is no closer to finding Jace Frost than he was when he started."

Sebastian's face hardened. "Have Tso assign three tenured men to assist Mr. Miller in his search."

Mirabella pursed her lips and was gone.

Sebastian stood up with a frown; his stomach was growling. Weaving between a maze of kiosks, he got on an escalator, thinking about how Jace Frost was missing and how Eloa Frost was currently living with Unknowings in Harbing, the same town, whether it be coincidental or not, where the boy who Sebastian had discussed with Harlow resided. It had been eighteen years since the Harlow conversation in the desert—the wait was over—and a few days ago, Sebastian had sent one of his men a telemast to start discreetly collecting information on Aggie Sterling's son. He had yet to hear back.

Sebastian narrowed his eyes, lost in thought for a few moments, then clasped his hands together, both forearms horizontal straight to the elbows. He blinked at the same exact time that a strange-looking kid in a T-shirt that read "Leave Me Alone. God Drinks Beer, Too!" dropped his cell phone at the top of the escalator. During that blink—during that quarter second of time—Sebastian went inside a specific compartment of his own mind where time did not exist. The compartment was his LO-MAK—Library of Memory and Knowledge—a giant structure the size of a city block that he'd mentally built centuries ago over the span of several months with intense internalized magic. Each story was covered with soft blue carpeting, filled with row after row of golden shelves that rose up thirty feet to the ceiling, holding millions of documented memories, facts and theories that he had accumulated since the very beginning.

As he walked down an end row toward Leam Holt's file, Sebastian thought about the effort it had taken to construct a LOMAK. He had completed it early on in the year of 1778, shortly after some of this country's greatest men had signed the Declaration of Independence. Over a beer one night, he had conversed at length about it with Benjamin Franklin, a popular, brilliant man of Light. Franklin had told Sebastian that he had spent many years toying with the idea, but humbly expressed that he didn't possess the magical capabilities to develop an internal storage warehouse. Sebastian remembered that Franklin had likened the LOMAK to smoke, saying he could see wisps of it out in front of him but could never grasp onto it. As Old City Tavern, Franklin's favorite drinking spot, was closing down that night, he was getting around to telling Sebastian, then known as Alon, about his decision to get out of the game.

"I know who I am, Alon, and I know all I'm not," Franklin was saying, his fingers curled around a pint of ale. "I see so much potential in you. I see a fresh-faced young man with a capacity of Light-mindedness unlike any other that I've come across. I invent the lightning rod and women are kissing me on the street. You create a library inside your own mind and they walk right by you because they'll never know! Doesn't seem fair, my dear friend."

"Don't feel too bad. I can get women to kiss me for other reasons."

"Ha! Now, that I believe, you handsome devil." After a large swig of ale, Franklin looked down at his hand, opening and closing it, watching the wrinkly rolls of skin contract and expand. "I'm getting out, Alon."

Alon searched the man's face for traces of uncertainty that he couldn't find. "Surely, you'll stay on in some sort of capacity?"

"Perhaps. On an advisory level, perhaps. But I plan to let age affect me as it does the Unknowings."

"But you're young, Ben. If you choose not to relinquish that constituent of purification, the youthful spirit of your soul could carry you another hundred years. I see that clearly."

"Yet this fascination of becoming old without out magical interference is strong inside me. The thought of it is too enticing to ignore."

Alon contemplated this and smiled. "You'll be moving along far too soon. I shall miss you. And the Light, your wisdom."

"I can tell you with complete sincerity, dear friend, that my life…well…is a life as fulfilled as there ever was. And as for wisdom, lend me your ear one last time." Franklin took off his bifocals, placing them on the wooden-planked counter. "You are pegged to do great things for the good of humankind, Alon. You rise so quickly. As I have said, your magical abilities and mental fortitude are unlike any that has come before you."

"I am in no need of flattery. Speak to me plainly, Ben."

Franklin wiped sweat from his face with the back of his left hand; his right still clutching his pint. "I foresee the war between Light and Darkness culminating while you still breathe the earth's air."

"And you envision this when?" Alon asked.

"As early as the close of the century."

Alon considered his good friend, who now looked much older without the optic duality of bifocals to obscure his eyes. "Why, Ben?"

"Science." A drip or two of ale curled down Franklin's chin. "In a hundred, two hundred years, mankind will be developing weapons that will reach their enemies in numbers that we *of this era of history cannot fathom. Weapons that Unknowings will create and use to kill one another... Weapons that Dark men with magic will create and use to poison the minds of those without it. Gaseous weapons, Alon, that's what I foresee, with chemical properties that allow for mass destruction or global pollution of mind."*

"And your advice?" Alon leaned in close. Franklin was whiter than salt.

"Protect the Unknowings best you can, Alon, but when science advances to that point—and you'll know—you'll know quicker than most—you must find the prophet. And be ready for him once you do."

"And what if he isn't there to be found?"

"Then he will come soon after," Franklin said. His normal volume of speech had trumped his whisperings. "If the world is on the brink, he'll be there. He'll be somewhere."

Alon nodded and put his hand on Franklin's shoulder. Franklin picked up his bifocals, perching them on the tip of his nose. His face was as pleasant and good-natured as before.

"Will you do me one last favor, Alon?"

"Settle your tab?"

"Ha! If you feel the need to, my boy, then by all means! But that, alas, is not my request."

"Anything."

"When you get to the top—"

"If I get to the top."

"—would you do me the honor of considering the name 'Sebastian'?"

"Sebastian?" Alon repeated.

"Yes. It was the name of my family's dog when I was younger, and I tell you, a more loveable, loyal and kindhearted being to pad this earth there will never be."

"If that is to be the path beneath my feet, I promise you I'll consider it."

A beaming smile spread across the squat little man's face. Across the counter, the owner of the Old City Tavern came over to the two men: one on his way along the short journey of mortality; the other just getting his feet wet.

"Closing time, gents."

"Ho, one last ale, Henry, and not on my tab. My dear friend here is buying!"

Back in the end row of the LOMAK, Alon, now known as Sebastian, located the file he came in search of, the tab of the yellow folder displaying two words written in thick black ink.

LEAM HOLT

He slid out the front most piece of paper—a visual copy of the telemast...

Leam Holt, Harbing, New Jersey

Mother, a woman of Light, killed by the father, a man of Darkness.

Gideon, too, will be interested.

Find out what you can, but leave no trail. That is of extreme importance.

A good place to start would be the heavyset man who presided over the boy's delightenment.

This man is believed to have gone into hiding from those of Darkness.

Be thorough. Be careful.

"Find out what you can but leave no trail," Sebastian muttered, nodding his head. *Good,* he thought to himself. *Had to make sure.* Sebastian knew it would be advantageous if Gideon didn't know he had gotten involved. Sebastian placed the paper back in the folder, slid the folder back into the file and clasped his hands together, forearms horizontal straight the elbows, eyes closed.

His eyes opened as the strange-looking kid with the "God Drinks Beer, Too!" T-shirt picked up his cell phone at the top of the escalator. Only a blink's worth of time had passed since Sebastian had gotten in and out of the LOMAK. As the step beneath him disappeared underneath the metal grate, he reflected on Franklin's prediction whilst making his way to the wide selection of eateries at the food court. Perhaps a Cinnabon and some Popeyes chicken would help ease the foreboding feeling growling deep in his belly.

CHAPTER 26

"Where are we?"

"Where does it look like we are, Leam? Up inside your butthole? We're in a field."

Leam brushed off the associate's lame remark, looking around in awe. It couldn't have been more than ten seconds since Leam had put the white winter hat on inside the associate's Cadillac, yet here he was, standing in an endless green-grassed field, beyond which lay absolutely nothing.

He turned full circle. No buildings, no mountains, no familiar bodies of water; only miles of grass beneath a soft, golden sky that suggested the sun had just now fallen into the horizon. But how could that be? Leam had walked out of the Coffee Sip less than a minute ago, or so it had seemed. He clutched the "hat of oblivion" in his hand. Had he really been hidden underneath its pitch black void for over ten hours?

"Hand me the hat, Leam."

Leam tossed it over through the warm breeze. The associate, whose perennial leather attire had been replaced by a black suit, black shirt, black shoes and a white tie, stood tall, sporting a dark, yet debonair expression. If Leam had to be completely honest with himself, he thought the associate looked fantastic.

"I look great, don't I?" the associate said. "Your face says it all." One at a time, with his palms, he straightened each Mohawk to a razor edge. "Looking pretty good yourself, big boy. I see you attack your abdominals at the gym. No harm in that."

Leam looked down to see himself bare-chested and barefooted. Dark brown Carhartt pants covered him waist to ankles—gone were the jeans he had been wearing when he'd slid into the Cadillac, which, like everything else, was nowhere in sight. He patted the hip pockets. Ice shivered up his arms, then down his legs, leaving his skin cold amidst the field's balmy air; his mother's acorn was gone.

"What'd you do with my clothes?" he said. The soft breeze tickling his chest had gone from pleasant to irritating.

The associate pocketed the hat of oblivion, a smug, rat-bastard grin on his face. "This wondrous place," he announced, stretching his arms up to the sky as if he had bounded off a vault and stuck the landing, "where the two of us stand in the grass so green, is a site where I can project your would-be magical powers onto you. Learn now that this is not an exact science. It's impossible to *precisely* predict how you, Leam Holt, would function magically in varying situations *as if you had been delightened*. But with samples of your blood and saliva, we can somewhat ballpark it."

Samples of my blood and saliva? Is this guy serious?

"Throughout this *process*," the associate went on, "the sky and the ground will be your constants. They will not change, you have my word on that. Sky will always be over your head, ground always beneath your feet, so it would be wise to use them as anchors when things get...hectic. Because besides ground and sky, anything and everything in between is fair game."

"But I didn't sign up for any of this," Leam said feeling helpless. Why was the flat field all he could see? He wondered if slick Chris Columbus would've still believed the earth was round if he had found himself in this weirdo place back in the fifteenth century.

"Do you want to go home, little boy?" The associate brushed some lint off his lapel. "Is that it?"

"I didn't say that."

"You're scared, then, aren't you, sweetheart?"

"I didn't say that either, *sir.*"

"So, what are you saying?" The associate's face stiffened, each eyebrow marking in full arch.

"I'm saying that I'm here, but didn't have any choice in the matter."

"Of course not." The associate stepped closer. "Destiny decided for you. You aren't so ignorant as to believe you're a normal eighteen-year-old boy anymore, are you? Nobodies aren't brought to places like this."

Leam felt a whiff of pride and had to hold off a smile, despite the skittering of unrest inside his gut—that instinctual, internal mechanism that warns the brain that the present environment is unsafe.

"This field is a somewhat simulated setting," the associate said, circling around Leam, arms postured like those of a bikini-clad model drawing attention to a hot new ride at a car show. "As you probably would guess, I've had a say in how things will unfold out here, but that doesn't mean I have complete control over it. It will, Leam, take on a life of its own, and believe me when I say that it won't be a small confrontation with some pigeons in a town park. Trust your initial reactions from this point forward. Instinct. The more you try to think things through, the more likely you'll get hurt...or maimed or burned or violated or eaten or...you know...killed."

"Killed?" Leam echoed, the skittering of unrest escalating to a stampede.

"Yes. Your magic is what's simulated. Any result of that magic will be real. If you're fastened between two trees and an ostrich sprints toward you and pecks through your chest bones, you will die while it devours your heart."

Leam could feel his heart hammering in his chest, as if it had heard it might become some giant *freak* of a bird's dinner.

With a cruel smile and glinting eyes, the associate added, "There are some peculiar and dangerous things coming your way, darling, because I want to see how special you really are." He walked up to Leam, pulling a syringe out of the inside pocket of his jacket. "Open your mouth."

"Wait a second—"

"NOW!" the associate roared and Leam obliged out of reflex. The hypodermic needle pierced into his gum below the bottom front teeth, extracting the aforementioned blood and saliva into the barrel. "Step aside," the associate ordered and again Leam obliged.

Before, there had been nothing but the two of them. Now, however, five feet behind Leam stood a five-foot-high table that looked to be made of smoothed-out, varnished tree bark. On its surface lay a small glass of cloudy water, into which the associate plunged the small amount of bodily fluid from the tube, which turned the liquid in the glass into the color and consistency of strawberry milk. He threw the syringe aside—it vanished before hitting the ground, as if the air had swallowed it whole—and placed his hand flat over the glass. At this, a metal cylinder shot down from his palm, encasing the glass. The associate snatched up the cylinder, turning to Leam with a beaming smile.

"Have fun," he said, his eyebrow tattoos pulsing white light.

"Wait, hold on a second," Leam said, trying, and failing, to sound composed. "This starts now?"

"Right now."

"Can I ask a question first?"

"Of course," the associate said. "Anything you'd like."

A smidge of relief softened Leam's features. "So I want to make sure I have this straight. You said my constants are the sky and—"

The associate laughed and disappeared, leaving Leam red-faced and shaking his head. "Thanks," Leam muttered, then said inside his head, *I hate that mother fu—*

BOOM!

Thunder crashed down from above—the field shook under Leam's feet like it was ready to cave in—followed by the noise of angry water smashing into a stone pier.

Rain, slow at first, began to pummel Leam's skin in sharp, painful smacks. He was reminded of the vision he'd had—the first one, the boat in the stormy sea—while holding Eloa's hands. He tried to push her from his mind, failing miserably, until out of nowhere, water came rushing at him from east, west, north, south, as if, just out of sight, four giant dams had broken. Furious, white-capped waves poured over the green grass, a section of which rose as the raging water covered the field. Eyes squinted—from both the pounding rain and the abrupt arrival of fierce, gusting winds—Leam soon found himself atop a small, square patch of grass amidst an ocean of rough, tempestuous water. Three breaths ago, there hadn't been a drop of water in sight. The associate's promise held, but Leam hadn't expected the "ground beneath his feet" to be a grassy raft bobbing in the ocean.

Struggling to keep his balance, Leam saw something, far off, nodding in and out of the ocean. A giant splash splattered his face, he looked again, and now there were several things out in the turbulent sea, things that looked out of place beside the wave peaks, things getting closer. At about thirty yards Leam got a good look at the nearest one; his legs buckled, dropping him to his knees.

A *huge* frog approached, slightly smaller than a walrus, its slimy brownish-green mouth open, revealing three levels of thick, sharp, disgusting teeth. Leam's heart felt like it had been dunked in ice water; the freakish thing wouldn't look away from him and it was smiling, too. Why was it smiling? Farther out beyond the lead frog, thirty more, at least, were poking up out of the water, all headed right for Leam, who shot to his feet, feverishly patting down his legs. He had no weapon, nothing to fight with. Was this it? *This* was how it was to end?

The lead frog hopped its massive body up onto the small raft way too easily, its toothy mouth snapping. Leam shouted a string of obscenities and booted it firm in the face. It crashed into the ocean several yards away, resurfacing in no time at all, paddling through the chop back to the raft, its army of now fifty behind it, a hundred bug-eyes all fixed on Leam.

He closed his eyes, felt the worsening rain ping against his skin, and thought to let it calm him. Almost instantly, it did. *"Find a weapon, Leam,"* a voice not his own said inside his head, and he felt a peculiar, bubbly power tighten around his muscles then shoot through his bones. His eyelids popped open and there, floating ten yards away on a smaller square of grass, stood the five-foot-tall tree-bark table, a cigar box glued to its surface.

Without a thought, Leam dove into the water, swam the small distance and pulled himself up onto the table-raft right as the lead frog hopped back up on the other. Leam lifted the box lid. Fifty or more cigars, glowing with amber light, trembled inside. He picked up one off the top—a mighty energy flooded first his hand and then the arm—and with the sharp snap of a whip, the cigar elongated. Clutched in his hand was a brown spear, six feet long, its pointed end sharper than the tips of the associate's ridiculous Mohawks.

Leam turned, waiting for the lead frog to spring from the other raft. When it did, he jabbed the spear through its eye. With a loud frog-cry of pain, it fell into the water, and the newly-invigorated Leam knew it wouldn't be coming back up.

With little room to maneuver on the table raft, Leam concentrated the energy to his legs. He jumped forward twenty feet up in the air, the box of magic cigars wedged securely under his arm, and landed on the original patch of land. He felt great—spry and capable. Was this how it was going to be if he ever received real powers?

Leam quieted his thoughts, focusing on nothing but the pending slaughter: to spear the swarming, mutant, leaderless frogs with swift precision. Whoever was watching was going to take notice; he wanted to make sure of that.

He grabbed another glowing cigar from the box—SNAP—whipping the spear at the closest frog, a big old dude, splitting its eyes. Leam laughed as he reached back into the box—another cigar, another spear—and he gored a third frog in its ugly mouth of triple-tiered teeth. Brown blood gushed from its throat as it sunk into the choppy water.

Cigar, spear, cigar, spear. Despite the monsoon and the bouncy, slippery grass-raft, Leam picked off the frogs with extraordinary accuracy. Inside of a minute, all but one had been slain, all but one sunken beneath the surface.

Leam watched the lone survivor swim toward him, a pawn sent by that rat-bastard associate, to kill or to be killed. Leam stared deep into its eyes. In another pair, he had seen the same look: those of Pamela, the Unknowing Leam had almost murdered and discarded in the wooded Cricket. Leam recalled how, as a last ditch effort to save herself, Pamela had begged Leam to sleep with her. *"It's what you want. It's what all boys want."* Her eyes, he remembered vividly, had been screaming terror one moment, and flatlining the next, drained of all emotion. Here in the stormy ocean, Leam witnessed the bug-eyes of the last mutant frog, now a spear-length away, do the exact same thing.

Leaving the last of the amber cigars in the box, Leam held up his hands, palms facing the frog.

"Stop," he said inside his head.

The frog did.

"Go with the others."

And the frog did, sinking beneath the surface, its eyes—holding Leam's—resigned yet peaceful, as was the water, which had begun to calm. The rain smacking onto Leam's shoulders and upper back lessened.

"Leam, Leam, Leam." The deep resonance of the associate's unmistakable voice purred through the misty air from a location unknown, perhaps the simulated heavens above. "Have you saved enough energy for the Witchlows?"

"What?" Leam shouted, wiping wet hair away from his eyes.

"Let us pray," the voice boomed, and Leam's feet were swiped by an invisible force. He fell to his knees—the irony not lost on him—recognizing this display of power as a reminder that he, Leam, was not in control.

The associate's words echoed, then ran off, dwindling away as a new sound, that of bath water being sucked down the drain, rushed near. Hardened, reddish-brown clay began to devour the ocean of water, and in a matter of moments, Leam stood in the middle of a sun-scorched desert of baking-hot clay and rock. He'd been shy about his shirt off at the start of the process, but now Leam considered stripping off his pants, too, to weather the suffocating heat. Again, he thought of Eloa and, again, was aided by an outside circumstance to push her image out of his mind.

Far away, rising out of the horizon, a small black cloud approached. Already dripping with sweat, Leam kept his eyes trained on the advancing mass of darkness while his bare feet cooked on the heat of the red clay. As the cloud got closer, the dark blur began to thin out, separating into smaller black clouds that quickly took the shape of humongous black butterflies soaring nearer and nearer. Leam staggered backward, his feet kicking up crimson dust, his mouth falling open. They weren't large butterflies at all. They were huge, fanged bats, wingspans of fifteen feet and ravenous eyes the size, color and shine of bowling balls.

Leam spun around, three hundred and sixty degrees of barren land, nothing else. The aiding tree-bark table must have gotten washed away with the water. The bats, or "Witchlows" as the associate had called them, were really humming, headed right for him. Leam figured he had no longer than ten seconds before his half-naked body became their dinner. He took a breath and closed his eyes, as he had when the frogs were almost upon him.

I need a weapon, he thought, and opened his eyes. Nothing but a giant Witchlow, fangs bared, screeching like a ghost owl as it swooped down upon him. Leam slammed his eyes closed in panic. *I NEED A WEAPON!* his inner voice screamed out. Again, nothing to aid him, nothing to fight with.

"Oh please, oh please," he gasped, sweat licking his face sloppy as the nearest Witchlow's claws expanded, twenty feet away or less, with five others trailing just behind. Leam crouched into a ball, covering his arms over his head, inside of which burst the thought of failing his father yet again.

"No," Leam whispered and forced a calm over himself like he had with the pigeons at the park and…

Thud… Thud, thud, thud, thud, thud.

The horrible screeching continued, but it was distant, distorted, barely audible—the air had cooled fifty degrees, easy—and to Leam's elation, his head wasn't gushing blood and bits of brain, severed inside a bat-monster's mouth. Jittery and a bit frantic, Leam was standing inside of a clear orb, safe and well-protected. Witchlows were crashing and bouncing off it. The ones who seemed to learn that penetration wasn't possible hovered close by, black saliva dripping from their mouths like leaky oil.

No computer screen of battle options materialized—the bubble was empty apart from a small red box, a keyhole welded in its center—which was fine with Leam. He wasn't going anywhere—the surge of magical energy within him had gone with the water and rain. As he was about to sit down and figure out his next move, he spotted something moving around far out in the red desert. It looked like a small boy, walking over clay and rock toward Leam. It *was* a boy, and he looked familiar. Too familiar. As he came closer to the bubble, Leam, with radiating waves of shock and dread, realized that the boy was actually *him*, eight or so years younger, with unblemished hands, naked of tattoos or scarring.

The boy's eyes widened joyously, presumably after spotting Leam in the bubble, and he began running toward his older self.

"Get back!" Leam shouted, banging his palms against the bubble. "Get back, you hear me? Get back! GET BACK!"

But it was useless. The smiling boy kept running forward as Leam kicked, clawed and cursed at the bubble. As it always does, the inevitable happened. A giant bat swooped down, its claws snatching onto the younger Leam's head and tearing it off the boy's body. Severed tendons and veins wriggled out of the neck as the Witchlow flew into the dry, blazing sky, leaving a headless body, twisting and writhing on the ground for its friends to pick apart.

The sky darkened as if a huge, black, semi-transparent sheet had slid in between the red desert and white sky. It was hundreds of Witchlows soaring through the air or setting down on the clay, batting enormous, leathery wings. Peering through their dark, blurry haze, Leam spotted another happy clone, this one about the age of thirteen. Behind it was a six-year-old Leam, smiling and moving nearer. Tears spilled from the real Leam's eyes, rage stomping in his chest with nowhere to escape. Four more younger Leam's had appeared, and there were others, scores of them, popping up all around. Powerless, Leam watched a grizzled old Witchlow, its giant claws stretching wide, swoop down, reaching for the smallest clone's head.

Leam looked away. His stomach was nothing but a tight, anxious ball of fury, but his body was sluggishly weak. Where the hell was the energizing power that he had attained to kill those mutant frogs? A paralyzing yet sensible realization stiffened Leam's bones: the associate had taken the projected magic back, leaving Leam with the same fate as the mutant frogs—helpless and, eventually, doomed.

Leam felt like a gutless coward, standing in the safety of his orb while the Witchlows wreaked havoc unopposed, but what could he do? He didn't care about his own safety; he cared that he was trapped. He wailed out obscenities, ferocious fists banging against the bubble. New clones kept arriving, popping up everywhere, all with the same stupid grins on their faces. Didn't they know their fate here? Didn't they have a clue to stay away? Every five or ten seconds, Leam witnessed a decapitation of a mini-Leam, who was then torn to shreds.

"WHAT DO YOU WANT FROM ME?" Leam roared up at the bright empty sky, and as his line of vision came back down, he saw it—something hovering over a headless, entrails-exposed body. A key. A red, oversized skeleton key, and the sight of it zapped another surge of foreign energy through Leam's veins. His magic was back. He could feel it ignite fire underneath his skin. His lips pulled back, exposing his teeth like a rabid wolverine.

He snatched the red box off the floor and without a thought about his own safety, strode forward, melting through the bubble without resistance into the awful heat that cooked above the blood-stained desert. His movements were swift, consuming next-to-no strength, his mind clear and focused in a way where he could've solved a Rubik's cube in five seconds flat but at the same time have trouble recalling his first name.

A silent, wiry Witchlow darted for Leam as he treaded forward. When it was close enough, Leam's hands shot upward, clasping onto the beast's claws. He yanked the two-hundred-pound bat down, driving its head into the ground, snapping its neck. Another Witchlow followed suit and got the same. So did a third, but one of its talons stabbed Leam between his shoulder blades, cutting a jagged, inch-wide gash down the center of his back through to the spine. Leam barely felt any pain. It was as if, in this state, his focus only registered what would help him, and nothing that wouldn't.

Sprinting forward, eyes honed in on his target, Leam brought another two Witchlows down to their deaths, hopped over a third, and dove forward, snatching the key out of the air, shoving it into the box's keyhole and twisting it to the right. The key was sucked into the box, which melted into a ball of fiery metal that shot up out of Leam's hands. His eyes followed its rise into the atmosphere until it was but a speck of a red dust.

When Leam looked back down, ready to fight, a splendid sight awaited him. Every Witchlow—those in the air and on the ground—was frozen still. The ground began to shake again, this time accompanied by an ear-splitting sound, as if the sky had cracked a giant walnut. An immense fissure began to split the red clay in two, zigzagging down the center of the hard-caked desert. Leam brought his arms up like Jesus on the cross, and thick strings of dark smoke emitted from his palms, entangling themselves around the gigantic, unmoving bats, pulling them down into the jagged crack. As the shaking ground began to separate further, the living clones faded into the background, like digital images on a computer screen diminishing to nothing. The unconsumed body parts of the slain Leams rolled toward the real Leam, merging together into a boulder-sized ball of flesh, blood and bone. As the ground tore apart, the ball levitated, revolving with escalating speed while the last of the shrieking Witchlows was pulled below. When the spinning ball had shrunk to the size of a grape—looking very much like a pinkish Milk Dud—it dropped into Leam's hand just as both his palms stopped spewing smoke.

Instinctively, he pocketed the ball of clones, not a second before the spot of ground on which he stood collapsed. Beside chunks of rock and red clay, Leam—screaming, angry, exhausted, shirtless and bloody—dropped like a barrel of lead into deep, cold blackness, away from the bright crumbling desert now so high above him.

Despite the notion of severe and certain pain waiting for him at the close of his free fall—well, either that or death—it was another thought that stung at Leam, right between the ears. His anchors—ground and sky—had been stripped from him. So much for the associate's promise.

CHAPTER 27

"Are you awake, dear?"

Eloa drew in a sharp gasp of breath, jerking her ink-smudged cheek up off the pages of her journal.

"Relax, Eloa, you're fine. I didn't mean to startle you, dear, but I thought you might want to join us for dinner."

Mary's voice. Her gentle hand on Eloa's shoulder.

Eloa must have dozed off. This morning's run had been a bruiser. A lukewarm breeze, more on the cold side than the hot, tickled the inch of bare midriff between her jean shorts and black cut-off T-shirt.

"Oh, thank you, but I'm not hungry," she said, yawning, turning to Mary as she covered her stomach with crossed forearms.

"Have you always eaten like a bird?" Mary asked, crossing in front of the desk to the front bedroom window.

Eloa shrugged. "I guess so."

"Dear, you mustn't leave the screen up with the window open." Mary released the latches on the bottom sides of the frame, lowering the screen. "The mosquitos get in." Even Mary's scolding was somehow kind.

"Sorry, I...I don't really remember opening it, to be honest." Eloa gazed out into the front yard. The late afternoon sun had dropped behind the leafy branches of the many towering oaks that lined Mary and Larry's street. Through the dusty screen—the upper left corner home to an elaborate spider web—her eyes found a small beige bird perched on a nearby tree limb. The bird seemed to be staring right through her. "I'm really tired for some reason." She squeezed her eyes closed, massaging the bridge of her nose. "I've been sleepy all day."

Wiping off some window screen dirt on the sides of her pale-yellow apron, Mary came back to Eloa and kissed her on top of her head. "Any news on your father, dear?"

Eloa rubbed the sleep off her face and looked back out the window. The bird hadn't moved, not a bit, and it looked too lifelike to be one of Larry's decoys that he kept scattered around the yard.

"I'm sorry, what?" Eloa asked.

"Your father, dear. Any news?"

Eloa shook her head, choosing not to elaborate with words. Mary put a comforting hand on the back of Eloa's neck, giving it a squeeze. Eloa let her head fall forward, longing for the warm wrinkled hand to stay put for a little longer, to warm the cold empty spaces she felt inside her body, to alleviate the near-constant stream of ugly, gory, Jace-related thoughts. But after a gentle stroke down Eloa's ponytail, Mary's hand withdrew.

"Well," Mary said, moving back toward the door, "Larry bought a whole bunch of food off of the value menu. McDonalds. He's just been. Come downstairs and eat if you get hungry."

"Thank you," Eloa said, half smiling, blankly staring out the window. "Mary, you're so good to me."

"We're both delighted to have you, dear. Despite the circumstances."

Something shiny near her iPhone on the corner of the desk glinted, pulling Eloa's gaze away from the motionless bird perched on the branch. Holding it between her thumb and finger—a clear, sparkly little gem—she turned to Mary, who was just about out into the hall.

"Mary, did this fall off of your bracelet?"

"I don't wear bracelets, dear."

"Well, is it yours?"

"What is it?"

"It's like a diamond."

"Not mine. Good night, dear."

The door scrubbed closed over the carpet, leaving Eloa to think about where the tiny jewel could have come from. After some thought, she went to the bed, lifting the mattress up an inch, and slid out the sky-blue envelope that tall, mysterious Porlo had given her a few nights back. Carefully dropping the diamond in next to her father's brief note—the one conveying that she must keep the starfish medallion "on her always"—Eloa slipped the envelope back under the mattress. As she sat down, a shopping bag crinkled next to her butt. Scooting a few inches to her right, she picked up the white paper bag. *Le Boutique Bordeaux* was written across its side in a slanted, cursive font.

Yesterday, in the pink Beetle on the way home to Mary and Larry's, Bridgette had convinced Eloa to stop off "real quick" at the fancy designer clothing store on Falcon Ave, which Bridgette referred to, in an absurd French accent, as "The Tique." She had led Eloa straight to a wall of skimpy dresses, unsuccessfully attempted to get Eloa to try one on—blood-red and no bigger than a washcloth—bought it for her anyway, despite Eloa's insistence that she not, and gushed for the rest of the ride home about how hot it would look on Eloa's body. Eloa had climbed the stairs to her room and tossed the shopping bag on the bed end, spending the remainder of the day-into-night thinking about a Flower Boy and a coffee shop.

Eloa inhaled deeply. The unmistakable aroma of Mickey Dees had infiltrated her room via the open window; Mary and Larry must be dining on the front porch. Eloa dumped the dark red dress out of the bag. It lay there, bunched up on the fluffy white comforter like a bleeding animal dying in the snow. She looked at it for a long while.

"Screw it," she said, no louder than a whisper. She crossed the room, pushed the circular button in the center of the doorknob locked, and came back to the bed. She removed her necklace and placed it on her bedside table.

Without too much concern as to whether anyone walking down the street—or resting on a tree branch—could see her, Eloa peeled off her shirt and stepped out of her shorts. She dropped the silk dress over her head and let it fall. It felt like light rain. The hemline just covered her backside...just.

She went to the thin, rectangular full-length mirror for a look. Despite being alone, a shy grin sat funny on her reflected face. Her bashful eyes traced downward, taking in the curve of her breasts, followed by that of her hips. Then, before her gaze could sink any lower, Eloa froze, as suddenly as if Larry had yelled up the stairs that her bedroom carpet was covered with invisible snakes.

"I got it," she said.

All business, she spun away from the mirror and crossed to the desk in a manner that said "Get out of my way or you're getting knocked over." Grabbing a red Sharpie from the cup and flipping to a fresh page of notebook paper, Eloa began to scribble down the poem she had memorized as a little girl—the one she couldn't quite piece together the night of the bloody lock of hair. The poem that summoned help to those of Light who needed it. Once finished, she straightened, and with eyes fuzzy, recited the four verses.

After, she waited, unwilling to move a muscle lest she miss a sound. She waited for an anxiously long minute, but nothing seemed to result from the recitation. She said it a second time, slower and more carefully than she had the first, then turned, her eyes darting around to every corner, every inch of the room. Again, nothing. Not a change in temperature, not a book over-turned, no glowing angel hovering before her to report the good health and safety of her dad. She let out a frustrated breath, but almost instantly found a calm peace as her gaze settled on the bed, which, with its white down and pillows, waited for her like a comfy cloud stuck in the sky. *The help will come when it's ready*, she thought. *Allow it the time to happen.*

So she went to the bed and lay down, her back and the undersides of her bare legs and arms all but melting into the plush bedding. The dress's crimson silk was but a soft breath over her skin.

She shut her eyes, relaxing her muscles and freeing her head of the clutter of Bridgette's next party, of Leam's alleged mental illness, of the magic in her hands yesterday morning at the Coffee Gulp. Instead she thought only of her dad, his head of hair, blood-free and flowing, as she recited the Ode of Aid over and over, with mounting confidence that answers were finally on route. Tonight it rang word perfect in her mind.

Help or hinder, not the latter,
I'm lost as what to do.
Genuinely urgent, is the matter,
Find me, I ask of you.

CHAPTER 28

Blackness. Nothing else.

Slowly, like the tide fading back into the sea, Leam became aware that he existed, but that was the extent of it. Later—how much later he didn't know, nor did it matter—a fuzzy crack of horizontal light spread out in front of him, pain blinding his eyes until they adjusted. The crack widened.

A perfect circle of fierce whitish light gaped at him. It took a moment for Leam to realize he was on his back looking up. A man leaned over him, obscuring some of the light on the left side of the frame. While Leam's eyes adjusted to the man's face, he heard the soft sound of liquid dripping onto plastic, the scent of soap strong beneath his nose. He couldn't move his limbs—he was strapped to some sort of table or board—and when his focus swapped from white light to dark man, his body pulsed with terror.

Leam's eyes shocked stiff as they took in the man's abnormally large face and dead eyes deep in sockets that caved above a nose and mouth covered by a surgical mask. On the right side of the frame, a huge hand holding a glinting scalpel came into view, tiny red ants crawling over the blade. Leam choked on his fear, and though he couldn't see the surgeon's mouth, he could tell by the creases near the man's dead eyes that a cruel, wide smile hid behind the thin powder-blue paper of the mask.

Before Leam could process it all, everything went black, and the hard surface of support vanished, sending him falling, falling through darkness, his memory coming back to him as he dropped, bright vivid colors forming recognizable forms and shapes. The field of green, the gigantic frogs and the Witchlows, the Leam clones, the desert, the ground splitting open, the fall, bracing for a bone-cracking impact, more falling, wind shearing past his ears and...

The wind stopped. The fall had stopped. Through the blackness bled a gentle yellow light that swung over him in slow soft streaks, faintly illuminating sections of a metallic floor, and four walls made of the same. Leam found himself sitting in a chair. The dim patches of light and the shadows that chased them came from a shiny tin lamp swaying above him. In front of him rested a small, four-by-four table, clean and silvery, like the walls. Across a slick of its surface, between a skid of light and shadow, Leam, for a tricky second, thought he saw the smoothed-out tree bark tabletop that had held the box of cigar-spears on the grassy raft, a stinging reminder of how the associate had re-neged on his promise of sky overhead and ground below. Here, in this place, was neither sky nor ground. This place, here, was a ten-by-twenty foot cage of solid metal.

As the lamp's swaying slowed, the shifting cone of dim light centered over an old, beat-up, black leather-bound book lying flat on the middle of the table like an island of coal amidst a silvery sea. Leam's eyes hit upon the worn-out page edges be-fore skipping to the faded lettering of the cover.

THE DICTIONARY OF DARKNESS

Leam figured that the Webster guy probably hadn't been involved in this edition. Without a look around—he knew there was nothing to see, anyway—Leam peeled back the stiff cover, which was sticky and left two of his fingertips blotted in some type of tar or curdled ink.

Millions of charred-black leaves—large, like those of an oak tree—flew out from the pages of the opened book, dancing and swirling around, swaying and sashaying in the room's dry, scentless air. After a moment or two, they began to assemble into groups until they're shaking slowed, and they became still, stuck to an invisible wall, shaped into letters that formed into words.

Leam read the clusters of words that hung in front of him:

You have opened The Dictionary of Darkness. In doing so, whether knowingly or not, you have thrust yourself into a mentally demanding, emotionally draining, task of difficulty and danger.

Once read, the leaves shuffled around, arranging into new letters and words:

Death may finally be yours, as anything other than the completion of the task spelled out before you will result in your agonizing demise.

Leam heard a clunk sound, like that of a basement furnace kicking over. He tilted his ear toward the wall on his right, his face scrunched-up-serious, desperate to hear the clunk again in order to decipher it. And when he felt hot panic ignite in his chest and send shooting stabs of dread down his legs like sharpened shoots of bamboo, it was not a reaction to sound but to sight. Each wall, all about ten feet away from him and the table was sliding slowly and silently inward.

The rustling of leaves pulled Leam's heightened sense of awareness back to the new set of words pasted to the air:

As you are now aware, the Walls of Doom inch closer, your mortal body in their sights. To keep them from advancing, and to delay their singular purpose—crushing your feeble body into nothing but skin, guts and turds— your task, no matter how daunting it may seem, is simple.

The Walls of Doom advanced, the room's square footage ever-shrinking. The circle of light illuminating the dictionary expanded. Leam looked up to see the entire ceiling pushing downward, the lamp chain aquiver. He tried to shut the stupid dictionary but smoke shot out of the pages, burning his fingers at their touch. The leaves shuffled again and he read on:

A word of Darkness will be presented before you, and you must locate that word and read its definition aloud. Exact recitation and proper pronunciation will temporarily halt the enclosing Walls of Doom, providing more time for you to flip through pages in search of the definition of the word to follow.

Beads of sweat seeped through Leam's forehead, cascading down the bridge of his nose, down his cheeks, like dew slipping down a giant beech tree leaf.

"Give me the first word already!" he shouted, the leaves swirling in the air, taking their time as they configured into new sentences:

But that will only delay their arrival. To stop the progression of the walls once and for all, you must define each of the seven words. If you don't, we say bye-bye and you die.

"GIVE ME THE FREAKING WORD THEN!"

Most of the ashen leaves flittered to the floor. Those that remained spelled out one word, the first of seven:

SPHYGMISM

Leam's fingernails cut through the edges of two pages about two-thirds down the dictionary, and he flipped to the S's. His eyes scanned downward, stopping when they fell on the correct word. He spoke, "Sphygmism: The rare ability to bring someone or something back to life."

Beneath Leam's scrutinizing eyes, all of the words typed onto the open page melted into hot ink, pooling together and forming into a dark sphere the size of a grapefruit. The swirly grayish-black ball hovered in front of him and, instinctively, Leam grabbed it. A jolt of energy flooded his body as the inky ball dissolved through his hand. He pressed his palm into the surface of the table—another instinctual action—and a deep boom, like thunder a town over, shook the room. The ceiling and all four walls stopped dead. It wasn't until a few seconds after the leaves spelled the second word that the Walls of Doom began to push inward again, their distance from Leam between nine feet and eight.

TRANSMORPHIA

Leam flipped through the small amount of pages between the S's and the T's, and found *Transmorphia* sandwiched between *Trailcorpsus* and *Trapclap*. He spoke fast.

"Transmorphia: The change from the stationary to the mobile form of an alternate being, and vice versa."

The words on the open page melted into another dark swirly ball. Leam grabbed it, felt the surge of magic soak his veins and slammed his palm down on the metal table. The enclosing walls stopped for a few seconds, then continued their squeeze. The air was getting muggy, thickening with Leam's panicked breath.

OCLIMODULATION

He tore through thirty or so pages, pinpointed the third word, and yelled it and the corresponding definition out as fast as he could without skipping over any syllables.

"Oclimodulation: Changing the weather to gain an advantage over the Light."

Leam snatched the ball of melted letters out of the air, felt the surge and slammed his palm into table, his eyes already focused on the rustling leaves, ready for them to compile into the next word.

MYRMIDIAD

The walls were close, five feet, maybe four. He flopped to the middle of the dictionary, startled by his luck. The exact page he needed was there on the first try. Leam shouted the word at the stationary leaves, his legs jitterbug shaking.

"Myrmidiad: A subordinate who, away from battle, takes the life of another without getting clearance from a superior."

A new ball of swirling darkness popped into the air, nearly shattering the dim light bulb that was lowering in time with the ceiling. "Sky above, ground below, huh?" Leam spat, his hand cupping over the ball of energy, slamming it to the table in one fluid motion. The Walls of Doom stopped, restarting in a matter of seconds. As the room got smaller, so did the leaves.

PROPNOTIST

Leam rifled to the P's, licked the tips of his shaking fingers and flipped to the page that contained the current word. The tin lamp was blocking his vision now. He punched it away; a comet of dim light streaked around him at random.

"Propnotist: Someone capable of traveling at such high speeds that they are undetectable to the Unknowing eye."

Sitting at the edge of the chair and starting to lose it, Leam held his palm down over the book before the newest sphere shot upward. When it did, it found his waiting hand, which squashed the ball of energy into the table surface. He was crying now—he couldn't help it. If he were to spread his arms as if crucified, the fingertips of each hand would find a wall.

Two more, c'mon, two more, you bitches, two more...

The leaves scurried around to form the sixth word.

INDESCENDENTATION

At first glance, the word looked to be a mile long. After a wasted glimpse at the wall that he faced, now close enough for Leam to see his horrified face reflected off its metallic shine, Leam scoped for *Indescendentation,* his eye snagging hold of it once his speedy fingers had shuffled to the correct page. The words shot from his mouth like exhaust out a tailpipe.

"Indescendentation: Aging backward. Having years taken off your life, but not your mind."

Leam's hand was on the inky ball before it had fully formed. As soon as he felt the magic fill his arm, he mushed his palm down, grinding the heel into the metal.

With the ceiling just a foot from his head, the chain had gone slack. He had to grab the tin lamp—a welt of pain singing his hand raw—and hold it like a policeman's flashlight at the seventh leafy word.

TELEMASTERY

The diminishing metal cube forced Leam into a catcher's stance. He tried to flip the pages forward to the T's, but at the mercy of the squeeze, the table had started to twist, crumple, and bend, and one of the legs snapped, knocking the Dictionary of Darkness behind Leam in between the lamp he'd dropped and his Achilles tendon.

The Walls of Doom were no more. Sandwiched into a tight, squatting ball, his sweaty chin pushed between his knees, Leam was trapped in a solid box, no bigger than a dog cage, but without the blessed, peek-through wiring that a dog cage would've provided.

Between his feet, a sliver of a page mutely shone in a slash of fading light. Leam could see it was still stuck on the last page, *Indescendentation* glaring at him, mocking him, a witness to his agony. Leam would give up his eyes and ears to indescendentate back to a time where he might be able to head off his fate: To be here, himself and a collapsed table, squashed and suffocating together inside a box of smoldering death.

"I CAN'T TURN THE PAGE!" he screamed. "I CAN'T TURN THE PAGE!" He could feel the ceiling make contact with the top of his head. His knees, framing his ears, pressed up against the side walls, his face shoved against the one in front. In a last ditch effort, and with all of his courage and will power, he closed his eyes, forcing himself as calm as his jackhammer heartbeat would allow and, incredibly, however briefly, he let go.

Leam Holt let go.

And in that moment of temporary unconsciousness—a miraculous separation of mind and body—the definition of a word he had never known squeezed out of lips that were flattened smack against an enclosing metal wall.

"Telemastery: Delivering news far distances through thought alone."

Pop!

The prism of dim light—the lamp's reflections off the many crumpled pieces and angles of table—was snuffed out by sudden darkness. The *pop* had somehow stiffened the shrinking metal cube firm. If it hadn't, moments later, Leam would have been a crushed sack of mush...but would that have been a good thing? The tiny cube that had formerly been the Walls of Doom had stopped dead, but Leam couldn't move any part of his body except his left big toe and the upper region of his left cheek. His mouth was flattened flush against the metal encasement. He could only draw in breath—hot, muggy breath—through a small quivering crack on the right side of his mouth.

Panic that Leam had never known set in. Ghostly silence screamed at him from all angles. Sweat coated every part of him, some areas sticky, others slippery, yet he was so compressed into unyielding confinement that not even body grease could help budge him an inch. His spine felt like it was dripping blood, and he remembered how one of the Witchlow's talons had torn a gash down the middle of his back.

He became highly aware of his left elbow, wedged into an upper corner directly behind his left shoulder blade. *Move!* his inner voice growled. *Move, elbow!* But it wouldn't. It couldn't. And, oh God, it was getting warm, warmer than warm. It was hot. All of a sudden it was hot, and this brought on additional stabbing, porcupine-quills of panic.

It was over. He couldn't move—muscles shuddering, spasms of fat, heavy, claustrophobic pain—then itching, he was itching, his nose itched, his side near the ribs and the under-folds of damp skin behind the knee. Itches everywhere, needling him, biting him, everywhere, no escape, powerless, he was powerless, he couldn't breathe—*I CAN'T BREATHE!*—lips splitting open, stretching and splitting, stinging blood, stretching flesh, teeth scraping, blood-stained teeth, as if painted with ketchup, clinking hard against flat metal—hot, it was so hot, it was too hot—*HELP ME!*—the box felt like—*HELP ME, PLEEEE-ASE!*—felt like it was closing in again, pushing in on him, oh please let it, please let it be, or was that his imagination—*I CAN'T MOVE!*—wishing for death, pleading for it, no matter how painful, praying for death, screaming for help, teeth scraping metal, itchy, sweaty paralysis, let it stop, have mercy, set me afire, light me in flames, poison the air, the thick air, heavy with heat...

...he could see his death in front of him like a mirror of the future, neck collapsing in on itself, bones cracking like snapped twigs, the associate watching, amused, blood everywhere, lips splitting, teeth shattering, the jags falling down his throat in a slow-motion waterfall of rusted nails...

...blurring out the mirror, blurring out death, pressing his body outward with putrid, weak strength, choking on blood, choking on snot and tooth and sweat. He couldn't do anything, he tried but he couldn't, he couldn't save himself, the associate grinning from beyond the blacks of Leam's crushed-closed eyes—*KILL ME!*—he couldn't lift his head—*KILL ME NOW!*—he couldn't move, his head it wasn't his own, he couldn't move it—*WHOEVER YOU ARE! JUST KILL ME!*—he couldn't lift his head, the associate smiling, smiling and lying and barking and laughing, he couldn't move, he couldn't lift his head, the heat consumed him, and...

...then, unexpectedly, when the associate's self-satisfied image infested his mind yet again, a sudden spark of desire to rip the man's face clean off his skull-bones ignited. As he pictured his hand pulling off the associate's skin and tendons and eyeballs and cartilage like a rubbery mask, Leam felt the markings on his hands throb with pain and, in unison, the prison box pulsed with white light. With compacted power, a pit of energy in his gut ebbed outward like lightning, like an ocean-deep nuclear blast spreading out through the water in a storm of speed and light, and with a deafening shatter—POW—his body sprang from crouched, coiled ball to standing straight and tall, and...

Clap...clap...clap...clap...

The dark heat was pulled off of him like a bed sheet yanked off a hiding child. The air was clean and intoxicating in flavors of cut grass and fresh dew.

Clap...clap...clap...clap...

Soft, golden, rosy light hugged every part of him, the voluminous sky welcoming him back to normalcy, to safety, away from the prison box, and yet...and yet, he felt no relief or freedom, nothing like that at all. His thoughts were dark, and every one of them vengeful.

Clap...clap...clap...clap...

The stinging applause approaching from behind Leam tunneled sharply through his eardrum like an ice pick chipping through a soft block of wood. He knew whose hands clapped the noise before turning around, and not because of more obvious factors, such as most recent association or context. Leam knew because it was just. He knew because it had to be. He twisted around, his mouth lopsided, a dehumanizing half-grin.

"Look at the fraud, everybody," Leam jeered, the markings on his hands going dim. "In his handsome black suit and fancy little tie."

The associate stood tall, his hands quiet as they fell to his sides. He was a dark, impressive figure against the soft glowing backdrop of the sky. "What did you call me?" he asked in his velvet voice.

"You're a liar," Leam said, stepping forward as the recognizable heat of the bull rose up his legs without the usual pinky-prickling, sole-warming, eyelid-fluttering warm-up. Apparently, with unlocked magic streaming through his veins, the powerful black bull had no need for preamble to rise.

"Have you forgotten who I am? Who I work for?" the associate said, his eyebrow markings flickering like a pair of fluorescent lights struggling to beam up. "You better watch your tone."

"Sky, ground, sky ground," Leam snarled. The rising surge of dark heat felt more powerful to Leam than the cleaner, lighter magic that had helped him defeat the frogs, the Witchlows and the Walls of Doom. "I hung on to those *constants* and you stripped me of them! Sky! Ground! Sky! Ground! You took them away and stuffed me in a box!"

"I said watch your tone," the associate urged, his weight shifting from foot to foot on the grass.

"Don't try to wriggle out of it like a coward," Leam said, advancing, blackish clouds storming inside him. The associate took a small step back, deep lines of concern burrowed into his face.

"Leam…"

"Don't further the fib like the snake-oil salesman you are." The dark burning swell bubbled up to Leam's chest like motor oil filling a spitting-hot engine. He felt unbreakable, despite his vision, which had begun to cloud over with gray speckles and black haze. "You're a *cheat* and you got caught." He took three steps forward for the associate's one back. "Cop to it. You did it. Say you did it."

"It was all a part of the training, Leam. Necessary observation."

"This isn't a test, Michael, not anymore."

"Oh, yes it is!" the associate shouted and—BOOM—he and Leam were inside the silver walled room, as it had been before the Dictionary of Darkness had opened. "Ha! Look around, you silly child! This is my terrain! Mine! Me! I run the show! It's all a test!"

"NOT SINCE YOU STUFFED ME IN THAT BOX!" Leam roared. "*Not since you lied!*"

"Oh, boo hoo, pee your pants," the associate said, grinning. "Whine, whine, whine."

Leam stared at the mocking man who had abducted him to this place, and in flat chilling tones said, "All this is now is me and you."

And Leam threw his arms open in an incredible display of force. The room's walls and ceiling burst into feathery strands of silver that clung like Christmas tinsel to the air above the field's green grass. With the rising, internal dark heat now level with his shoulders, Leam bore in on the associate, who stumbled backward and fell on his butt. Below the Mohawks, bursts of white light shot at Leam from tattoos that sat high up on the.

associate's petrified face. Whether their aim was to injure or kill, Leam wasn't sure; they bounced off his half-naked body like handfuls of pebbles flung at a brick wall. Gone from the associate's arsenal was the pompous smile, the intimidating stare. A role reversal had occurred: the red-eyed mouse towering high over the scientist.

The fiery surge hijacking Leam's body finally swelled up into his head. He pounced on top of the associate, pinning the man's shoulders down with his knees, relishing the crybaby screams fleeing the man's mouth in high-pitch cackles. Leam lifted the associate's head up off the ground by coiling the man's tie around one hand. He raised the other into a fist of lead and amidst the associate's screams, the bull finally consumed Leam whole...and all went dark...all went quiet.

Blackness. Nothing else.

CHAPTER 29

*S*he was sprinting down a long, narrow alley, bright rays of *sunshine beaming onto the back of her sweat-soaked shirt, chasing her toward a dark street a hundred yards ahead, above which black clouds churned in the thunderstorm. Thousands of diamond-encrusted starfish spun in the air around her as if kicked up by a glittery tornado. Deliriously out of breath, she quickened her already hectic pace.*

She was closing in on the line in the sky where the furious sunshine crashed into the heavy black rain—about fifty yards until the day became the night. With arms flailing at her sides, feet pounding atop asphalt, she noticed her hand was a brownish, yellowy green. Sticky and bubbly, the green crawled up her arm like a jungle snake swallowing a long, white limb. Yet it caused her no panic. If anything, she seemed to welcome it, as she shortened the distance between herself and the rain, closing in on the street, the storm, the dark, the night.

Eloa awoke with a start. Lying on her back atop her fluffy bed, she kept her eyes closed, her body still. The room was silent. Too silent.

Something's wrong.

Quickly and quietly she reached to her right, her fingers grasping for the silver starfish on the bedside table. In her haste, she knocked it onto the carpet where it landed with a small thud. She opened her eyes a crack and sat up in one fluid movement, her long legs sliding over the side of the bed. Before her bare feet could slip onto the carpet, though, her body stiffened with terror. The sound of something heavy being dragged over the carpet brushed through her ears. She gasped, frozen with fear.

Through the darkness, the pitch-black silhouette of a tall man was moving toward her. When her scream pierced through the quiet of the sleeping house, the advancing shadow was only an arm's reach away.

"Shhhhhhhhhhh!"

Eloa recoiled to the center of the bed, opened her mouth and screamed again, panicking that, this time, no sound came out.

"Stop trying to scream!" a hushed voice urged. "Eloa, it's me, Porlo!"

"*What are you crazy?*"

"It's just me, okay? It's just me."

"I can't see you!"

"No, leave the lights off," Porlo's voice commanded.

"Why?"

"Your grandmother's coming up the stairs."

"Oh, Jesus…"

"Try to calm down."

"*You* calm down!"

"I'm always calm."

Eloa could tell by his tone that he was grinning. "What are you *doing* here?"

Dead quiet suffocated her again, then Porlo's words found her through the darkness. "I had to see if you were alright."

"In the middle of the—" She slapped her hand over her mouth. "Oh my God! It worked, didn't it?" she asked, the question muffled by the muzzle of her fingers.

"I'm sorry?"

"The Ode of Aid!" she exclaimed. "I said it and now here you are. I *knew* it would be you—"

Knock, knock, knock.

"Eloa, dear? Is everything all right in there?"

As forewarned, Mary stood outside the door, undoubtedly disturbed out of sleep by the first scream. Eloa had a feeling that Porlo had silenced the second with magic.

"Yes, I'm fine, Mary," Eloa said, keeping her eyes on Porlo's form. "I'm so sorry. I thought I saw a mouse along the floorboard. I'm sorry, I'm sorry I woke you up."

"That's quite all right, dear. Larry'll put down traps in the morning. Goodnight."

"Goodnight," Eloa called back, listening to the sweet old woman's slippers shuffle off down the hall. As the creaking of the stairs diminished, Eloa yanked down the bedside lamp's gold chain. A muted glow cast over the room.

Porlo was standing right in front of her in jeans and a gray T-shirt, as before. Her eyes went to the bag hanging off his shoulder before flicking up to his face. She withdrew several feet back on the bed. Something shining in his eyes had startled her, a shocked and somewhat lascivious glimmer. As she watched his eyes trace downward, a tiny squeal squeaked out of her mouth, color hotter than fire flooding her cheeks.

The dress!

She had forgotten she had put in on. No bra, just underwear and a tiny blood-red silk dress; her shoulders, arms and every inch of her legs exposed. Porlo seemed to recover smoothly, peeling his leer away from her by crouching down out of sight to put his bag down on the carpet. Eloa quickly covered her lap with a white pillow while cursing Bridgette's name.

"I had forgotten I had recited that poem," she said, in hopes of quickly hurdling over the fence of awkwardness that had spread between them. With Porlo bent over, she couldn't see him apart from his shoulders and the back of his neck, but her ears caught his voice clearly.

"I figured as much."

Eloa waited for him to rise, wishing there was a T-shirt or a smock or parka within grabbing distance. Her heart was beating fast. She'd never been alone with a man before, and certainly not in a closed-door bedroom with ninety percent of her skin displayed, leaving her feeling like a naked salami hanging in a butcher shop. She felt more blood rush beneath the skin of her cheeks.

"Thanks for answering it," she said. "The Ode of Aid."

Porlo rose from his crouch, her starfish in his palm, the chain coiled into a small pile of silver thread to its side. "Of course," he said, standing beside the bed. If she extended her legs, the soles of her feet would be flush against his thighs. "Which reminds me," he said, "I need you to recite it once more."

"Why?"

"Protocol. I have to make sure you're the individual who spoke those verses."

"Who else would it have been? Nobody else of Light lives here."

"There are things about magic that the unpurified can't yet understand." He sounded tired. "Do me this kindness."

As he leaned over, placing the medallion on the bedside, the lamplight threw itself over the majority of his face. Eloa immediately noticed that he looked weaker, paler, than last she saw him, however, it didn't detract from his mystique. If anything, this new vulnerability seemed to be pulling her closer.

"Will you say it again for me, Eloa?"

"Of course," she said, speaking the poem a breath later, during which Porlo's eyes scanned the room. Eloa saw that the palm of one hand faced the door, the other the front window.

"Thank you," he said after she finished.

She nodded with a smile.

"May I sit down?"

She nodded without one.

Porlo took a seat at the bottom of the bed with a groan, rubbing his face in his hands.

"Are you okay?" Eloa asked. She pushed the pillow off her lap toward the others that were stacked at the headboard, and nudged her butt to the edge of the bed, leaving about three feet between herself and him. She crossed her legs as she hung them over the side.

"I am," he said, the pads of all four fingers of his right hand pressed into his forehead just above the brow. "I'm tired, but I'll be fine."

Eloa nodded, hands clasped together over her lap below the hemline. "So?"

"Hmmm?"

"So *tell* me."

"Hmmm?"

"My father, Porlo! The Ode of Aid, that's why you're here, aren't you? What's going on with him? Tell me everything. I've been driving myself crazy!"

"Eloa," he said, removing his hand from his brow, "I can't tell you anything about that."

Her mouth dropped open, eyes squinting daggers at Porlo. She made to get up, but Porlo asked, "Where are you going?"

"To get my journal. I want to *show* you something."

"Allow me," he said. The journal rose off of the desktop, floating across the room, landing in her lap.

Her smile betrayed her contempt—she had rarely seen magic firsthand; her dad never used it in her presence. She composed herself, flipped the notebook open and found the page she needed. "What you said, word for word: '*I am sure our paths will cross again, and when they do, I hope to have the time to answer any questions you would like to ask me.*' So...do you have the time?"

"It's not that I don't *want* to tell you. It's that I *cannot* tell you."

"Why? What's the big deal with you guys? Please. Enlighten me. Why all the secrets? Is the world going to blow up if one of you has the courtesy to talk to me candidly about my own dad?"

Eloa found herself pacing the room, though she couldn't consciously remember standing up.

"Tell me what you know, *Porlo*, I know you know something. If you're his friend and were the one trusted to bring me the starfish, you can't have been left completely in the dark."

"Eloa, listen to me. I can't talk to you about him because I don't know anything more than I did the night you wrote my words in your diary."

"Journal," she corrected him defiantly, like a cranky child awake at midnight telling his mother that he's not tired.

"My mistake. Journal," Porlo said, rubbing his throat. He's eyes flicked to his bag, which rose up off the carpet, hovering into his hands. "I didn't have any answers for you then, and I still don't. I happened to be on route to report back to my boss—"

"About my dad?"

Porlo put his four fingers to his forehead again. "No. I'm gathering information about someone else, which hasn't been easy, but that's neither here or there." His eyes looked drained, but his hands moved like a blur: pouch unzipped, pipe removed, pouch zipped closed. "What I'm trying to tell you is that I was the nearest person of Light when you recited the poem, so here I am."

His eyes narrowed at her; Eloa stopped pacing, a chill running up the backs of her legs. Porlo's eyes closed as he pulled smoke heavily from the pipe. When they opened, his brief glare of...frustration, was it? Anger?...had been replaced with an expression of warmth.

"Eloa, I...I feel there's a...bond between us, and..." She looked down at her feet, curling her toes. She heard him exhale a stream of smoke. "Anyway, it's classified, but purified or not, I feel you have a right to know something. I have nothing else to offer you, but I *can* tell you with a hundred percent certainty that Jace is alive."

A long pause; a few tears slid down Eloa's face, slipping down her neck and disappearing beneath the blood-red dress. She looked over at Porlo—sitting there on her bed smoking his pipe—and told him thank you.

"Don't tell anyone I told you that," he said.

"I have no one to tell." After a moment's hesitation, she came back to the bed, inching the hem of her dress down before sitting, this time a mere two feet from Porlo, maybe less. "It smells of apples, the smoke. Crisp apples. Is that how it tastes?"

"It does, but not to me anymore."

"What happened?"

He considered her. "I burned my throat long ago during a procedure that went longer than it should have. Ever since, I can't taste anything."

"Really?" The brown of his eyes looked so soft from so small a distance. "Nothing at all?"

"No. Not chocolate, nor a woman's lips. And not this." He held out the pipe.

"Why smoke then?"

"When my throat flares up, the smoke eases the pain."

"May I try?" she asked, taking it from him before he could answer, noticing his eyes had closed during the moment his hand had grazed hers.

"I remember you worrying it would hurt your chances of Purifying," he said, and the look between them was long.

"I don't care anymore." Her eyes smiled at his as she pulled the apple-scented smoke deep into her lungs where she felt it swirl like a feathery cocoon until it escaped from her mouth in a series of muted, jabbing coughs.

"The night we met," Porlo said, grinning, "you told me you weren't sure if Purification—you know, the war—was a right fit for you."

"I hate the idea of war, even if I believe it to be necessary."

"The camaraderie, then," he said, massaging his temples. "You don't crave it?"

"My friends are Unknowings. The one who bought me this dress, for example."

Porlo looked down at her as if the last she had said was an invitation to take her in. "Most kids stay with other to-be-purifieds. Not many hang out with the Unknowings."

"Your world has yet to really appeal to me." Eloa handed the pipe back to Porlo. "That stuff is *fantastic,* by the way. It's like a hot air balloon." Porlo grinned again. "Ummm, what was I saying?"

"Our world and theirs," Porlo said, zipping the pipe into its pouch, the back of his hand brushing her bare thigh as he dropped his bag to the carpet.

"I hated the idea of camp with other Light children," Eloa said, pretending not to have felt anything. "It sort of felt like a cluster of arranged marriages. Unknowings are much more interesting to me." Even through the smoke fog, she immediately thought of Leam.

"That can't be true," Porlo said.

"For me growing up, a world without magic seemed more exciting. If you never know that it exists, you'll always be able to find a reason, if you want to, as to why something happened the way it did. If you blink, and the desk is on the other side of the room, we both assume it was magic. The sky turns black and stays that way for three days: magic. So if you can forever assume that magic is the reason, the world is less exciting...at least to me."

"Do you still feel that way?" he asked, his eyes blazing, locked on hers. She nodded. "You really do?" he asked again.

Eloa downed a gulp of nerves and blushed. The act of swallowing had sounded so loud inside her head, she knew he must have heard it. Lord, were they close, their thighs almost touching—his covered by jeans, hers speckled with gooseflesh. "But there are moments," she continued, "when I think the magical world might bring me something I need."

"How so?"

"But only moments."

Porlo hesitated. "Like what?"

"I called for you, you know. From that window, the night after we met. I called for you, thinking you'd come back."

"I know."

"You—wait, what? How did you know?"

"I knew you must have and..." He scratched at the fine stubble beneath his chin. "I had told you so little, I figured you'd be keen to hear more. In a situation like yours, anybody would. Especially after seeing what was in the box your dad entrusted me to deliver, in case he ever... Anyway, I'm glad here now." He shot out his palm. In a blurry streak of silver, the starfish zoomed off the bedside and into his hand. "I thought I had conveyed the importance of this last time," he said, leaning in close, clasping the necklace together behind her neck. The cold medallion slid over her breastbone. "Your dad wanted this on you always. Make me a promise you won't take it off again."

Their faces were intimately close. Eloa could taste the apples on his breath, feeling all sorts of different things. Things she didn't want read from her mind, if he was capable of that. Things that Bridgette would die just to hear. "I promise," she murmured.

"Good. Thank you." Porlo's breathing sounded labored.

"Did you know my mother?" Eloa asked before she could stop herself, her chin on her chest. When the length of silence thickened the small area between them with unbearable discomfort, Eloa looked over at Porlo. He seemed like he was struggling with the decision to answer her or not.

"I did not," he said. "I wasn't around for those years of Jace's life."

Eloa nodded, looking down again, feeling the cold weight of the starfish against her skin—a comfort she hadn't known she needed until now, until it was hanging from her neck again after a brief absence. "It's okay. I thought you might have, that's all. He never speaks of her. He told me he would talk to me about her once I was purified."

"That seems like reason enough to go through with it."

Her mouth twitched. "I guess."

Outside, the sensor light secured beneath one of the eaves facing the garage popped on, brightening Porlo's lamp-lit face as he turned toward it. Eloa saw him squint, his mouth grimacing at whatever had his attention outside the window. He stood up.

"You're leaving?" Eloa asked. "What's wrong?"

"Nothing's wrong," Porlo said. It sounded like a lie. His bag rose up, the strap cinching over his shoulder. "Will you do me one last favor?"

Her response was immediate. "Yes."

"Watch who you hang out with."

"What do you mean?" she asked. "What makes you say that?"

Porlo shook his head in an it's-not-a-big-deal kind of way.

"Am I in danger?"

"No." He peered out the window again. A small frown crossed his face. "I shouldn't have said anything. I just want you to be careful. I mean—" he gestured from her head to her toes, "—you're going to attract all kinds wearing stuff like that, if you haven't already."

Eloa covered her lap again with a pillow. "I told you I didn't even want this. It's mortifying."

Porlo bent down a little clumsily—Eloa got the impression he was flustered—pulling up the left pant leg of his jeans to scratch an itch. Before he pulled the pant leg back down, she got a glimpse of a brownish-red tattoo that covered his entire calf.

Porlo was standing up as the light outside switched off. Eloa sensed his departure was imminent. She had maybe seconds left with him, and there was one last question she wanted to ask.

"Do you have a wife, Porlo? A family?"

He was quiet, and then the lamp went out. Bridgette, Eloa thought to herself, would have thought the bulb had burned out. Eloa knew the bulb was just fine. Through the sudden darkness, she heard Porlo's voice, raspier than it had been the whole visit.

"I do not. Never had much of a reason to."

———

The night was still. Only the quiet chirping of lonely crickets breathed any life into the summer air until—POOF—a tall man appeared on the rundown porch, vanishing from the bedroom above a moment ago. His eyes flickered up to those of a small bird perched on a nearby tree branch, barely visible in the dark of night.

The bird was immediately aware of the man's presence. In fact, he had been expecting it, and when the man looked in his direction, the bird took off into the sky, flying over the tree line, heading anywhere that the man was not.

The bird had already put a mile between himself and Eloa's house and was soaring over a black lake when the man on the porch's mufflemiff reached his ears. It startled the bird, for this was his first time receiving this rare form of communication where a sender's silent words spoken from afar become audible once they reach the ears of the recipient.

"I know who you are! Stay away from the girl! I know who you are!"

Fear crippled the whiplap, his wings failing him as he plummeted down toward the lake, the message ringing over and over again inside his head. Struggling to stay airborne, it was his own internal squeaky voice, not the man's, that helped steady himself.

Whatever happens, I got it to her. Whatever happens, it's hers.

The bird regained control and tiny tears streaked out of its tiny eyes. It would never be safe to see her again; too many others knew. The whiplap's heart broke open, pain and sorrow flowing out from within. He climbed higher and higher into the night sky.

The whiplap's gift to her would not be his last attempt at betrayal, however. Gideon would find out eventually—that was a certainty—and the punishment would be savage, ultimately resulting in death. But more damage could be done before that time.

That's what happens, ya know, the whiplap thought, speed and vengeance drying his tears. *That's what happens when promises get broken.*

CHAPTER 30

Standing in the center of a guestroom, which had been nothing but white hollow space twenty minutes ago, Sara tried to quiet her jittery hands as she listened for the tap-tap-tap of approaching footsteps against the floorboards just beyond the closed door. Out there—the third story hallway that ran the length of the Manor—everything was how it always was: musty, candlelit and, since Zach and Leam were not permitted on the third floor, quiet. In here, the surroundings were always different and new, because, with a flick of magic, the perpetually empty room temporarily filled with furniture and belongings of the conjurer's choosing, remaining as such until the conjurer vacated the space.

But she had made sure that everything was just right, for if it wasn't…well, she didn't want to even think about that. The curtains that masked the windows were black, same for the carpet and the bed linens, as per his request. Hundreds of black candles floated around the room like cylindrical planets hovering in outer space. Their wicks were cherry-red, as were the flames, flickering softly.

Certain as she was that once he saw how she was dressed, he wouldn't care about the carpet or the linens or the squeaky cleanliness of the giant mirror above, she scanned the room for mistakes. It was safer just to get things right. Had she forgotten something? She closed her mouth and inhaled. A pleasant aroma of Febreze greeted her nose.

"Oh, no," she muttered, realizing her error. "Oh, my, my."

She shot her arms out to the side, palms down, cramping her icy-white fingers into claws, as if weighted strings hung off her fingertips. The incongruous sound of a drinking straw slurping up a glass's bottom drops filled the room, then died, passing the room-noise back into the cherry-red hands of the whispering candle wicks. Her arms fell as she leaned over the bed—several floating candles bobbing out of her way—and sniffed again. With him, smells were different from, say, curtains. With smells, she had to be sure.

"Perfect," she whispered. The deodorizing enchantment had left the room without an aroma, as she had her own body, earlier, in the master bathroom's twenty-spout shower, by scrubbing a scentless bar of soap over every inch of her skin until the bar was nothing but a gelatinous nub.

Something shuffled outside in the hallway. Her eyes darted to the faint stream of light between the carpet and the bottom of the door, as the shadow of two tiny feet—at least that's what they looked like—scrambled past. As she took a step toward the door, a voice came at her from behind.

"Sara."

Her heart skipped a beat—several beats, in fact—and she twirled around to see the Head of Darkness, cinched up to his neck in a trench coat, standing just a few feet away.

"You scared me," she exhaled, her eyes open wide.

"Good."

Gideon's bulging eyes examined her, starting with her blond hair—which was pulled back into a tight bun—and working down. A shimmering black sweater, white underwear and black stockings that climbed a few inches above her knees.

"And Bram?" he asked. "Tell me. Where is he?"

"He left several days ago. To where I don't know. He's yet to return."

"Is that right?" Gideon muttered, stepping up to her, the tip of his finger caressing her naked lips like a tube of ChapStick. At his touch, they became saturated with lipstick that matched the flames of the floating candles.

"Let's not worry about him now," Sara said, removing her sweater, revealing a white see-through blouse. She sat down on the edge of the bed, slowly crossing her legs, and Gideon's opaque eyes bulged even farther away from his hollow, skull-like face.

"Don't tell me what to do," he said, his big lips spreading into a clown-mask grin that sent a chill spiraling down her spine.

"I wouldn't dare," she said.

"You just did." His grin widened.

"A slip of the tongue." She unfastened the buttons of her blouse, starting with the topmost. "I never tell a man to do anything. I'd only ask."

The corners of Gideon's lips stretched almost to his ears. "What would you like to ask?"

"It's about Zach. My son."

"I know his name," Gideon said, taking a step closer to her and the bed.

"He's obedient. He's devoted to the Cause. And I know he's been yearning for the chance to prove himself to you."

"It is my hope that he'll someday be of great use to me."

"Someday?" Sara asked, standing up off the bed.

"That's what I said." The crackling wicks of fire hovering around Gideon made his eyes bubble with red fizz.

"Is there anything I can do, anything at all, to maybe influence you into...utilizing his talents now?" The blouse fell to the black carpet, and Gideon's eyes danced over the multitude of small, black markings that were speckled on the skin around her black lacy bra, markings all over, that stretched across her ribcage and covered her stomach.

"Zach's on reconnaissance right now," Gideon said, his bony face flushing with color, "as are most during their first calendar years of Darkness."

"Do you think he might be useful to you for missions that have a little more substance?"

A long pause. "Perhaps."

Sara went to him and removed his bowler hat. Stubborn tufts of orange hair sprung outward like Slinkys. "Oh, my," she giggled, running her fingers through the unruly mane. His hot breath steamed against her face, and each time it did, a quiet moan escaped her mouth.

"If certain events unfold as I foresee them," he whispered, "Zack could be of use to me."

"I'd be forever grateful." She quivered as she pressed her body against his, her pale hands working to remove the trench coat off his bony shoulders.

"There's an assignment I've been considering for him."

As she was slipping off the coat, Gideon's hand snuck into an inner pocket and removed a small glass bottle. The coat floated across the room, hanging itself on a golden hook that formed on the wall.

"Spray this on yourself," he said, holding the bottle out for her.

She submitted without question, spritzing the perfume all over her trembling body. It smelled like garbage. It smelled like wet dog food and dirty diapers. Normally, she would have been revolted, but as she watched his eyes roll back into his head, the stench began to excite her, too.

An invisible force threw her away from him across the room. She landed on the bed, quickly pulling out a bobby pin and shaking out her blond hair so it fell down her naked back.

As he went to her, Gideon's black clothing slid off his spindly body like a molting snake shedding dry skin. She watched his frailness expose itself, her breath heavy and damp. As his fingers brushed over her ribcage, the black speckled markings tingled with pleasure. She had been yearning for this for many years, and the fact that her son would be moving up the slippery chain of Darkness because of it was sure to make what was about to ensue even better.

"And what does the assignment involve?" she breathed, her hands rubbing against his waist for a moment, and then climbing to his emaciated chest. "Torture? Revenge? Murder?"

"Better," Gideon said, his eyes alive with the red fire dancing all around the room.

"What could be better than murder?" she whispered into his ear, closing her eyes.

"Betrayal."

CHAPTER 31

Leam! LEAM!"
A familiar voice pushed through his ears, wedging into the grogginess of his brain. He opened his eyelids with difficulty, every part of his body heavy and sluggish. Behind the blurry image of a girl peering down at him, the familiar leaves—blacks and grays amidst the fog—of Capnick Street's oak trees swayed in the background. His head felt like it was splitting open from the center of his forehead to the top of his scalp, as his pupils strained to focus on her.

"You're alive, aren't you?" Eloa asked, crouching down in front of him. "Jesus Christ, Leam, I thought you were dead. You're lying on a sidewalk! What happened to you? You look terrible."

Leam groaned, struggling to pick himself off the ground. Eloa stood up to give him room. He sat up against a wall, leaning his head back against the Coffee Sip's front window. Poking out of the legs of his jeans, the soles of his white Nikes lay flat on the sidewalk. The sight of the jeans bothered him, but he didn't know why. Everything before now was a black, nothing, void.

He scrunched his eyes closed, desperate to remember anything through the aching fog that had hijacked his memory. He swam in black, for how long he didn't know, until a hanging lamp from above flooded his mind with light, and brightly colored moments of the near past played against the backdrop of his eyelids like short video clips pieced together into one vivid reel. The metal box closing in. The metal box bursting open. The grass, the sky, the associate on the ground, eyebrow tattoos shooting light. Him, Leam, advancing…and then…then…

And then the void. That was it, that's all there was. The void and, as Leam opened his eyes, her.

"You really do look terrible," Eloa said, clutching a silver object that was hanging from her neck. Her long ponytail was curved around her neck, slipping over her left shoulder. "Are you okay?"

Leam rubbed his bloodshot eyes with the heels of his palms.

What happened to me?

From the last time he had been with Eloa, up to now, could all of it have been real? Had none of it been real? The associate had made him put that hat of oblivion on in the maroon Cadillac—then all the madness happened—and now he was back. His sneakers were back on his feet, his black T-shirt back on his body, his jeans…

Leam shot his hand into his right pocket. A small wave of relief washed through him the moment his fingers wrapped around Aggie's acorn, not lost forever like he had thought in those first few confusing minutes at the field of green. He patted over his left pocket: keys and his iPhone. He had them back—the acorn, too—which meant *he* was back, back in reality, no doubt about it.

"Leam… Hello?"

But back from what? The associate, the field… It had seemed so real, every minute of it, but was it possible, *possible*, that it never actually happened, that it was all in his head? Maybe. But then why was his body so beat down?

"LEAM!" Eloa yelled. "Geez, where is it you go off to when your eyes get all hazy like that? Have you been listening to me?"

"Sorry."

"I haven't seen you since the coffee shop. Where've you been?"

"Right," Leam said, shaking more smog from his mind. "The Sip. Yeah, I wanted to talk about how we ended things yesterday."

"Yesterday?" Street lamps gave the night some life, and Leam could sort of see her eyes, larger than he'd remembered them to be. "That was a week and a half ago, Leam!"

Leam gave her Zach's hey-sweetie-what-have-you-been-smoking look. "What are you kidding?"

"No! I'm *yelling* at you, why would I be kidding?"

"I've been gone for...no...no, it hasn't been..."

"TEN DAYS!" she finished for him. "Yes, it has!"

"*What?*"

"How do you *not* know that?"

"Please don't mess around with me, alright?"

"How does somebody *not* know something like that?"

"*Ten days?*"

"He's asking *me* not to mess around with *him*," Eloa said to the night. "Of course, ten days! I figured your family went on vacation or something."

"Ha!"

"What?"

Leam waved it away with a hand. "We don't vacation."

"Well, that's what I thought at first. The flower shop's been empty since you've been gone."

Leam rubbed the front of his neck. "Empty? Wait a second, how—"

"My friend recognized you outside the Coffee Gulp when you went driving off with that man. She knows you from school and Bram's Florist."

"Who does?"

"My friend. Bridgette."

"I don't know who that is!"

"Just follow the drool." Eloa leaned her butt back against a newspaper box that displayed an advertisement for a Leif

Garrett concert—whoever that was—taking place tomorrow night at the town theater. "She's obsessed with you."

Leam rested his hand over his eyes. Even his face felt tired.

"Anyway, I went there to check things out, and—"

"You went where?"

"Your dad's florist, *Leam!*"

"You did?"

"I remembered your number but you weren't responding to my texts. I don't have any idea how long I'm gonna be in this stupid town. I don't know anybody here but Bridgette, and she's driving me crazy and—"

"So your father's still missing?" Leam cut in. His mind felt like it was starting to clear.

"What?"

"You said he had disappeared, didn't you? The ten days ago? I thought that's what you told me."

For a quick moment, Leam saw her eyes soften. "Yes, I did say that."

"So what's the deal? Is he still missing?"

"Yes, but never mind him." Eloa looked exasperated again. "What I'm trying to say is that even though *your* dad closed up your shop, it didn't feel right to me, that your family went away 'cause I knew you would've texted me if you could have. You would've responded to my texts. I know that."

"I didn't have my phone on me," Leam said, rubbing his forehead. He pulled out his iPhone. "I just got it back." His thumb found the circular button at the bottom, the screen illuminated, then his eyes found the time and date at the top, above a darkened strip of screen displaying seven unread messages from the girl in front of him.

"I knew it!" Eloa said. "They took it from you, right?"

"Who did?"

"Uhhhh...who?"

"Yeah, who took my phone?" Leam sat up straight. "You said *they*. Who's *they*?"

"The, uhhh...the doctors at the, ummm...the mental hospital."

"Come again?"

"Bridgette told me about you," Eloa said, and then seemed to be occupied by her feet. "The bipolar stuff."

"You're joking with me, right?"

"She told me stories. Rumors and things. How you ran around the town naked and stuff like that."

Leam gritted his teeth. "What do you want? My life history?"

Eloa squinted at him, leaning up off the newspaper box. "What is your *problem?* You've been snapping at everything I say."

"'Cause what's the point?"

"What point?"

"Nothing can ever happen, Eloa."

"Happen? What do you mean?"

"It doesn't matter, that's the—"

"You mean like *happen* happen? Me and you?"

"Eloa, there's no point, okay? I'm a psycho. I'm a frail little mental patient, remember? I can't be your friend."

"I don't care about any of that. I don't believe half of it anyway. There's something special about you. I can feel it."

"What about you?" Leam asked, trying to smudge the dirt off his fingers, the markings on his hands a ghostly gray.

"Me?" Eloa said, as if that was the most preposterous question anyone had ever asked her.

"Yeah, you. There anything special about you?"

"No." Her response flew out of her mouth before the end of Leam's question was swallowed up by the street noise humming down Capnick from Falcon Ave. The small amount of orange-yellow light casting down from the nearest street lamp kept too much of her face draped in shadow to tell if she was blushing, but Leam saw her look at her own hands and then his.

"So what happened to you?" she asked, a landmine blatantly sidestepped. Leam said nothing, slouching forward.

"Are you hurt?" she asked. "Should I call the police?"

What could the cops possibly do?

"You've got bumps and scrapes all over you," Eloa said. "Tell me where you've been."

"I don't know."

"What does that *mean?*" She crouched down in one graceful, fluid movement, studying his face.

"It means what it means." He could feel her breath, warm on his mouth. "I don't know where I've been."

"Hold on. Wait a sec…" Eloa said, eyes wider than before. "Don't tell me…Was it the same as what happened at the Coffee Gulp?"

"Coffee *Sip*, Eloa. It's the Coffee *Sip*. The name of the store is *right above my head!*"

"The Coffee *Sip*, then. Geez."

"What about it?"

"What do you mean '*What about it*'? Those things that happened to you—the visions, you called them—when you held my hands. It wasn't like that, where you've been, was it? For the whole ten days?"

"No. No, not like that."

"I didn't think so." She pursed her lips, moving them side to side as if in thought. "Okay," she said. "So it was an episode."

"An episode?" Leam's eyebrows arched up his forehead. "You mean a manic thing. The bipolar?"

"It must be. Some sort of hallucination."

Leam looked at her, disgusted.

"Well, what else could have been, Leam? Enlighten me."

Because of Darkness! Leam felt like screaming in her face. The *Darkness* within him was why he couldn't be with her. The *Darkness* was why he had disappeared for ten days.

Oh golly, what else could it've been, Eloa? How 'bout I was warped away to a place without time to battle giant frogs with cigar spears! To fend off hundreds of blood-thirsty bats the size of Toyota RAV4s! To get squashed into a metal cube with a leaf-spewing dictionary! THAT'S what else it could have been!

"What is it?" she asked. "What are you thinking?"

Leam took a breath.

"Leam, you can talk to me."

"Look...these mental issues," he said, his hand loosely over his mouth. "Your friend Widget or whatever. She was right. I'm not stable. I can't be around you. I'm a danger to myself and to others, they told me. I'm not normal."

"Nobody is."

"You don't want me around, okay? Seriously. It wouldn't be good. It doesn't work."

"Why?"

"Because I have secrets."

"So do I."

"I have big secrets."

"Like how you won't tell me where you've been for the last week and a half?"

"Exactly!"

"Trust me, Leam, I have a bigger secret than you do."

"No, you don't."

"Yes, I do."

Leam paused. He looked right at her, their faces a foot and a half apart. Then, with the staunch conviction of a man who knows he's right, he said, "I *know* your secret, Eloa."

She looked ready to respond with something quick—some little lie—but stopped herself, tilting her head to the side. Her mouth opened a tiny bit, her eyes went wide, unblinking, but the rest of her face had been scribbled in with skepticism. Then she went blurry. He was looking at her but not really seeing her, as her voice repeated itself in his head.

"Like how you won't tell me where you've been for the last week and a half?"

Like a sharp needle through the skull, it was Sara's voice now, spoken at the Manor during her and Leam's last conversation, which pierced into his mind.

"You're out on your own, Mr. Big Shot. Starting the first of next month, you'll no longer be granted entry here. The Manor, alas, no longer your home. You'll never walk its halls again. It's time for you to go away."

Leam and his "trash," he now remembered, had to be out of the house by the end of the month, which, if the whole damn excursion with the associate had really been ten days, was tonight.

"I have to go," Leam said, getting to his feet.

"Right now?" Eloa stood, also.

"I have to go home and take care of a few things. I'm getting kicked out and it's a long story and I don't have the time right now."

"Then later," she said. Her suspicion was nearly blinding him. Her eyes were different, judging. "Later then, Leam."

"Fine. Later."

"What time?"

"Uhhhhh…midnight, I guess." Leam pulled out his keys. "A little after midnight." His eyes were drawn down the street just past Bram's Florist. He thought he saw a group of men in trench coats, but a blink later, there was nothing but quiet train tracks and the darkness beyond them. "Is that all right with you, does that work?"

Eloa nodded. "I'll text you Mary and Larry's address. You have your phone now, right?"

As she pulled her iPhone from her the pocket of her jeans, Leam looked at her, *really* looked at her, hating the difference between them, the difference that would keep them apart forever…*if* they had had a chance to begin with. But as he watched her text, her face a blend of fascination and worry, he knew he didn't want it to end right here and now. Not just yet.

He felt his thigh buzz; his phone had caught her text. "I'll be there," he said. "Midnight."

"And you'll tell me everything?" she asked, reaching out as if to touch his arm. If that had been her intention, she resisted, instead placing her hand over the something silver hanging from her neck.

"I will," he answered.

"Do you promise?"

Leam grinned. "Why the hell not?"

Through the fog, he crossed the street to the Range Rover and got in, not surprised that it was still parked where he had left it those many days ago. Who would have come for it? Sara drove a cherry-red Audi, Zachary the Spoiled had his new Jeep Grand Cherokee birthday gift, and Bram, evidently, was a non-factor. Eloa had said the flower shop had been shut down the entire time Leam was gone, which meant the Holt patriarch, who had disappeared a day before Leam's little expedition had begun, was still missing.

But why?

CHAPTER 32

A large, well-built man was slowly—very slowly—walking down the center of a dark road, the frayed edge of the bottom of his black trench coat swooshing over the pavement as he moved toward his destination.

Swish, swish, swish, swish.

The man liked the road. He was comfortable; there were very few houses and no street lamps. The only light was that of moonbeams filtering through the leaves of the oaks that lined both sides of the street. The branches from each side had long ago stretched together, intertwining into a plush canopy woven over the road. The man liked the sense of solitude and confinement it provided.

He didn't know *how* he had gotten into this tunnel of branches and leaves, didn't know where he had come from, or what had led him to this particular place at this particular time. All he knew was his destination, and that's all he wanted to know.

Swish, swish, swish, swish.

Down the center of the road he went. His eyes didn't blink; his lips didn't move. He could feel his tired knees and achy elbows brush against the inside of his coat. He could feel the warm breeze, slight against his bearded face. But, inside his body, he felt nothing. No worry, no bewilderment, no emotion at all. The fact that he couldn't remember his past didn't bother him. The fact that he didn't even know who he was didn't bother him. This was not an amnesiac situation where a man wakes up from a coma and desperately tries to remember who he is and what his life was like before his memory had been washed away. This man, the man walking, the man in the trench coat, had no inclination to discover anything about his past because, in his mind, it was as though he had never existed.

Peering through the darkness, far into the distance in front of him, he could just see that the end of the road came to a T. He'd have to go to the right or to the left—east or west—when he reached it. With the bottom of his coat dragging across the pebble-dusted asphalt—*swish, swish, swish, swish*—the man felt something peculiar in his stomach, something that was getting warmer. It was a strange sensation, but he didn't mind it. It was simply something that was happening because it had to happen.

The warmth began to rise up to his chest, leaving his stomach cold and empty as it traveled up through his esophagus, past his throat and into his mouth, which remained closed. The warmth sat patiently on his tongue as his feet continued to carry him along the road.

Swish, swish, swish, swish.

With his dark eyes still trained frontward, the man opened his mouth wide, and the warmth steamed out into the night air, accompanied by words, words that didn't belong to him, words that hadn't formed inside his own mind.

> "*Uncloak the approach...*
> *Unsettled brewing, long the throes, a storm of swans*
> *and crows.*
> *The earth's reliable spin balks;*
> *For it is coming.*
> *Midst of uncertainty, thou are flung, a spike of oil*
> *through the tongue.*
> *Blood scars the flat shapes of chalk;*
> *For it is coming.*

*Stung by denial, wayward be lost, enduring minds set
    for fire and frost.
Steady onward the dueling walk;
For it is coming. For it is coming. For it is coming."*

The man's mouth closed, and the message that had escaped
it traveled out into the night, leaving only the sound of heavy
fabric brushing over pavement. His eyes aimed far down toward
the end of the road, where, at the intersection, a pair of white
headlights streaked by from west to east. The man put his hands
in the empty pockets of his trench coat, moving closer to his
journey's end, his mind as blank as fresh paper.

Swish, swish, swish, swish...

CHAPTER 33

The beams of its white headlights were cutting through the night fog as the Range Rover curved left off of the Boulevard that dissected Harbing, peeling down Whitewax Way towards the end of the cul-de-sac. There it turned into a cobblestoned driveway, coming to an abrupt halt in front of the gate that protected the Holt Manor from uninvited intruders, such as wayward UPS drivers and eager-eyed Jehovah's Witnesses, who, at this address, would be in way over their heads.

Leam blew toward the left gate post, atop which sat the rusted statue of the crow, which, at the touch of Leam's breath, gleamed brightly, dropping the now silver flower from its beak to start the unhurried procession of gaining access into the estate.

"C'mon, c'mon..."

While Leam waited—staring at the metal ivy leaves laced throughout the black wrought-iron gate—his mind ran away from him in exploration. Would there be any surprises awaiting him inside? Could the mysterious hallway creature he thought he'd seen the other day have used Leam's bed for a toilet? Could Zach have magicked all of Leam's boxer shorts into panties? Would his room already be empty, his stuff thrown into boxes that were now lined along the entranceway's black marble walls?

Could, perhaps, his father be in the sitting room, waiting to hear all about his eldest son's adventure?

The cloaked monk's red laser eyes scanned Leam's, at which point the gate creaked open. *Finally.* Leam slammed the accelerator and the Range Rover screeched across the cobblestones, cruising past the northern end of the mansion—candlelight pulsing behind the blinds of the music room; all other windows within eyeshot dead and dark—before skidding to a stop at the end of the pebbled driveway in the back.

He hopped out, gingerly, his body still tender and sore, and crossed the back patio. He tasted a hint of charcoal in the air and saw that the pit at the property's edge was alive, its layer of coals glowing like a quilt of lava. Fog, though, had swallowed the rest of the yard.

Leam walked in the back door, went through the kitchen, which was unlit and smelling of all-purpose cleaner, and into the main hall. Facing the front door at the home's center, he could hear a pair of toned-down voices tossing it back and forth from inside the music room, which was all the way down the north end on his left, past an enormous open-spaced entertainment/theater area, twenty La-Z-Boys facing a TV screen the size of a billboard. Equidistant from Leam, and down at the southern end of the Manor on his right, was the sitting room, gracious host of delightenments, the door cracked open, yet void of any light within.

Leam turned back for the center staircase, but, two steps later, in singsong fashion, a woman's nasally voice stopped him cold.

"I know you're there, Leammmm. Come say hello to meeeee."

Leam scrunched up his face, releasing it in a surrendering manner. A thirty second journey later, he stepped up to the music room door, where Sara waited holding a glass of wine the same color as her dark red knee-length skirt, her black sweater tighter than usual. Leam wondered whether it had shrunk in the wash or if she had magically enlarged her coconuts.

"Welcome back," Sara said with a phony smile, putting her blond hair up in a bun tighter than the sweater, her wine glass hanging motionlessly in the air.

"What do you want, Sara?"

"I'm fine, thank you for asking, aren't I always?" She laughed. "You've been away for quite some time, haven't you, Mr. Leammmm? I thought you might've been my husband returning home, but no. No, it's you...just you."

"When's he coming back?" Leam asked, knowing full well the chance of her throwing him a scrap about Bram's whereabouts, whether she knew anything or not, was slimmer than Gideon's waistline.

"It's actually been quite nice not having your little daddy around," she said, after a healthy sip from her glass.

"Where is he, Sara? Come on, okay? Please. I have to talk to him."

"Aww, do you?" she said sweetly, her thin eyebrows highly arched. "What about?"

Leam turned his hands up and let them fall. "Do you really care? Do you, Sara? All of a sudden you're ready to take an interest?" Leam looked left toward the entertainment unit. Through the dark massive space, acid green digital numbers stared at him from the cable box. 9:44 P.M.

"Leam, there's something I want to tell you before you, *tsk, tsk*...start packing." Sara's face was unreadable. "Follow me."

She led him into the music room, which smelled of melting candle wax and dampened wine corks. Zach was in small black gym shorts in the middle of the finely-buffed, wooden-paneled floor, his tattooed arms jutting out of a red sweatshirt without sleeves. He flipped onto his back with an ease that only a magic-wielder could possess, starting in on some crunches.

"Hello, brother," Zach said, grinning. Sara sat down on a rich, navy blue couch, behind which, on a rustic brick wall, hung a few violins, some French horns and a pair of bassoons. The entire room was filled with an array of pristine musical instruments, whether showcased on the walls, or atop golden stands scattered in front of them. And the windows, which faced the pebbled driveway that led to the back yard, were shaped like clefs and musical notes. Dreamy classical piano music complimented the room's dim, wick-crackling aura.

"Where's Father been off to, Zach?"

"*Uh, uh, uh.* Whether or not my baby knows," Sara said, again in singsong, "he won't be sharing with youuuuuuu."

"Yup," Zach said, locking his elbows around his knees on the upswing of a crunch, candlelight flickering off his sweat-shiny face. "You're not a part of the Cause, big brother. Sorry. And anyway, to be honest, even if you were, you'd be a bottom feeder."

"You tell him, boy!" Sara chimed in, before her own wine hiccup mildly startled her.

"But me?" Zach said, holding out his hand, into which floated a cold bottle of water from the mini fridge across the room. "Well, I guess Gideon's been happy with the work I'm doing, 'cause it looks like I'm moving up." The fridge slammed closed. "New assignment!" he added joyously.

"Darling, of course he's happy with you. How could he not be?" Sara said, her fingers nipping and tucking over her sweater, adjusting the bra straps hidden underneath.

"Whatever," Leam said, massaging his temple. "Sara, can you please just tell me whatever it is you brought me in here to say?"

"Certainly not," Sara replied, nearly spilling her glass. "I will talk to you when I feel like it, and not a moment sooner. As it so happens, however, that moment is now."

Leam shook his head, lips tight. Unparalleled smugness smiled onto Sara's pointy face. Leam thought to sit down and rest his bones, but straightened instead. The idea of showing any physical weakness at present was an ugly one.

"So what is it?" he asked. "I'm well aware you're tossing me out of the house—a house that, in terms of blood, would be rightfully mine not yours."

"Leam, Leam, Leam," Sara said, uncrossing her pantyhose-less legs, switching the right, which had been on the bottom, over the left. Leam felt vomit rise to his throat. "For someone so keen on living here, you surely have a queer way of showing it. Absent for all of your final, allotted days."

"That wasn't my fault. I had no control over that," Leam said. Zack rubbed his fists beneath his eyes in cry-me-a-river fashion.

"That's precisely my point," Sara said. "You need to find a way to *control* yourself. To get your life together, like my beautiful Zach here. He's much too modest to tell you, but—" she hiccupped, "—he's been assigned to a highly essential case to further the good of the Cause."

"He actually *just* told me that," Leam said. "You were sitting right there, it was thirty seconds ago." Sara took a gulp of wine. Leam noticed that her glass seemed to continually remain full. "Besides, Gideon has his eye on me, too."

"The mission to which Zach has been assigned is real, Leam," Sara said. "Not fantasy."

"Really? What is it? To eat more soup?"

Zach smiled.

"Gideon's interested," Leam said. "You guys have no clue what's going on with me."

"Zach's been *working*," Sara spoke, with a growing, wine-induced slur. "Actual work—not goofing around for ten days at a time sniffing Unknowings' butts, or whatever sick sorts of things you've been up to."

"Yeah, Sara, that's what I've been doing, sniffing—"

"And if you keep living in this fantasy land of yours all the way to your death bed, you'll never be able to respect the small nothing of a life you've led."

"And his death bed approaches quicker than ours, Mother," Zach stated, smiling, content. "He was never delightened."

"Too true, my darling." A faint, purple vein twitched down Sara's neck. "My, oh, my, Leam, sometimes I forget what a failure you are. What a mistake you have been. I'm sure you're too ungrateful to remember, but there were times I did try to help you despite knowing then what a lost cause you'd ultimately turn out to be."

Leam clenched his fist. Zach noticed and went to stand up, but Leam shot him a look that kept Zach's toasty buns glued to the floor. Sara, having seen none of this, kept on talking.

"I'll just say this, and then I'm done with you forever… never to waste a thought on you again. Find somewhere where you belong, Leam, because it isn't with us. Find…*your purpose.*"

Her words chimed like church bells, hitting Leam clear and true. Two things had sprung him from the cold, lightless well of depression he'd been mired in every single day he had been seventeen: Gideon's newfound interest in him, and Eloa. But Eloa, because of who she was, couldn't happen. She was a fantasy, a never-could-be. So that left Gideon and the testing and the associate and Bram, wherever he was. So if Leam was to find a purpose, as his stepmother had drunkenly advised, it would have to be found in the world of Darkness. He'd pack up and leave, go tell Eloa the truth so she'd understand, then go wait for whatever Gideon had in store for him next.

Zach's voice brought Leam back to the warm room, the cozy glow of the candles with their wicks crackling beside the soft tones of a piano concerto. "I have already discovered *my* purpose, brother, and in a twisted way, I kind of hope you stop sniffing people's buttholes and try to get delightened properly someday. The sharing of secrets, the tradition, the honor. Maybe there'll be a spot for you…you know, if you stop sniffing butts."

Leam sighed, turning to Sara. "Anything else?"

"Pack your things, Leam. Pack them up and go."

Leam's mouth tightened. "I'm taking the Range Rover."

Sara glared at him over her wine glass. "If that's what it takes to be rid of you forever, then by all means."

"Good," Leam said. "Enjoy your wine." He stormed out into the corridor and strode to the stairs. As he climbed the first few steps, he heard Sara, in sodden tones, yell, "I will! Been toasting your farewell all evening, *Leaaaaaaaam!*"

Leam shook his head back and forth, biting his lip, his feet pounding the stairs as he ascended. All he had gotten out of that pleasant little visit was an affirmed hatred of his stepmother, a stronger dislike for his muscle-head sack-of-meat brother and a $90,000 Range Rover that he would sell tomorrow and parlay into a cheaper car, a hotel room and cash. What Leam had wanted to gain, though, was knowledge of his father's whereabouts, but no dice on that front.

Sara didn't seem to care that her husband was missing. No, she was having the time of her life, slugging wine, crossing and uncrossing her legs, watching precious Zachy-poo do calisthenics. Could she have had anything to do with Bram's disappearance? It was possible. And if so, Leam made a vow that he would pay her another visit someday somehow, and shove her farewell toasts back in her face.

"Some powers would be nice, though," Leam muttered, reaching the fourth floor landing. He'd kill Sara right now if he thought he could manage it, but despite the woman's slight figure, Leam was aware of how accomplished she was, both in her magical abilities and her malicious scheming. She had been around the war, surviving, for a very long time. Plus, Leam was quite certain she had Gideon in her corner.

Which begged the question: Where did Leam stand with Gideon, especially now, after the whole blackout/associate ordeal? What was Leam's future involvement, if any, in the war between Darkness and Light? A war that had been raging for several millennia, since the *creation* of man, if some of the books in his father's library were accurate, or since the *evolution* of man, if Leam's old science textbooks and slick Charlie Darwin's theories proved to be true.

In his bedroom, Leam thought about a quick shower, but instead crossed to his closet, removing a large black gym bag, into which he began stuffing sneakers and clothing. As he did, something Drunkie Sara had said swelled toward the forefront of his mind riding a nasally wave.

"*The mission to which Zach has been assigned is real, Leam...not fantasy.*"

Fantasy... Fantasy...

What was real? What was unreal?

Leam thought back to the magical field of green, straining to remember what had directly preceded his blackout—the rise of the powerful black bull. He closed his eyes and saw what his memory had for him. The associate on his back, face twisted in terror, stabs of white light shooting from his eyebrow tattoos. After that...nothing. So had that overwhelming darkness actually been real? It felt like it, but if it wasn't, if it all had been completely inside his warped head, then what else during the past three weeks hadn't necessarily happened? Could Eloa have been a figment of his imagination, too? Just the queasy thought of it made Leam think about trotting to his black-tiled bathroom.

Finished with his closet, Leam moved to the desk, sliding an assortment of random items off the top shelves into the duffel bag, followed by the contents of the drawers. He didn't pay much attention to what he was taking with him, and what was being left behind to walk the plank into the fiery pit at the back of the estate under Sara's watchful eye.

He dropped the stuffed bag down and checked under the bed and beneath the bedside tables for anything hiding from him on the floor. He stood, scanning the rest of the room. His eyes honed in on the delightenment robe hanging in the closet, white and ghostly, with a bulge in the hip pocket. He went to it, pulling out the small metal cylinder. Leam couldn't care less about it as a Harbing High memento. What fond public school memories was he holding onto? It was what was inside that mattered. The small diamond Bram had given to him at the flower shop with the instructions to find out where it came from, and, in a magical sense, what it was and what it could do.

Pocketing the cylinder, Leam heard it clink against something that sounded like glass, which immediately ruled out the iPhone and the car keys. Out the latter two came, hastily tossed on the bed, before Leam took out a small circular object that felt like smooth crystal. With a jolt to the heart, he recognized it in an instant. The ball of flesh and bones of Leam-clones that had been massacred by the Witchlows.

Leam didn't know whether to laugh or cry. Here, in his trembling hand, was proof. Proof that his time with the associate was real, and that whatever Leam had done to the associate before and during the blackout was real.

Leam started shaking and sweating as his memory reminded him of what Gideon, with his scary eyes and grinning clown lips, had said to Leam in regards to the associate the night of Zach's delightenment.

"*I am fond of him, so anything other than politeness and compliance will be taken as a personal insult to me. Have I made myself clear?*"

The backs of Leam's knees went gooey, dropping him butt-first onto the edge of the bed. He hadn't a clue as to what had transpired during those dark moments before waking up on the sidewalk outside the Coffee Sip, but it was an easy guess that he hadn't been polite or compliant. What he *did* know was that whatever Gideon decided to do about it—whatever the punishment for personally insulting the Head of Darkness entailed—it, like the ball of flesh and bone, would be real.

CHAPTER 34

Harbing, New Jersey. 10:00 P.M. EST, July 31, 2013.

Sitting on the bed clutching the ball of flesh and bone in one hand and his mother's acorn in the other, Leam closed his eyes. His heart was fluttering like the restless wings of a wasp, as he tried to piece together his next move. Three flights down, Sara drank from her glass, watching Zach do another set of pushups and crunches—his tenth, if she had counted correctly through the lovely haze of the wine.

Pasadena, California. 7:00 P.M. (10:00 P.M. EST). July 31, 2013.

Coming from her Tuesday/Thursday 5:10 p.m. Rarefied Aerodynamics class, a young black woman in an orange-and-white Caltech Beavers T-shirt walked briskly down California Boulevard on route to Piggy's Pet Shop, where she worked part-time to supplement her financial aid. She checked her reflection in the front windows of Von's grocery store as she went by, poufing up her short cropped hair, dyed black, with streaks of gold.

A tall man with cold gray eyes stood across the street, his black trench coat buttoned up to the neck despite the warm and breezeless air. He unclenched his fist, palm up, and a small sphere, the color and size of a small arcade-machine pinball rose from his hand and floated over late-evening street traffic. It came to a stop directly beneath the nose of the young woman, who had slowed to attach a pink-colored pin to her shirt, shaped like a pig's face, with the name KATHERINE stamped across the middle in blue capital letters.

Hovering silently, the pinball—undetectable to Unknowings—puffed out two invisible smoke streams of gas that spiraled upward through the young woman's nostrils. A moment later, while the pinball retreated back over to the tall man with the gray eyes, the young woman looked around, nose twitching, wondering, as she came upon Piggy's, if a new bakery had just opened shop nearby. A score of chocolate Lab puppies loped around inside the display window case, some yipping playfully at the glass as the young woman entered the shop.

Just inside the bell-jingling door, the young woman's boss, Chip, a shiny-faced, forty-something man with wispy blond hair, had been waiting for her, looking harried.

"There you are. Katsy, I have to run out for an hour, maybe a little more. Deb wants this soup, some kind of soup...I think it's Thai or something...lemongrass, she said, that they only make at this place somewhere in downtown LA, and... *Jesus...* Katsy, are you *feeling* okay?"

The young woman faked a smile, her black eyes clear, yet oddly lifeless. She nodded.

"Okay...good," Chip said uncertainly. "It's just...you don't look like yourself."

The young woman shrugged.

"You look...*scary*," he whispered, following it up with an uncomfortable laugh.

"I'm fine," the young woman said, flashing her boss a second mannequin smile, which she gave much less effort than the first.

"Good." Chip's hand was on the doorknob. "Okay good, that's good. I hate to leave you here so understaffed, but I don't know, this trimester... Holy cow, her emotions have been insane, if I'm being frank, and if she's craving this soup, then I'm getting it for her, isn't that right? I mean Deb...you know how Deb is. I'll see you in an hour. Or maybe a little more," he finished and out he went, the door jingling closed behind him.

The door remained closed and the bell quiet, until the young woman known as Katherine on campus and Katsy at work, left Piggy's Pet Shop nearly ten minutes later, rubbing antiseptic gel into her hands. Fifty minutes later, or maybe a little more, Chip returned to find every dog, puppy, cat, kitten, bird, mouse, hamster, gerbil, Guinea pig, ferret and rabbit mutilated, inside of cages and out, soaked in blood, and either dead or close to it. A warm container of Tom Yum soup fell from Chip's quivering hand and burst open, splashing onto the thin green carpeting that was littered with shards of aquarium glass and lifeless fish, lizards, snakes, turtles and frogs. The wispy-haired father-to-be gagged profusely, and then fainted as the stench of the massacre consumed him.

Buenos Aires, Argentina. 11:00 P.M. (10:00 P.M. EST). July 31, 2013.

Seated cross-legged on the edge of a plush white ottoman pushed up against the wall in the red-lit bar area of Belgrano hotspot *Sala Trece*, Ilta Jokinen, a nineteen-year-old exchange student from Aalto University of Business in Helsinki, clutched her third glass of Fernet and Coke in both hands, the straw never more than an inch away from her glossy lips.

At the bar itself—which glowed in florescent green light like a looming praying mantis on the planet Mars—a tall local boy with long dark hair that fell over his face like curtains turned away from the counter, a one-liter Quilmes beer in his muscular brown hand.

He spotted her easily, as he did all his girls, his practiced eye noticing, in order, how she was alone, how she was squeezed into a tight black dress so very unlike local Argentinian style, and how, at her side, there were two empty glasses perspiring atop a small table with clean, hard, modern edges. He approached slowly, seductively, the top four buttons of his white linen shirt unfastened, revealing a dark, tanned chest which he tried to keep as smooth as his charm and polished flattery.

"Hola, linda."

"Hola," Ilta said, her drinking straw resting on her shiny bottom lip.

His dark eyebrows jumped; he had never heard an accent like hers before. "Estudiante?" he asked.

Ilta nodded. "Cómo se...mmmmmm... I'm not sure how it's..." She paused. From the adjoining discoteca, the beats of a techno-version of Madonna's "Like a Prayer" could be felt pulsing beneath her feet. "Hablas inglés?"

"Un poquito, linda," the local replied. "Little bit." He set his eyes right on hers, well aware that even under the camouflage of the bar's red, alien lighting, his conquest was blushing.

"I'm an exchange student...at la Universidad Torcuato Di Tella," she said.

"Sí. Yes, Torcuato Di Tella." His gaze lowered down her body, flicking back up in the precise amount of time where she couldn't be sure if he was checking her out or not. "Tu acento? You from come where?"

She smiled. "Finland."

"Finlandia! Es hermoso!" He held out his hand, knuckles and thick veins bulging. "Nicely meet you."

"Me llamo Ilta," she said as he took her hand and began kissing it much too passionately for a first encounter. She felt her insides squirm. "Ilta Jokinen. Y tú?"

"Me llamo Hugo."

"And your last name? Your surname?"

"Hugo."

She laughed, and he kissed her hand again, his flush lips parted over her delicate white skin. "Nice to meet you, Hugo Hugo."

"Sí. Hugo Hugo." He took a deep pull of his Quilmes, its blue label damp with condensation, and set the amber bottle down on the modern table next to her empties. "Baila conmigo! Come dance? You dance with me?"

Ilta felt her face go flush, and she sucked the remaining half of her Fernet and Coke up through her straw—an action that seemed to please Hugo Hugo very much—her ice-blue eyes not daring to stray from his, so deep brown and smoldering.

"We drink more after," he said. "Before now we dance."

And he led her through the red space, past the sleek praying mantis, away from the dining area and into the discoteca. It was dark, yet bright with colorful flashing lights, hot and crowded and rich with the smell of sweat and alcohol, vibrant and loud, 80s music blaring beneath the sparkly, spinning disco ball.

Just outside amidst the dark, humid heat, in the faint shadows between two street lamps on Avenida Olleros, a short squat man in a black trench coat—a red Spanish crest woven on the lapel—peered inside an open window at the multitude of lasciviously-dressed coeds, drugged-up and drunk, spinning, grinding and gyrating on the crowded dance floor. He opened his fist, and a small pinball floated away from his doughy hand, sped inside the club and hovered beneath the nose of the young woman in the sexy black dress, who was getting close and bumpy with the dashing and suave Mr. Hugo Hugo.

Ilta's nostrils twitched and she snuggled her face up against his neck, her nose pressed into his bulbous Adam's apple, at which point the invisible pinball cruised away from the dance floor and shot out the window into the hand of the squat man in the trench coat.

"Your cologne...me *gusta*," Ilta breathed. "It smells of sugar cookies."

"Colonia? No uso," he said, pulling her close. He kissed her, her tongue countering actively to his, swirling and sliding inside the cocoon of their mouths.

Shortly after, the seducing local drew away from his would-be conquest; her tongue had stopped responding, as did her lips and the sexual push of her lithe body into his. He released her, and she fell dead to floor. Hugo Hugo casually stepped away, walked back through the bar and then bolted out of *Sala Trece* and down Avenida Olleros into the night.

The party continued inside the discoteca for several minutes before the pounding techno music screeched to an abrupt halt amidst the piercing screams of a youthful Argentinian bent down on the dance floor trying to revive the deceased, nineteen-year-old Ilta Jokinen.

Beijing, China. 10:00 A.M., August 1, 2013 (10:00 P.M. EST. July 31, 2013).

Well south of the hustle and bustle of the spacious and renowned Qianmen Street, fifteen-year-old Lin He, wearing the prestigious white and blue of Beijing High School Four, cut through the late-morning heat of the cloudless summer day. He navigated through groups of narrow streets and alleyways known as Hutongs, his sketch book in one hand, a charcoal pencil in the other.

Ambling along the Hutong Jiuwan—a slim, torturous alley full of curves and bends—Lin's intimate reoccurring daydream of his older sister's surprisingly busty friend, Yanmei, was interrupted by scuffling noises up ahead, then a shriek of pain. Propelled by frightened curiosity, Lin's stumpy legs carried him around a tight turn toward the commotion, where he stopped short at the cruel sight playing out in front of his wire-rim, bespectacled eyes.

A childhood friend of his—the two had grown apart during adolescence—a skinny, ugly boy named Minsheng, was getting slapped and pushed around by a couple of older kids that Lin didn't recognize. Minsheng, through shiny tearful eyes, recognized Lin and screamed for his help.

"Stop!" Lin yelled, as a wizened old man in a black trench coat—banana-yellow trim along the collar and cuffs—sauntered by, unaffected by the relentless bullying in his wake. A small pinball fled from the old man's opening hand, hovering for a moment before chasing after Lin, who had dropped his art supplies and was hurrying over to try to help Minsheng.

"STOP!" Lin yelled again as the invisible pinball floated up to him, hovering between his upper lip and nose.

"You want it to be you, fatso?" the smaller of the two bullies said while the bigger one continued to slap Minsheng's reddening face. "Mind your business."

Lin inhaled deeply, suddenly overcome by the desire to find some sugary-sweet baked goods. *Mantou*, he thought, salivating; or his favorite, *youtiao*, all nice and deep-fried. All signs of panic and worry that had surfaced on his face moments ago sank below.

"I said get lost!" the smaller bully shouted, poking Lin's pudgy chest with his finger.

"No chance," Lin said, more seriously than anything he had ever said before in his life. "You're going to leave this little weasel to me."

"Hey, Yunxu!" the smaller bully called to his buddy. "Four-eyes here wants a piece of the action! What you think? Give him a go?"

Yunxu grinned like the mindless goon he was and plodded a few feet backward from the crying and puffy-faced Minsheng. Lin stepped forward, stuffed his index and middle finger up Minsheng's nostrils, and ripped off the front slab of the boy's nose, flinging the chunk of cartilage onto the Hutong's flat, dirty cobblestones. Minsheng howled, crumbling to the ground, the remnants of his nose gushing thick dark blood. The two older kids slapped each other high fives, wearing smiles that spread out longer than the Great Wall.

Standing over the boy cowering at his feet, Lin He exposed himself, and amidst the guffawing of the bullies, as well as the gaze of the old man in the trench coat standing near a dusty sketchbook by the bend, Lin began to urinate on his skinny, ugly, little childhood friend.

Washington, D.C. 10:20 P.M. EST. July 31, 2013.

Hunched over in thought, Gideon rested his bony forearms on the surface of an unusual table, where dull streaks of yellow light from two overhead lamps slid across the gloss of its black marble. He looked up, his opaque eyes flicking in the direction of the south wall, impossible to see so deep and dark in the distance. The wall, of his own design, was as black and bare as the others that comprised the room—a large, nearly empty room, big enough to hold ten of the one lone table situated in its center. Gideon straightened, annoyed, and pulled himself away from both the table and his thoughts.

He moved toward the south wall, behind which stood the source of this inconvenient interruption. He looked back just before he reached it. To those few of Darkness who had ever laid eyes on the table through the door that was now constructing itself in the south wall, it looked harmless. For no one but Gideon knew of its powers.

"Raxton," Gideon said, stepping from the black room into a thin gray-stoned passageway, cold yet torch-lit, the brownish flames enchanted to smell like animal carcasses of all sorts and types. Through the hollow between Gideon's shoulder and his mane of hair, Gideon caught the battle-tested Raxton sneaking a peek at the table beyond, but the door collapsed in on itself, and the wall of the passageway was, again, just a wall. "Tell me, Raxton. How are things progressing?"

"As smooth as a stream of blood, sir, and just as lovely," Raxton said, scratching at the thick blue-veined scar that stretched from the lip of his eye to the edge of his mouth. He motioned to his right with a scabbed hand and said, "This way, if you will."

Gideon took his time—small steps, slow movements—the rustling of his black clothing a constant, feathery-light whisper. A half step behind, Raxton waited to be further prompted. Like the handful of others who had made it near the top and were granted clearance to the secret tunnel-like corridors of the building, Raxton understood that seeking out the leader of Darkness was a delicate procedure reliant on reestablishing the chain of power at the start. Amused at how Raxton was breathing only through his mouth, Gideon made the man wait, though not for long.

"Tell me."

"Certainly, sir," Raxton said gruffly, his bulky body lumbering down the tight passageway that squeezed and stretched parallel to, and hidden from, the massive, blinkingly-bright front room of Darkness Headquarters. "Gujin7B has been the most challenging undertaking in Weaponry's history, as you know, chiefly due to the three-pronged complexity of its objective: for it to have a different effect on them, us and the enemy."

Gideon listened to his grizzled subordinate. Raxton might look like a giant sack of rocks, but the tough old coot was well-spoken and well-educated, a man who, even without magic, could beat the snot out of twenty grown Unknowings, and then recite them a Shakespearean sonnet or explain to them the intricacies of their stock market.

"So, in terms of the Unknowings," Raxton was saying, "as you so wisely decreed, the aim was to darken the Skunks who are *capable* of being darkened—that is to say cultivate and encourage the untapped pouch of evil *potential* sewn within their magic-less bodies. Those who are *incapable*, however...well, more useless creatures there cannot be. Therefore the first of Gujin's three-pronged objective required two prongs of its own: alter some of the Skunks, destroy the rest. Whittling it down to a tangible solution became a question of *potency*, and after taxing trial-and-error experimentation, we were able to identify the proper molecular levels suitable for this particular dual action and isolate the specific properties conducive to both."

"And tell me, Raxton." Gideon held his hands behind his back as he walked, slender fingers interlocked. "Have you succeeded?"

"We encapsulated samples of the most recent prototype inside small hollow spheres coated with a lubricant that morphs into an undetectable chrome-like skin. The gas itself, which has been manufactured to smell like sugar cookies, rises from the capsule in two streams, one per nostril. I scattered thirteen of my men across the world to administer random Gujin testing, each to have taken place precisely twenty-four minutes ago. Anchorage, Beijing, Buenos Aires, Lagos, Melbourne, Pasadena, Rome, Tokyo, Toronto, Warsaw and three more in Afghanistan alone. All reports back have been favorable and, to answer your question, do indeed corroborate success. Some of the Skunks died instantly—quicker than you can slap a toddler in the face. Those who survived contamination committed Dark acts shortly after infection."

"Good. What else?"

An uneven smile spread across Raxton's hardened face. "I had a gas mask with me, sir, last we spoke."

"You must think me a fool with a child's memory," Gideon said, cocking his head toward Raxton, whose smile vanished like smoke up a nose.

"I do not, sir. Poor tact, forgive me. I only mention it to highlight that I have no need for the mask now. Our delightened souls are what separate us from both the Unknowings and the Light. On that basis, a joint task force of Weaponry—" Raxton gestured to himself, "—and the persons down at Physiological Advancement, incorporated properties extracted from samples of delightenment vapor to be fused into the Gujin to protect us from potential side effects of the malevolent variety. In theory, utilizing what's already inside of us as an antidote to what we're developing. This has, as we believed it would, rendered the gas useless on men and women of Darkness. It has no effect on us at all, sir. To breathe it in is to breathe air."

The narrow passageway tightened some more as it tunneled upward several feet, and the echo of the men's footsteps became less hollow.

"So you've reported on us and the Skunks. Tell me, Raxton. What does exposure do to the third of your three prongs?"

"An opportune question, sir," Raxton said, slowing to a stop, "because the answer is found here at our destination." He rapped his mangled knuckles on a piece of empty wall between two golden torches, one smelling of dead fish, the other a rotting mountain goat. A door materialized, a side entrance to Cells A and B.

"As you know, sir, I administered the gas to Jace Frost and his gold-toothed, sack-of-bones friend ten days ago," Raxton said, as Gideon slithered past him into the sickly green light of the dungeon. Raxton cracked his knuckles a step behind his leader. "Let's see how they're doing."

CHAPTER 35

Standing up off the bed, Leam decided not to waste any more time in his room. After all, Gideon could come to kill him at any moment if he so chose, once he found out how Leam had treated his associate. With a soft groan, Leam slung his duffel bag, which was stuffed with clothes and keepsakes, over his shoulder as he took in his bedroom for, conceivably, the last time. If he'd bet his blemished hands earlier that this impending moment would bring about feelings of goodbye nostalgia, he'd now have nothing but bloody stumps hanging off his forearms.

The weight of the bag on his shoulder was a working symbol of moving on and starting anew, both of which he viewed as necessities to a better life. That was not to say his memories of Manor life had all been bad, not in the least, but whether these recollections came with smiles or frowns, they were in the past, a part of his childhood, which Leam planned on leaving behind when he walked out the back door. Regrettably, it looked like he would be leaving knowing nothing more about his father's disappearance than the little he had known upon his arrival: that Bram had gone missing the day after Leam had met the associate in Black Patch Park.

One step toward the door, Leam heard something scurrying off down the hall. Rushing out, he turned to the back staircase...and there it was, all the way at the hallway's end. Covered in a small dark cloak with a hood over its head was what looked to be a diminutive morphing of a human and a warthog. Its beady eyes glared at Leam before it hobbled down the stairs out of sight.

Whatever the thing might be, Leam realized at once that this was his last chance at finding out. He tore after the tiny beast, rushing by the huge wicker armoire and zipping down the long, windowless hallway, passing the statues, then the sword, the showcase of trumpets, the rusted daggers. Leam flew by the painting of sheep on a train dressed in old-fashioned business suits, his individual frustrations—Eloa, the blackout, his father—fueling the fire that was building inside him to catch the fleeing creature so hell bent on eluding him.

At the end of the hallway, Leam sprung left, descending the steps that would take him to Bram's library, his hand slid-, ing down the silver railing so cold to the touch. As he bounded past the third floor landing, his duffel bag swishing at his side, his index finger brushed over one of the hundred silver crows that hovered motionlessly inside the stairwell, and it burned him like fire.

"*Jesus!*"

His fingertip was bright red and throbbing, sizzled by the fierce cold of the bird, as if the small hovering statue had been carved out of dry ice. He shot a look over his shoulder and could have sworn he saw the crow flattening a smile.

At the bottom of the staircase, Leam ducked into the library. Like a cozy swarm of fireflies, the perpetually burning candlewicks lit up the room in a soft glow. Leam's gaze was darting around the room as if following an agitated housefly, when a strange flare streaked across his mind.

He was standing on the blue carpet of a similar room, yet much bigger and unfamiliar, filled with rows upon rows of golden bookshelves.

The flash was so quick—one snap of a moment, like the crack of a whip—that Leam dismissed it, catching his breath.

The warm air of the room smelled faintly of burnt bacon. He dropped his bag onto the cushy maroon carpeting and saw slight indentations mark their way across the carpet toward one of the dark, finely-polished desks in the corner of the room. Candlelight flickered off of a small reddish-gold object resting on its surface.

Leam walked the opposite way, to the French doors that led to the spiraling staircase in the center of the Manor, closing them quietly before pulling the strings of the door's blinds so no one could see in.

He then crossed to the far-corner desk, passing his father's large ivory Find-a-Thought at the library's center and realizing that he'd seen the glittery object before. Hundreds of times, in fact. It was the gilded bronze handle of Bram's knife, which until now, Leam assumed, had never strayed from its scabbard on his father's hip.

Leam slid into a worn leather chair next to the desk, studying the handle, which was shaped like a hooded, bent over creature—a miniature, metal version of the thing he had seen hobbling hurriedly away from his bedroom a minute ago. Leam flicked it with his seared fingertip and the knife knob spun around and around into a shiny blur. The very moment it became indistinct, a pop of bright light stung Leam's eyes closed. He blinked away blurry stars and, there, hunched over, its stout feet shuffling in place on the slippery desktop, stood a three-foot cloaked monstrosity that, as Leam had thought before, looked like a mix between a diminutive human being and a deformed warthog.

Leam's eyes widened, and the hog man jabbed them with his stubby fingers.

"Oww!" Flailing his arms, Leam blindly grabbed hold of the beast's cloak. The hog man twisted out of it and hopped off the desk, scampering toward the back staircase. Leam grabbed a heavy book off of the nearest shelf and slung it at the retreating creature. The corner of the book spine thudded into the back of his head. The hog man wailed, turning back and baring an expansive bottom row of jagged, brownish-yellow teeth.

Leam kicked out his chair, shooting to his feet, his eyes stinging daggers. He approached the hog man, who eyed the French doors before deciding to huddle halfway under a nearby reading bench made of dark marble.

"What in the hell are you?" Leam barked, unnerved by this bizarre transformation of an inanimate object into living beast.

The hog man let out another raging squeal, his beady eyes difficult to see in their cavernous sockets.

"You understand me?" Leam asked, advancing. "Do you speak?"

The hog man's crusty mouth snapped open and closed, open and closed, but Leam couldn't make out the sounds.

"What's that?" he asked, nearing the creature until he was close enough to hear that the hog man's mumbling was actually impressively coherent.

"I said that I speak very well." His hushed voice took Leam by surprise, as if all the other hog people he conversed with on a daily basis were of a more boisterous variety.

"What are you?" Leam asked again, peering down. "An animal?"

The hog man's mouth opened. The human half of him looked as if he was smiling; his hog half looked like he was about to bite the flesh off of Leam's face. "Two questions of yours that I would rather die than answer," the hog man said.

With the swiftness of a hawk, Leam swooped down to the hog man's level, pinning its coarse-skinned neck into the seat edge of the reading bench. "Answer me, hog man. Trust me, I'm not in the mood to play games."

"I am a being of magic!" the hog man croaked, its beady, reddish eyes going purple. "That's what I am, which is more than can be said of you!"

"Why are you here, hog man? Why have you been lurking around my room?"

"From what I gather, that room is not your place of rest any longer."

"Keep being cute." Leam squeezed his grip tighter around the creature's neck.

"*I am here,*" the hog man sputtered out, "because your paternal superior has left me here."

"Bram?" Leam loosened his grip, furrowing his brow. "He forgot you?"

"I have not been *forgotten,* Leam." The severe purple of the hog man's face quieted back to reddish-brown. "He left me here by his own choosing." Saying this out loud seemed to upset the hog man. Leam could see moisture developing in his recessed eyes that he didn't attribute to pain.

"But what *are* you?" Leam pressed, loosening his grip. "How do you know my dad? How do you know my name?"

The hog man squirmed out of the hold and bit Leam's left hand right next to the white marking stretching from index finger to thumb. Leam yelped in pain, pinning the hog man to the seat edge again, this time with a forearm across the neck. After several eye-bulging gasps, the hog man surrendered.

"He is the...beneficiary host to my...symbiotic parasitism," he wheezed.

"What?"

"HE IS THE BENEFICIA—"

"Shut up! I heard you! I just don't understand what you mean."

"He and I are connected, Leam. He would say I am an extension of him, however, I am of the belief that we are supplements to each other."

"Wait a second, wait a second..." Leam felt like he'd just seen the fat man walk by all buttered up in a string bikini. "Are you trying to tell me that you and my father have sex and stuff?"

The hog man broke into a fit of laughter, his foot-hooves scuffling atop the dark red fibers of the carpet. "How wonderfully barbaric! What a simpleton! I am not your father's lover, Leam. I am his alternate being."

Leam had come across the term *alternate being* a few times before, while skimming through some of the very books that surrounded him now. Its exact meaning, however, escaped him. "What is that?"

"Will you please unhand me?" the hog man gasped. Leam obliged and sat down on the carpet as the hog man shook out his head. "After a man of Darkness—or a woman—reaches a certain, spiritually-awakening point in his life, an alternate being of that man grows within him, taking a form—a form consisting of actual physical matter—that is somehow connected to his physical makeup, his character, or his soul. There is nothing it cannot be. Often, the alternate being is linked to the marking or markings received during delightenment, but not always. And not for your father."

"I know. His is on his throat."

"Yes, it stretches over his Adam's apple, and as you can see for yourself, I have nothing in common with an Adam's apple."

"So, you...live, or whatever...you *exist* on the end of his knife handle?"

"No, I *am* the end of the handle."

"So, you're just frozen there. A figurine."

"Think of it as short-lived hibernations." The hog man climbed out from under the bench and hopped up onto it. Leam was happy to see the well-spoken monstrosity was making himself comfortable.

"And then when he needs you or wants you to do something..." Leam said.

"Then there I am."

"Like a servant."

The hog man gritted his teeth. "No, Leam. What *he* needs and wants is what *I* need and want. We both were formed from the same spirit."

Leam took a better look and could see that the skin, or hide, of his father's alternate being had a golden, glittery glow to it, just like the knob of the knife.

"So does everyone have an alternate being?"

"Like I said, when a man of Darkness reaches a specific juncture in his life *spiritually,* then yes, his alternate being—previously an indefinable presence within his body—takes form and presents itself."

"Then me too someday," Leam said, looking at his hands.

"No. You are undelightened."

Leam leaned in, whispering, "How would you know that?"

"My God," the hog man said, looking up at the ceiling of book spines. "It's a wonder this boy ever learned to tie his shoelaces! I know this, Leam, because I live aside your father's hip."

Leam thought carefully, disregarding the jab. He wanted to avoid wasting time with pointless inquiries when the hog man could shrink into a tiny piece of metal at any moment, at which point Leam would be forced to toss books into the Find-a-Thought to further educate himself on the subject of these remarkable alternate beings.

"So do you have to stay attached to the knife most of the time? You know, are you allowed to jump back and forth between that and how you are right now?"

"Two very different questions." The hog man narrowed his eyes at Leam, presumably sizing him up. The creature rubbed the base of its glittery, reddish-brown throat with its stumpy fingers and continued. "I am able to transform from knife handle to what you see, and from what you see to knife handle, at my own discretion. How you couldn't piece that one together in light of the last five minutes is baffling, but, alas, so is so. As to the former inquiry, when an alternate being is in direct physical contact with its host—e.g. me against Bram's hip—the AB is stuck until the host chooses to release it."

"So, he knows you're here?"

"He *wants* me here," the hog man whispered.

"And what he wants, you want, right?"

"Yes, Leam. Congratulations. You have been paying attention. Your father left me here. The reason why is none of your concern. He had to take care of a personal issue—not an unusual occurrence—so I do his bidding here at home while he attends to other matters outside the Manor."

"I'll decide what's my own concern." Leam scooted forward. "Tell me what you know."

"I've given you enough."

"Tell me the personal issue, hog man."

The eyes of the loquacious animal glazed over, soupy drool spilling from what looked to be a grinning mouth. The hog man shook its head no.

Leam ran a hand through his hair, and in one quick moment, grabbed the hog man beneath his arm pits, carried him back to the corner table and dropped him on the hard wooden surface.

"Listen to me, hog man. I'm not a violent person, but lately—" Leam grinned, his eyes wild, "—lately I catch myself *becoming* a violent person. It's gotten to the point where I'm starting to enjoy it." Leam leaned in farther, his hands flat on the table. The hog man crouched into a ball. "Don't force me to hurt you, hog man. Because when a person starts to savor the act of inflicting pain—"

"I am an extension of your father! Would you hurt him?"

"—the pain tends to be severe."

"Don't kid yourself, Leam," the hog man growled, though Leam heard nerves in his voice. "I know what kind of person you are. Since your birth, every time you have been in the company of your father, I have been there, as well."

"He was never around!"

"*Be* that as it may, I know much about you. Yours is a gentle spirit. Your scare tactics are nothing but—"

Leam punched the hog man in the snout, hard, and it gushed sludgy, purple blood.

"WHERE HAS HE GONE, YOU GARGOYLE? I WANT TO KNOW!"

The hog man wailed and sobbed, desperately trying to cover the blood streaming from his nose, but his hoggish-handed arms were too stumpy to reach.

"Everyone I care about is either missing or a goddamn dream!" Leam shouted into the hog man's face. "He's been away longer than I have! Where has he gone? I'm done playing games!"

"He goes to the Graveyard of Gaddiel!" the hog man cried out, in a strained, hoarse voice, human tears sliding down his coarse hog face. "It is where he always goes around the anniversary of your mother's death!"

Leam stumbled a step backward, as if he had just been hit in the chest with a brick. He pictured the Graveyard of Gaddiel, located on the other side of Harbing near the movie theater complex, the bright lights of which had always left the graveyard dark and inconspicuous, masked in shadows. He had biked and driven by that cemetery countless times and she, *his mother*, had been buried there, so close this whole time, his whole life.

"He goes there?" Leam asked. Every part of his body felt tight and jittery. "He goes to her grave, is that what you're telling me?"

"Yes," the hog man whispered. "It is the only time he leaves me alone."

"Lies," Leam said, after a dawning recollection. "When he took me to the shop the other night or whenever it was, only the blade was in his hand. I specifically remember that."

The hog man bared its jagged teeth. "Yes, yes, fine, fine! He told me he had a project for you that...that I was not to know about." The words seemed to be painful for the hog man to voice.

"What does he do at the graveyard?" Leam asked. "He goes there to see her for ten days at a time?"

"No." Worry flooded the hog man's face. "It's never more than a few hours. I know not where his is. I need him. I grow weak. I depend on him. He depends on me. He is without me, wherever he may be, and he is alone!"

"But the day he left you...that was the anniversary of her death."

The hog man nodded.

Leam did the math in his head. "So, she died on my birthday."

The hog man nodded again. "She died giving birth to you. Put another way, Leam...you killed her."

Leam's head clouded with heat. "What'd you just say?"

"You killed your mother."

Leam clenched his fists together so tightly they went sugar white, releasing them a moment later, the white flooding with red. "No, that's not my fault. I get what you're trying to do and I'm not gonna let you do that."

"Have it your way."

"And if it turns out you're lying, I'll find a way back inside this house. If this was a lie, I'll come back to kill you."

The hog man sat back on his haunches, responding, "Then I'm afraid it won't be you who ends my life. Not for this."

"Besides for that, though," Leam spoke, eyeing his duffel bag, which lay beyond the Find-a-Thought by the back stair-case, "I'm never coming back." Crossing to the bag, Leam rolled his head back to smooth the kinks out of his neck, and his eyes locked onto a book wedged into the ceiling of spines. A yellow book. He scanned the rest of the ceiling, then all four book-shelved walls. It was the only yellow in an entire sea of muted, earthy-toned book covers.

Leam dragged the nearest desk beneath the yellow spine and hopped on top.

"What do you think you're doing?" the hog man asked.

"The yellow book," Leam muttered, anger clinging to the edge of his voice.

"What about it?"

"I've seen it before."

"Of course you have, you're in here every day."

"That's not what I mean," Leam said, his mind delving into his visions, picturing the illusive tome that had been hiding in them, now unveiled above him in actuality. The woman had been holding it in the sailboat, as had the youngish man with the purple Nikes in the giant white room. "The painting, too," Leam mumbled, reaching up, his feet planted on the desktop, remembering a yellow book in the hands of one of the sheep in the back of the train compartment. He grabbed the spine, pull-ing the hard-backed volume away from its peers and the almost magnetic hold of the ceiling. The cover bore no title.

"Leave that where it is!" the hog man yelped from atop the corner desk, his brownish-red hide presently more red than brown.

"This means something." Leam jumped down from the desk. He went to the duffel bag and stuffed the book inside.

"Where are you going?"

"Gaddiel's."

"You mustn't take anything from this room, Leam!" The hog man was shaking, clearly more upset about the theft of his host's book than by any of the physical intimidation administered by the host's son. Glittery sweat dripped from his face like beaded jewels.

"Yeah right," Leam said.

"THAT BOOK IS CURSED!" the hog man howled, his eyes blinking laser red inside their sunken sockets.

"I don't care."

And Leam moved to the French doors, pushing them forward as he yanked open the blinds. Hurrying away from the candlelit library, his mind was on his mother and the graveyard. Just before he turned the corner, he looked back through the glass-paned doors of the library and saw the squat little hog man, draped again inside its cloak, whirl into a dark cloudy blur atop the desk, and then—POP—all that remained was a spinning, gilded bronze handle in the shape of a hooded figure, slowing to a stop as Leam took off for the spiraling stairs.

CHAPTER 36

Gideon stepped out of the side entrance of Cells A and B into the passageway, orange flames crackling atop the torches, Raxton right behind him, the door disappearing as the wall stones merged back together, snuffing out the dungeon's queasy greenish light.

"It's better than I hoped for, Raxton, you've done quite a job."

"Hardly recognizable, the great dumb beast, isn't he, sir?"

"If he's in pain, he doesn't show it."

"He is, sir, he's just a tough old horse. That kind of physical change is unavoidably excruciating."

Gideon tilted his head back, breathing in the stench of what one of his top men referred to as the Corridor of Carcasses.

"Tell me," he said. "What's next?"

"Once you release me, I head straight down to Chamber 5. It's the air-sealed compartment in Weaponry where we've stored the Gujin7B. There, I and a few of my men will extract a small amount of gas, dilute it, and then release it in a larger community."

"Dilution? For what purpose?"

"The ten o'clock tests validate how quickly the effects of Gujin take place once administered. A high-concentrated dose released in a relatively larger area—say the size of a small town—will kill a large number of Skunks, shooting up immediate red flags. That we must avoid. As much as I would like to see the swine slaughtered, we have to think big picture here, sir."

Gideon nodded.

"If, however," Raxton went on, his blue-veined scar twitching down his face, "we water it down, so to speak, the effects of the gas won't materialize right away. This allows us to continue to monitor and modify Gujin, see more precisely how it works."

"Go to it, then," Gideon said. "I have to leave but I'll be back later tonight. Make sure you are, as well."

"Yes, sir."

"And, Raxton?"

"Sir."

"I have foreseen this night to be one of greatness for Darkness. I hate to think of the punishment inflicted on any of my men who hurt the chances of tonight's potential glory."

"Yes, sir."

Gideon stared at Raxton with a grin, his eyes wide, his face perfectly still. Raxton, awaiting his release, did not look away. He didn't have to wait long.

"Go."

CHAPTER 37

The vast sky had darkened. A few scattered stars twinkled above two men walking through a field, nearing the tree line that led to an old-growth forest of green ashes and white pines.

The younger-looking man, the man in the sea-green long-sleeve T-shirt—Ski Vail stamped in red across the chest—had been talking animatedly for several minutes now, arms swaying this way and that, hands bobbing up and down. The man listening, the man in a faded navy blue V-neck T-shirt and jeans, the man with silver hair, looked to be in his early forties despite being born over three hundred years ago. He listened intently to the report, sometimes looking ahead, sometimes looking down at his bare feet, one stepping in front of the next, taking him toward the forest.

"...but," the younger man was saying, "this comes from a source whose motives are somewhat unclear."

"Whatever his intentions, Miller, you believe the source is telling the truth?"

"I do. He says he was lied to, betrayed, deceived... You know, I don't know if it was Gideon specifically who wronged him, but the source is dead set on vengeance."

Sebastian raised his eyebrows. "Go on."

"The boy's preliminary test took place in the town park. This was Friday the nineteenth. Two days later he was taken in for further examination."

"That soon?"

Miller nodded. "And he hasn't been seen since. Which to me, sir, means they see something special in him. They must. And *that* to me means he has more prospect potential than they've come across in a very long time." Miller looked up at the black sky, an infinite backdrop for the radiant moon, which was a beauty, full and bright. "Or they put him down."

"If Gideon killed him, it would've been done in a way where we would have heard about it." Sebastian furrowed his eyebrows. "Since the boy has been under heavy examination by the forces of Darkness, Gideon not only knows a lot more than we do, but he also can shape and influence the boy's mind before it develops according to its natural maturation."

Miller nodded, and the rhythmic swishing sounds of their feet crossing the field accompanied them to the edge of the grasslands. Right before entering the woods through the threshold of two magnificent pines, Sebastian stopped and looked over his shoulder toward the middle of the enormous field, hidden by the eerie mask of nightfall.

"Did you hear something?"

"Hear what?" Miller asked.

"A baby crying. Somewhere out in the field."

"Nope. And I have excellent hearing, sir. My mother always told me I had a talent for hearing, but not so much for listening."

Sebastian peered through the darkness, then turned, stepping into the forest with Miller keeping pace.

"I had no idea this place was so big," Miller said, brushing his hand over the branches of a sparse pine tree. "Lakes, fields, forests…" he peered through the brush, squinting, "…jungles."

"It is impossible to explore every acre, as is its nature."

"Sort of silly to be called a room, sir," Miller said, rubbing his earlobe between his thumb and finger—a habit of his, Sebastian had learned, when excited. "How big is it, sir?"

"The prospect has two paths laid out in front of him," Sebastian said, staying present on what mattered. "The one he's walking on right now, where Gideon, with his wiles and trickery, sinks his teeth into the boy, or the other, the path where the boy runs into me and hears what I have to say."

"I like that path. The second one, that's a good path."

"It's rushed." Sebastian rubbed his temple with the heel of his hand. "He's not yet supposed to know who he might be."

"Are you not ready for it, sir?"

"No, I'm troubled by it. I'm always ready."

"But we don't even know where the boy is."

"He's in Harbing."

"How do you know that?"

"Because I can feel it."

Miller smiled. "You're working on a whole other level, aren't you?"

"Gideon's forced my hand. As regrettable as it may be, the choice is a simple one."

Miller nodded, his eager eyes beaming as the two men continued on, moving deeper and deeper into the woods.

"You know what though, sir?" Miller said, and Sebastian could tell that the words were being chosen with care. "There's one thing you might want to prepare for, and I only mention it because I can see how troubled all of this is making you, and I think you might have overlooked one other possibility."

"Which is?"

"Maybe Gideon has deliberately used the boy as a stepping stone to get information that he's been trying to obtain for a long, long time. Maybe he set this whole thing up to put you in a position where you felt that you had to talk to the boy about specific things, things that Gideon has wanted to know for centuries...things you have been so careful to keep hidden from him."

"It's plausible." Sebastian cleared a tree branch out of their way with his mind. Even in the soft blacks of near darkness, it was evident that the pines and ashes of the forest were giving way to jungle vegetation. Cecropias, various epiphytes and other plants were flourishing beneath banana trees and three hundred-foot kapoks wrapped with vines as thick as the many Burmese pythons Sebastian knew to inhabit the tropical areas of this glorious place. He could taste the heat clinging to the sultry air. "But what can I do? There's no other way around it. I have to act."

"Right now, sir?" Miller asked, slowing his pace, the brush so thick that the little bit of moonlight peeking through the canopy of the rain forest no longer provided adequate visibility to navigate through a jungle. "Then let me quickly give you the rest."

"Take your time. I haven't found what I came for yet," Sebastian said, holding up his hands. Speckles of pink, purple and white light broke away from his fingertips, hovering in the air around them like a cloud of glowing glitter as they walked.

"Jace Frost has completely vanished," Miller said, turning up his hands as if at a loss.

"That's all you have? I gave you more men. You've had nearly two weeks."

"I know. He's gone. Which can only mean one thing, *if* he's still alive. Darkness has him at their headquarters."

"He's not dead."

"He's not? You can feel it? Like with the Leam thing?"

"No, this I flat-out know. And if he's alive but can't be found, then I agree, Gideon has him. That's the only way this makes sense."

"How do you know he's alive, though?"

"A decade ago I crafted an Ocean Goblet for him to drink from, along with Zalika and Broox," Sebastian said, moving along inside the cloud of flickering light, which swung through the black jungle like a light bulb swaying in a dark closet. "If any one of them dies, the others, and myself, will know. It was necessary. All three were given operations in the same dangerous mission, which you're as familiar with now as is possible."

"Break Lock."

"Precisely."

"Tso mentioned it when he first put me on the search for Frost, the night Frost vanished." Miller sidestepped a large Venus-flytrap, its hungry lobes opening wide. "He didn't elaborate. Neither did Zalika or Broox when I sought their input. Not really."

"Most who know of Break Lock know only its name. Few know the specifics. That's the way it is because that's how it has to be."

A weak smile saddened Miller's face. "I didn't mean to pry."

"You've earned the right to see the brush strokes," Sebastian said. Miller tugged at his ear. "Ten years ago we unearthed a buried secret of theirs as old as the moon. A secret they are certain we know nothing about, or so I once thought. The Blanket of Darkness."

"Like our Layer of Light?" Miller asked.

"The Layer of Light is a term that represents the varying strength of the protection we can provide the Unknowings from Dark interference. The Blanket of Darkness, however, is not a figurative term. It's tangible, in a magical sense. A shielding enchantment unlike any other, protected by codes of letters, symbols and numbers. It hides an entity unknown to us that I believe is pivotal to their existence and power, guarding the most significant information of theirs that we've ever tried to expose. It's why I enlisted the smartest and bravest to Break Lock—the very best—and Jace, Broox and Zalika have been working to find a way to break through, in their own different ways, for the past ten years."

"I personally spoke to Zalika about Jace," Miller said, "and sent one of the men you lent me, a man by the name of Kiskadee, to question Broox. Zalika knew nothing, but was unnerved when she learned of Jace's disappearance. Broox, however, once Kiskadee convinced him how dire things were...he had something to say."

Sebastian stopped. "One second." He bent down beside the trunk of a small drooping tree. The tree looked lost—unhealthy and gray amidst such vibrant and colorful life, like a dead mouse floating atop a brilliant lily pad. He skimmed his palms over the bark, eyes closed. Ten seconds passed before he stood up, frowning. "I'm sorry, Miller, go on."

"Kiskadee said that Jace had recently confided in Broox that he was uncovering data on a new weapon of Darkness's in development. A poisonous gas-like substance capable of global contamination, he said."

"What does the gas do?"

The men were moving again, the cloud of sparks—pink, purple and white—with them.

"I asked. Kiskadee said Broox didn't know. All he said was that Jace was working on it exclusively, nothing else, and that…"

"And that what?" Sebastian prodded.

"He said he got the impression that Jace kept wanting to look over his shoulder…you know, to peek back, but was willing himself not to. Like he was expecting something or someone by surprise."

Sebastian put a hand over his stomach—it was growling, a deep hunger setting in. "If Darkness took Jace prisoner, then Gideon must've discovered what Jace was doing and snatched him up as soon as he could. It's what I would've done. Gideon got him before Jace could tell me what the threat is and how to go about stopping it. It could mean the weapon's ready for release, or close to it." Sebastian let out a long breath, shaking his head. "Global contamination? How am I only hearing the first of this now?"

"Kiskadee just told me, couldn't've been twenty minutes ago. I came straight here, sir."

"How did I not get involved sooner?" Sebastian muttered, increasing his pace. "Gideon has him. Jace's completely off the grid."

"I asked my Leam Holt source where Darkness Headquarters is," Miller said. "Thing is, it looked like he wanted to tell me but he couldn't say anything, like he physically couldn't speak. His mouth would open, but nothing but choking sounds came out."

"Taciturnal spell," Sebastian said. "No one who knows DHQ's location can speak of it."

"Well, at least we know Frost isn't dead."

"If you want to know the truth of it, his disappearance is just as damaging." Sebastian bypassed what he knew to be a large patch of quick sand. "All the codes he's been deciphering are inside *his* head and nowhere else. I forbade him and the other two to document any of their work." He touched his stomach again. "I don't like it. I don't like any of it."

"It's that serious, huh?"

"This isn't solely about the new gaseous threat, Miller. Jace has collected ten years' worth of data. Leam Holt is here, right now. I won't jump to say that Leam is who we seek—it's way too soon to dub him the prophet, that goes without saying—but if he is...*if* he is, then we don't have another ten years. Notify every department across the board. Jace Frost is now a red-flag top priority. He has to be found alive. That means all data relating to the location of DHQ ever collected has to be thrown together in a bowl, mixed up and spun around until some sort of pattern materializes, a connection, something that we've overlooked in the past. Something discernible that gives us a chance."

"Right away," Miller said.

"And Miller?" Sebastian said, standing tall and still. "Let it be known that if we find DHQ, we go immediately and we go in heavy."

Miller nodded and closed his eyes. Twenty seconds later, they opened, as Miller's telemast shot out into the night to alert the heads of every department throughout the COO. "It's done, sir."

"Good," Sebastian said, picking up again, striding through the jungle sounds and humidity.

"But, sir," Miller said, jogging to keep up, "what if nothing comes of it? What if DHQ can't be found? Or what if they kill him?"

Sebastian thought on this, running a hand through his silver hair. "Then we'd need a miracle."

Right then, as Sebastian could feel the reality of the situation dawn on the excitable man a few paces behind him, shards of unnatural yellow light illuminated the jungle floor in jagged patches. Both men looked up at the taxicab-yellow beams that burst through the jungle's glowing green ceiling of leaves.

"What's happening, sir?"

"The tube," Sebastian said, peeling his eyes off the above. "Stay directly behind me, attach yourself to my force and we run as fast as we can. It'll be enough."

Sebastian took off, shedding the pinkish-purple cloud of sparks, running in a straight line like a blur, trees and plants and wildlife moving and bending out of his way, repelling from his magic. He could feel his magnetism pulling Miller like a sleigh, keeping him close. A few seconds later they shot out of the dense jungle, skidding to a stop at the bank of a giant, flowing river. Sebastian's eyes went straight to the tube jutting through its middle, displacing the current. The tube, the width of a large oak tree, extended too high to see and enclosed a flat piece of rock on the river's surface. The strip of yellow sky above the river darkened, returning to the moon-bright shade of night. Bright red lights emerged from every tree trunk, flashing in sync with the piercing sound of a car alarm. Across the river, several men and women stood waiting, their expressions mingled with excitement and fear, the latter trumping the former.

Sebastian looked up to see someone dark and bulky chuting down the tube with great speed and slamming onto the flat rock. Clambering to his feet unharmed, was a large, bearded man... Or was it? The edges of his black trench coat and skin seemed fuzzy and tricked with strange light. Sebastian couldn't tell if the man was a computer image or the real thing, but he knew either way it didn't matter. The message is what mattered. The bearded man stared out of the tube, seemingly unaffected by his surroundings. As he opened his mouth to speak, both the alarm and the red lights shut off with a snap, and silence draped over the men and women inside the Room of the River like a damp, unnerving veil.

> "Uncloak the approach...
> Unsettled brewing, long the throes, a storm of swans
>   and crows.
> The earth's reliable spin balks;

For it is coming.

Midst of uncertainty, thou are flung, a spike of oil through the tongue.

Blood scars the flat shapes of chalk;

For it is coming.

Stung by denial, wayward be lost, enduring minds set for fire and frost.

Steady onward the dueling walk;

For it is coming. For it is coming. For it is coming."

At the close, the bearded man's entire image went fuzzy, not just his edges, like the static of an old black-and-white TV, but in color. His feet rose off the rock, and in the next instant he was sucked up the tube, gone.

"The Spirit of the Coming!" Miller whispered to Sebastian, who was watching his people on the far side of the river take off for the Water Glass that separated the Room of the River from the COO's offices and training facilities.

"Perhaps," Sebastian said. "Perhaps not. They've tried to trick us with decoys before." His stomach ached, but now he felt something else, something behind his eyes and around his heart, something full of power and anger and clarity of purpose. Miller stared at him, wide-eyed.

"Sir, is it or isn't it?"

"Are you asking for my guess?" The anger in Sebastian's voice tipped off the emotions stewing beneath his outwardly calm demeanor.

"But, sir, with all that's happening," Miller stammered, "it's like there's too many coincidences going on right now for this not to be the real—"

"We proceed as if it's real. That should suffice for now." Sebastian knew fire was burning in his eyes, and he could see Miller was scared of it. "I'll tell you one thing, Miller, and I'll tell it to you straight. Whether this is it or not, things change right now. Gideon has Jace—*My* Jace! *My* man!—*and* he's developing a new toxic weapon, *and* he's been influencing Leam Holt for who knows how long before I've even made a move. It's all on me, I don't deny that, but I'm telling you that things change right now."

"Yes, sir."

"Do you hear me?"

"Definitely," Miller said. "I exactly hear you."

"Everybody here at the COO is on Jace Frost. I'm going to Leam Holt. Are you staying with them or are you coming with me?"

Miller smiled, rubbing his earlobe between his thumb and finger. "What do *you* think, sir?"

CHAPTER 38

Parked at an unlit side entrance to the cemetery where his mother's body was buried, Leam shut off the headlights as the nightly summer fog curled itself around the Range Rover, the silver paint quickly lost in its haze. Before it could consume the SUV whole, Leam peered out into the spooky graveyard, a place he'd never once set foot in.

But why?

Why hadn't he ever searched for her grave? Had he subconsciously not wanted to acknowledge her death? If he never saw Aggie's grave, then had he imagined she might still be alive?

He shifted his weight to the left, pulling his mother's acorn from the right pocket of his jeans, letting his fingers roll it around his palm. With his eyes swimming in the broth of the hanging fog, he thought back to his conversation with Sara in the kitchen—the same place the acorn had come into his possession. He had left Bram's library and was raiding the refrigerator when Sara had approached him.

"Here's the other set of car keys," she said, handing them over to Leam, who was cramming bottles of water and Gatorade into his already overloaded duffel bag.

"Thanks," Leam replied, turning back to the fridge to take what he pleased. He could sense that Sara was watching him with disgust.

"Don't come back, Leam," she said.

"I won't." He ducked his head inside the fridge. The chill felt good.

"Don't come back, Leam," she repeated.

"I heard you the first time, Sara."

"Don't sharpen your tongue with we, you ungrateful little skunk."

Leam straightened to look her in the face. The drunken haze that had clouded her eyes in the music room earlier had cleared. "Why would I give you gratitude?"

"How about we start with the keys in your hand?"

"I thanked you for the car, Sara. I'm not gonna kiss your feet."

She took a step back, her lips pursed. The drone of the refrigerator nagged Leam like a bee.

"I can tell you know how close I am with Gideon," Sara said.

"I've always known." Leam closed the fridge, turning to the island to zip up his bag.

"Yes, I think I'll have a little chat with him next he's over," she said. "Yes, I think I will, and I'll say whatever I need to, and offer whatever I need to, to get you taken out. And do you know why, Leam? Because more important to me than myself and my own son's success in the throes of Darkness, is your failure. Your demise."

"Go for it. You think I care?" Leam hoisted the bag over his shoulder and stepped toward the back door, his Range Rover waiting for him beyond the back patio. "Go right ahead."

"Don't come back, Leam."

"That's three times you've said that." Leam turned back to face her. "I am aware that you don't want me to come back, Sara."

"I've set up precautions, Leam. Booby traps, protective magic, enchantments that your feeble mind can't comprehend. I *hope you hear me when I say that this truly is the last time you'll be standing in this house."*

"Got it. Thanks."

"Whatever it is Gideon sees in you," Sara said, "it's not what you think."

"I don't think much of anything anymore."

"There's been hundreds of snot-nosed teenagers just like you who never panned out to be anything. You're no different."

"And you, Sara? Do you think you're so special? Has your frigid heart convinced your tiny brain that you're any different than the rest of the pigs that Gideon sleeps with?"

"Yes," she said, and Leam could see that she meant it. He turned and went for the back door.

"I guess we'll both find out where we stand, then," he said. "Sooner or later."

"Goodbye, Leam."

"Goodbye."

Squinting through the windshield, Leam could no longer see anything that surrounded him apart from the swirly fog. He experienced that same feeling of helplessness that attacked him when looking out an airplane window while flying through choppy clouds.

He looked away and unzipped the duffel bag, taking out an orange Gatorade and the yellow book that he had stolen from his father's library despite the warnings of the hog man. He downed three-fourths of the Gatorade, still rubbing his mother's acorn in his hand. Bram never spoke to Leam about her, never gave off the impression that he even thought about her, but if the man came here, at a minimum once a year, every year, then maybe there was more to the story than that.

Leam opened the yellow-bound book. His eyes jumped from the clock inset on the dash—11:11 P.M.—to the bold capital letters of the title page.

EAST OF EDEN

Leam started to flip through the pages, unsure why he had thought this book held answers for him. *East of Eden?* Was it solely the fact that he'd seen it in a couple of his visions? He had been expecting something like *Digging Deep for your Delightenment* by Mud Toppler, not John Steinbeck's *East of Eden*. He thought there would be something of significance inside this book, something between the front and back covers—a map, maybe, showing him some secret route that would guide him to some secret place.

He stopped turning pages, the half-opened book on his lap. *You're losing your mind, Leam. Get a grip.*

He felt like slamming the book shut, flinging it out the window, but the last words the hog man had yelled at him echoed in his head.

"That book is cursed!"

If it really was just an ordinary book, why would the hog man scream something like that? Was it just because he didn't want Leam taking anything that belonged to Bram...anything that was property of his host, as the hog man had put it? Probably not.

So Leam flipped through the rest of the book, and when he turned over one of the last few pages, a folded piece of paper—dirty and well creased from overuse—lay flat in the wedge. Leam unfolded it as newfound excitement replaced the uncertainty that had been poisoning his mind. His eyes darted across the lines.

Bram Holt – Operation Duncan

Prospective Victims:
GRAHAM, age 55, of Light
MADELINE, age 53, of Darkness
ABIGAIL, age 22, daughter
CHRISTIAN, age 19, son

Site:
Harbing, N.J. Sidwitch Lane. Three quarters of a mile after turning off Eaton Street. Wooded area on the left.

Time of Arrival:
Backus to deliver Graham on the 18th at 11:05 P.M.
Huxley to deliver Madeline and Abigail on the 18th at 11:08 P.M.
Holt to deliver Christian on the 18th at 11:10 P.M.

Method of Termination:
Cardiobliviation
(Special attention: Christian. See attached)

Leam flipped the loose-leaf paper over. Nothing was on the back, just the hardened creases of the folds. He looked back down at the book and, sure enough, another piece of paper, in the same condition as the first, was wedged between the open pages of the last chapter of *East of Eden*. Leam opened it, his fingers a blur.

CHRISTIAN JOSHUA DUNCAN
D.O.B: September 31, 1976
Observed/examined since October 1993 (DL Hybrid)

- *Patient*
- *Composed, well-tempered (even under unforgiving circumstances)*
- *Exhibits excellent physical aptitude*
- *Superior level of intelligence amongst peers*
- *Undelightened (note: never attempted)*
- *Confides in, and takes after, father (Graham)*
- *Avoids mother and sister (Madeline/Abigail)*

Leam refolded the paper, processing what he had read. He went back to the first sheet.

Method of Termination:
Cardiobliviation
(Special attention: Christian. See attached)

Note:
Due to hybrid sensitivity, Christian's existence is
a threat to the Cause and because of that, he shall
be terminated. As evidenced by the decreed date of
death, the completion of this mission is of a timely
matter. Wasted time enables our counterpart to
interfere. Every precaution is necessary, and thus
the execution of Christian's family, despite our ties
with Madeline, has so been mandated.

–Ward Thorne, O of D, D.O.P July 16, 1995.

Leam's brain crawled with questions as certain words and
phrases jumped out at him. Cardiobliviation. Undelightened
(note: never attempted). Hybrid sensitivity. Sidwitch Lane.

The Duncans had been killed by his father and two guys
named Backus and Luxley, and it had been because the son's
parents were on different sides of the war.

But how could they have been together? Leam thought to
himself. *It's not possible for Darkness to be with Light. It's mag-*
ical law.

And then, below everything else, clearly written several
years after the other somewhat faded words that a man named
Ward Thorne had typed up back in the mid-nineties, Leam recognized his father's handwriting, a few sentences at the bottom
of the page.

The Duncan's were the only married couple that
I'm aware of where one is Dark and one is Light.
What would my life have been like if I had fought
for a similar union? I wonder what would have
been if I hadn't carried out my orders. I wonder
what could have been if I hadn't killed her. Her.
Aggie. The Light of my life.

Leam grabbed at his chest. It felt like his heart had caved
in—that everything had caved in, leaving his body hollow. Hollow just for a moment, though, as anger filled the space like

helium into a balloon. Rage slid through his veins like poison. His hands began to shake. He tried to quiet them by gripping the steering wheel, which seemed to only make it worse. It made no difference to him that Bram had been ordered to kill her, it was that he *did* kill her. She hadn't died giving birth to Leam. She had been killed. And, Leam thought, if his father had loved her—which Leam assumed was the case since the man kept visiting the Graveyard of Gaddiel every single year—then Bram was a weasel and a weakling, a coward for going through with it. Leam had only met Eloa a couple of weeks ago, but it was hard for him to imagine he would harm her if ordered to do so.

Leam gasped down breaths, trying to calm himself, to ease the trembling. The sheet of paper shuddered in his hands, drops of tears and thin straws of drool smattering the ink.

Her. Aggie. The Light of my life.

He read the last of it once more, and it was then that everything fell into place like scattered jigsaw puzzle pieces suctioning together to become something recognizable. The *Light* of his life... His mother wasn't a member of Darkness, she was the exact opposite, a woman of Light. No wonder Sara loathed her, forbidding anyone in the house to utter her name. No wonder Bram had told him by the pit all those years back that a coupling like the Duncans could never exist. No wonder Gideon wanted Aggie out of the way. And if Leam's mother was of Light and his father was most certainly a man of Darkness, then Leam—like the slain Christian Duncan—was a combination of both. And that meant, just like Christian, that he could also be murdered for the simple fact that his parents were on opposing sides of the war.

But why would anybody be a threat because they were of both Darkness and Light? That's what didn't make sense. Leam wiped his face—glazed over with a combination of sweat, drool and tears—with a black hooded sweatshirt from his duffel bag. He wondered if the associate had taken Christian to the field of green to fight Witchlows. Had Christian failed where Leam had succeeded? Or had Christian been successful as well and killed because of that, meaning Leam would be next?

Leam closed *East of Eden* and tried to peer through the fog, wondering if his killer was out there now, waiting for Leam to step out into the graveyard. He wished now more than ever that he had been delightened—wished the fat man had just gone through with the ceremony, because if the fat man had, the dormant magical powers inside of Leam would be wide awake, they'd be alive, and then Leam might stand a chance to defeat whatever might be lurking just outside the car and far beyond it. Christian hadn't been bestowed his powers either...

Undelightened (note: never attempted)

Was it because the blood that coursed through Leam's veins was half Light, half Darkness, that he had failed *his* delightenment?

What was it that Gideon had said to Bram about Leam before leaving the Manor after Zach's delightenment?

"And also be reminded that some of the greatest men of Darkness were slow starters. It is as if their souls need to be darkened at a snail's pace in order for them to achieve their potential. Potential for great things."

Was Gideon right? And if he was, did Leam's soul need to be darkened at a snail's pace because half of it was as bright as Light?

Potential for great things...

Could he, Leam, be destined for greatness? Was Gideon—through the tests monitored by the associate—preparing Leam for the moment when his soul would finally be ready to darken? And where had Christian Duncan gone wrong? Why had he been killed? What grievous error had he committed that apparently Leam yet had not?

Leam picked up the second sheet of paper, his hands jumpy, the blood pulsing in his veins like the cry of a distant alarm growing louder.

D.O.B: September 31, 1976.
Observed/examined since October 1995 (DL Hybrid)

So, if the powers of Darkness began watching Christian in October of 1995, that would mean he had just turned seventeen, the day of delightenment for most children of Darkness, the night before.

...Observed/Examined...Observed/Examined...

Leam thought of the first time he had been examined by Gideon's associate. Just like Christian, Leam had begun his examination around the time of his birthday, though according to Bram's papers, Christian's testing had started a year before Leam's, when Christian was seventeen. This, however, did nothing to quiet the eerie feeling in Leam's gut that he was on to something big here. He was pretty sure that he had been "observed" since he had failed his delightenment over a year ago, perhaps even earlier.

He checked the date that the itinerary was issued.

July 16, 1995.

So the murders occurred in 1995, two days later, the 18th of July.

Leam's body froze, his mind already afire with sparks of discovery and scalding revelations, one after the next, with more, it felt like, standing in line waiting to be lit. This last firework, the one that had sent a sizzle down his neck—and he double checked the dates to be sure—affirmed that everything he was finding out could no longer be miscued as a string of coincidences. It couldn't be.

Christian Duncan had been murdered by Leam's father, Backus and Huxley, during the twenty-third hour of July 18th, 1995, just a few minutes before he, Leam Holt, had been born at the stroke of midnight in St. Giles Hospital less than eight streets away from Sidwitch Lane.

Holy shit.

Sheer seconds before a woman of Light had given birth to Leam, his father had killed a nineteen year-old boy that had gone through exactly what Leam was going through now for no discernible reason other than being half Dark and half Light.

Crazy.

But why hadn't Bram ever warned his son of the danger that might befall a hybrid? A hybrid, he was a hybrid, which had to be rare, no doubt about it, but again, *why* did that pose a threat, pose some sort of danger? Why would a hybrid have to be monitored?

Leam sat back into the contours of the leather seat, slowing it all down, quieting his mind. For a moment, he thought of the open lanes of the Garden State Parkway South, and could see the big green signs with white letters of destinations and the corresponding numbers beside them letting you know how far away you were. But then the green signs faded into the background, and Leam was seeing his old room now, his bed, and he thought of the safety and warmth of being underneath its covers. But Leam shook his head free of highway signs and bed linens, slapping himself on the cheeks. The graveyard outside held his mother and was the last known whereabouts of his father. This was a time to get out there, not stay in. A time to show himself, not run away or hide. To spring toward the unknown, not recoil from it.

"Go," he said and opened the car door, pushing a thick puff of fog out toward the dark grounds dimly lit by strewn moonbeams filtering through the trees. Leaving his duffel bag and every possession he had to his name, Leam got out and headed toward the nearest of the many long rows of tombstones at Gaddiel's, disappearing into the fog's ghostly grasp.

CHAPTER 39

On the fourth floor of the Manor, Sara was in the hallway staring at a set of rusted daggers bolted to the wall. They began to quiver.

The doorbell chimed three stories below her—a long, majestic tone—and she turned and headed for the spiral staircase, black high heels staccato-tapping the wooden floor panels as she smoothed out the bottom folds of her sweater, then fixed her hair. She peered through the crack in the door as she passed her stepson's old bedroom, smiling. *If he wants back in this house, the little weasel, I'd like to see him try.*

Hurrying down the steps past the third floor, her smile broadened as she thought about the exploits that had taken place in the guestroom she had crafted down the hall a little over a week ago. Her pale legs—jutting out beneath her candy-red skirt—carried her past the second floor and down the last of the steps where she reached the main corridor. She crossed to the grand threshold and placed her hand flat against the center of the front door. It swung inward and she gasped.

A nanosecond moment of pleasure at seeing her lover broke apart like a stained-glass window shattered by a rock. Gideon stepped out of the fog and into the Manor, the door shutting closed behind him as he removed his black bowler hat and slung it on one of the silver beak-shaped hooks. Something in his bulging eyes scared Sara straight to the bones. Gone was the yearning and lust that she usually saw in them—the glimmer of playfulness. The lifelessness that sat in them now was cold and cruel.

"May I take your coat?" she asked, head downward, her neck bent by magic, her eyes on the shiny black shoes on his feet.

"We won't be staying long," Gideon said, walking past her toward the music room. Sara caught up with him.

"We?" she asked, doing her best to stay glued to his hip. He shot her a look that caused the word "sir" to babble out of her cherry-red lips.

"Yes, you and I," Gideon answered. "This pleases you, I'm sure."

"Yes, it does. Yes, it does." She turned her head away from him toward the huge entertainment/theater area on the left, fogging breath into her hand, which she sniffed for traces of wine. "Zach's down there in the music room," she added with pained effort at sounding casual.

"Why else would I be headed this way?" Gideon asked, and Sara squeaked. "This, too, pleases you, as it comes about of your request."

"Of course, sir, yes, of—"

Gideon held up a bony hand to silence her.

Sara swallowed hard as they came upon the music room, worried thoughts tap dancing around the floor of her brain, loud clacking that was void of any melody. Had she done something wrong? Or worse, had Zach done something wrong? Two steps from the closed door, Gideon opened it with a flick of his hand and ducked beneath the doorframe. Sara shuffled in behind him.

Lying with his back on the floor, shirtless and sweaty, Zach looked up, his eyes widening at the sight of the man entering the room. Zach slung himself to his feet, knocking the largest cymbal of a nearby set of drums to the floor, where it crashed and wobbled like a spinning top. He looked over at his mother as if in need of direction while the cymbal took an agonizing amount of time to teeter to a stop.

"No need for haste, Zach," Gideon said. "Remain calm until given a reason not to."

Zach blushed, hands in the pockets of his tiny running shorts. Gideon cocked his head, holding out his hand. A rush of thick dark smoke swarmed from his palm like a swirly nest of crows, swathing Zack's entire body in seconds. Watching her child disappear, Sara covered her mouth with both hands. Gideon grinned before pulling the smoke back into his hand, clearing the air. Zach was now dressed in cargo pants and a form-fitting T-shirt, both black.

"Better," Gideon said. "What I have asked you to prepare for—it might happen tonight so you must be ready. Do you understand?"

Zach nodded, brushing his hair behind his ears. "Anything you want me to do, sir, I'll do."

Gideon's eyebrows bounced. "Is that right?" he asked, smelling his own fingers. Zach nodded again. "A little proof, I suppose couldn't hurt. You've undoubtedly been honing your magical skills. Practicing, I'm sure. Tell me. Could you conjure up a batch of hot tar?"

"I could do that."

"Then let's make sure you're not a little liar, Zach, for anything I want you to do, you'll do, yes?"

"Yes."

"Then boiling-hot tar, from your hands, into your mother's face."

Zach's face went white as salt. He was silent for a moment—very still—then he raised a tattooed arm, his pointed hand aimed right at his mother's face. Expecting to be overwhelmed by the terror of having her face scalded, Sara was surprised that what she felt more than any other emotion right now was pride.

"At the third chime, young Zach," Gideon said, his smiling face frozen and mask-like. A padded mallet rose from a table in the corner, floating to the large bronze plate that was suspended from two gold-threaded ropes.

The mallet struck, a deep resonating punch of noise. Sweat dampened Zach's forehead. The mallet struck again. Sara gave her son the smallest of nods, then shifted her eyes to Gideon, whose grin had risen to eye level. Long seconds passed as the gong's second chime slowed and quieted. The mallet struck a third time and—SNAP—Zach jabbed his hand at Sara, scalding beads of black slop shooting right at her trembling face. The flood of tar was but an inch from striking when Gideon's hand shot out, his palm absorbing every drop. Sara shrieked, falling to the floor, covering her face as if she had actually been burned.

"YES!" Gideon roared. "*That* is dedication, young Zach! The choice between duty and family is simple, but not always easy. Well done."

Zack lowered his arm, breathing hard. Sara, who was cowering on the floor, saw that Zach was avoiding her eyes.

"A necessary test, Sara," Gideon said as she patted her unharmed face as if checking its temperature. "Don't fret, silly woman, no harm has been done to your appearance. Why would I want yours to be a mangled face of blotches and scars? Now get up off the floor, you're not a dog."

Sara rose to her feet and adjusted her skirt at the waist.

"Zach," Gideon said, "if you want to prove yourself to the Cause, this is that chance. Stay alert. Be ready. Do not fail."

"I'll be ready, sir," Zach said, his voice hollow. "I'll wait right here."

"Good," Gideon said, pivoting back toward the door. "Your mother comes with me."

Gideon walked out of the room. Sara had maybe a second before she had to follow suit, and used it to glance at Zach, who stood tall in his new black clothing. There wasn't time to share a moment with her son, but if there was, she wouldn't have taken it. She left the room, following Gideon to the Manor's center, leaving Zach and the quieting gong behind.

"You wanted your son to submerge deeper into Darkness and now he has," Gideon said. "But with that comes responsibility, which in turn warrants either reward or punishment. Your brazen request to expedite his rank has ridded him of any learning curve. It's good you know this now."

Sara nodded, fighting off tears. Gideon laughed.

"Say goodbye to this place, Sara."

"Well, what…why are we…where…"

"Out with it."

"Bram. Where…wha…what about Bram?" she whispered, struggling to look Gideon in the eye. "When he comes home—"

"*His* home."

"—he'll be wanting me."

"Bram's gone, silly woman."

"Gone how?" Sara glanced back at the music room. "Gone dead or gone missing?"

"Somewhere in between," Gideon answered. "Regardless, if he *resurfaces,* Bram will come to me." He stopped at the coat hanger to pluck his bowler hat off the beak-like hook. "As of this moment, your life has changed, Sara. Some of it you might like, a lot of it you won't. It makes no difference to me. Either way you're mine now."

Sara wrapped her arms around her front, suffocating on the type of fear that sneaks up from behind, fear for which there's no time to prepare. Gideon closed his eyes, tipped his head back a touch, and sniffed the air.

"Leam has gone, too, hasn't he?"

Sara nodded. "An hour ago. Maybe less."

"That's good. That's necessary."

"It is I who told him that he can't return." Sara's eyes narrowed. A smidge of the panic that had been tainting her voice lifted, as if the irritation and disgust caused by the slightest mention of her stepson could push the fear of her jeopardized wellbeing to the back burner.

The door swung open, and she followed Gideon outside into the night. "I was booby-trapping the mansion just now. When you…came for me."

"I see," Gideon said, walking by the tall statues that lined the Manor's approach, the fog up to his waist, the moon shining down on him like a giant spotlight hung from the center of the sky. He slowed, touching the side of his temple, then removed his hand, resuming his pace.

"Leam won't last two days out there on his own," Sara said, her high heels clicking down the cobblestoned driveway, arms still wrapped around her sweater-covered bosom. "Away from his cozy bedroom and his spoon-fed meals."

"You don't truly believe that, do you?" Gideon asked, turning to look at her. Sara kept her face neutral, careful not to commit to a yes or a no. "Never underestimate someone purely out of loathing. You might think differently of Leam's daring once we get to Headquarters."

"I will?" she asked, taking a tentative step closer. Gideon watched her move, and she saw his Adam's apple bob as if swallowing down a rush of saliva. He licked his big fish lips.

"A telemast just came in. I hope you're not feeling queasy tonight," he said, pulling her close. His breath attacked her in a cloud of nausea. "An associate of mine has returned, and you'll need a firm stomach to see what condition your stepson has left him in."

CHAPTER 40

He couldn't see a thing. Every so often his eye would catch the hard edge of a grave marker or the outline of a low, leafy branch, but for the most part, all that surrounded Leam was fog. Periodically, he'd crouch down in front of a line of tombstones, bending in close to read the names, but everything so far had been family plots, and his mother, Leam had a feeling, would be on her own.

Now, deep in Gaddiel's, the white haze looked to be shifting unnaturally. Leam narrowed his eyes, slowing his already cautious pace. He could see something…something coming at him from the depths of the fog…something getting closer…something—Leam gathered his nerve—taking the shape of a person.

Like a mummy emerging from a giant wall of toilet paper came a man who seemed to be an extension of the fog itself. As the man closed the space between himself and Leam, who had stopped dead with a hammering heart, his pure white color separated itself from the light gray haze. White hair brushed against the shoulders of his white suit, through the sleeves of which poked chalky-white hands. A sugar-white face, white shoes…it was as if the man had taken a shower with his clothes on where the water had been switched out for white paint.

Leam successfully fought the urge to run away. How often did a person come across someone like this? Even the guy's lips were white, Leam noticed, when the distance between the two had shrunk to a couple of yards. Leam's feet were glued to the ground by the time his gaze dipped and saw the hatchet at the man's side, also white, the blade edge sharp and gleaming in spite of the lusterless surroundings.

Leam couldn't find his voice. Any screaming thoughts of "Stop!" or "Get away!" got snagged in his throat. The man grinned, his thick fingers strumming the blade of the hatchet. His teeth, the one thing that should be white, were red.

"I guess it'll be up to me to start the introductions," the man said.

"Gideon..." Leam mumbled.

"What's that?"

"Gideon sent you to kill me?" Leam didn't recognize his own voice, soft, a low tremble. The man in white bared his red teeth. "Whatever happened out in that field I blacked it out."

"You're speakin' slop, laddy. I don't catch the meanin'."

"The associate."

The man in white shook his head, the expression on his face tantamount to shrugged shoulders.

"Gideon..." Leam hinted. "You don't work for Gideon?"

"Nope." The man in white leaned in, pushing his head closer to Leam, his black-dot pupils bleary, like a drop of ink on a napkin. "And you got as much magic as an Unk, don't ya? If I was sent to kill you, the stink of a corpse would already be stripin' down the grass as I dragged you out of here."

"You here to hurt me at all?"

"The blade of this hatchet ain't marked for the skin stretched over your neck, buckaroo."

Leam wobbled a step backward. "Who's it for, then?"

The man in white grinned red again. "I've been expectin' you, Leam."

Leam's eyes stayed locked on the man, ignoring the tips of the tombstones peeking out of the fog like rounded teeth jutting out of dirty white gums. "You must've been waiting long. This is the first time I ever came here."

"I said expectin', not waitin'. I ain't ever been to Gaddiel's either." Leam's eyes went back to the hatchet, prompting the man in white to add, "I promise you, bucky, I ain't here to hurt you."

Leam nodded in the slight but constant way a gambler wills his racehorse down the stretch. "Then what do you want from me?"

"Manners, manners." A smile of red. "I want to give you somethin'. That's all." From the inner folds of his white suit jacket, the man withdrew something shiny and black, dangling it from his finger for Leam to see.

"I *have* a watch," Leam said.

"This one's not for tellin' time." The man in white dropped the hatchet into the fog. Leam heard it thud into the grass. "There's somethin' I want you to see."

And the man in white threw his arms down viciously. The fog in the vicinity flattened toward the ground, then bounced back up and pushed backward, away from Leam and his new acquaintance, creating a hazy barrier around them. They now stood in a giant fog-free cylinder, like the calm center of a tornado that had stopped revolving. To Leam it seemed like a nut-job thing to do, until he saw the five tombstones lined up before him.

"The Duncans," Leam whispered, his eyes, in a swoop of wonderment, landing on the grave marker next to Abigail, bearing the name Christian.

"Right you are," the man in white said. "So you heard of 'em?"

"Yes," Leam said, without elaboration. He knelt down, tracing his fingers over the indentations of the carved out letters that spelled out the name of Graham and Madeline's son.

"Funny," the man in white said. "You don't find it odd to be in the company of a stranger who's got you trapped inside a tube of fog?"

Leam focused in on him. "Like you said, that axe doesn't have my name on it, and I've seen magic before."

"You believe the things I say then?"

"You're really not with Gideon, are you?" Leam asked, standing up. The man in white shook his head. "The Light, then?"

"The ballot box I step to is marked independent." The man in white folded his arms behind his back; the watch stayed, hovering a foot from his chest. "I pass this watch from prospect to prospect but I don't choose sides."

Before Leam could open his mouth, the man in white changed gears.

"I see you're drawn to Christian's tombstone, four in a rank of five. Fittingly, it's his left wrist this was last been wrapped 'round."

Leam kept his eyes on the watch and listened.

"As it becomes yours tonight, it did him eighteen years back. You feel a kinship to him, don't ya, the boy buried beneath your feet? His parents were *mixed* in their beliefs like yours. It's because of that he was murdered. You, Leam, are in no less danger now than he was then."

Leam felt his breath get short. "Did he do something wrong?"

"Can't help you there, laddy-buck. He was dead twelve days after I gave this to him. Overseas, I was, when it happened. Couldn't get to Harbing 'til a full week later. Got the watch out of evidence. Cops hadn't a clue what happened to them, the Duncan's. Hadn't even found out who they were. I left the detective their names and some money on his desk to see to it the family got buried proper. You can see he did a good 'nough job."

Leam thought he heard a whisper behind him and looked to see that no one was there. When he turned back, the watch was flying toward him. He snatched it out of the air. Both the band and dial were black. It had no face, no numbers, no hands, and it was as cold as ice.

"The watch is now your most important possession. I need you to understand that."

Leam thought of his mother's acorn and Bram's diamond, both locked in the Range Rover, which was devoured by fog somewhere outside of this frozen tornado.

"From a magical standpoint, it senses things that you can't," the man in white said.

"I don't know you," Leam said, his pinkies prickly below the skin. "This watch is my most important possession? Why? I'm supposed to believe everything you say? You're bleached white from head to toe standing in a graveyard. You're a cartoon character. And whatever you are, I've only known you for about five seconds. *The watch is my most significant possession? I don't even know your name!*"

The man in white smiled red.

"Tell me your name, please," Leam said.

"No."

"Do it."

"No."

"Why not?"

"Because I don't have one," the man in white said.

"Perfect!" Leam cried out and flung his hands in the air as he started pacing from one side of the cylinder to the other. "Great. Good. Very normal. You have a hatchet and a weird watch. You're covered in paste, or whatever, *and* you don't have a name. Why would you? That's not how things are. Why would *anything* be normal? Good. This is good. Fantastic. It's perfect." Leam stopped moving. "You know, you could've had the decency to make a name up—"

"The name's...Trevor."

"You're gonna mock me now. You're not finding me at a good time, okay? For Christ's sake, I just found out my mother was ki—" Leam cut himself off. The man in white took a step toward him.

"Was what, bucky?"

Leam shook his head. "Never mind. It doesn't matter."

"What does matter, then, lad? What do you really want to know? 'Cause the both of us know it's not my name."

"What's the watch for?"

"Hopefully you'll find that out."

"Not good enough!" Leam cocked his arm back and threw the watch as hard as he could at the man in white's face.

The man caught it with clamping red teeth and spit it out into his paint-white hand. Leam read the face opposite his own; it seemed more sympathetic than annoyed.

"If I knew, I'd tell you. Theories. That's what I have, nothin' more. I send them away with this…" he held up the watch, "… next I see them, they're dead."

"Who?"

"The prospects."

"Prospects? What do you mean?"

As he stared in at Leam, the man in white's shoulders dropped with a big huff. "*You* are a prospect, laddy. That's what this's all about."

"Prospect for what? What prospect?" Leam asked, shaking his head.

"The one spoken about in the prophecies."

It was Leam who grinned now, white not red. "Yeah right."

"Do I look like the kinda man who kids around?"

The sincerity in the man in white's eyes slapped the grin off Leam's face, stiffening Leam's body as if the blood coursing through him had frozen, his veins rivers of solid ice.

"*The* prophet? Me? The one who will win the war?"

The man in white nodded. "Prophet…messiah…savior…whatever you want to call it. You're the top prospect in the world, Leam."

Something Leam heard in the man's voice rang true—whether it was or wasn't, that was a different story, but Leam could tell that the man in white believed what he had said was the truth. Leam staggered backward, grasping for support. His unsteady hand found Abigail's tombstone, which he sat on, clutching Christian's to brace himself.

Prophet…prospect…prophet…prospect. Two weeks ago Leam was picking lint out of his toes in his bedroom, hiding from the world.

He shut his eyes hard. It felt like someone had shaken a can of seltzer and cracked it open inside his brain, a different question, a different consideration, rising from each popped bubble.

One thought, though, rose highest through the fizz, a bit more ticklish than the rest.

"Prophecies..." Leam pinched the bridge of his nose. "That's what you said. You're saying there's more than one?"

"Always has been."

"But I don't get it. How does Gideon and all the rest of them know which prophecy to believe?"

"You're not getting' me," the man in white said, shifting his weight from foot to foot, his hair sweeping across his shoulders like rubber car wash noodles over the hood of a white car. "There's only one Prophecy of Darkness. The other's for the Light."

"The Light?"

"Lots you don't know, huh, laddy? That'll change."

Leam shook his head. Everything lately seemed to make him shake his head.

"They're the same, just worded a little different," the man in white elaborated. "I don't know them exact, it's like the game telephone cuz words heard from many mouths over the years don't get repeated right. As it is, as I know it to be, is that Darkness's says a prophet will be born half Dark, half Light who will possess the essential piece necessary to their victory. The Light's is the same, with a prophet born from parents of opposite sides, who they say will destroy what Darkness needs to win the war."

"So a half Dark, half Light...a *hybrid*," Leam said, thinking of the term used by Ward Thorne in Bram's murder itinerary, "could be the prophet of either."

"Right you are, bucky-boy."

"It's absurd. It can't be me, I'm not—"

The man in white held up a hand. "*Prospect*, laddy, that's all I said. You're a prospect now, nothin' more, so don't go gettin' ahead of yourself."

"That's all? *That's all?*" Leam was struck with sudden lightheadedness.

"But if it is you," the man in white said, "then in the future, at some point...it'll be you who decides the fate of the world. You'll defeat one or the other."

Again, whether right or wrong, Leam was certain that the man in white believed what he was saying to be the truth. Leam swallowed hard, looking down at his hands, still gripped over the top of Christian's grave marker. His mouth was as a dry as a rice cake. Something black and polished floated into his line of sight as the man in white's words—gentle but clear—found his ear.

"I give this watch to you eighteen years after it was removed from the young man's hand, cold and lifeless, whose tombstone you are now touchin' with your hand, warm and blemished."

Leam plucked the icy timepiece from the air, fastening the band around his wrist. In a few seconds, the watch had warmed as if heated by his blood, and the circular wall of fog began to thin, spreading back toward Leam and the strange man, filling in the space, the cloudy gray air returning to where it had originally been.

"That's yours now," the man in white said, coaxing a few wayward strands of white hair behind his ear. "I ask that you never trade it, sell it or give it away. It's no ordinary watch. If it becomes lost, you won't be replacing it at Walmart, laddy-buck, that's for damn sure."

"But if everyone it was given to before me has failed—"

"Failed and died," the man in white cut in.

"—then why would I want it?"

"Because one day a prospect will survive." The man in white grabbed the handle of his hatchet, yanking the blade out of the grass. "And you should know the most unique difference between you and Christian, and all the others, is those tattoos."

Leam looked at his hands. The delightenment scar on the left one was whiter than normal in juxtaposition with the black watch strapped beneath it.

"You're not a fool, Leam Holt, you know you're odd, even in a world filled with magic. Everythin' I've said won't seem so crazy or impossible in a few weeks' time. If you last that long. Like I said, you're in terrible danger, from here 'til the end, whenever the end is for you, or for the world. It's my guess that those tattoos will help you to stay alive."

"I never delightened, so…" Leam looked up at the man in white, "…so I just wonder what they could be for."

"Where were you when you got them?"

"The sitting room at my house," Leam breathed. "My father's house, I mean."

"If you want to find out…you know, find out why you failed…that might be a good place to start."

Leam pictured the Manor, imagining all the defensive enchantments and traps that Sara had most certainly put into place. The man in white swung the hatchet up, resting the handle on his shoulder.

"Out of curiosity," the man said, walking away backward, smoothing out the breast of his white suit jacket, "how do you feel about Unknowings?"

Leam took a moment to think before answering, "I don't see how it's their fault they don't know."

The man in white grinned his red grin, the rest of him meshing with the fog crawling around the trees and tombstones. Leam expected him to say something else—a goodbye, a good luck, a good knowing ya—but he said nothing more and disappeared, his outline fading away a few seconds after the inside had vanished.

All that remained was the fog and Leam, who was trying to decide whether to seriously freak out about everything he now knew, resume his search for his mother's grave or get going on figuring out why his delightenment had failed, which, of course, began at the one place he'd been forbidden to ever return.

CHAPTER 41

There's no freaking way. A prophet? The prophet? What is he crazy, I couldn't even delighten! Zach got delightened, and he's the biggest ass-jack in the world!

Leam was driving the Range Rover through the streets of Harbing like it was a rat on steroids juicing through a maze. He'd left Gaddiel's without finding his mother's grave or any clues about Bram's disappearance, but he'd figured he could return to those quests later. Right now there was someplace he needed to be. The air conditioner was blasting, a background of white noise for the incessant beeping of the seatbelt alarm alerting Leam it had yet to be fastened.

I can't defend myself. I can't light things on fire with my mind. I can't throw a rock through a window without using my hands.

"But if it is you," Leam said out loud sarcastically, "it'll be you who decides the fate of the world."

Get real, he thought, as he pounded the accelerator, the Range Rover flying down Monroe Avenue, fog lights working overtime, head lamps illuminating a small huddle of people gathered together on the sidewalk as Leam spun out onto Falcon Street and gunned it past Black Patch Park. It was the third grouping he had spotted since leaving Gaddiel's, each person draped in a black neck-to-foot trench coat.

Leam's heart had been beating like an electric mixer set on stir ever since Bram's knife handle had spun itself into a hog man, but all the craziness he knew about himself now, and the sight of trench coat people everywhere he looked, had flipped the switch all the way to blend. What was the deal with these trench coaters? He knew they were men and women of Darkness, but why were they convening in Harbing? Had Gideon sent them looking for Bram? Or were they all here because of Leam? To find him? To kidnap him? Kill him? *Praise* him? About twenty minutes ago, Leam's initial shock at the man in white's revelations had been switched out for utter disbelief of everything. But now...

A glint of light from one of the headlights bounced off the *S* of a stop sign Leam was blowing through, ricocheting off the black faceless watch on his wrist and piercing into his eye. He squinted at the watch, gripping the steering wheel vice-like, knuckles bone white, questioning if the watch had significance, and if it was indeed *possible* that he, Leam, was a prospect.

The man in white had warned of danger, and Leam felt it following him like kids chasing an ice cream truck. The fact that his eyes were in the rearview mirror as much as they were on the road hadn't escaped his notice.

The thing about it, though, was that he couldn't dodge the danger, he couldn't stop Darkness from coming for him. If Gideon wanted him, Gideon would get him, Leam knew that. And whatever the reason—Leam could think of several, starting with the whole associate dilemma—they were going to come for him at some point. All he could control were the things he would do until that time came, two of which spoke to him louder than the rest. One was to get to the sitting room of the Manor where his hands had been branded with white tattoos—the starting point of discovering what went wrong with his delightenment, according to the man in white. The other action—as Leam screeched off Falcon onto Stoneladen Lane—was coming up about twenty houses on his right.

———

Amidst the midnight deadness, Eloa was sitting in a white wicker chair on the front porch gazing out at the heavy woodlands across the street, her iPhone in her hand, Barry the beagle lying beside her, looking up at her with an occasional wag of his tail. Behind her, bluish-white light from the TV flickered behind the drawn curtain of the living room window; Mary had stayed up late to watch Pierce Brosnan on Letterman. Laid out before Eloa, beyond the yard, the dark night sky took turns vying for her eye with the white fog.

It had to be past midnight by now and it felt like she'd been outside for about half an hour. She was still dressed in today's black sleeveless blouse and jeans, though earlier in her bedroom for a blink of madness, she had almost stripped down to slip on the slutty red dress Porlo had caught her wearing over a week ago. Instead, she had settled for a little bit of mascara.

Her phone buzzed: one new message from Bridgette.

Staring at her friend's illuminated name, a stab of guilt and a mild sort of vindictive satisfaction hit Eloa equally hard. As tough as it was to admit—and in fact she hadn't admitted anything to Bridgette concerning the enigmatic Flower Boy—Eloa liked how this weird, complicated and possibly mentally sick boy had *for years* ignored Bridgette, the Unknowing with whom Eloa had always wanted to trade lives. And he had sought out Eloa, instead, displaying obvious feelings of attraction.

She swiped her finger left to right, tapped the lock code in and read, *Like 50 guys from my party want ur #, u sexpot!*

Before Eloa had a second to process the message, a *smacking* sound snatched at her ears. Her head tilted in the direction of the rundown garage on her right, only to recognize after *smack* number two that the disturbance was coming from the left near the stairs. Barry's tail slapping the weathered wooden panels of the porch floor.

She pocketed her phone and leaned over, scratching the furry folds of skin beneath his collar for a few seconds, smiling at the funny look it gave him. She sat up, shutting her eyes and letting out a long, quiet sigh. She wished Leam would get here already. Ants had crawled into her pants, sitting here waiting with nothing to keep her company besides the dog and the fog, which was now starting to disperse. In a few hours it would be completely gone, until late tomorrow evening. She hadn't been living in Harbing long, but each night she wished this gloomy haze would stay away for good—that if it didn't return, maybe her dad would—but each night her wish remained just that.

His absence and the unshakeable memory of the bloody lock of blond hair embedded in their living room carpet had been weighing her down as much as the heavy starfish hanging from her neck. She guessed it was because she had no one to really talk to about it. She hadn't heard from Porlo in nine days, and he was the only non-Unk she'd had any contact with since forever.

A pair of headlights swept around the street bend coming from the left, getting bigger and closer until an SUV stopped in front of the yard, the lights cutting off with the engine. Barry sat up stiff, watching a young man get out and stride toward the house. Eloa thought Leam still looked pale but better than he had earlier tonight lying on the sidewalk.

"Hey," he said, coming up onto the porch. He stopped dead as if he had smacked into an invisible wall. "Whoa you look hot," he blurted out. His cheeks caught color as his eyes shifted somewhere else.

Eloa felt her stomach flip. She ran a hand through her hair from scalp to shoulders and realized he'd only ever seen her in a ponytail.

Leam bent down to pet Barry, who, to Eloa's amazement, didn't bark or scurry away. She heard a *squeak-squeak* and saw Leam set down a blue plastic-bone squeeze toy between the dog's front legs.

"What's that?" she asked.

"I thought he might want it. I found it clearing out my room."

"You have a dog?"

"We did," Leam said. He stared off for a moment. "It didn't work out."

"Oh." She patted the wicker seat of the empty chair. "You want to sit?"

"No, thanks."

"You don't want to sit down?"

"I can't."

"Why?"

"I don't know, I just can't. I'm too...I don't know." He ruffled Barry behind the ears and rose out of his crouch. "So, I have to tell you some stuff, but I wanted to say I was sorry first."

Eloa clasped her hands together. "Okay, what for?"

"Everything earlier, when we talked, it was all about me. We barely talked about you and what's going on with your father. That's not right, so let me hear what's going on?"

"With my dad?"

"Yeah. Do you want to talk about that, or..."

A silence sat between them for a few flickers of blue TV light.

"Leam," Eloa said, blinking, her fingers over her mouth. "Oh, Leam," she said again, feeling her face change, feeling it scrunch together in the somewhat ugly way it did the moment before crying, the moment before the release—a release from the worry and anxiety that she had refused to let go of—and with that release came wet eyes and a flood of words.

"I'm so worried about him, Leam. He's all I have, and I have this pit in my chest that I try to ignore but it's there and it gets tighter all the time, and that tightness, I think it's saying that he's never coming back, that he's dead or something, that he's gone.

"And he'd do anything for me, Leam, like yours would you," she went on, sitting in her chair looking up at him, as his face went red, went angry, if that was possible, his head cocked to the side as he listened. "When I was little, I overheard him telling Mary that no matter what happened to me, or whatever situation I got into, he would be there to protect me, to love me, to help—" her voice broke, "—to *help* me, to keep me safe, no matter what, that's what he said, no matter what, no matter what, and that nothing could ever stop him. He said that his heart would keep pounding as long as I still needed him, that nobody could get in the way of that, Leam, that nothing could be as strong as the love I had put in his heart the moment he first saw me. And I do, Leam, I need him, I still need him, I…"

Leam took a half step forward, to comfort her, maybe, but she waved him away.

"I'm a mess, I'm sorry." She wiped beneath her eyes with the pads of her fingers. "I never get like this. I just, I guess I needed to—"

"You had to *vent*," Leam forced out, his jaw muscles clenched.

"I guess I did," she said, sniffling. "And I did, so…so talk to me."

He was standing with his back against one of the railing posts, looking down, looking uneasy, his chest rising and falling in the tempo of a man in need of regaining control. She was flattered by how much he was affected by her anguish.

"You said you had some things to say to me?" she asked, trying to coax his eyes away from the floor.

"You look like a duck when you cry."

Eloa chortled. "Okay…" His face remained set, as if he was trying to see through the floor boards. "Will you talk to me?"

Leam scrunched up his face, and then let it fall. "Outside the Sip, I said that I'd tell you the truth and—and I told you I knew your secret—" his eyes snapped up at her, "—and I do. I know who you are, Eloa."

Eloa felt her breath catch in her throat like it was barbed wire.

"I know you're of the Light."

She couldn't move—frozen—just staring at him, rooted to her seat. *How does he know? He's an Unknowing. Unknowings don't know.*

"Leam," she breathed. "How could you possibly…?"

"A man told me in the coffee shop that day. Strange guy…a Light guy."

"Then how are you so—" She studied his face, got a sense of his posture. He was acting as if this was normal conversation, the same way as if he had said he wanted to go to Dairy Queen. "Wait…"

Leam grinned. "I'm magical, too."

She felt her eyes widen larger than normal and her mouth fell open. "Of course! *Of course!* How did I not see it? You're Light, too!" She hopped up, a smile coming over her face as his vanished like a scared bunny. "You jerk! You kept it from me this whole time?"

"I'm not of the Light."

"Why wouldn't you say anything? This is amazing!"

"Listen to me! *I'm not of the Light!*"

"What? What are you talking about?" She looked at him, she looked at him hard, and his eyes weren't lying. "No..." She felt her face go ice numb.

"I'm Dark. Actually, I'm half Dark, half Light, but I just found that out. All I've ever known is Darkness."

Eloa covered her mouth, tottering backward toward the blue-blinking window, behind which emitted a muffled drone of studio-audience applause.

"Hold on." Leam took a step forward. "Listen to me, okay?"

"Don't you move one more foot. Not a foot or I'll scream."

"Eloa—"

"Get away!" Barry hopped up, growling. "Barry, *stay!*"

"Let me explain," Leam said. "It's not what you think. Trust me."

"Trust you? You tell me you've been lying to me, you tell me that you're evil, and you want me to trust you. Are you insane?"

"Please stop looking so scared. I can't deal with that, I'm not a monster. I don't want to hurt you. I'm not gonna lie to you. I've kept this from you, but I never lied."

"Like when you told me that horrible man with those Mohawks was a family friend?"

"A family friend, not my friend."

"Right."

"That was before I found out what you were. Don't stand there and try to say that you didn't keep things from me. To hide your identity?" Leam inched forward again but stopped when he saw how it made her shiver. "I wanna explain myself, and then I'll go. You wanted the truth, then I'm gone and I'll stay gone."

She read his face, finding her hands held out protectively, like she was trying to push an invisible dresser. He looked so earnest and she remembered his awkward pursuit of her. She nodded and Leam pounced.

"Tonight, after I saw you, the weirdest things have happened, you wouldn't even believe, and the craziest is that my mother, my mother, I found out, wasn't Dark. And she wasn't an Unk. So that means I'm not all Dark, I'm just as much Light. So what I gotta do is I gotta find out what side I'm meant for. That's all I can try to do, and I have one lead, and that's what I'm going on."

"So, why'd you come here?" she asked, still shivering.

"'Cause I told you I would."

"Well, you can go."

Leam swallowed hard, and she saw his pinkies twitching, his weight shifting from foot to foot. "Didn't you hear what I said?" he asked.

"What'd you think?" She felt her chest getting hot, despite the cold touch of the starfish arms. "That you'd tell me you were some evil murdering psycho, and then we'd get together and start dating?"

"Hey, I get you want nothing to do with me—"

"How perceptive!"

"But listen, what I told you in front of the Sip...how I could never be with you, it...well, I guess what was black has grayed a little, you could say."

"What are you talking about, *Leam?* You're Dark!"

"I know that! But I didn't pick to be."

"So!"

"So, you gonna yell at a left-handed guy for being left-handed?"

"My *dad*—whatever happened to him—*your people* probably did it! YOUR PEOPLE!"

"Again, I'm Not. All. Dark. The other half of me is whatever makes up the whole of you."

"You deceived me!"

"And what would you call what you did, huh? You're acting like I intentionally lied to you, Eloa, it was Widget who fed you all that bipolar crap, not me. If you'd let me talk, you'd be hearing me say that none of it matters anyway."

"None of it matters anyway... You said that once already tonight."

"But that was..." He took a breath with tiny little shakes of his head. "It's for a different reason now."

"What's changed?"

"It's not a firm no," Leam answered. "It's *possible* now—"

"You're out of your mind."

"It's been done before, is what I mean." Leam clasped his hands together, rooting his feet to the floor boards. "Pretending you didn't hate my guts, it's possible now."

"So, if you're saying it's possible now, why does none of it matter?"

"How 'bout my life expectancy is somewhere around eight hours. It's not safe for you to be around me."

"How was I supposed to know that?"

"You're not," Leam said, "I'm telling you now."

"So, you came here, *to me,* because it's not safe for me to be around you?"

Leam smacked his palms together, the fingers grabbing tight. "*I'm not staying.*"

"So what's the big danger?"

"All prospects—" Leam stopped. He wiped his brow, his right foot tapping the porch floor, the knee above it jumpy. His face looked strained, like he was aching to tell her something that he knew he shouldn't.

"Because what?" Eloa asked again.

"Because they're coming for me," he said, but she could tell by his face that there was plenty more to it than that.

"Who, exactly?"

"They. The half of me that disgusts you. Haven't you seen any of the trench coat people around?"

Eloa felt her body tighten up, like her ligaments were strung-together fishing lines yanked taut by the jerk of a rod. "I've seen them."

"Tonight?"

She nodded. "Before I found you passed out on the sidewalk. I didn't think anything of it. The trench coats, that's Darkness?" She remembered the men that had come out of his dad's flower shop before Bridgette had given her a ride home that day.

"Yes," he answered.

"And they're after you?"

"I think so."

"But you're one of their own!"

"Thank you, I know that."

"Then *leave,* Leam!" Her eyes swept the length of Stone-laden Lane. "Mary and Larry...I haven't purified, I can't protect them!"

"I am leaving. I'm going right now. I have to get home before they get me."

"Why home?" The question had run out on its own and there was no way to harness it back in.

"I don't get it," he said. "Do you want me to stay or to go?"

She pulled her eyes away from the darkness beyond the yard, beyond the street. "I want you to go, but I wanna know why you're going." Inside her head it hadn't sounded so bratty. "I hate you for that."

"Good," Leam said. "'Cause I'm not gonna tell you anyway."

"You brought it up, not me," Eloa fired back, amidst a conscious effort to keep her ears more alert for the rustling of trench coats.

"No, I'm not gonna say anything..."

She hadn't noticed when it shifted, but the expression on his face was that of a nervous little schoolboy.

"...you'd think it's stupid," he was saying, "or egotistical, or—"

"You don't know that."

"Do you smell that? I smell cookies. Do you smell sugar cookies?"

"Stop dodging!" Eloa snapped, and Leam's eyes came back to her. "You said you got kicked out of your house, so why are you going back?"

There was movement in her periphery. Barry, maybe, or something past him, but she stayed on Leam.

"My hands," he said. His chest deflated and he looked even younger. "The markings."

"I thought they were scars."

"Whatever they are, I think they mean something."

"Mean something?"

"They have to."

"Okay, so say they do. What's at home?"

"It's where I was when they formed." Leam held out his shaky hands. She saw the white shape on each, like a horseshoe from pointer to thumb. His fingers were moving without pattern, maybe to offset the trembling, as if they were manipulating puppet strings.

"That's the reason they're after you, isn't it?" she asked, her top teeth scraping over her bottom lip.

"Maybe. I don't know."

"It is. It's your hands."

"*I* think they're important, Eloa. I have no idea if they do."

"Yeah right."

"I don't. But I know they know I'm a hybrid, and they—"

"It's your hands, don't you see?" She couldn't believe he didn't see it.

"What are you doing?" he asked as she moved closer to him.

"Your hands. *Your hands*." Her skin was tingling. "That's the connection. It's why you like me."

As Eloa went to him, she could see his Adam's apple bounce. She could see he wanted to back away—in another step, the space between them would snuggly fit a stack of dance mats—and yet he didn't. He stayed, and she gazed down at his hands, took one step closer, and grabbed them with hers.

He was standing in a dark forest, fog hovering over the soil and hiding the ground upon which he was standing, swirling almost up to his knees. It was like a forest that had grown out of the clouds. Black leaves were falling off the branches of black trees, raining down all around him and melting into the whitish-gray fog, which began to darken as more and more charcoal leaves were sucked into its hold. Between the trunks of two black trees, pure white smoke emerged, and twisted and puffed itself into the head of a magnificent white horse. From its mouth spewed dark red vapor, until the stallion vanished behind the trees, and all Leam saw was a forest of dark clouds.

He felt his feet go numb and looked down to see the dark fog ascending, climbing past his knees, up his thighs, covering his waist, swallowing his stomach and reaching up his chest to his neck. The fog immobilized every part of his body as if he had been fastened inside an invisible straight jacket. As the fog engulfed his face, he gulped air, sniffed it in streams through his nostrils—it smelled of wet cigarettes—and the instant pure panic grabbed his system, the ground broke and he was dropping now, falling through the dark clouds.

He dropped and dropped in a massive free-fall, gaining speed, his skin getting cold, falling, falling, falling, until, for a short second, he saw an infinite amount of wide open sky above an ocean of water, and...

CRACK!

His feet slammed down onto what felt like concrete. Pain rippled throughout his body, his legs buckling beneath him as he crashed through the surface. His lungs constricted as he shot twenty or thirty meters deep into freezing cold water.

He opened his eyes and ice water slapped him in the eyeballs. He could see a sheet of light glowing beneath him. His instinct to live, to swim to the surface and breathe, was bludgeoned by his curiosity, and his feet kicked with vigor, his arms propelling him deeper into the lake toward the light. He passed a dark living creature that was swimming upward. Leam looked into its mean, black eyes. It was the fox he had seen before, a white bird, dead, clenched between its teeth. The fox shot up to the surface, Leam continuing his descent, his lungs losing air.

As he plummeted deeper, the spread of light was expanding. When he reached the shining lake floor, he realized it was also the glass ceiling of a gleaming white room, stationary beneath the icy water.

Again, Leam's will to live pleaded with him, begging for him to swim upward to the surface and devour the oxygen so far above, yet the grip of his curiosity was too strong and he pushed his face against the glass. It was the same room he had been in during the coffee shop vision, and he could see the likeness of himself from that vision, standing in the room below.

From his bird's eye view, he watched that vision's fox slink up to the white bird. A sound clinked to his right. Leam looked away from the glowing room and saw something several feet away. It was the dirty, wooden oar that the wind had torn from his hand in one of the first visions, where he had been rowing a small boat in a thunderstorm, a woman covered in unnaturally white scales seated at the bow.

The oar began to change color as it floated away from him, clinking against the glass, its earthy, wooden hue turning school-bus yellow. He was completely out of breath, with no chance of making it to the surface, so he surged after the yellow oar, chasing it through the crystal clear water, and...

"LEAM! Look at me!"

Leam inhaled sharply. He looked like he was in pain, squirming on his back on the porch floor.

"Leam! You're here! You're safe!"

"Put me back," he croaked, his hands wringing out his dry T-shirt as if it were soaked through.

"You fell over! Your hands ripped away from me and you fell to the ground!"

"Put me back."

"Are you hurt? You should've heard the horrible noises coming out of—"

"PUT ME BACK!" Leam yelled, sitting up off the floor.

"Wh-what? What do you mean? I can't just—"

"Put me back, Eloa! Take my hands, I have to go back in, I have to follow it! I know this is important! Take 'em, take 'em, take 'em, take my hands, right now, take 'em!"

A crazy glint maddened his eyes, both scaring and arousing her. As he climbed to his feet, she flicked her eyes across every inch of his face, searching him, feeling something, feeling connected. He said her name once more and she lunged forward and clasped her hands over his.

Water again. Cold water shivering against the skin of his flailing arms and legs, his lungs beginning to suffocate once more. He could still see the yellow oar, but faintly. It must have drifted away when he had been sucked back to the porch. He tore through the water high above the white room, chasing the oar that was leading him farther into the unknown. With his eyes glued on the oar, he wondered what was going on in the room beneath him, wondered if that Leam was watching the fox tear the white bird to shreds, wondered if he were ever inside that room again, would he be able to see himself swimming above the glass. He swam and swam, and the glow of the room faded, disappearing in his wake. The water darkened.

With his lungs in a fit of convulsions, the fleeing yellow oar beckoned him still. He thrashed through the water until, again, it began to lighten, but with an emerald greenish hue. He could see what was around him more clearly, the yellow oar slowing as it approached two other oar-shaped sticks of the same size floating in front of it.

He was gaining on the three, but his body was showing signs of surrender, the fight in him mere moments away from conceding to the cold water, allowing it to surge into his lungs and drown away the pain, which had become unbearable. He was going to die, he was sure of it. But then he felt a spark flicker from within, and he willed himself into the same state of tranquility that had come over him right before the appearance of the bubble in the park; the same brief sense of calm that had spread over him as the Walls of Doom had boxed him into a tiny metal cube.

His mind relaxed. His body relaxed. He swam with fluid motion, darting toward the three oars that were now almost touching: the yellow one that had guided him here; the second one, which looked like a normal, wooden oar; and the third, which now seemed to be made of glinting, gilded bronze.

He was so close. He knew if he was able to reach them in time, he would survive, that he would live to keep fighting. Only a few meters away from him now, the tips of the three oars were inches from touching each other, about to make a triangle, and as they came together, within the triangle they were forming, began to glow an abyss of emerald green. Leam was almost upon it, ready to swim through, into the brilliant green, and...

She felt him suck in a huge pull of air, then his eyelids twitched, his breathing instantly back to normal; hers, however, was jagged and uncomfortable. She was sprawled on her back, the floor boards giving a little, with him face down on top of her, their lips almost touching.

"Leam." She felt the heat of his breath meet hers. "You're crushing me."

He rolled off her and stood up like a bolt. "Hurt you, didn't mean hurt you, no," he muttered, his hands shaking as his gaze darted around at everything and nothing.

"Leam, what's wrong?" He paid her no attention. "What are you seeing when we touch?" She could hear fear and panic in her voice, understandably, yet the inflection was tainted by a sort of pathetic concern for his wellbeing that spilled onto each word. "Something's happening, you're not yourself."

"What?" he said. "What? What?"

"You're unhinged, Leam!"

"Who?"

"I can see it in your eyes!"

"Forget that!" His words showered out in a spitty blur. "What happened? What happened *here*, right *here*?"

"To me?"

"WHAT HAPPENED HERE ON THE PORCH?"

"Nothing, I don't know. Wh-wh-what do you mean? Your—your—your breathing kept getting heavier...louder... you thrashed around and we fell over. I kept hold of your hands but you were so... Your face was all contorted like you were hurt, or being hurt and I...I just let go."

She watched him, horrified, as he paced from door to window, his face twitching, smiling, frowning, his teeth biting air. Behind the veneer of lunacy, he still looked so young, innocent, scared. And just as she felt herself softening, he burst into a fit of laughter, his face going red for a fleeting second before revving up into an unsightly mess of purple.

"What the hell is wrong with you?" Eloa snapped. It felt like a long thin nail had split her skull, yet a jolt of anger had resulted, not pain.

"The visions," he cackled, his temple veins throbbing like squeezed worms, his shoulders taking turns brushing against the house as his legs took him from side to side. "It's like they're attacking my psyche or something. My head feels all swimmy, like I can't grab onto my thoughts. They're so real, they're so so real, so they can't be visions anymore, can they?"

Before she could answer, the laughter intensified, his lips pulling back so far away from the teeth she could see his gums.

"You're *laughing*," she sputtered out. "You're *insane*—"

"It's all I can do to keep from breaking down crying! Is that what you want? Huh? Is that what you wanna see?"

Eloa slid to the front railing, putting more distance between herself and Leam, who had stopped dead in front of the curtained window, the flickering light emanating from the room behind him playing tricks on her eyes; the soft, bluish-white glow seemed to blur his edges fuzzy, like he had been transported from old time TV.

She looked away, out past the front yard, drawn by a sense of being watched, and though she saw nothing, that same sense imparted to her that whatever she couldn't see was big and moving steadily by.

When she turned back, she screamed. Directly in front of her was Leam's snarling face, an inch away, while in her periphery a few porch lights of neighboring houses popped on, and a scattering of windows awoke.

"The white bird," Leam whispered.

"*What?*"

"Tilt your head."

She did so; an instinctual reflex. He staggered back a few steps, his face less contorted, eyes less wild. Eloa fled to the far end of the porch, letting out a gasping, shuddering breath, as if she had narrowly dodged being violated.

"On your neck," he said. "The dove."

"My birthmark?" She could feel the sharp pulse of her heart in every vein.

Leam stood statue still by the two empty chairs. "I've seen it in the visions."

"I was in there with you? You saw me?"

"The bird, I saw, okay? The bird!"

"Okay! What was it doing?" she asked, aware of the muted noises coming through the wall: creaking stairs, hurried footsteps.

"It gets killed and eaten by a fox."

"What?"

"Does that mean anything to you?"

"No."

"A fox, Eloa, are you sure?"

"I've never even seen a fox!" she hissed through a whisper, not that it mattered anymore, the whole street was up.

"Listen to me," Leam said, "if these freaking things I'm seeing, or living inside of or whatever, if they have meaning, then you might be in danger, right? I mean, maybe, right?"

"You said *you're* the danger!"

"Not like this."

"Oh my God, *Leam*! Get out of my life!"

The front door, with a great squelch, swung inward. The screen door flung open, slammed against the house and tore off at the hinges, Barry scurrying out of its way. Right before Leam bolted, Eloa caught something deep in his eyes, far back behind the madness that had seized them. Defeat.

"GET GONE!" Larry shouted, shuffling out onto the porch, led by the belly of his robe.

After two quick steps, Leam's hands slapped the railing and he projected himself over some sorry looking bushes, his Nikes hitting the shabby grass on the move.

"WHO IS THAT?" Larry roared, shaking his fist in the air, the other hand grasping what it could of his lower back.

"Hey!" Eloa yelled to Leam, finding her voice. He was already halfway across the lawn. "Leam, your hands!"

Beneath her bare feet, the floorboards shook all the way back to the door as Larry shouted something about calling the police.

"LEAM!" Eloa cried out, and this time he swung around. "Your birthmarks, they were glowing! During the vision, they were white, they were glowing!" She saw him hold up his hands; it looked like he was holding a pair of dying flashlights. The transformation from poker face to childlike euphoria was instantaneous.

"Something's happening, all right," he said. "Something's stirring up tonight!" He spun away, beeping the car door unlocked as he bolted to it and swung it open.

Breathing heavily and clutching the silver starfish against her chest, Eloa watched him hop into the driver's seat and turn the engine over with a roar. The silver Range Rover sped off down Stoneladen, leaving her to wonder if either the cops or the trench coaters would intercept him, this manic-depressive Unknowing turned half Dark, half Light boy on the run.

CHAPTER 42

"Garrick!"

Gideon swept through the entrance door, brushing his fingers over the gilded bronze *Dressing of the Unk* statue that depicted two men in trench coats lowering a cloth over a naked Unknowing. Sara was a step behind him, marveling, for the first time, at the huge gleaming space that was the front room of the Headquarters of Darkness.

"Where is he, Garrick?" Gideon called out, his voice amplified over the constant wasp-like drone of the blistering hot room. Garrick's head poked out from a door just appearing in the gold-plated back wall, his body able to stay hidden courtesy of his neck's length and elasticity.

"They took him up to Cleanwalker's," Garrick called back.

"Is he alive?"

"Was when he went up."

"When?"

"Twenty minutes ago."

Gideon strode to his right for the ivory staircase. "Come," he said to Sara, who obeyed immediately, her black high heels clicking against the off-white squeaky-clean floor for a sixty-yard stretch. On their quick journey from New Jersey to D.C., she'd remained three steps behind Gideon, as he had instructed her, and she did so now up the stairs.

At the top of the landing was a three-pronged split. A hallway known as the Bolt ran straight, cutting down the center of the second story of DHQ, which housed departmental offices, conference rooms, and small scale training facilities. The hallway that branched off to the left, dimly lit by tiny globes of yellow light, led to Gideon's private quarters. The hallway to the right, which Gideon and Sara began to walk down, was unlit— somewhere in the middle of pitch black and dusk—with a dot of bright white light beckoning at the very end.

"What's Cleanwalkers, sir?" Sara asked. Gideon took his time with the reply, feeling the chill of the passageway that greeted him.

"Cleanwalker is a man, not a thing or a place. He's a doctor of sorts. Deals with illness and curse wounds that others are unable to heal. Solves medical quandaries that others cannot or dare not try."

"And your associate was brought to him because of something my stepson did?"

"Yes." Gideon turned his head back as he kept moving forward, seeing the faint illumination on Sara's face brighten with each step. "Mind your tongue."

As they neared it, the dot of light took a square shape, and was soon definable as the window on a small steel door. Gideon held out his palm and the door swung open, sucking him and Sara through its frame as if they were magnetically drawn by what lay inside. Gideon heard Sara shudder, reveling at how her eyes danced around their new surroundings in revulsion.

Both side walls of the narrow room consisted of eight cube-shaped display windows, four on each side, with a second steel door straight ahead. Other than the glass panes through which to view, the other seven sides of the display boxes were comprised of solid sheets of cold, bluish-tinted fluorescent light. The room had the feel of an Apple retail store, but the items being shown were not laptops or iPads. These items were alive, but just barely.

The cubes, which Sara peered into one by one in horror, displayed an eight-step sequential deterioration of a healthy, fully-grown Unknowing man into a withering, bloody animal that by the eighth window box resembled a horribly beaten, hairless baby panda. Gideon, who had many times seen the experimental effects of Cleanwalker's poison, dubbed "Liquid Justice," watched Sara's reaction to the room's marvels. It seemed like she tried to play it cool at the start, but when she got to the fifth window box—home to a writhing creature akin to a skinned, slimy, teenage gorilla covered with blood-crusted patches of hair—her face went deep red and her body started to convulse. Gideon stepped back, grinning, a moment before Merlot-colored projectile vomit spewed from her mouth, spraying all over the glass and dripping down into watery sludge piles on the clean steel floor.

"Get out," Gideon said, flicking out his fingers. The vomit evaporated. "You wait downstairs for me." Sara covered her mouth and ran for the entrance door, which Gideon opened with another finger flick. She jetted down the darkening passageway without a look back. Gideon went through the second door, arranging his facial expression to neutral.

The room he entered had the same lighting and feel to it as the room he had come from, yet was considerably bigger albeit with much less to look at. In fact it was empty, save for the far left corner where a body wrapped in spools of white gauze lay unmoving on a flat, dentist-like chair. A tray of tools and gizmos hovered in the cool air nearby. Through a glass door in the far wall, Gideon could see the back of a man in a white doctor's coat who was putting down a blow torch and leaning in to inspect something Gideon couldn't see. Gideon walked to the dentist chair and looked down at the body. Three slits had been cut into the gauze over the face: the two eyes—black and bleary—and a dark-lipped mouth. Gideon leaned in close. The eyes beneath the slits registered recognition, and the lips parted.

"I'm...in so much pain."

"You've been gone a long time. Triple what was authorized."

"Ten days?" The associate's voice was as soft as the gauze. "I...I sensed we were under...a long time."

"You were right."

"He was with the girl when I went for him. The one from the park. I wanted...to make sure I told you that."

"I see."

"A tasty—" The associate coughed up a mouthful of blood, the gauze beneath his mouth one giant red stain. "A tasty piece of tail, she is."

"How well did Leam submerge?" Gideon asked.

"No incidents," the associate wheezed. "On the journey there, his body lay limp the whole time. How we got back...I don't know."

"Tell me. You saw the butcher while submerged, yes?"

The associate nodded with his eyes. "At...at one point the boy woke. I don't know what he saw...or if he felt anything."

"That we'll know in time." Gideon was quiet for a moment, caught up in the soft hypnotic whirr of a ventilation grate overhead. "In the field, then. Did you adhere to my stipulations?"

"To a T, sir."

Gideon could tell by a small swelling of gauze where the associate's cheeks were that a smile was trying to form.

"Physical aptitude and courage both...both creamy as my mother's corn," the associate said. "And how he stayed disciplined and focused under pressure...reminded me of someone I read about after...after being recruited by Prophecy Intel. A prospect named All-ja Koobah... He lived back in the 1500s."

"How so?"

"All-ja Koobah...from what I remember...was put through a series of tests while tied to stakes under water with—"

"Not Koobah! Tell me of Holt!"

"R-r-right. Of course," the associate stammered, coughing and wheezing, thin strings of blood spraying from the mouth slit. "With Leam I...I enclosed a metal box around him despite incredible efforts of his to keep me from doing so. I was watching the screens from the pod, and it was clear that he started to panic. I thought ...I thought it was over, that he was done, but he...he *willed* himself calm, is the only way I can describe it, and then broke the box wide open." The section of gauze over the associate's chest rose up steadily, as if being pumped up with helium, then fell like a popped balloon. "And then…"

Gideon leaned in. Reflecting off the associate's dark shiny eyes, he could see his own, so very big and clown-like.

"And then…he came after me."

"The Darkness?" Gideon asked, dipping his face closer. "It was there?"

The associate nodded.

"Tell me."

The associate closed his eyes. It took several seconds. "When Leam broke free of it, his mannerisms…his conversation…it all indicated a singular purpose…one thing only on his mind. That I wronged him. *He* knew it, he knew *I* knew it…and he was going to settle the score."

"Is that so?"

"To make things right."

"And that's when…"

"I have no excuses. My…powers had no effect on him." It sounded like the associate was about to start crying. "The boy, he…he pounced on me, and…" With an eye roll, the associate indicated the extent of his injuries.

"Tell me. What happened *exactly?*"

"The ribbon here…see it? On my neck?" Gideon peered in at a break between the head bandages and those wrapped around the body. A purplish-white scar was belted around the associate's neck. "Cleanwalker says the boy choked me…but other than smacking my face around before that, the choking was it."

"Then these bandages…" Gideon muttered as the glass door slid open and a plain-looking black man in a white doctor's coat entered, his alert, yellow eyes flicking up from the futuristic clipboard in his hands.

"These bandages cover what was once his skin," Cleanwalker said, his voice delicate and clear. "The inflicting magic functioned as a venom. The fingernails and toenails fell off, same with his Mohawks, and…" Cleanwalker snapped his fingers; the full-body bandaging rose off the associate like a boat net pulled off a giant pile of shrimp. The associate looked away. "...the skin."

Gideon raised his eyebrows, but Cleanwalker seemed unaffected by the sticky, red-coated, skinless body lying in the dentist chair between them.

"His skin was seared down to the stratum germinativum, the fifth and deepest layer of the epidermis. From the stratum corneum all the way down, the successive layers peeled off like flakes of Parmesan cheese. The jolt of magic transferred from the prospect's hands to the mutilated body of this hideous freak you see before you was so powerfully concentrated that the damage done, I'm afraid, depending on how you want to look at it, is irreversible. The pain will be constant and considerable, but whether or not it's the patient's will to continue on—"

"Or permissible," Gideon said.

"—I'm confident I can fashion him a sort of full-body synthetic membrane. A quasi-skin casing that will protect, as well as aid in the regulation of body temperature, but be void of sensory nerve endings."

"Why all this pain, then?" the associate croaked.

"It's internal," Cleanwalker answered. "Any harm inflicted externally will go unfelt. And aesthetically...we'll see when we see."

Gideon closed his eyes for a moment, initiating silent communication with Cleanwalker via telemast.

"Are his delightenment scars gone?"

"Seared off clean."

"Has his mind been damaged?"

"Too soon to tell."

"Is he a risk?"

Cleanwalker shrugged. *"Better safe than sorry,"* he telemasted back. *"Plus, I'm always in need of white mice."*

Gideon nodded, dismissing the yellow-eyed Cleanwalker with a wave of his hand.

Cleanwalker stepped back to the glass door looking at his clipboard. "Whatever becomes of the prospect, Gideon, I'd like to examine him. Dead...alive...any condition." He snapped his fingers and the gauze cast dropped back over the associate like a lowering curtain, nestling over the contours of his body. On his way out of the room, Cleanwalker added, "Remarkable magic. Remarkable."

Gideon bent low over the dentist chair, sniffing through the bandages at the slow decay of the associate's face.

"The boy," Gideon said. "What do you like about him?"

"The most?" The associate winced, as if he had tried to shift his body. "It's that *inside* the boy...his tendencies to become worried or frightened lessen when the danger *outside* of him...is at its greatest peril."

"Tell me. Could...he...*be?*"

The associate met Gideon's stare and nodded, a movement so faint that ninety-nine out of a hundred Skunks would have missed it. "Where do you have him, sir?"

"He's in Harbing."

"On his own?"

"I have my reasons."

"What about interference?" the associate gasped.

"Sebastian knows nothing." Gideon sniffed at a smudge spot on his palm. "The mother kept the pregnancy a secret and was killed after the birth."

"Sir, if the boy is proven *not* to be," the associate wheezed, "I ask to be the one who ends him."

"These requests," Gideon said brightly, straightening up. "You're worse than Cleanwalker."

"Let it be me, sir. Please. Look how he's left me."

"No," Gideon responded, flicking a shred of lint off the sleeve of his black shirt. "You've served the Cause well, but an employee in your condition...*tsk, tsk, tsk.*"

"Sir?"

"A man of mine, a late player in the Leam Holt case, is to arrive downstairs shortly with news. I will transport you for you to be present, as your firsthand knowledge of the boy's abilities may be advantageous to our conversation. However, after that," Gideon said, peeking through the slits at the terror glistening in the associate's dark eyes, "as you are, you're no use to me."

"I have to be healed, that's all!" the associate wheezed, hacking up another mouthful of blood. "Sir, I need to heal and to rest—*oh please no!*—and then I'll be fine, I'll be of use again!"

"If Cleanwalker merely *hints* that it's pointless, than that should be good enough for you, too."

"Cleanwalker? Sir, plea—"

"Plus, Cleanwalker needs test subjects for pain serums and other ghastly things, so your death, like your life, will be one of service."

"Sir, listen to me, I promise you, let me live and you won't regret it. I am smart. I have ideas—"

Gideon held up his hand and brought his lips to the nearest of the associate's ear slits. "I'm not an unreasonable man. I recognize you've done good work with this prospect. After the meeting, I'll permit you one minute to convince me to spare your life. Yes?" The associate blinked. "That will be your only chance."

Gideon raised both hands, palms up, and the associate's mummified body rose off the chair. After a quick look through the glass door—Cleanwalker's back was to him, the good doctor pouring beakers of bubbling, brightly colored liquids into a steel pan marked *Fry 'em Up!*—Gideon headed back the way he had come. The associate hovered behind him at an unvarying distance of five feet, muttering thank-yous. Through the door, past Liquid Justice and out into the dark hallway, the pair headed for the patch of light that was the landing at the top of the ivory staircase.

Gideon took his time, his body motionless above the waist. An equally unmoving grin graced his face, as he thought about how great a night it had been with the acquisition of Sara and the still-in-the-game-after-round-two Leam Holt, who would be delivered to DHQ before daybreak. When Gideon reached the landing, he went left, descending the ivory staircase into the deli meat stench of the massive front room, the floating mummy five feet in his wake.

Reaching the shiny-tiled floor, Gideon spotted Sara on the far side of the room, observing the deathly-thin mutt. It was tied up in its cage just out of reach of a pair of bowls, one for food, one for water. She looked over at Gideon, opening her mouth as if to speak, but the whirring noise of the laser outside sounded, and the iron door clunked open. Gideon's man—his go-to man—had a talent, amongst a million others, of arriving at exactly the opportune time.

Out from the dark silence and into the buzzing light, strode Gideon's man, his carrying bag over his shoulder, clouds of blue smoke puffing from the pipe wedged in the corner of his mouth. Behind him, slinking inside before the door clinked closed, trotted a fox, its eyes mean and black. The man bent down near the *Dressing of the Unk*, lifting up the left pant leg of his jeans, exposing a large, reddish-brown tattoo that covered his calf. The furry alternate being pressed up against his host's leg and melted into it, its bushy tail—the exact shape, size and color of the tattoo—the last part to seep through.

"Porlo," Gideon said, coming forward, feeling his springy orange hair bounce on his shoulders. "What news have you?"

CHAPTER 43

Gotta go, gotta get there, gotta keep going, gotta keep moving..."

The fog was all but gone, and the Range Rover was humming down Blaff Street, the sporadic blinking of its brake lights disturbing the blackness that had fallen over Harbing. Leam's mind was racing, randomly strung together words tumbling from his mouth.

"...gotta keep going, Leam keep going, can't stop going, Leam keep going..."

His eyes were fixed on the road, his duffel bag—still filled with his few possessions, some clothes, Gatorade, water and his father's yellow-bound copy of *East of Eden*—on the passenger seat next to him. Coming up on Harbing High, a flash of déjà vu brightened his mind and he slowed to see if there was another message written in the branches of ivy clinging to the wall, as there had been the morning he'd tracked Eloa down, the morning the associate had abducted him to the field of green. Or could that message have been a figment of his imagination? What was real? What wasn't?

"...keep going, yeah yeah, gotta keep moving, keep moving forward..."

Out the driver side window, Leam squinted through the darkness, unable to get a good look at the school. When he put his eyes back on the road—BAM—he slammed the brakes, cuing a wailing screech of tire against pavement.

There, standing in the middle of the road, were two men, both as calm as the night around them, despite the out of control SUV skidding along the street, coming to an abrupt stop about five feet from their kneecaps.

Leam threw open the door, jumping out of the car. "What are you crazy?" he yelled, stepping right up. "Don't you see, don't you see, I could've flattened you like mush, you idiots, I could've killed you!"

"Oh, I doubt that, slick," the younger-looking man said, pushing up the long sleeves of his sea-green shirt, cuffs bunching up at the elbows. "Not yet, at least."

"I've seen you before, okay? Alright? You hear me? I've seen you." Leam had his finger pointed at the man's chest.

"Maybe," the man laughed, bending at the waist, stretching his fingers to the toes of his purple Nikes. "Maybe not."

"I've seen you, guy, I've seen you."

"I don't believe he's lying to you, Miller," the other man said—a man with silver hair, who looked slightly older than his smirking friend. "He just hasn't seen you as he sees you right now. But perhaps in a dream…"

Leam said nothing, his finger still pointed at the man named Miller, who was looking at the watch on Leam's wrist, or maybe the markings on his hand. Words kept slobbering out of Leam's mouth, his eyes flicking back and forth from Long John Silver Hair to "Miller."

"…gotta go forward, keep keep forward, keep going going, going going going…"

Miller raised his eyebrows. "This kid's lost it, Sebastian. I would know."

"You've had a lot going on these last few days," the man named Sebastian said to Leam, before turning to Miller. "One's sanity can be damaged by an overload of shock and stress. Let's bear in mind what he's been through." He held his hand up, palm facing Leam, and hot air pushed into his face like he was staring down a blow dryer. The nonsensical drivel spewing from Leam's mouth stopped instantly. He felt a fog lift, clarity of vision and a refocused mind.

"Hello, Leam," Sebastian said, dropping his hand.

Leam looked the man over. "How do you know my name?"

"I've known your name for eighteen years."

"That's helpful," Leam said, moving to his car. "I don't like this. It's too weird."

"You said you've seen this man before—" Sebastian gestured to Miller, his voice remaining pleasant yet commanding authority, "—but we both know it wasn't at the movies or in the grocery store."

Leam turned back to him, shaking his head. "It wasn't in a dream, either."

"I believe you. I also believe you saw my friend, Mr. Miller, in a place that transcends the worlds we stand in right now, but also lies far beyond the realm of dream worlds we visit while sleeping safely in our beds."

Leam stopped fidgeting. The man had his attention now.

"Do you know who I am?" Sebastian asked.

"Obviously you're a member of the Light."

"Try *leader* of the Light, kid," Miller chimed in.

Leam studied Sebastian's face. Sebastian nodded, and Leam felt like the man's eyes were sucking him in.

"I ask for but a few minutes," Sebastian said. "You quite clearly have somewhere you need to be, and I have to neutralize a threat before it actualizes. Time is not on our side."

Leam looked down at his hands for a moment. He couldn't tell if the markings were glowing ever so faintly or not at all. "Fine," he said.

"Excellent," Sebastian said. "But before we get into that, Leam, I have one quick and rather odd question for you."

Leam raised his eyebrows as if to say *What is it?*

"Have you noticed a man with a mouthful of gold teeth following you?"

"No."

"You don't have to think about it?"

"I haven't seen any gold teeth."

"Not at all these past few weeks? I'm worried. He's a good friend."

Leam shook his head.

Sebastian frowned. "Another mystery to put at the top of the wobbly stack of things we do not know."

"Why would I have seen a guy with gold teeth?" Leam asked.

"You said you don't lie, Leam, and that's good to hear. I've never lied once in my life, and besides, you deserve to know the truth. I had sent this man—his name is Griffton—out to obtain information about you and your current circumstances quite a while ago. I fear he has been taken by Dark hands."

"What do you mean?" Leam's voice cracked. "Like he was following me around?"

"Yes." Sebastian turned to Miller. Leam had to strain his ears to hear. "I should have known something was off. Griff has his own way of doing things, but there had to be reason he never returned my telemast."

"Gideon has him. Probably grabbed him when he grabbed Jace."

Sebastian sighed. "Who tipped you off about Darkness's involvement with Leam?"

Leam could feel the back of his neck getting hot. They were talking about him as if he wasn't there.

"It all came from the mouth of a little bird," Miller said, smiling.

"Not the best of times to be cute," Sebastian said.

"No, literally. It's this little brown bird that turns into a tiny man. He's traitor to Gideon. Feared they were going to hurt the woman he loved…or it might have been the bird he loved, now that I think about it… Either way, he says for as long as Gideon doesn't discover he's turned, then he'll keep flying back to me with the goods until they kill him."

Sebastian turned to Leam. "Have you been aware of a brown bird flying around you? Or perhaps a tiny man watching you from behind some blades of grass?"

Leam shook his head, and kept shaking it. The leader of the Light was asking him insane questions in the middle of the road in Leam's home town, lending this prospect stuff a little more validity. His mouth was dry. Things were getting beyond overwhelming.

Sebastian looked quiet in thought, then he clapped his hands together. "Now, Leam, if you'd be so kind," he said, gesturing to the school. "I only need a few minutes."

Leam looked over at the Range Rover, whiffs of smoke puffing from the exhaust pipe, the whirring engine restless.

"I won't keep you long," Sebastian said, with that same commanding quality that had demanded Leam's attention earlier. "I promise you, you're going to want to hear what I have to say. What I mentioned earlier...the otherworldly place you've been visiting..."

"How do you know about that?" Leam asked.

"Why? Is it a place you believed only you have been?" A smile lit up Sebastian's face. "Judging by the look of you, I'd wager you'd like to hear more about it."

Leam peeked over at Miller, with his foot impatiently tapping the road. "Five minutes," he said.

"Come," Sebastian said. "There's good cover behind the school. It's not safe for us to be exposed."

Leam turned to move the Range Rover, but the engine cut before he could take a step, the driver side door slamming shut as the SUV slid off the road, over the curb and onto the grass, stopping just before the woodlands adjacent to the high school. Leam's pulse quickened as he watched three bushy pines pop out of the ground—one, two, three—smack in front of his Range Rover, masking it from any passing driver or midnight stroller.

"Why isn't it safe here?" he asked, looking across the street at menacing shapes of darkness perceived as irrelevant and innocent only moments ago. "The threat you mentioned?"

"That's part of it," Sebastian answered.

"Those trench coaters I've been seeing?"

"That's the rest of it."

"But if he called you the leader of Light, and that's really who you are, then what could any of them do to you? They're not Gideon. You'd just slap their faces with your magic."

Under a large patch of clear sky, distant clouds were approaching.

"I don't fear their harm, Leam," Sebastian said, as he and Leam strode toward the back of the school, the latter unsure whether his first step had been taken under his own initiative. Miller, the last to step off the black pavement of Blaff Street, followed a few paces behind. "But it wouldn't do either of us any good if they were to see us together tonight."

CHAPTER 44

The waspish buzzing of Darkness Headquarters greeted
Porlo as it always did upon entry, like a rusted screw digging through his ears into his brain. Gideon stood before
him, clad in black, as a skinny blonde woman near a dog cage by
the wall looked on with interest. Porlo's eyes went to her legs—
pale beneath a short candy-red skirt.

"You look tired, Porlo," Gideon said.

"I'm fine," Porlo said, unsure whether Gideon would believe it. The lie was worth the risk, though. If Gideon found
out that Porlo had felt unwell ever since the fat man threading, there was a good chance he might have Porlo replaced. And
when Gideon had someone replaced, that someone was often
never seen again. Luckily for Porlo, he entered with a shield of
good news.

Gideon took one step toward him. "Tell me."

After a glance at the blonde, who was inching closer wearing the look of a person who was not inching closer, Porlo closed
his eyes for a second, sending Gideon the telemast he had been
drafting inside his head during the short and mercifully-dark
trip from Harbing to D.C.

"I see," Gideon said, a smile tightening the skin stretched
over his pronounced cheek bones. Porlo watched inky strings of

words materialize on a piece of paper that had appeared out of thin air in front of Gideon.

"Garrick," Gideon called. A man with a freakishly long neck came out from a door appearing inside the gold back wall. Porlo looked at the giraffe man with disgust. "Deliver this message straightaway, making sure you get his confirmation that it's been received." The giraffe man hurried back through the wall.

"Saw Raxton no less than ten minutes ago," Porlo said to Gideon, with a small smile. "Gujin7B is an absolute go. A diluted sample has been released at the town's center. Many of your devoted followers are there nearby, all sorts of excited, ready to witness it in person. Raxton was as frothed up as a tit mouse and I won't say it wasn't contagious."

Gideon's taut face twisted up in glee. "Excellent news. And yet you look so tired, Porlo."

"I'll be fine." Porlo brushed the back of his hand across the front of his neck, feeling a rattle inside his head that wouldn't go away. "A little rest is what I need, nothing more."

Gideon spread his emaciated arms. "Then sit with me. The gas, the boy...it should be a night of glorious proportions." He turned and Porlo followed him toward the center of the room where a massive table awaited them inside a rectangular, Romanesque colonnade. A mummy, floating horizontally six feet above the immaculately clean floor, tailed behind Gideon. The instant Porlo opened his mouth to ask why a mummy was floating horizontally above the immaculately clean floor, Gideon was answering the unspoken question.

"This is an associate of mine, Porlo. He can't move much, but he can speak. He was creating and administering young Leam Holt's examinations."

"What happened to him?"

"Leam Holt happened to him. The boy's got a Dark side, I think."

"It would appear so."

"Have a look at his face." Shreds of gauze shed off the mummy's head like toilet paper sucked into a wood chipper, revealing socket-less eyes set in a skull-like countenance that looked to be lathered in strawberry jelly. Porlo cringed as the shreds, which had stuck to the air, rematerialized into the bandages covering up what he assumed was once a normal face.

"And the woman?" Porlo asked, eyeing the blonde, who stood by a corner column, her hands fidgety, picking at the cuffs of her tight black sweater.

"She's mine," Gideon answered.

Porlo raised his eyebrows at her, wondering if, by the bizarre look on her face, she was torn between honor and fear that the leader of Darkness had declared her his. Porlo, though, going up the three colonnade steps, couldn't care less. He took the nearest chair, as Gideon conjured a black-marble throne on the opposite side and sat down, all the while magicking the mummy upright, where it hovered vertically a few inches off the table edge on Gideon's right. The blonde stopped just outside the colonnade, and Porlo could tell by her face that she was unsure whether or not she was permitted to inch any closer.

Porlo seeped gratefully into his chair. He zipped his pipe into the side pouch of his carrying bag, and withdrew a jet-black starfish-like medallion from down deep, placing it on the mirrored surface of the table.

"I've...I've seen one of those before," the mummy wheezed through a slit in the gauze, then groaned in pain. "A silver one... The girl that was with the boy."

"A simple precaution," Gideon said, "that became more useful than intended. Isn't that right, Porlo?"

"It is."

"Well, share, share. Speak freely, Porlo. After all, this might be his last conversation," Gideon said, gesturing to the mummy.

Porlo grinned and he and Gideon shared a laugh.

"Well, then, Mummy, at least it'll be interesting. The girl's father, a man by the name of Jace Frost, had broken through some of our code, had learned of Gujin7B, and had nearly gotten as far as to develop magic that would render Gujin7B useless when we took him down and brought him in. We figured with a higher-up like that—a code decipherer—Sebastian would set off a manhunt to track him down, so I gave the twin of this one—" Porlo indicated the black starfish, "—to Frost's daughter.

We wanted to know if any of the Light came sniffing around asking about him."

"It's the only reason she's alive," Gideon said. Porlo felt his hands get clammy.

"How's it work?" A wheezy question, the mummy's voice faint.

"When Silver is touching the daughter's skin," Porlo answered, "it transmits anything she says, and anything anybody around her says, directly to Blackie here." Porlo placed his hand atop the black starfish, which emitted quiet radio static, followed by an old woman's voice.

"Those groups of people, dear. What are they doing out in the street?"

"Probably just wondering what all the screaming was about."

"Come away from that window, dear. I'll fix you a cup of tea."

"I'm fine. Like I told Larry, that boy's harmless. He's just got some mental issues and...anyway, everything's fine now, Mary, just stay in—"

Porlo removed his hand and the radio noise cut dead. "Pretty simple. It also alerts me if contact between her flesh and the medallion is broken." Porlo's eyes gazed over to Gideon. "Oh, and you'll be pleased to hear that when I went to her the one time she *had* taken it off, she thought I had been summoned by a poem she called the Ode of Aid. Apparently it sends help to those of Light who recite it. I figured she must've remembered it wrong, but I had her repeat it for me, so we can play around with the wording. Could be useful." Gideon's giant lips twitched; he gave a slight nod. "Plus, if I need to find her," Porlo said, looking back at the mummy, "it points me to her exact location."

"How did..." The mummy coughed—muffled and wet. "How did you persuade her to keep it?"

"Under the ruse that her father had entrusted me to deliver it."

"But—"

"Clean out your ear holes and think a little," Porlo said. "She doesn't know who I am, friend. A little forgery and all of a sudden I'm a man of Light, her dad and I are great friends, we've known each other forever, and he wants her to wear it should anything ever happen to him—it would keep her safe as long as she kept it on her. I fed her lie after lie after lie, and she ate up the slop with a soup spoon. But it wasn't until a day later that these seven-legged beauties delivered us a piping hot trump card, fresh off the presses."

"What was it?" the mummy wheezed.

"She bumped into a boy by the name of Leam Holt."

A strange noise came out of the mummy, like a combination of a laugh, a bark and a scream. "I know, I was there!" he cried out hoarsely.

"Good for you."

"He...has a crush on her. That's your big news?"

"ENOUGH!" Gideon roared, baring his teeth at the mummy, smacking his hands down on the table. Reflected in the mirrored surface, Porlo saw the pupils of the mummy's eyes rattle beneath the slits, but whether this was a product of fear or a simple distortion of the wavering tabletop, Porlo couldn't be sure.

"He's right to call it a trump card because it gives me what I need," Gideon spat. "A way inside the boy's head. How does he feel about the Light? Or Darkness? Or the testing? How does he handle ripping an incompetent man's skin off? How does he *feel* after he finds out he's a prospect?"

"You, you, you...you get him...you bring him in...you, you ask him—"

"RUBBISH!" Gideon bellowed, and Porlo saw the man's eyes bulge a half inch out of the sockets. "You're signing your own death sentence! Whatever the boy did to you has warped your mind!"

Porlo felt his heart dip down into his stomach. He swallowed down the dry little bits of saliva caked into the bumps of his tongue, and found that his hand had gone to his head.

"If I had brought him in too soon," Gideon went on, "I'd never have known the truth. I pull him toward me, to the dungeons, to anywhere, and I ask him things, who knows what he'll tell me. He may not spin me a spool of lies, but if he's intimidated or scared, then he's going to tell me what I want to hear, and as pretty and nice as that may be, it's useless. I need the *truth*, it's the only way to know precisely where I stand. A man speaks perfect truth only if he believes himself to be free. But tell me. With whom is a free man honest?

"You see there are two forces inside Leam Holt, and as an undelightened he's more capable of love than you or you or her," Gideon spat, throwing his thumb at the blonde, whose face, Porlo noticed, had gotten redder every time the boy's name was mentioned. "And a side effect of that sickness is that people tell the ones they love the things they wouldn't tell anyone else—just as they're more inclined to listen to those they love," he added, with a quick glance at Porlo.

"His family's a dead end. He hates his lovely stepmother like poison—the brother, too—and Bram was soon to go...*missing*, shall we say? So when my whiplap comes to me—he'd been on the boy for some time—to report this unlikely connection, I saw it for what it was. Useful. Now Leam may not be in love, but she's as close as he's going to get. And his thoughts, the conclusions he's been drawing, his plans...he's confided in her. And by confiding in her, he confides in us."

"Is...he...the one?" the mummy asked. Porlo looked at him, impressed by the bold question coming from someone whose life was apparently on the line. But if Gideon felt taken aback by the mummy's brazenness, he chose not to show it.

"If we combine your reports with the information Porlo retrieved from the depths of the fat man's brain, we'll have the most accurate assessment we've ever had of a prospect's potential."

"The fat man?" the mummy said. "My telemast...that Thomas had tracked him down south somewhere...that the fat man was in a permanent state of...you received my telemast, didn't you? The fat man's brain had been cooked and...so how did you...how could you have gotten any information out of him because—"

"Calm down, friend," Porlo said. "Catch your breath."

The mummy opted to spit up reddish fluid instead.

"I saw in your eyes last we met that you were caught up with your examinations and had no interest in the fat man," Gideon said to the mummy. "You're an adequate tracker but clearly you were more suited for prophecy-testing. It was then that I called on Porlo to find the fat man and get the information he'd held for almost a year."

"But, I sent you—"

"I got your telemast," Gideon said, a fish-lipped smile swimming up his face. "Thomas did very little for you down there. For both our sakes, my judgment to enlist Porlo was sound. Show him, Porlo, as he walks his plank."

"Of course," Porlo said, nodding. He closed his eyes and after four or five seconds, slid down his chair an inch or two, his shoulders hunching a bit. When he opened his eyes, they were the exact brownish color of the fat man's, and when he spoke, it was in the fat man's tongue.

"*It was a perfectly round globe. A planet, if you will, churning in space, though not the infinite blackness of the universe that exists outside of earth, no. No, far from it. This space was bright, as difficult to look at as the sun, and within it spun his soul, a breathtaking sphere, comprised of two opposing swirls of mass. One dark and slippery, like ink swirling around in the clear water of a fish bowl. The other was wavy and had a reddish tint to it, like rose petals still secured to the stem, gently billowing in a soft breeze. And these two amazing entities were splashing into each other, sticking to one another, pushing together and pulling apart. Pools of red and black swimming inside each other, coexisting, yes, but both seemingly fighting to conquer the other. If it was all there was, it'd be all we ever needed.*"

As Porlo's eyes flickered back to normal, Gideon spoke. "Do you see? The boy's soul, what a remarkable entity it is? How far from common?"

The mummy groaned. "How'd you get him to talk?"

"Threading," Porlo replied, seeing from his own eyes again. "Same as the girl, I duped the fat man into believing I worked for Sebastian. I watched him suffer over the belief that he was giving secrets away to the enemy."

Blood gurgled out of the corners of the mummy's mouth slit. "And the fat man's fate?" he asked.

"Your boy Thomas brought him into Cleanwalker."

"*Watched him suffer*," Gideon echoed, scratching at his chin. "Watched him suffer, did you? Tell me, Porlo. Did you not see the fat man for the wonder that he was? The way he spoke about that soul, the spectacle of it all, the rhythm of pace, the fluidity of speech." Gideon bore in on Porlo as if his eyes, his bulging eyes, were ready to scream. "Tell me. Were you aware that he was just as gifted a chef as he was a linguist?"

Porlo shook his head; it felt like loose change was rattling around the walls of his brain.

"To him, the philosophy for both speaking and cooking was the same—there must be order to make something the best it can be. Salt and pepper season the steak before it's ready to sizzle on an oily pan, just as suitable adjectives bring out the taste in nouns, and a verb becomes suppler when a delicious adverb is added right before it."

Beneath the table, Porlo readied his hand, the palm facing the black throne and the man sitting in it. *Salt and pepper season the steak? What the hell is going on?* Porlo was uncertain of the motive, but when Gideon got into something like he was now, he was dangerous.

"Every word he used," Gideon continued, eyes getting bigger and bigger, "was always enhanced by the word that came before it as well as the word yet to come. He *lived* the stories he told, and there was artistry to the way he spoke."

"I know. I know he was special, that isn't lost on me," Porlo said, rubbing his throat with the hand that was still in plain sight. His smoking pipe rose from his bag and began to pack itself with blue tobacco. "But the fact is that the fat man went into hiding to keep that information from reaching your ears and without mutilating his brain we wouldn't know the full extent of what that failed delightenment truly meant. I did it for the Cause, sir, and like it or not, that fat man fried for the Cause. His last minutes helped us see something we otherwise would've missed. He was a hero, and his death a noble one. That threading has shortened the route to victory, and if he was able to come back, he'd do it all over again in faithful service to you." Porlo calmly blew two streams of blue smoke from his nostrils to disguise all the squirming beneath his skin.

"I don't care that you threaded him into a puddle of mush," Gideon said softly. "He was a coward. Yet you, Porlo... you brand him noble? He withheld information from me in spite of the Cause. Tell me, my dear Porlo. Is that your definition of heroism?"

Porlo's heart was pulsing so violently it hurt. He didn't know what to think. Was he being toyed with or was Gideon just that insane? And it was the grin that scared Porlo most, that giant, unmoving grin. Porlo had to act, though, and he took a calculated risk. "I tried to get it from him through conversation first, sir, but I'm glad that fat man fried and I'm glad I'm the one who fried him."

The look between Gideon and Porlo was long, and to Porlo's surprise, Gideon blinked first.

"My bird did mention you talked to the fat man for quite some time before the threading."

Porlo's skin was jumpy, but he felt his blood cool a touch. "The bird that felt the connection between Holt and the girl? The whiplap, right? I remember you mentioned him to me once."

"He tracked the fat man down, too, presumably to get back in my good graces."

"I thought I saw him down there." Porlo relaxed the hand beneath the table. "He was perched on the canopy when I walked out. I saw him again, too, peeking through Eloa's window when I had to go back to her."

"Is that so?" The iciness in Gideon's voice cut through the sauna-like air. "It appears he cannot leave her alone."

"It's her beauty," Porlo said, instantly regretting it.

Gideon's head tilted to the side. "Have you developed an attraction?"

"Hate lust," Porlo said, exhaling another drag.

The white noise of the buzzing wasps hummed unbroken for several moments, until the mummy, to Porlo's relief, posed a question.

"If he's confided in the girl...what was said through the medallions?"

Porlo gave Gideon a look that said *Shall I?* Gideon took his time, but nodded.

"He knows he's a hybrid, and it appears he knows about the dueling prophecies. He says his hands have something to do with all this, and he's on route to a location he believes holds answers."

"And...where's that?" the mummy said softly through the gauze.

"Home," Porlo replied.

"To my home?" the blonde shrieked. "To the Manor?"

Porlo had forgotten she was there. The woman looked livid and, for the first time, formidable.

"That place is no longer your residence, Sara," Gideon corrected her. "This is." He held up his arms and laughed one of the all-time creepiest laughs Porlo had ever heard.

"If Leam manages to get inside there," she said, her hands like claws, her arms shaking, "he's not coming out alive. I promise you."

Gideon sniffed, seeming to savor her angry breath and her displeasure. Apparently, her hatred for her stepson really licked his chops. "It's the final test," he said, smacking his lips. "If he is killed by your enchantments, then he was never to be our prophet."

At this, the mummy floated to the middle of the table, facing Gideon.

"Unfortunately, this seals your fate. You've been a devoted servant, but are unnecessary for the future."

"*Wait—*"

"You're damaged."

"But you—"

"Do not grovel."

"Upstairs, sir! When we were upstairs, you said I'd have a minute to change your mind!"

"I did?"

"Yes! Yes! You did! You said it!"

Gideon turned to Porlo and grinned. "That doesn't sound like me." And with a wave of his hand, the slits over the mummy's eyes and mouth stitched up with red yarn, leaving the head looking like a mummified baseball. The muffled squeals and groans seemed to have no effect on Gideon in any way, as, under the guidance of his slender hand, the mummy's body shot across the room and whipped up the ivory staircase toward Cleanwalker's. Gideon set his bulging eyes back on Porlo.

"You, however, Porlo, take the day. You look like you could use it."

"Thank you, sir," Porlo said, still feeling that clattering in his head, but taking extreme care not to give this away.

"What shall you do?"

"I don't know." Porlo stood up, tossing the strap of his carrying bag over his shoulder. "There's a Leif Garrett concert tomorrow at the town theater in Harbing. Heard he puts on a nice show. Might check it out."

"A good place to be," Gideon said, diverting his eyes to the tight-sweatered, short-skirted Sara, and adding as an afterthought, "for there will be much more than Leif Garrett greeting the citizens of Harbing tomorrow."

CHAPTER 45

Secured above the rear entrance of the school, a weakening lamp cast a soft, golden puddle of light over the stairs that descended to the back lot of Harbing High, but reached little else of the peninsular expanse of land enclosed by a sea of heavy woodlands. If one were to fire a spell from the base of the stairs all the way to the frontline of oak trees opposite, it would shoot over a white concrete basketball court, a wide stretch of hardened mulch, on which stood empty picnic tables and an occupied set of swings, and a large section of grass, that by the smell of it, had been mowed no later than lunchtime today.

With one ear on Sebastian, Leam couldn't help putting the other on those dark and distant oak trees, almost certain he could hear an unsettling sort of rustling beyond. He was also levelheaded enough to consider that his head wasn't exactly level at present, and the noise seeming to emanate from the forest deep might actually be a distraction originating in the depths of his mind. He could feel eyes on him, too, though, and not just those of Sebastian, seated to his right on the swing nearer the school, or Miller, who was several feet away leaning against a flag pole near a receptacle unit containing a blue bin for recycling and a green for trash.

"And it's the *things* that you want to pay attention to, if or when you find yourself back in that place," Sebastian was saying. "They all mean, or will mean, something to you. That's my belief. Nothing in that world is random, so don't treat it as such. Absorb every detail you can."

"Should I keep a journal or something? So I don't forget?"

Sebastian shook his head, his silver hair slightly translucent despite the dark. "You strike me as someone who remembers."

Leam fell silent, debating whether or not he should confide in this man of distinguished kindness who represented his mother's people. Leam was desperate to get up, get going, get moving—for the Manor could be a place that held certain answers—but next to him, wearing a patient smile, was a *person* who might have other kinds of answers. But what should Leam disclose? What was most pressing? On one side of his mind swam a triangle of oars filled with brilliant emerald green. On the other, floating just above the imaginary floorboards of her porch, was Eloa.

"I keep seeing a white bird and a fox," Leam divulged, brushing his finger over his lips. "Do you have any idea what that could be?"

"No," Sebastian said, "but that's my point. If you focus in *that* world, and pay attention in *this* world, you'll stand a chance to figure it out. Leam, inside your phantasms, or what you refer to as visions, every pothole, every can of beer, even the hair sprouting from a wart on a person's nose, has a purpose. They're there for a reason. The bird, the fox...they could be symbols. They could signify things in your past that need your attention now. They might even represent alternate beings."

An image of a squat, glittery hog man conspicuously slipped in and out of Leam's mind. "I didn't even know those existed 'til tonight."

"Alternate beings?" Sebastian said. "Another creation that both helps and hinders. You can imagine how hard it is to protect ourselves, and our secrets, from things and beings that can truly be anything. Entities that do what their masters make them do. It leaves us, and them, constantly vulnerable."

"Can they take any form?"

"Oh yes. And the more magically capable the host is, the more complex that form can be, to the point where the being can talk and think for itself."

Leam saw Sebastian looking upward and got the urge, too, gazing up at the sky while wondering if he himself would ever have an alternate being, and if so, what form it might take. For some reason he was picturing a loon when he heard Miller clear his throat.

"Sir, we're tight on time." Miller was looking over his shoulder at where the farthest blades of grass welcomed the woods. "I feel something."

"Thank you, Miller." Sebastian looked at Leam. "So remember, when you find yourself inside that world, take in everything you can."

Leam nodded a few times until the emergence of a disconcerting query changed it into a shake. "What I don't get is that in the street you immediately knew I had had visions." Leam's hands were tight around the swing's chains. "You had never even met me and you knew."

Sebastian sighed and across the shine of his eyes, Leam read pity. "There are signs. Your speech was erratic. You were having trouble staying oriented to your surroundings. The pupils of your eyes were unsteady...shaken...as if they had taken in more than should ever be seen."

Leam looked at the markings on his hands, which, like Sebastian's hair, had an almost imperceptible glow. "You're basically describing every single TV psych ward mental patient."

"But there's a difference between them and you."

Leam waited for it.

"You possess magic, Leam. And not your ordinary variety either. Being able to travel to that phantasmal world we've been speaking of is extremely rare within the magical community. And the uncommon few that are, or were, ever capable of it share a commonality."

The blood in Leam's veins spiked. "They're hybrids."

"Exactly."

"So Christian Duncan, then?"

"And many others before him." A doleful look came over Sebastian. "Ever since the ancient Lights began documenting our history, there's only been one known non-hybrid who was able to get there, be there, and inhabit that place."

"Who?" Leam asked.

"Me." Leam turned to see what he could of the man's eyes. "I haven't been in there in a very long time. But speaking from my past experiences, I'd advise you not linger there. It is not a place, I found, that one is meant to stay. Take it all in—it holds valuable clues—but to make a conscious effort to remain there might set off a disastrous string of consequences here."

"What if I don't want to go back?"

"I doubt that what you want will have any bearing on the matter."

"Yeah," Leam said, flexing and unflexing his hands. "I mean, going or staying, I guess now that I'm thinking about it, it hasn't really been up to me. We touch, I go. She breaks the connection, I come back."

"She?" Sebastian asked.

"Mmm-hmm. Her name's Eloa."

Sebastian's eyes grew wide, then his whole face froze in an expression that reminded Leam of Gideon. Miller stood up off the pole, drawing Leam's eye. When Leam's awareness came back to the swings, Sebastian had his fingertips pressed into his own face like a muzzle, unnatural whizzes and clicks coming from his mouth. Leam shot his eyes back at Miller, hoping to discern if this was normal behavior, but Miller just stood there in his purple Nikes, his expression blank.

"Eloa," Sebastian mumbled, after the whizzes and clicks fell dead.

"Do you know her?" Leam asked. "She's one of yours."

"You've been in contact with Eloa Frost?"

"Yeah, if that's her last name. It's contact with her that's sparked all my visions."

Sebastian threw a look at Leam that nearly knocked him off his swing. "How deep are you in all of this, Leam?"

"In all of what?"

"I'll break it down for you, shall I?" Sebastian said, and Leam's nerves began to panic. "Gideon's heavily involved in your life, and *you've* obviously developed some sort of relationship with Eloa Frost if you've been in her company on more than one occasion. Can you really expect me to believe that you're not mixed up with whatever Gideon has planned?"

"What?" Leam exclaimed. "Gideon's plans? I met him once."

"The whole Jace situation, Leam, don't play coy."

"What? What are you saying? I don't even know a Jace! Who the hell is he?"

"Eloa's father!" Leam felt the force of the words push his swing a few inches toward the forest. He caught Miller smearing his palm over the air hanging between himself and the swings, as Sebastian shouted, "Don't be cute with me, I'm finished playing games! Gideon's molding you, manipulating you like a puppet, whether you've been aware of it or not. *You* are tangled up in this!"

"I'm not a puppet!"

"Then tell me what you know!"

"Nothing!"

"Spit it out right now, Leam, because you don't want to force me to get it out of you in other ways!"

"ALL I KNOW IS THAT HE'S MISSING!" Leam cried out. He felt tears rising forward, and he gave like hell to will them back. "That's the only thing she told me! A Jace Frost situation? I don't have a clue what that is! Look at you! You don't even know me and you're threatening me and telling me I'm this big player in everything! Go find somebody who knows something if you need to get him back so bad! I met her in the park, is that what you're so desperate to hear? We talked a couple times and I got sucked away into some freaked out visions! That's it! And you wanna hurt me for that, what are you a savage?"

The anger and skepticism Sebastian had been wearing on his face softened. Leam slouched forward, putting his forearms on his knees, his face in his hands.

"Jesus Christ, *Sebastian*, do you have any idea what I've been put through these past however many days? I've got a hundred guys in trench coats hunting me down. I don't have a family, if you can believe that. And if you want to know the truth of it, I'm not that...I'm just not that *brave*, okay? I'm scared."

"Leam?"

"I mean how much of this do you think I can take? My dad—my own father!—*killed* my mom—"

"Leam, listen to me. I know about your mom."

"—*and then* when I go to see her grave, some bleach white zombie—"

"Leam, calm down."

"—he says to me that I, *ME*, might be the world's *prophet!*"

"Hold on a second, Leam."

"He just springs it on me, like it's no big deal to tell *me*...a misfit, depressed, friendless *weirdo*, that I could be..."

"*Leam.*" Sebastian put a comforting hand on Leam's shoulder, but Leam shrugged him off.

"...that of all the thousands of years that people have been on earth, the fate of the Unknowings, the magical world, I'm the prophet of it all!"

"You're not the prophet," Sebastian stated.

"And—"

A loud, compact *POP* banged through Leam's ears, as a flash of light from Sebastian's palm shot at his feet sending a scattering of mulch all the way across the basketball court, startling Leam into truly hearing what Sebastian had said.

"You're not the prophet, Leam," Sebastian repeated.

Leam felt dizzy, an ache in his head. It took him a moment to find his voice, which came out shakier than the hands he couldn't stop himself from staring at. "I'm not?"

"No, you're not. And whether or not that's what you wanted to hear, that's the way it is." Sebastian clasped his hands together and sighed. "Leam, I didn't really believe Gideon had you mixed up in this Jace Frost mess, but it doesn't hurt to be sure. I hope you can understand that. Because of his link to this threat, it would be unforgivable for us not to cover all our bases. For whatever it's worth, I can understand how you're feeling. These recent weeks must have been a nonstop overload of information…emotions flying up and falling down. But you can relax if it's the prophet stuff that's been unnerving you, because it will not be you who decides the fate of the world."

Leam scrunched his face up real tight, then let it fall back to normal.

"In a way, Leam, Darkness is courting you, as if you can be molded into their prophet. Gideon's done this before—it's the way he thinks this works. I would bet the sky and the sea that the testing you were put through was the most exhilarating time of your life. His aim is to draw you in and make you feel powerful."

"But I… You don't know what… You didn't see what I did in that field."

"Exactly—*in that field,*" Sebastian said. "I imagine you were capable of incredible feats of prowess and valor *in that particular field.*"

Leam felt his face get warm, and the ebb and flow of un-shed tears.

"His deceit and trickery, he has it down to a science, Leam. Gideon's an old pro. You're not the first to be torn between sides, and certainly not the first to think you're something that you're not." Sebastian looked in the direction of the receptacle unit and added, "You may withdraw your silencing spell now, Miller."

Leam kicked his heels into the mulch, pushing back and swinging forward…going back and coming up. The earthy aroma beneath the strewn wood chips took him back to a time when he was small and he would dig holes under the black rose bushes and bury Zach's toys, only to help his brother unearth them later on, all the while cursing the evil Tommy Toy-Snatcher…a time when he knew very little of the Unknowing world, and even less about his own. Shaking away the memory, Leam tried to swallow, his mouth bone dry. A second later—POOF—a cold bottle of water popped into his hand. Miller gave him a quick wink and said, "It's not all about you, kid."

"But even though you're not *the* hero," Sebastian went on, "that doesn't mean you don't have the opportunity to do something heroic. Who you are prophesized to be isn't in your control. What *is* are your choices. No matter what's stacked up against you, no matter how dire the circumstances, you will always have a choice, Leam, and you should believe in yourself and let your brain and your guts and what's *inside you* be your guide. As with anything, you'll get a tiny serving of help from some, and big fat entrée of interference from others, but your heart is yours and no one else's, and I hope you listen to it no matter what happens when we part, because if you don't, you'll be the first to know it, and the things we do cannot be undone."

Leam dug his heels into the ground, skidding to a stop. He stared upward at a black void sprinkled with faint starlight. He thought to close his heavy eyelids when he heard Miller say, "I can feel something, sir. Nearby, getting nearer."

"There's time," Sebastian said. "Leam, I know you've been through more than anyone your age and in your circumstances ever should. But now that you know the world isn't sitting on your shoulders, you can catch your breath."

Leam groaned, rubbing the back of his neck. "Whatever."

"It's okay, son, you can breathe now."

"I am breathing," Leam said, staring lasers into Sebastian's face. "And it doesn't matter what you think. I have a purpose, okay? I know I do."

"I didn't say that you didn't," Sebastian urged.

"I can feel it—and isn't that what you said? To let what's inside me be my guide? I won't sit around like some goon twiddling my thumbs. I'm meant for something and I'm gonna find out what. I choose to seek, not wait."

"Yes, but you shouldn't set your sights on something that can't be tracked down. No one can discover their destiny before the fact. It happens *when* it happens."

Leam shook his head. "Then how can you say I'm not the prophet?"

For the second time in their conversation, Sebastian looked sad. "A valid question. The answer of which I wish I could share. It would aid in my efforts to earn your trust, but not without needlessly complicating the future."

"See? Whatever," Leam muttered again. His shoulders, which had risen with mounting angst from the entire conversation, fell alongside a loud exhale of breath.

"I'm sorry, Leam. I hope you don't mistake my caution for rudeness."

"Then I guess we're done here," Leam mumbled at his feet.

"I suppose we are." Sebastian extended his hand through the space between himself and Leam. "Remember. The things we do cannot be undone."

Leam looked up at Sebastian sheepishly, twisted toward the man, reached forward, and shook the hand awaiting his own.

He was inside of an orb, running his fingers over the hard and waxy material encapsulating him. The orb's general color was a warm orangey gold, like the wick of a burning candle, but there were also subdued patches of earthy green, rose-petal red and sandbox brown formed into complicated shapes.

He put his eye up against one of the clearer portions of the orb's skin, but the things he saw on the other side were blurry and distorted. A table, perhaps, with fiery light flickering on its surface...something bluish, that might be a bookshelf or a TV. Something else, dark and flat, was in the far corner of the shadowy gloom, on top of which lay a shivering woman, her arms cradled around her belly...a distortion of darkness up in one of the corners, something small and rigid in its center.

As he was committing as much as he could to memory, the orb began to move and fill up with red smoke, rolling toward the flickering light, gaining momentum. He was walking with it now, like a hamster in one of those balls, picking up speed, faster and faster, redder and redder, until it pushed through the fiery sparks of light, and the orb's glowing skin extinguished, the red smoke gone, as he and the orb kept rolling into darkness, rolling into nothing, rolling, rolling, rolling...

The grip around Leam's hand lifted, and he felt a lukewarm Harbing breeze greet his skin. He glanced at Sebastian, who was looking up at the sky.

"May I ask you one last thing, Leam?"

"Sir," Miller cautioned, his agitation evident in one word.

"There's time." Sebastian's voice and aura were both remarkably serene. "May I, Leam?"

"Fine," Leam replied, his fingers fidgety, the tapping of his toe incessant.

Sebastian smiled, eyes still aimed above. "What do you see when you look up at the sky?"

The breeze tickled the hairs on Leam's arms. He looked hard at this man with the silver hair, and, reluctantly, tilted his head back. A soft raindrop or two patted his face; only two stars remained, both faint. "I don't know," he eventually said. "I see what's up there, I guess. I see the stars."

"One day you'll have a very different answer for that question," Sebastian said.

"Why, what do you see?"

"Many things. But lately I see water." Sebastian peeled his attention away from the sky and stuck it square on Leam. "I see waves."

Leam furrowed his brow when—WOOSH—Sebastian sprung to his feet, the rattling chains of his swing tangling around each other. His eyes were on the woods, darting between tree gaps. Leam stood, too, following Sebastian's line of sight when the lamp above the stairs of the school snuffed out. Miller was already running toward a particularly dark patch of forest where Leam thought he could hear something moving, something stepping on sticks, brushing against bushes and branches.

"Why is he—?"

"Go now, Leam," Sebastian urged, as he took off after Miller, and before Leam could say anything else, he was being pushed by an invisible force toward the front of the school, his feet an inch off the ground. Movement in his periphery lassoed his gaze left—the set of pine trees that had been hiding his Range Rover dropped through the ground as if the sheet of grass supporting their weight had been yanked out from under them. The SUV slid toward the road in pace with Leam, both converging on the same point, and before Leam knew it, he was seated inside as the Rover slid to a stop, straddling the yellow lines of Blaff Street exactly as it had before.

Gripping the steering wheel, Leam spotted the white markings on his hands, their glow less faint than the last time he had looked. He could feel energy radiating from them, too, and though cognizant that his mind was apt to playing tricks, he could feel himself being drawn to the Manor, drawn to the sitting room on the first floor, drawn to the place where the man in white had suggested he should begin his quest. Just as Leam's mind began to wander away further, his own inner voice was abruptly cut off, replaced by that of Sebastian.

"Leam, go now!"

And Leam hit the gas, unsure if he had consciously pounded the pedal or if it had been done under the same magical power that had swept him away from the swing set. Tires spun against damp pavement—the scattering of rain drops had yielded to a constant drizzle—before their treads caught the road and the Range Rover shot off toward the Manor, away from Sebastian, Miller, and whatever troublesome entity or force was so close by.

Leam stared through the windshield, his eyes chasing the endless stretch of yellow lines disappearing beneath the grill, all the while peppering the rearview mirrors with a barrage of brief and frenzied inspections for any danger that might be coming from behind. His senses were tuned on the Range Rover and the surroundings outside of it, but his mind was focusing in on the only thing that mattered to him right now.

"Let's see what you got, Sara, you bitch."

CHAPTER 46

Heavy rain battered the roof of the Range Rover as Leam sped to the end of Whitewax Way, jammed on the brakes and skidded into a pocket of darkness just off the cul-de-sac. He switched the lights off and cut the engine. Reaching over the center console, he fumbled to unzip the duffel bag, his unsteady hand fishing around inside and hooking onto an orange Gatorade, which he reeled in and downed in a matter of seconds. It was sugary and warm, but soothingly so, and Leam felt his jagged pulse ease, despite the unnerving image forefront in his mind. An image of a man's horrifying face; a man who had been standing calmly beside the Boulevard just a mile down the road; a man who had been smiling, eyes crazy; a man who had shown no concern for the rain dumping onto his greased-back black hair that fell past the shoulders of his trench coat.

Leam was freaking out because the man had just been waiting, staring and smiling. If he had been trying to stop Leam or chase him down, then Leam could at least make sense of it, but if the man knew Leam was coming, which Leam believed to be the case, then what was the purpose of just watching the Range Rover fly by?

Leam grabbed a water and chugged that, too, trying to steady himself, for it hadn't only been the greasy-haired smiling creep. Closer to the school—and the center of town—Leam had spotted a few Darkness groups along the roadsides, and oddly, none of them had paid him any notice. He was getting the feeling that the slew of trench coaters hadn't convened in Harbing to come for him, but there was no way to truly know.

So he concentrated on what he did know. He knew that his visions were important; Sebastian had confirmed that. Sebastian had also let on that other hybrids were capable of traveling to the "phantasmal world," like the slain Christian Duncan, the last prospect to have worn the watch banded around Leam's wrist.

But was Leam still a prospect? He knew Sebastian's answer to that was a definitive no. But he sensed that in Gideon's eyes, Leam still remained a possibility. If the greasy-haired smiler was just standing in the rain like a total creep instead of firing a kill spell between Leam's eyes as he sped by, then it stood to reason that Gideon hadn't yet ruled Leam out, which was probably the only reason he was still alive.

But as he peered out the rain-beaded window up White-wax Way, it dawned on him that whatever Gideon and Sebastian thought they knew was irrelevant to Leam *here,* a cigar spear's throw from the Manor's gates. Leam had been told so many things by so many people, but now was about what he could figure out for himself, by himself.

The delightenment markings—their glow dim, yet constant—had been branded on *his* hands, and whatever lay between him and the sitting room, ought to be getting itself ready. Leam had been put through a lot of crap and, up to this point, had physically and somewhat mentally endured. So if keeping her rotten stepson out of the mansion was Sara's goal, she had better have laid it all out there best she could, because Leam had a pair of glowing hands and a heat in his chest sending flames shooting out to his fingers and toes. He didn't have magic—no, he didn't have that—but he had a growing fire in his chest, and a volatile bull that he could feel starting to snort. A bull that he would not attempt to control if it chose to rise.

Leam got out of the car, his clothes soaked through by his fourth step toward the wrought iron bars and intricate, ivy leaf patterning of the gate. Something in his gut told him that the gate would open for him—that Sara would want to lure him inside before unleashing her worst. If not, though, he had a backup plan in the form of a low hanging oak tree branch three quarters of the way down the estate's west wall.

As he stepped off wet pavement onto slick cobblestones, Leam sensed that the small statues that sat atop the gate's end posts had been expecting him. Trying to peer down the west wall, all he could see was darkness and sheets of cascading rain. Reluctantly, he blew a stream of breath toward the crow, which, as it always did, transformed from rusty and motionless into silver and animated. The progression began, and after a quick look behind him for the smiling man, Leam smiled himself, watching the gleaming flower drop from the crow's beak, its petals separating, one of which floated onto the rusted shoulder of the monk, who sparked to life, tossed back its shiny hood, and scanned Leam's face with its red laser eyes.

Normally, the gate would have clinked open, however tonight it stayed closed and locked. Leam waited for at least thirty seconds and was just about ready to set off through the dark sheets of cascading rain toward the west wall when the shiny crow, with its talons clawed to the post, feverishly flapped its wings. It opened its mouth. The voice that squawked out sounded like Sara's.

"If you cherish your rotten, embarrassing life, go away. Nothing but death awaits you here. If you feel otherwise, try to come in, but tomorrow they'll be tossing your body into a grave beside your whore mother."

Leam slapped rain away from his eyes and said, "Oh go fu—"

But a loud crash, like a metal safe smashing onto the street from high above, ate up Leam's words. Simultaneous to the deafening noise, a translucent sheet of blue light settled over the entire estate, from the top floor natatorium all the way down to the walls that bordered the property. It faded a moment later, but despite its invisibility, Leam knew that whatever he had unwittingly activated—some sort of protective spell or barrier enchantment—was still there, still intact. And jumping over the wall from a tree branch was no longer an option. The crow squawked, though this time it sounded like a cough of laughter.

Leam stood there, soaking wet, glaring at the silver bird without a clue as to his next move. His head fell limp as he leaned forward and put his hands on the wrought iron bars.

When his skin touched the gate, the centermost metal ivy leaf began to glow—warm, golden light that was soon spreading concentrically outward, igniting other leaves, one by one, until a large portion of the middle of the gate was glowing. Heat blustered into Leam's face. Some of the metal began to melt, hot drippings of orange and gold falling between the cracks in the cobblestone. In the heart of the gate, a hole had presented itself, its edges sticky and smoldering, and without hesitation, Leam dove through, a few scrapes on his face and arms as he got to his feet, wiping the mud off the front of his shirt. He peeked back and saw that the gate's leafy patterning and iron bars had reconstructed themselves, as if the temporary metamorphosis had never happened. But it had, and because it had happened upon his touch, Leam felt that maybe some of his magical powers from the field of green hadn't totally worn off.

"Me one, Bitch zero," he muttered as he started jogging up the long winding driveway, quickly formulating a plan. His new black watch didn't tell the time, but the time didn't matter. Leam knew that he didn't have a lot of it.

He figured the front door, off to his left, was probably his worst chance at getting inside, so he decided to run along the side of the house to see if anything presented itself. When the cobblestones beneath his soggy Nikes became the pebbled pathway that led to the back of the property, Leam veered left on a whim. He hurdled over a hedge of black roses and cautiously approached the largest of the music room's windows, a giant G-clef. He put his hands on the glass to push it up and—ZAP—the window flashed blue and he was knocked off his feet, an intense electrical charge surging through his body and throwing him back onto the hedge, its black roses burning through his clothes and skin until he twisted himself off onto the path.

Leam got up, patting out the smoking singes on his jeans and T-shirt, curses spitting from his mouth as he plucked thorns out of his arms, neck and cheek. He went to give the hedge a piece of his mind, but mid kick he slipped and fell on his back like a circus clown. As he lay there getting pummeled by rain, he thought he heard a distant squawk that sounded like *"Tie game."*

He shot to his feet and ran to the back of the mansion, stepping onto the red-bricked patio and moving to the sliding glass door that opened up into the kitchen. Peering far across the lawn, Leam noticed that the fire pit at the very edge of the yard was twitching, as if the ground was quaking beneath it. Despite the unrelenting rainfall, thick black clouds were puffing out of it, like it was a smokestack of one of those old-time factories in the height of the industrial revolution. Wasting precious seconds by watching the pit's unrest, a shiver slipped down Leam's body that he knew had nothing to do with the rain.

He turned back toward the house, putting a tentative finger on the handle of the sliding door and—ZAP—his hand was thrown backward with such force that his entire arm swung around and around like the blade of a jet propeller. His pinkies prickled as if stabbed by needles, but was that from the *ZAP* or the huff and puff of the bull?

Leam grinned, his face feeling warm as he ran through the side garden around to the other side of the Manor, which was a massive, ivy-laden stone wall pocked with a few windows looking out from each story. Leam knew beforehand it was no good, but he yanked out a chunk of muddy grass anyway and heaved it at one of the two windows that bookended the ever cold and inactive sitting room chimney. The clump hit the window with a sizzle, and was zapped into nothing, as if the glass pane, which flashed blue for a hot second, had eaten it whole.

Picturing Sara's nasty smug little face, Leam felt the soles of his feet get warm—a welcome sensation—as he sloshed around to the front yard, a huge space of endless grass, oak trees and plush shrubbery. After a quick scan of the mansion, Leam's gaze settled on the front door. The front door. Part of him had known all along, but he had avoided it because of the larger-than-life statues that lined both sides of the approach. If Sara had bewitched them, they could spring to life at any moment and clobber him with the marble swords, clubs and pickaxes held in their giant hands or resting at their chiseled sides. He knew it was going to be trouble, how could it not be? But he had to try. He'd rather be killed by a statue than relinquish victory to a stepmother who deserved to be buried alive.

The soles of his feet were burning now, like he was walking over a bed of hot coals. Leam felt his heart pounding quicker and harder as he started splattering up the pathway, cutting right between the two lines of statues. Their jeweled, pupil-less eyes glinted down at him as he trudged by with deliberate and slow movement, his breath held in his chest as he tensed for an attack.

But his eyelids began to shutter as he harnessed the small amount of fear Sara's traps had instilled in him and converted it into anger, an anger he was now losing control over, an anger whipping the bull in its hind legs, forcing it to charge up his body. Leam swiftly stepped past the last of the statues unscathed, hopped up two steps and stopped. Could it have really been that easy? Sara must have thought he couldn't make it this far.

There, in front of him, was the huge iron door. Leam grinned, swiping rain water away from his face as a suffocating heat swelled into his head. He felt his eyes go dark and he stepped forward and pressed his palm into the door's center.

Two things happened in the blur of a second. He removed his hand; and a large blackbird with yellow eyes burst through the section of door where Leam had left his palm print, stabbing him in the gut with its long pinpoint-sharp beak.

Leam cried out, falling backward as the bird yanked its beak out of his bloody flesh and shot away through the lessening rain. Something caught Leam before his back could hit the ground, wrapping itself around his limbs as he stared at the hot crimson goo gurgling out of the pinball-size hole in his stomach, only faintly aware that his body was being dragged upward through the air.

He pulled his eyes off the wound to see that several ivy strands had torn away from the Manor and were pulling him up the facing of the house. Before he could brace himself, the entwining arms of ivy flung him in the air, launching his flailing body over the lip of the roof, shooting him close to thirty feet above the apex. His heart caught in his throat as he dropped downward, heading right for the middle of the glass ceiling that spread over the enormous indoor pool that ran the length of the Manor's top floor, and with an angry, come-get-me yell, he hugged himself into a fetal position and—

SMASH!

—crashed through the glass, falling down into the warm water of the pool alongside thousands of tiny jagged shards of broken roof. He plunged to the bottom as what felt like acid poured into the hole in his abdomen. Hundreds of aqua-blue lamps glowed at him from all sides, but all went black as his head met the pool floor with a sickening thud.

CHAPTER 47

Did you see him? Did you see his trench coat? That was him! The Spirit of the Coming! The guy we saw at the COO, he shot through the tube in the Room of the River! That was the same guy!"

"Relax," Sebastian said, standing on muddy grass behind Harbing High, his silver hair soaked, matted down over his forehead. The rain was dying down. His eyes were trained on the woods, about twenty feet away.

"What do you make of it?" Miller tugged at his earlobe, pacing back and forth parallel to the tree line. "I mean this is crazy! Why would the Spirit choose a man of Darkness as its vessel?"

Sebastian was quiet for a few breaths—it was a good question. "I don't know the reason. But whether spoken of as the Spirit or, as they do, the Word, its wisdom speaks to both sides. When there's time to think, I'll scour my LOMAK for answers."

"Better it took one of them than one of us, I guess."

"On the surface, I'd agree. But Gideon might be able to finagle it into an opportunity."

"Where do you suppose the Spirit is guiding that guy?" Miller was wringing the rain out the bottom of his sea-green shirt. "He looked right through me. Gave me the willies."

All Sebastian offered was a shake of the head. His eyes had the woods and wouldn't stray.

"So this is got to be it, though, right, Sebastian? Think about it. You take the poem that that guy said in the tube, or what his image said anyway…the warning…'*Enduring minds set for fire and frost,*' remember? Now add that to Break Lock… add *that* to the gas threat—"

"Uniquely-shaped coincidences seem to be sliding into a perfect fit." In Sebastian's periphery, Miller was tugging on both earlobes now.

"So, c'mon, Sebastian, I can't handle this! I struggle with patience, sir, you know this about me already. I'm asking you, do you think this is it?"

There was a pause. "Yes, Miller. This is the start."

"Whoa…I thought so. I just… I had a feeling."

"Human existence will be separated into two periods: from the birth of man until now, and from now until it's over. With the dawn of Leam Holt, the fight has given way to the war."

"You're saying that all of this, from way back when… that's just been a fight?"

Sebastian nodded.

"And now comes the war?"

Sebastian nodded.

Miller stopped moving. "So then…you lied to him."

"I told him what he needed to hear."

"So he *is* a true prospect. I knew it, *I knew it.*"

"He *was* a prospect, Miller. The last prospect."

A twig snapped beneath Miller's feet as he resumed pacing. "Then the search is over? Leam is the prophet?"

Sebastian looked at Miller through shiny eyes and nodded. "Ours or theirs."

Miller was quiet for a moment. A plane swept low overhead, descending to Newark Airport. "But then why—?"

"I had to play down the magnitude of it all, for his sake. It'll be far easier for Leam to carry on if he doesn't realize who he truly is."

"Ours or theirs," Miller murmured. "I guess we have to hope the good within him overpowers the evil."

Sebastian smiled. "Faith is our strongest asset. It will always be, Miller."

Miller touched his slick forehead, eyebrows lowered in thought. "But your tirade, sir—"

"Tirade's a bit strong."

"You broke the kid down."

"And he got back up."

"I get that," Miller said, "I do. But the heightened security and the hidden secrets of Break Lock...You knew that poor kid had nothing to do with it. There's no way he'd be involved on their end."

"I needed him to see me angry. I can't allow him to think I'm the ever-kindhearted and all forgiving Christian ideal of God."

"But you are, sir." Miller pulled a wet leaf off his neck and flicked it to the ground. "Just a bit more of a bad ass."

Sebastian held a hand up, pressing the other against his ear. An unseen person, or persons, was within earshot, having stepped over the invisible alert line that Sebastian had cast out right before he and Leam had sat on the swings earlier tonight.

"*They're in the woods,*" Sebastian said to Miller via telemast. "*Coming right at us.*"

"*How many?*"

"*Four. Now five.*" Sebastian faced his palm at Miller. A flashlight and a small blue plastic bag of dog feces popped into Miller's right hand, while into his left, formed the leather handle of a leash, the clip at the end of its line clasping onto the collar of a Siberian husky that wiggled itself out of the air.

"*What's the plan?*" Miller telemasted.

"*Stand your ground.*" Sebastian's hair shortened as if his brain was a sponge of tiny mouths sucking in every follicle, the strands of silver turning wheat-field gold.

"*I can get reinforcements, sir!*"

"*It's not that—I can take these men down with a shimmy of my hips. I've spotted eyes. They know we're here, but not who we are. Right now we're Unknowings. You snap your finger and disappear, we're the enemy. Gideon cannot learn I was here."*

"I get it, sir, but no one's going to believe two Unks are taking a dog for a walk behind a school at one o'clock in the morning."

"We're drunk, it just stopped raining, Wolfgang needed a walk. If anything we'll get information out of them. Stand your ground and play the part."

Miller pressed the flashlight on, a cone of light spreading over the husky, which was happily pawing at the wet ground. A moment later, two men in black trench coats emerged through the trees, followed by three others, big old dudes. The moon reawakened after a thirty minute snooze behind the fleeting cloud cover.

"What are you guys doing out here?" one of the two front-most men said, smoothing his sharp-edged goatee with his middle and index finger.

Miller let out a belch reeking of rank booze, and then giggled. Sebastian pulled a can of a Miller Lite from his back pocket, cracking it open and downing it in seconds. He flung the can over his head, held up his arms and hollered, "CAN YOU HEAR ME, NEW JERSEY?" The husky howled at the moon.

"Drunks," the man said, as the man next to him—short and dumpy—plodded forward, stubby fingers poking out of his sleeves. "You keep that mongrel on its leash," he sneered at Miller.

"Who Wolfgang, here? He wouldn't hurt anybody, if anything he's pleased to meet you." The husky gave a playful bark.

"He doesn't wanna know me," Dumpy said, creeping closer. "I don't like Eskimos, do I, Flint?"

The man with the sharp goatee grinned, the group shifting forward. The distance between the two Light and five Dark was now that of a picnic table.

"So, what are you doing out here, Giggles?" Dumpy snarled, glaring up into Miller's face, which was a good foot above his own. "Funny time of the night to be taking that mongrel for a squirt and a push."

"I'm not doing a thing." Miller hiccupped, shaking his head rapidly and taking a cautionary step back. "Nothing at all, we was just passing by."

Sebastian wobbled back and forth on his feet, watching Miller feign fright.

"They're a couple of drunks, Kavitch. Always the suspicion," the one named Flint said. The three behind Flint and the dumpy Kavitch—all enormous Shrek-like goons—sniggered like fools.

Kavitch spat at the dog and shifted his glare to Sebastian, who shook sprinkles of water out of his short golden hair, adopting an expression that would fit him right in with the goons. Kavitch waved his palm in Sebastian's and Miller's direction, and the air between him and them crinkled like it was made of Saran wrap—a crinkle, Sebastian knew, that Kavitch thought only his men could sense or see.

"This one looks ready to piss himself," Kavitch said, a stubby finger aimed at Miller. The words were muted—muffled—as if they had traveled through rubber.

"You'd be too if you were him," Flint said, his voice carried by the same rubbery current.

"Exactly! So why isn't the other one scared?"

On the other side of the crinkle, Sebastian avoided Flint's eye.

"Because he's an idiot," Flint said to Kavitch. Sebastian started strumming an imaginary banjo, pretending to be taken by the sky. "Look at him. He's too oiled up to know what's going on." Flint smoothed down his goatee, keeping it sharp. "You want to scare him, pull down your pants and show him that podgy cottage-cheese ass of yours."

The goons guffawed, and Flint, who seemed rather pleased himself, began to walk away toward the school.

"Do you think that maybe he's playing at it?" Kavitch called to him. "Because I don't see stupid in those eyes."

Sebastian sensed Miller's body stiffen with tension, and he telemasted, "*Stay the part.*"

"He's gonzoed," Flint yelled back. "He doesn't know what planet he's on. Let's go."

"If you ask me," Kavitch said, baring a set of ugly, mismatched teeth, "he looks like pictures I've seen on the Light board. Pictures of—"

"If that was him," Flint shouted over his shoulder, "we'd all be strung up by our toes by now. It's two drunk Skunks and a dog, nothing more, and if they're acting extra kooky, it's that they're already feeling the effects. Now, c'mon now, the show's not waiting for us."

The three goons set off after Flint. Kavitch stayed put. From Blaff street Flint yelled, "Let them be, Kavitch. It's the Gujin's that's to mess them up, not you. Raxton's orders."

Only the pupils of Kavitch's eyes moved at first, beaming in on Sebastian's face. Satisfied or not, he gave the belt of his trench coat a good cinch, and then swiped his palm against the air like he was cleaning it with Windex, the crinkles stretching smooth.

"It's your lucky day, sweethearts," he sneered, his voice freed of all rubber. He turned and plodded after the others, hocking a splat of tartar sauce-like spit at Wolfgang's hind legs as he sloshed by. Sebastian waited for Kavitch to reach the slick asphalt of Blaff, and when the dumpy man vanished out of sight, the husky that Miller had bent down to pet vanished, too, along with the beer can, the flashlight, the blue plastic bag of feces, and the drunk demeanors.

"Gujin?" Miller asked, standing upright. "That has to be the gas, right? Do you think they already released it?"

Sebastian rested his hands on his hips and looked around. "There is something in the air." His nostrils twitched. "Other than grass and mulch and the stench of Darkness left in the wake of those men. It's very faint."

"Sugar cookies, sir."

Sebastian pulled another pocket of air through his nose. "Is that what that is?" He felt his eyes getting a little itchy.

"Definitely. I eat them all the time." Miller paused. "Wait, hang on a sec." His eyes closed and opened a second later. "Sir, the search for DHQ has yielded nothing. Broox and Zalika are still combing through the last of the Jace-related data, but...it doesn't look good. There seem to be no loose ends, sir, just dead ones."

"Get back to the COO and stay with those two until there's nothing left to sift through. If anything pops up, you let me know immediately."

"You're staying around here?"

"If something's about to go down, I want to be right on top of it."

Miller rubbed his eyes, gave his leader a quick, short-lived smile, and was gone.

Sebastian stared blindly at the woods, strands of hair pushing through his scalp like millions of tiny silver snakes slithering to the proper length as their golden heads seared off into nothing. He walked over to the swing set and knelt down, rubbing his hands over the upturned mulch where Leam Holt had rested his feet. The feel of the wet chips of wood and soupy dirt was but a fleeting comfort as Sebastian thought about the boy who had kicked into the ground, swinging back and swinging forward, coming down and soaring up.

CHAPTER 48

He was swimming through clear water, the three oars—one dirty and wooden, one bright yellow, one bronze—getting smaller as they fled, their six ends almost touching together to form a triangular abyss of brilliant emerald green.

He made a move to chase them, but something had his leg. Tangles extending from a forest of shiny gray seaweed had snared around his left ankle, pulling him downward. He thrashed around, kicking wildly to free himself, but it was no good. His muscles began to tire as he lost breath, the fight within him growing weak.

But as his mind clouded, close to slipping into darkness, a naked woman slithered out of the silvery weeds, red veins covering her white scaly skin, and she broke the reedy binds around his ankle. He peered down at her through the water, which was suddenly getting colder and redder, as if polluted by clouds of frigid blood pushing in.

The woman's uncommonly blue eyes grabbed hold of his, her veiny face calm and happy, and as the hungry seaweed swallowed her back below, she spoke to him. He couldn't hear her—the blood clouds carried a loud hiss—but he had no trouble reading her lips.

"Swim up, Leam. Swim up. Do not stay down here any longer."

And he darted up through the crimson water, his eyes closing as he sped toward the surface, red getting pink, pink getting clear, clear getting blue and...

Leam's entire body sprung out of the glowing water, shooting up out of the pool with such force that he was completely above the surface before dropping back in, his feet padding onto the jeweled pool floor. Drawing air into his aching lungs, he doggy-paddled to the nearest edge, gasping for breath. He pulled himself out of the water and collapsed on red tiling that was sprinkled with shards of glass. He rolled onto his back and the most recent events came back to him in distorted sounds and hazy color: a dive through a melted hole in the gate, an electric shock from a locked window, an anxious walk between two lines of monstrous statues, a blurred hand extending for the front door and...

Leam gasped, yanking up his soaked T-shirt, his hand covering the gash where the blackbird had stabbed him through the stomach...yet he touched only smooth wet skin. The wound had sealed, a small circular scar above his bellybutton.

As he sat up, distant memories flooded his mind, a slide show in blacks and whites of the numerous times he had been unhappy and depressed as a kid, how he would submerge himself into the pool and it would somehow cheer him up, somehow ease his worries, if only for a small breath of time.

The pool heals! Leam thought, immediately feeling foolish he hadn't pieced that together until now.

He got to his feet and caught his reflection in one of the large single-paned windows sandwiched between the warmth of the natatorium and the blackness outside. The pool water had healed all the visible scrapes, bruises and welts that had been inflicted by Sara's protective magic. Leam poked his fingers through the small holes that the black rose bushes had singed through his Ramones T-shirt, but felt no corresponding burns into the skin underneath. He pictured Sara's ugly, smiling face—it was his favorite goddamn T-shirt—and felt the low rumble of the bull in his belly. He turned from the window and got on the move.

Between the pool and the back staircase that led down to the fourth floor hallway by Zach's room, stood a thin unsupported porcelain doorframe whirring like a gentle hairdryer. Leam strode through it, emerging with his hair, skin and clothes as dry as rye. He moved to the stairs, descending to the fourth floor, looking and listening with keen eyes and ears. It was his feet, though, that sensed trouble first.

The staircase's purple carpeting began transforming to brown soil like that of a forest, and a great rumbling noise came at Leam from behind. He stopped about halfway down the stairs and looked back to see a huge wave of thick sludgy mud pouring down from the natatorium. After the mental equivalent of smacking himself in the face, Leam bolted down the remaining steps, ducked into Zach's room, banged the door closed behind him and screamed. Hundreds of bleached-white snakes—huge ones, small ones, in-betweeners—were writhing around the room, on the carpet, bed, dresser, everywhere, and all had bent their heads at him, widening their mouths with a loud, collective hiss.

Leam flung open the door, smacking an approaching three-footer into a collage-covered wall of hot celebrity girls and the main guy from One Direction. He jolted back into the hallway—now covered with over a foot of brown slop that drowned his sneakers in two steps—praying he'd make it to the center staircase that would spiral him to the first floor.

The mud was rising as more and more of it rolled down from the back staircase, almost to Leam's knees as he ran, and snakes as thick as teenage trees were gaining on him, slithering atop the mud, flicking their long forked tongues. He tried to calm himself and magic-up a protective bubble, like the ones in the park and at the field of green—he concentrated on the word "bubble" in his mind—but no help came, only panic.

Leam heard a hiss right on top of him, and turned to see the fangs of the nearest snake, less than two feet behind his shoulder. Leam ejected a primal growl, and was pushing forward, trudging through the thigh-high sludge when all of the closed doors along the hallway banged open.

Billiard balls fired at Leam as he roared past the game room. He dodged and ducked away from a few, but most pounded into his body, one whacking into the side of his head. A torrid headache burst through Leam's ear nearly shattering his brain, but Sara's face, laughing and jeering inside his mind, kept him tromping forward as he came up upon the art studio and—THWACK—a can smacked hard against his shoulder, splattering thick black paint all over the side of his face and neck as a boxful of sharply-pointed paint brushes pierced into his flesh.

Screaming curse words and running on pure nerves, Leam finally saw the center landing, the main staircase hidden from view just off to the left. He threw a vicious elbow at the snake poised to clamp onto his shoulder, turned to hop down the steps and slammed smack into a brick wall that was barricading the staircase, flattening him onto his back.

He sat up, cringing, ready for fangs to sink into him, and a ravenous muddy tidal wave to gobble him whole, but Leam felt and heard nothing but strong wind. A half-second of time played out in front of his eyes in detailed slow motion.

The massive armoire that sat opposite his old room slid toward Zach's end of the hallway with tremendous speed, narrowly missing Leam and crashing into the flood of mud, stopping it dead, along with all the rest of Sara's bewitched objects and killer snakes. It blocked off the entire south end of the fourth floor and a quiet calm sat heavy in the air.

Leam clambered to his feet, gaping at the wondrous piece of furniture and running his fingers across the wicker, woven into floral and ivy leaf patterning. One of the leaves burned orangey-gold at his touch, and he felt a vibration inside his pocket that wasn't his cell phone. He reached in and removed it...and then he knew. The bones in his legs folded like rubber, and he slumped up against a wall mirror, feeling blood drain from his face and run hollow down his body...because he knew. He knew. Clutching his mother's acorn, Leam knew what had moved the armoire. She had. His mother was ivy. It made perfect sense. Aggie's alternate being was ivy.

The only alternate being he had ever come across, at least that he was aware of, was his father's, so Leam had assumed that they all must be animals or tiny people, like the hog man. But as Sebastian's voice sounded in his head, that assumption was wrong.

"You can imagine how hard it is to protect ourselves, and our secrets, from things and beings that can truly be anything."

That would mean that it was possible for Aggie's alternate being to be something like ivy, which didn't necessarily breathe, but was still alive. And not just *possible*, but *likely*, because Sebastian had said that the more magically-capable the host, the more complex the alternate being. It made sense. Leam's mother was killed young, well before she could attain and master the complicated types of magic that Bram had. But still, moving that giant armoire via its ivy-leaf patterning seemed pretty impressive to Leam.

A second voice came up from the back of Leam's head, sounding awfully like Sara.

"She's dead. She's been underground in a coffin for eighteen years."

"Shut up," Leam murmured.

There wasn't a doubt in his mind that Aggie's mystical ivy had acted here tonight, despite her death so long ago. And that meant that she had set up protection for him, here at the Manor, before he was born, perhaps sensing that her days were limited and her newborn son was going to need her someday, after a childhood filled with loveless neglect she was powerless to prevent. Leam wasn't sure if he needed the acorn on him for her enchantments to be effective, but either way, the woman had saved his life.

With the spiral stairs barricaded, Leam pocketed the acorn and had only taken one step down the long stretch of hallway between him and the back staircase that led down to the library when another revelation weakened his knees. Outside, after being stabbed in the gut by the yellow-eyed blackbird, it had been strings of ivy that had broken his fall, carrying him up to the top of the Manor, and throwing him through the glass roof into the healing water of the pool.

He smiled wide, and then—PING—another thought, another realization. The strands of ivy on the high school wall, the warning he had seen on his way to Black Patch Park to meet the associate for the first time…that was his mother, too.

"Be brave. Help will come when you most need it."

Leam's body was tattered with new bruises, swellings and gashes, but the only thing he could feel at the moment was a warmth in his chest that had never been there before. His father had killed his mother almost two decades ago, but if she was able to warn him about the dangers ahead, and even come to his aid, like tonight, that would have to mean that her spirit, or even something tangible, was still alive. He covered his face with his hands, shaking his head, eyes scrunched closed, letting the warmth fill him up, a warmth so unlike the suffocating heat of the bull.

Feeling toasty all over, Leam wiped his eyes and started down the hall again, but had to dive to the ground to avoid something shiny spinning right for his face. Leam looked back at the quivering handle of a dagger, its blade pierced through the center of one of his mother's wicker leaves. Anger stabbed Leam as he hopped up, his gaze down the hall as several dozen other daggers wiggled free from the wall, and one by one, fired his way. Ducking under the second, he bolted down the hallway directly at them, dodging dagger after dagger, revenge infused in every sweat bead seeping through his pores.

He stole a look at the painting of the sheep in business suits as he flew by. He wasn't sure—it had just been a glance—but he could have sworn that the sheep were no longer chatting up each other or reading the Wall Street Journal. Instead, they all looked terrified, as if the train had derailed.

A dagger glanced off his shoulder, but Leam ran on. A collection of trumpets broke free from a glass case, blaring loudly, bouncing through the air, banging down onto his head and body. He covered his face, blindly running forward, and smacked into the wall just beyond the side landing, falling down flat against the floor. The trumpets smashed into the wall, and crashed down upon him, becoming still and without magic.

Leam climbed out from under the pile of horns, fresh cuts and bumps acquainting themselves with billiard ball bruises, paint brush welts and the like. He sighed, hoping the worst was over, but with just one step to the top stair he froze, his hand an inch away from the cold silver railing.

"Jesus Christ..."

Just as the snakes had done in Zach's room, every one of the hundred silver crows that hung motionlessly throughout the stairwell turned their sleek heads at Leam, a malicious glint in every eye.

CHAPTER 49

Climbing to the top of the ivory staircase, Gideon looked down the dark hallway to his right and grinned. The dot of bright white light at the very end meant Cleanwalker was still having his fun with the skinless associate. Straight in front of him, however, the stretch of hallway known as the Bolt was void of activity, which Gideon attributed to the late hour and the release of Gujin7B, which had shot restless excitement into the men and women of Darkness like a B-12 injection. It was, Gideon understood, a time to be out celebrating. He, however, holding a spray bottle, had a different sort of festivity in mind.

Gideon pivoted left and set off down the third hallway, the tips of the fingers on his right hand touching the tips of those on his left. Tiny globes of faint yellow light floated around him like lightning bugs.

With his mood serene and his head perfectly still as he walked, Gideon thought about how poetically the recent events had fallen into place. The only man with a remote chance to neutralize Gujin7B had become the first person of Light to be exposed to it. Gideon was just now returning from a pleasurable little visit to Cell A, and the blond-haired leviathan had hardly been recognizable. As for mass exposure, any town, of course, would do, but what a stroke of beauty it was that, under his order, the diluted sample of the gas had been released in the very town where the brute's daughter had fled after precious Daddy had been snatched up.

Gideon came upon the hallway's dead end. A wall of stone. "Open."

The wall vanished, exposing a dark room faintly lit by candles on a table in its center and the turquoise glow of an aquarium off to the right. Gideon walked in and the stench of the room greeted him with open arms: the constant and delicious flatulence of Li Li, his pony-size armadillo pet with a half lizard, half turkey face. The creature—smacking its leathery lips—was plodding away toward the far wall, shedding yolky flakes of dandruff onto the filthy stone floor.

Gideon placed the spray bottle on the table and went to aquarium—dead goldfish and glittery diamonds floating together in harmony. His eyes got lost in the blue. A quick spell of weak coughing broke his trance, and he looked across the room at the shape of a woman on a dirty mat, lying on her side with her back to him, pulling a blanket over her naked body as Li Li neared her. Gideon swallowed hard, his heart rate elevating as he stared at the small black markings that pocked the woman's arms, upper back and ribcage before the blanket slid up and hid them.

Gideon grinned and returned to the table. His loosely-fitting shirt peeled off his body, a shiny, black medallion rising out of an inside pocket, its starfish-like tentacles setting down on the wooden table.

"I see you and Li Li are getting acquainted," Gideon said. His black pants tore off his skeletal legs, and, along with the shirt, skimmed across the length of the floor into the base of a vertically-spinning globe.

"It won't take its eyes off me," the woman shuddered, the massive creature a few feet away from her, wheezing and flatulating.

"*She* won't take *her* eyes off of you," Gideon corrected her. "Tell me. Would you like me to remind you that she's been here longer than you have?"

Sara's cheek was flat against the thin mattress. He couldn't see her face, but he heard every trembling word. "Does she... mean more to you than me?"

"Shut up or you'll spoil my mood." Gideon stood still in nothing but a yellowing pair of tighty whiteys. "And lay one magical finger on Li Li and I'll bite it off," he added, placing his hand on top of the black medallion. Radio static crinkled out, followed by a muffled voice—male—beneath his palm.

"Stop your crying. Can't you hear him? Can't you see it's almost time?"

"Splendid," Gideon breathed, removing his hand from the starfish and snatching up the spray bottle. As he took slow steps toward Sara, his underwear shed off, the glow of the aquarium reflecting off his pale body. She turned away from the wall to see him and shuddered, her eyes wide and shiny.

"Again?" she said, slapping her hand over her mouth as if the word had only been meant to sound inside her head, immediately adding, in a much more sultry tone, "You are insatiable."

Gideon flicked his finger; the blanket slid off of her, freeing more black markings on her shoulders and chest from suffocation. Getting closer, Gideon marveled at how helpless she looked, her eyes glued to the spray bottle. He felt a huge grin cut up his mask-like face, as, outside the small high window, early sunless sky waited for the first light of what was sure to be a glorious day.

CHAPTER 50

Why? Leam thought, his body battered with pain as he stood dead still atop the back staircase that tunneled two floors down to Bram's library. *Why? Why?*

Hundreds of now-animate silver crows were staring at him, their sharply pointed beaks glistening, their eyes shiny and mean. In eighteen years up and down these steps, the birds had hovered without motion, and with each vulnerable step down into this tightly confined space, Leam would be playing right into their claws if their aim was to attack, and how could it not be? But what choice did he have? This was the only way down, and down was where he had to be.

Leam had a feeling these birds had been waiting for this for years and years, and now had come the reward for their patience. Leam flicked out his hands as if to say *Screw it* and dove forward onto the chrome-plated stairs, sliding downward on his belly as crow after crow shot at him with speed and vigor.

Leam tore past the third floor in seconds, screaming out as beaks stabbed into his back, and talons tore at his shirt and the skin beneath. Gaining velocity, his stomach slid over the stairs like a mallet swept across a xylophone board. Leam covered his head, braced for impact, and—CRASH—he pummeled through the glass door between the bottom step and the library, somersaulting over sharp bits of glass and banging into the large ivory Find-a-Thought at the center of the candlelit room.

Leam opened his eyes just in time to swat away crows aimed for his face, his palm bruising against their metallic solidity. He whacked one of the smaller ones across the room into a bookshelf, and it dropped to the plush maroon carpet, landing inches away from a stubby foot, reddish and glittery. Standing thirty feet away was the hog man, waving for Leam to rush over, the hood of his cloak pulled over his small hoggish head.

Leam hopped to his feet—angry crows pelting into him from all angles—and bolted toward the hog man, who was pushing aside a bookshelf with surprising ease, revealing a hidden, brightly-lit cubby about the size of a two-door closet. The hog man hobbled in, and Leam dove through a half-second later as the bookshelf was already gliding back into place. A crow the size of a cereal box shot through the crack just as the bookshelf closed, and Leam caught it out of the air before it could stab into the center of his chest.

"Where's the book, Leam?" the hog man said.

Leam wrestled the bird to the cement floor, its wings thrashing as it pecked violently at his bleeding hands.

"The book, Leam. Where is it?"

"What book? *What book?*" Leam shouted, pinning the crow down and watching the gleaming luster in its eyes fade away along with the magic that had given it life.

"The one you stole. Have you for—"

"There's no time for that!" Leam flung the dead hunk of metal aside, breathing heavily and grabbing at his side. "I gotta get downstairs!"

"Have you stopped here to return your father's book?"

"What are you kidding?" Leam laughed madly, lifting up his shirt, exposing the hundreds of wounds covering his arms, chest and stomach. "Do you think I'd go through all of this to bring you back your stupid book?"

The hog man threw off his hood, the coarse hide of his face glimmering with the same bronze that comprised Bram's knife handle. Leam felt his pinkies prickle and the bottoms of his feet get warm, as he wondered, for the first time, if his father's knife had been the instrument of his mother's death.

"I see you've managed to meet some more alternate beings tonight," the hog man spoke, his beady eyes trained on the crow.

"What are you talking about?" Leam yelled, sucking down air that smelled like horse stables. "There's seven thousand of these things out there! Sara bewitched them!"

"Of course they are bewitched, but they are more than simple magical statues that spring to life. They are extensions of her alternate being."

"What?"

"Her alternate being's alternate beings, you could say."

Leam sat back against the cinderblock wall, the stitch in his side healing as he pictured all the silver crows darting around the library, most likely awaiting his return so they could grant Sara's most coveted wish, a wish that she had vocalized often during Leam's childhood—that he die a terrible death. It was at this moment of reflection that the circular scar above his bellybutton tickled his attention, igniting the memory of the large yellow-eyed blackbird stabbing through the front door into his gut.

"She's the blackbird," he whispered. "Her alternate being is the crow."

"Yes, it is," the hog man said. "And every other crow in this place is an extension of that blackbird, and thus an extension of her. From up close—and frequenting the bedside table, I have been *up close* many times—the black markings speckled over her upper body are shaped like tiny crows. She's a filthy cow, your stepmother, but her magic is quite prodigious."

Leam nodded, his fingers rising and falling over the lumps growing atop his head, courtesy of the enraged trumpets two floors up.

"You know what?" he said. "Yeah, yeah that makes sense 'cause I don't know what exact strand of ivy is my mother's *true* alternate being—it could even be buried with her beneath the ground at Gaddiel's—but every leaf of ivy that helped me tonight has gotta be extensions of the real thing."

"You've figured that out, have you? Perhaps you aren't as stupid as you come across."

"Yeah, I did figure it out." Leam glared at the hog man. "She helped me. Looks like your *master* didn't completely kill her. Her spirit, or whatever, lives on inside of all these supplementary extensions."

An ugly smile of jagged brownish teeth darkened the hog man's face. "With that in mind, what can you tell me about the Manor's front gate?"

Leam's eyes opened wide. "Insane," he whispered, the word a feather fallen from his lips. "The hole I dove through... she melted the bars. The ivy-laden patterning all over that gate... that was her."

The hog man's proud chest deflated a bit. "And?"

"The bird on the post... Jeesum crow, it's another of Sara's, isn't it?"

"*What else?*" The hog man pulled the hood of his cloak back over his head. "How did I know you were coming tonight, Leam? How do you figure you never once until two weeks ago spotted me in my form as you see it now? How you never ever caught me off guard?"

For a brief second, deep inside the folds of the hood, the hog man's eyes shimmered with a reddish glow.

"That's you on the other post," Leam said. "Guarding the gate."

"An extension of me, yes. Very good."

Leam was quiet for a moment, then he shook his head. "But why'd you save me just now if you didn't help me at the gate?"

"I figured you had no chance at making it this far, a non-magic wielder thwarting magic. But since you have, I thought why not ask about the book." The hog man lowered his head and added, "I thought why not ask about your father."

"HEY!" Leam said, and the hog man's head snapped up. "You want answers, you gotta help get me out of here!"

"How could I ever trust you?"

"Use your gate eyes. Right now, do it. You see the Range Rover off to the side? The book's inside it. If I survive this night, it's yours. So help me, 'cause if you don't, those crows are gonna eat me alive."

The hog man closed his eyes. A red-laser dot glowed mutely behind the eyelids, extinguishing as they opened. "And what about your father?" he said.

"I didn't see him at the graveyard, and Sara doesn't give a crap that he's missing. That's all I know."

The hog man was quiet, scrutinizing Leam's face. "Fine," he said. "But I can only get you through the library. Beyond that you are on your own."

Leam murmured in agreement and felt his wrist go numb, as if an ice cube was melting on the skin. He held up his new, very old watch. Three digital numbers had appeared on the faceless dial, all glowing, their color as fluorescent red as the hog man's gatepost eyes.

3:00.

Before Leam had a moment to think, the numbers changed—2:59—and changed again—2:58. Coinciding with each second of the countdown, the markings on Leam's hands blinked white—a visible flash undiminished by the cubby's bright lights.

"What are you doing, Leam?"

"I didn't start it. Did you see me do anything?"

"What do you make of it?" the hog man asked, squinting at Leam's hands.

"I don't know, but I gotta get going. The watch senses things I can't."

The hog man grunted, his foot-hooves scraping the cement as he reached for the door. Leam grabbed the waist of his cloak and spun him around.

"Tell me if you were there," he said. "When he killed my mother, were you with him?"

The hog man stared at Leam unblinkingly. "Your watch ticks down, Leam. You don't have the time for that answer."

Leam met the stare, and then some. "Then I'll be back when I have more time."

"With the book," the hog man said. He swiped his cloak free but it took two tries.

"With the book," Leam said. "Let's go. Are you ready?"

The hog man nodded, his droopy hog ears straightening. "Stay. Stay until I tell you to run."

And with that, the book shelf slid open with a bang, the hog man scurrying toward the middle of the room beneath a swarm of birds—a blurry silver halo spinning above the library, thinning as crows plunged downward in attack. Bent in a runner's crouch inside the cubby, Leam watched the hog man stuff nearby books into the Find-a-Thought, as birds stabbed into and clawed at his thick rough hide. Leam peeked at his watch. 2:29.

Give me the signal, hog man, come on, give me the signal...

The hog man jammed one last book into the ivory contraption and rubbed his stubby hoof-hands together over the mouth. Bronze shards of glitter grated onto the small mountain of books crammed inside.

"GO!" he yelled at Leam, and dove under the nearest bench. Leam sprung forward, dashing for the French doors as a swirl of silver rained down, clouds of crows plummeting at him from the book-laden ceiling. Leam could feel them behind him, could see them in front. They came from everywhere, their sound a mixture of howling wind and rattling chains, but all of a sudden, with a loud crackle, shiny book parts shot out of the Find-a-Thought, exploding into heavy, jagged fragments of gilded bronze that burst out in every direction. Every single bird was hit by the shrapnel, and upon contact they were immobilized, stuck to the air.

Leam went untouched and threw open the French doors, looking back as he sprinted toward the main staircase. For a moment he was struck by the sheer beauty of the candlelit library, filled from wall to wall, floor to ceiling, with hundreds of exquisite, silver birds frozen still in the air. Beneath a bench, a shimmering knife handle spun to a stop.

The distance from the library at the northern end of the Manor to its center was long and progressively getting darker.

The sound of wind and chains returned, coming up behind him; Sara's crows must have broken free from their trance and were closing in. Leam made it to the stairs, lost his footing and skidded on his butt down all forty spiraling steps. He peeked at his watch—1:44—before his feet found the first floor and his eyes found darkness; not a light bulb on, nor a candlewick lit. The Manor, it seemed, was empty. No Sara, no Zach.

Leam shot into the kitchen on his right, sliding over the slippery floor tiles and banging into the marble-topped island. Hanging from hooks above his head, quivering knives and cleavers glinted with strange sparks of orange light. Leam froze stiff after scrambling to his feet, the pulsing of his markings falling dimmer as his gaze burned through the window to the edge of the backyard.

Viscous glowing lava poured over the sides of the pit, a fiery swirl devouring the dark inky lawn as it raged toward the house, and—

Thump, thump, thump, thump, thump.

Sara's crows, Leam knew by the sound, had caught up, banging into the kitchen door Leam had closed. He spun around to the door that opened into the living room, while out the back window, the spread of lava churned forward, scorching the patio furniture to ash, the back of the estate nothing but a bubbling lake of fire.

Run, Leam, run! Right now! Run!

And he took off, barreling into the enormous living room, knocking aside a coffee table and hopping over a black leather couch. He could feel the lava's heat on the back of his neck, its fire illuminating his way. He bolted toward the open hallway that led to the sitting room on his right, as his hand markings blinked with each cold second—0:29, 0:28—that ticked off his watch. Leam skidded onto the hallway looking left.

Bursting out of the silver coat hanger, the pegs of which, he remembered, were molded into the shape of giant beaks, larger crows than those that lived in the back staircase shot toward him, flapping and squawking. Leam sprinted the other way, toward the sitting room, his whole body throbbing and bleeding, his lungs raw. He guessed he had a shot at outrunning the ocean of lava—maybe—but after a frantic look over his shoulder, he realized there was no chance he'd beat the flock of giant birds to the sitting room door.

But the heavy flapping sounds of their wings took him briefly to the park, to the pigeon attack, to the calm he had settled over himself and the protective bubble that resulted, similar to the orb that shielded him from the Witchlows, also brought on by the calm, the same calm that had freed him from the associate's enclosing metal box.

Running for the sitting room, Leam cooled his mind, cooled any lingering embers of the bull, found the calm within, cracked it open and let it flood his nerves. He felt a burn in the pocket of his jeans and reached in, fingers grasping onto something small and round, and it wasn't Aggie's acorn. Leam yanked it out—the ball of concentrated flesh and bone of his clones from the field of green. He threw it over his head. Like popcorn in a microwave, loud pops and bangs sounded over the backdrop of the lava tidal wave gushing forward, and Leam braved a look back, his hands ticking brightly.

With every pop, his full-size clones were emerging from the ball, snatching birds out of the air and crushing them into clouds of silver dust. The sight of it pulled new strength through Leam's eyes, energizing his core as he raced forward, twenty yards away from the sitting room, his body springy, his mind clear—twenty feet away—the scalding hot lava nearly licking his heels—ten feet away—the watch dial blinking from 0:03 to 0:02—five feet away—the door, slightly ajar, right in front of him, an arm's reach away—two feet away—his markings searing with blinding white light...

The door snapped closed behind him.

He was in.

The room was quiet, odorless and still, and as far as Leam could tell—after a quick sweep from corner to corner and end to end—void of any visible spells, enchantments or booby traps. This unnerved him. Sara's Dark magic had preyed on him throughout the entire mansion. Why had she left this room alone? But before Leam could think on this longer, he felt a magnetic pull for his markings to unite, to draw his glowing hands together. He had come for clues, for anything that might shed light on why his delightenment had failed—why *he* had failed—but the light bursting from each hand was all that mattered right now.

He bent down near the far wall opposite the door, his knees and toes pressing into the Oriental rug. It felt like his shining delightenment scars had caught fire, though not in a painful way; the sensation was warm and oddly soothing. The tips of his index fingers and those of his thumbs were drawing together, hand to hand, two halves itching to become whole, just a few small inches away from connection, Leam fighting the urge to shut his eyes, the entire room glowing now, like a cave of shining ice, and—

"No, no, no, no, Leam. I wouldn't do that if I were you."

CHAPTER 51

Leam dropped his hands. He recognized the voice immediately. The mystical glow of his markings vanished, and only soft light breathed through the foot-wide gap between the door and its frame, leaving most of the sitting room coated with a filmy darkness. With the right side of his body still in the hallway, which oddly wasn't spewing in lava or silver birds or Leam clones, Zach stood, his arms folded, his grin smarmy. The fireplace hidden in shadows on Leam's left roared to life, casting flickering patches of gold over the arms of the magnificent chairs and the legs of the low table standing between him and Zach.

"Get up," Zach said. "You're coming with me."

"No chance of that. None."

"You know, I thought you might say that." Zach reached into the hallway and yanked a young woman into the room who kept her head down, her eyes fixed on her feet. Her dark shirt and jeans blended with the drapes folded over the massive front windows behind her. Leam strained to make out her face. He felt the bottom of his stomach drop, and his heart lurched in his chest.

"Eloa! What happened? What's going on?"

She said nothing, as if she couldn't move her lips.

"*You* know Zach?"

Leam sensed an almost imperceptible shake of her head, which Zach immediately confirmed.

"Hang on now," Zach said, grinning, reaching out for her, but she retreated farther into the room.

Leam jumped to his feet. "You stay away from her."

"Did we not meet at one of Bridgette's parties, Eloa?" Zack asked.

"For two seconds," she said. Her voice was barely audible over the crunch of fire eating through kindling.

"Did he hurt you?" Leam asked.

Again she shook her head...maybe. Leam could tell her eyes were wet and shiny because of how the flames swam in them.

"If only I had known who *she* was." Zach had aimed his grin at Leam. "They told me you had fallen like a turd over some skank, but I didn't find out who until tonight when it came time to snatch her up. And there she is...Long Legs McGillacutty from the party, who all the other girls seemed to despise. I thought she might've been somebody's hot cousin or something, but Zoey was all over me so..."

Zach's voice trailed off—who knew what sick things were taking up his mind. Eloa was warily surveying the large, unfamiliar room. The corner behind her, the furniture, the shelves... everything but Leam, whose pupils snapped to Zach.

"Why is she here?" Leam asked loud enough to jar whatever went on with Zoey at Bridgette's party out of his brother's head.

Zach let out a melodramatic sigh—*God, what an asshole*—and casually flung himself into the nearest chair, one of his feet on the rug, the other dangling over a dark-oaked arm. "Ahhhhhhhh....much better. You wouldn't know it, obviously, but it's tiring being so good at everything."

"What'd you bring her here for?" Leam snapped.

"Well, I think it's probably best to let your little honeysuckle answer that one for you, Leam. She'll be able to capture the true emotion, you know, that might be...well, that might be lost on me."

"You're such a prick bastard," Leam said, then looked to Eloa, whose eyes were on the floor again. "Eloa, tell me what's going on?" Even from across the room—about forty feet—Leam could see Eloa's face go so red she looked ready to explode. "ELOA!" he shouted.

"They kidnapped my dad!" she cried out.

Leam looked at her incredulously. "Who did? Zach?"

Eloa finally met Leam's eye. "*They* did! Darkness!"

"But—"

"I *told* you he had been taken, didn't I? They took him! *Your people!* Just like I told you!"

Leam put his hands out. "Wait, I had nothing to do with that."

"Who cares? Aren't you listening! He's been abducted!"

"*I* care. I don't want you to think I had—"

"I know you didn't," Eloa cried, smearing the mascara tracks that were running down her cheeks into smudgy gray clouds. "I figured that out when he told me everything," she added, slouching against a great desk wedged in the front corner of the room.

"You've got something to do with it now, though, brother," Zach said, appraising his fingernails.

"How so?"

"*Because,*" Eloa cried, her face so scrunched up her eyes had been forced closed, "if you don't come with us wherever they're making me go, he said they'll kill him! They'll kill my dad!"

Zach nodded. "We're gonna string him up, we're gonna cut his throat, and then we're gonna skip down Broadway and let the confetti fly!"

"Shut *up*, Zach!" At his sides, Leam's fists were tight compact balls.

"Well, it's true. Unless you surrender."

"To who?"

"To Gideon. That's the deal."

"Please, Leam," Eloa sobbed. "Do what he says. It's my dad."

Leam dropped his gaze to the circular indentations his knees had left in the rug, but the terror in Eloa's voice brought him back.

"This house…" she shuddered, "…your brother…"

"Did he do anything to you?" Leam's voice broke.

"No, but how do I know he won't? I don't like it here. I don't want to be here. I don't want to—"

Eloa's own scream cut her sentence short as a hundred chalk-white snakes of all sizes pushed into the room, slithering toward Zach, who was laughing while pushing up his sleeves. As they wriggled across the rug, each snake began to shrink and morph together, melting into each other until only a pair remained, sliding up Zach's leg, their white scales beginning to glow. Up his torso they parted ways, one wrapping around his left arm, the other his right, curling past his biceps and slithering to a stop directly over the rope-like markings on his forearms. Once in place, they sunk into his skin, their light extinguishing as if they had never existed outside the joyous young man laughing and beaming with pride.

"Did you have a little run in with some snakes, brother? My humble contribution to Mother's spells."

Leam glanced to Eloa, who looked fit to die, and then to the door, which rested a couple inches inward from the jamb. "Where's the rest of it? The lava? The mud?"

"All of Mother's enchantments were created for you, so they only activate in your presence. As soon as you twinkled in here on your tippy toes, everything else out there went back to normal, exactly how it was before your smelly ass showed up here tonight. How'd you not see us in the music room? We were sitting in there like old friends. Her, crying like a baby…me, watching WWF on my phone. I saw you through the window before it zapped you into the hedges."

"You were waiting for me?" Leam asked, becoming aware that his pinkies were tingling.

"Yeah, on Gideon's orders."

"Well, how did he know I was coming here?"

"Does it really matter? It's over. Gideon let you have your fun, but that's it. You don't like it, bitch to him when we get there. But if you run—" he jerked his head at Eloa, "—it's bye bye Daddy-oh."

Leam straightened, porcupine quills now stabbing at his pinkies.

Zach laughed from his chair, rolling down his sleeves, taking his time with it. "Did you honestly think that you could do anything you wanted, and that Gideon wouldn't be paying attention while you ran around town like a fart in the pants?"

"*What?*"

"C'mon now, Leam, you're smarter than that. Gideon knows everything."

"But you don't. You've only sniffed a *whiff* of what's happened to me tonight."

"Then how come I'm here, smart guy? Your life's in Gideon's hands, not yours. You're one of us, Leam, like she said. Take it as a reminder."

Leam's head was swooning, the bottoms of his feet getting hot, as the room—tricked by the fire light—shifted from side to side.

"But yeah, it's gotta sting that it's me, doesn't it? Yeah, it's just got to." Zach laughed. "Ohh, look at you! Look at his face, honeysuckle, this couldn't get any better!"

Leam was gasping for breath, his eyelids going jittery, like they were ready to shuffle like a flip book. That powerful black bull was coming on, rising up, only now Leam didn't want it to, not anymore. He couldn't hand over the reins—he couldn't black out—not with Eloa in the room, she could get hurt. Leam fought the bull with the little control he had left, squeezing his hands tight, pushing down the rising burn from within.

Stay, Leam, Stay. Don't slip away. Anchor yourself. Grab hold. Grab hold.

Leam concentrated on Zach.

Zach... Why'd it have to be Zach? Zach, who Leam had helped all throughout childhood, making him laugh, protecting him... Zach, who had grown up to treat Leam like garbage, to never offer rescue while Leam was under Sara's attacks, or reciprocate anything that could have ever remotely been considered a semblance of love. *This* was to be the person to take Leam down? Fire crackers sizzled between Leam's ears.

"Please, Leam, do what he says, I'm begging you." Eloa's voice was small, her eyes looked bleary, and the combination of the two spilled cool water through his scalp. "I have no one else, so please, please, ple—"

"SO HE CAN WIN?" Leam shouted at her face from across the room, the cool water evaporating in a dusty billow of heat. "NO! He does *not* win! He's been handed his life on a *platter!* He's done *nothing*—"

"I've done nothing?" Zach said, swinging his leg off the arm of the chair, sitting up bolt straight.

"—nothing but putz around and chase girls and eat soup, and now *he* wins?"

"*I've* done nothing, is that what you're saying to me?"

"He gets to beat me!" Leam yelled. "And why? For what? Because he was gifted powers and I wasn't?"

Zach snapped to his feet, his wild eyes eating holes through Leam's. "I'm sick of your crying, you whiny little brat. You think you're so weird and special, and you think you know everything because you read *books*, but you don't. You don't know anything at all. Would a *nobody* already have an alternate being so quick after popping his delightenment cherry? Does a *nobody* get enlisted to do work like this, and have a one-on-one *talking* relationship with the HEAD OF DARKNESS?" Zach shot a loud pop of magic out of his finger, and Leam felt it whizz over his head. "You want powers? Do you, you *brat!* Try being buried in sand and getting your face eaten off by fifty thousand rats. Then you come talk to me."

"I know what happened, I was there and it was insane." Sprinkles of cold water tingled inside Leam's head. "I tried to help you."

"Guess I didn't see it with my eyeballs getting chewed up inside a *rat's mouth!*"

"I know and I'm saying it's messed up what they ask of us, *Zach!*" Leam's hands were shaking. Eloa trembled in the corner of his eye. "It hit me when I was watching a goddamn *hog man* rub skin-glitter off its hooves into a Find-A-Thought like it was Parmesan cheese! Is this not insane? Is it? Do you think there's three Unks our age standing in some room somewhere talking about people getting killed and one of them's blowing fireplaces on, and snapping magic from his finger, and they're getting gutted by crows and fighting pigeons and prophecies and bubbles and visions and graveyards and *graveyards!*"

"Somebody get this guy to St. Francis's," Zach said. "He's lost his mind."

"I was here," Leam said. He dropped his head, his shoulders drooping down, too heavy to hold up. "I had made it. I was alone. I was here for a reason. I was ready. Something was happening…I could feel it…and now…"

Zach clapped his hands together once—SMACK—and said, "Boo hoo, Leam, and now what? You tell us."

Leam slunk into a chair, gazing in at the roaring flames. He could hear Eloa trying and failing to mute a fit of sobbing. Zach told her to shut up and crossed to the empty fireplace that faced the door, the one sulking between two enormous windows draped in dark fabric that cut off the room from the world.

Leam buried his face in his hands, and then slid them down his neck. He felt the flames lick his skin. "Could you imagine if you could just break free?"

"But it would never work," Eloa said. Her voice sent a shiver down Leam's legs, almost as if he was hearing her for the first time.

"I thought I told you to shut your mouth," Zach said. "They don't listen, these girls."

"You can't shed it, Leam, no matter how hard you try. It's impossible. If you try to get it off, you'll get roped back in tighter than before."

"Smart chick," Zach said.

"So if you're in it," Eloa went on, "you have to hold onto the other people who are in it, who you love and who love you back…who you know you can't live without."

"And who's that?" Leam asked, but he knew the answer.

"My dad."

Leam stood. "I'm sorry, Eloa. I really am, really, this is all messed up. But I can't surrender." He pointed at Zach with a laser-straight arm. "He doesn't get to win. Not him. Not against me."

"I know how you feel about me," Eloa pleaded, wiping her nose with the back of her hand. "I do, and I...I need you to help me."

"Why's it have to be this, though?" Leam said. "Why this?"

"I can't lose him. He's all I have. I need you to do this for me. You have to save him. I'll make it up to you, I swear. I'll owe you, Leam. Forever, I'll owe you."

"It's not about that. I don't want you to owe me—"

"Please..."

Leam's shoulders dropped and he said, "On your porch you looked at me like I was evil. Like I was a monster without a soul."

Eloa put her hands on the sides of her neck. "I *feel* something for you. Of course, I'm terrified, but I still feel it. I'm not a liar, that's the truth."

"Or you're just trying to get me to do what you want."

Eloa dropped her hands dejectedly. Her eyes closed, re-opening with fresh tears.

"Believe what you want, Leam, but remember it was you who played me. I had no idea what you were until a few hours ago, but you knew about me since inside the Coffee Gulp. But you're right. Things are so messed up who knows what to think anymore. I'm asking you to save him. That's all I can do, whether you do it or not."

"And what if Gideon kills me the second I get there?"

"Then you die," Zach said.

"My dad will be killed if you don't go, Leam. That's a certainty." Eloa lowered her gaze from Leam's eyes. "We don't know that for you."

"Exactly," Zach said to Leam, "so stop acting like a jerk. Do what Gideon wants, surrender, and save honeysuckle's father. It's not rocket science."

Leam's mind felt like it had caught fire, his brain smoldering under a hot plate.

"And who're you kidding anyway," Zach said, rubbing the back of his neck as if to smooth out some kinks. "You know I'm stronger. You know I'm better. You know you can't beat me."

Leam's hands were shaking so ferociously he had to clamp them together behind his back.

"Oh my god," Zach went on. "You really thought you had a say in the matter, didn't you? That you had control over—"

"HEY!" Leam snapped, and Zach stumbled backward, the drape folds nearly swallowing him up. "I'm not a pigeon! I can see! Your future's in *my* hands! If I don't surrender, it means your ass, Zachy poo!"

Zach narrowed his eyes. "You don't get to call me that anymore."

"Gideon would have an absolute field day with you if you came back empty-handed!"

"But you're forgetting something so obvious I'm surprised it hasn't stabbed you between the eyes." Zach pushed his palm forward, cracking a pop of magic into Leam's face. Leam fired back a variety of obscenities. It felt like he had jammed a fork into an electrical socket. "I mean how many times can I hint at it? If you don't come willingly, you're coming anyway."

"I beat Sara's little tricks, didn't I?" Leam said, wiping water from his eyes.

"Hardly."

"I beat your snakes."

"Yeah, my snakes, not me. You see in here it's me who has magic, and it's you who's a sad little loser." Zach turned to Eloa with a grin. "I mean, who do *you* think's gonna pull this one out, honeysuckle?"

"See?" Leam said, turning back to Eloa. She was hugging herself as if to keep warm. "Do you see how he is?" The bull's hooves were kicking up large clouds of dust. "He's had everything his whole life—the attention, the support—and he's too stupid to even know it! I would've loved to see how he would've done if things were switched around! If I was beloved and nurtured! If it was me having my diapers changed real special—"

"What are you saying? That you crawled around with crap taped to your ass all day? Your diapers were changed, too!"

"BUT YOUR MOTHER WAS LEFT ALONE!" Leam shouted, and the walls seemed to shake. If his stomach wasn't empty, more than words would have vomited from his mouth. He felt even worse when he saw that Eloa's face had broken for him, despite how horrible and terrifying this had to be for her. In her eyes, Leam saw cold pools of water, and the heat inside of him cooled, which, in turn, strengthened his grip on the reins.

"What are you talking about?" Zach asked. "Left alone?"

Leam answered Zach, but stayed on Eloa. "It doesn't matter."

"Then why even bring it up, stupid?"

"It does matter," Eloa choked out. "Leam, I don't have a mom either, I know how it feels."

"I know," Leam said softly.

"So don't let them take my dad away, too."

"Just so we're clear, here," Zach cut in, eying Eloa carefully, "we're going to *murder* him. I feel like you're not getting that. He's already *been* taken away. If Leam doesn't surrender… if by the biggest miracle in the world he somehow gets away, then your precious Daddy gets killed." Leam watched pain eat at Eloa's face as Zach added, "And you know what? Maybe he'll get the rats, too."

Eloa made a half choke, half sob sort of sound, covering a hand over her face.

Leam stared in at his brother, who couldn't have looked more pleased with himself, he was just that smug. Looking in at Zach's pompous, pretty-boy face, Leam's want for magical powers stung its strongest. What he wouldn't give to tear the skin off his brother's face with one sweep of the hand. "You didn't always used to be like this." he said.

"Like what? A winner?"

Leam swallowed hard. Zach's eyes looked dead—like whatever spark they had once held had gone missing. Leam looked away, to Eloa, whose eyes were on the rug. That duck-like expression that had saddened her face on Mary and Larry's porch a gazillion hours ago had returned. Leam clenched and unclenched his hands, feeling no energy—no hum—beneath the skin. His markings were invisible in the soft firelight.

"I guess you're right," Leam finally said to Zach.

"That's right you guess I'm right," Zach said, flexing his bicep. Then his face smushed together as if trying to remember if he had guzzled down his protein shake this morning. "Wait… why do you guess I'm right?"

"Because I'll do it," Leam said. "I'll surrender."

Eloa covered her hands over her face up to the eyes, which shined like sunrays at Leam.

"Imagine having a father that…" Leam pursed his lips, and swallowed again. "Anyway, I'm doing it, so—"

"Say it louder," Zach demanded.

"I said I'm doing it!"

"And there's the victory, folks. We all knew it was coming." Zach laughed, strutting in place, like a peacock with nowhere to go. "I win! What a shocker! Who's the Zachy-poo now?"

Leam went to speak, but stayed quiet.

"Oh man, that is sweet," Zach gloated. He clapped his hands together. "All right, kiddies, let's hit it, then! Gideon's expecting us."

The short-lived relief in Eloa's eyes drained away. The recognition of what was to happen next settled over her like a poisoned veil, as the magnitude of where they were likely going now crippled her face. Leam wondered if her pained expression mirrored his own, for he knew who would be waiting for them with bulging eyes and a clown-face grin. But why had it all worked out this way?

If Gideon had known all along that Leam would be coming to the Manor and specifically the sitting room, then what else did Gideon know? Leam thought about the groups of trench coaters he had dodged all night; how he still had no idea what unspeakable horrors he had inflicted on the associate, of whom he knew Gideon was so fond. Leam's teeth started to rattle at the thought of it—how he had sat down on a swing with Gideon's sworn enemy and nemesis. It suddenly seemed very likely to Leam that it would be he who would be getting the rats next.

Leam blinked out of his musing to find Eloa's fretful eyes waiting for him, and for her he willed his panic to remain internal, offering a small smile and an assuring nod. But before he could say a word, the room was hijacked by the sudden snapping hiss of crossed electrical wires. Fluorescent white ropes sprung from Zach's forearms; those from his left lassoing Eloa's body, the right entangling around Leam with a burning singe.

Leam heard Eloa shriek, just as his Nikes began to skid over the rug. Zach was reeling his big catches in. If there had been a third electrical connection—one stretching between Eloa, who was screaming her head off at the front of the room, and Leam, who was trying to calm her from the back of the room—a bird's eye view would offer a perfect triangle shrinking smaller and smaller.

The singe of pain subsided, as did the ropes' shining light, which weakened to a soft glow, but Leam had to shout over the high-voltage sizzle to make sure Eloa could hear him.

"Eloa, look at me! Relax! It's gonna be okay! I'm here! Look at me, look at me!"

She did.

"We're going together, Eloa! Stay with me! We're going to get your dad!"

Though Eloa remained equidistant from both brothers, Leam could see in her body language that she was straining to gravitate toward him.

"We're gonna be okay," Leam said.

"How do you know?" she mouthed so quietly Leam had to read her lips. He grabbed her with his eyes as her lips repeated, "How do you know? How do you know?" and from Leam's mouth sprung words that felt unlike his own.

"Because for something to happen, all you need to do is believe."

The grandfather clock struck one. Eloa closed her eyes. Her tension seemed to release, her body letting go of all resistance against Zach's magic, which continued to pull the triangle smaller. Her beauty in this unlikely moment of tranquility was so great that Leam made a conscious effort to blink her face, as it was right now, into memory.

From the corner of the sitting room, the second hour chimed. A shaky breath shuddered from Eloa's mouth and she opened her eyes. Leam kept her with him, kept her eyes firm on his, and as they came together, he smiled at her and she smiled, too, the space between them folding in.

"Eloa..." he breathed, and she kissed him.

Though the clock announced three, time, for Leam, had seemed to stop.

As Eloa pulled her lips away from his, the particulars of the kiss were instantly lost on him. He would only remember that it was magical. Her warm breath climbed his neck to his ear, and she spoke—nothing more than feathery whispers but perfectly clear. His heart should have soared but it sank.

Leam knew that soon he would never again see the warmth in her eyes, at least not directed at him. The markings on his hands were once again beaming, feeling just as tingly as the breath Eloa had left on his ear.

And then her face fell cold—the gratitude, the sympathy, gone, gone. Did she know? Had she seen it on his face? Could she feel what was about to happen? What he was about to do?

Leam heard Zach jeering—something about how Eloa was a whore and how incredible it was that Leam's first kiss wasn't with a dude—but Leam kept his focus on Eloa, on the tiny lines of confusion traced between her eyebrows. He thought—as he brought his hands together, both markings ablaze—to say sorry. But that wasn't the right word. Sorry didn't really fit.

Leam looked across Zach's right-arm ropes, watching the derision that was staining his brother's face flee from what was now becoming an onslaught of true concern.

"What the hell are you doing?" Zach shouted, watching Leam's hands brighten. "What are you doing? What are you do-ing?" Over and over he said it, but Leam tuned him out.

And just before the tips of his fingers and thumbs connected, Leam stole one last look at Eloa. In that tiny hiccup of time, although her face conveyed a slew of lesser emotions, overwhelmingly it shone with hurt. And not the physical kind.

The physical kind would have been a thousand times better. This would be the face of hers he would remember.

Leam's hands became one, and a bright white flash blinded the room.

His tightly-shut eyes burned for only a second. The flash soon died, but Leam kept the barrier of his eyelids firmly in place. He could still hear the crackling of flames, though the surroundings now were significantly cooler, the rug beneath his feet as hard as bricks, and a nasty stench of what he guessed might be decaying corpses hugged the air. With trepidation, he opened his eyes.

He was standing alone in an unfamiliar passageway. The crackling in his ears came not from the sitting room fireplace, but from purplish-blue torch flames licking a low ceiling made of flat gray stones, the likes of which also comprised the floor beneath Leam's Nikes, as well as the narrow walls stretching into darkness both ways. A strange sensation of both knowing and not knowing where he was, sent rapid heartbeats spiking to his fingertips and toes.

The stink was overwhelming. Covering his nose, Leam deduced the torches were the source, their assault undoubtedly more potent due to the pleasantly intoxicating aromas they had replaced: Eloa's perfume or shampoo, or both. Leam held up his free hand, which squirmed with life, yet no longer light, examining it, as if pertinent questions were raised on the fingerprints, and along the curve of his palm tracks raced the answers. Throughout this process of inspection, Leam sensed a calmness trying to get in at him, pestering him with the promises of serenity and a clearer head. He let it in.

When he did, he straightened, pushing his palm at a distant torch. A torrent of power fired from his mind, through his arm and out his hand, shooting a silent cloak of invisible energy at the purplish-blue flames, snuffing them out cold and leaving nothing atop the torch-stick but a charred, hissing wick.

Leam turned back his palm and, gazing into it, he just had to grin.

CHAPTER 52

From the corner of the sitting room, the second hour chimed. A shaky breath shuddered from Eloa's mouth and she opened her eyes. Leam kept her with him, kept her eyes firm on his, and as they came together, he smiled at her and she smiled, too, the space between them folding in.

"Eloa," he breathed, and she kissed him.

He was sitting in a lawn chair on a small outcropping of grass facing an expansive lake, the water flat and still, no wind to nudge a ripple. Puffy white clouds hung from invisible strings in the brilliant blue sky. A forest thick with trees filled with leaves of all colors wrapped itself around the lake, unbroken. Leam closed his eyes, recognizing the vision, and breathed in the fresh air. It felt like autumn. The grass tickled his bare feet.

"Beautiful, isn't it?"

He turned toward the sound of the melodic voice on his right. A thin woman in a yellow sundress was sitting next to him in a lawn chair of her own, a small table between them. A pitcher of iced tea and two glasses rested on its surface. He didn't recognize the woman. She was pretty and seemed relaxed.

"Where am I?" he asked.

"A place of reflection," she said, half a smile on her face. "A place to clear your head so you don't march yourself into a mistake. A place for a person to first consider all the factors before a life-changing decision is to be made."

"What's to decide?"

The woman kept her gaze on Leam, half smiling. "Presently, you are not only here at this lake, are you, Leam? You are also somewhere else, and at that somewhere else, you have a decision in your hands."

Leam looked out at the lake. He could see something far out, above the water, little more than a dot. A rowboat, maybe. He couldn't be sure. "I've already made up my mind," he said.

"Have you?"

"Yes."

"But as of now you have yet to act on it."

"I'm surrendering. It's the only way to save her father."

"Tell me," the woman said, the smiling half of her mouth mimicking its serene counterpart for a moment. "Would she do the same for you?"

Leam considered it, but briefly. "My mother's life was taken by a father who's dead to me. I have no family, no friends... Eloa's a pipedream, I'm not an idiot, but without her, who do I have left?"

"So was it simply your guts and will power that got you through your stepmother's obstacle course?"

Leam said nothing.

"Leam, if Al Qaeda wiped out themselves and the global population except for you, you still wouldn't be alone. But, yes, this girl is physically there, planting a good one on your lips, and no one I know would dare argue that you don't deserve a friend. Sparing her the pain of this loss, I understand it. But regardless of that, there is much more at stake than your would-be-could-be relationship with Eloa Frost. You know this, Leam. You are well aware that you are now a part of something much bigger than that. Despite what Sebastian says," she added.

Leam sighed. His eyes swam in the potpourri of autumn that surrounded the quiet water. He thought about how at that somewhere else, his lips were flush against Eloa's, and he wished he hadn't been sucked away from that to be brought here.

"I know of something you don't," the woman said, pouring iced tea into each glass, one baring an etching of a bird, the other what looked like a mouse. "There is another way to go about saving Jace Frost. A better way." The woman held out both glasses, but Leam shook his head.

"How do you know that?"

"Because, if I didn't, it wouldn't be me with you inside this phantasm of yours. Leam, the intense urge you've undoubtedly been experiencing to connect the markings on your hands pleads for a reason. When they connect...when those two halves combine together to create that circle of light, the magic within you that has been sleeping for so long will be awoken. For whatever reason it was given, the advice to return to your father's sitting room was sound."

"So you're saying it's possible for me to activate my magic?"

"The magic that will give you a leg up on saving Jace Frost."

"But without delightenment?"

The woman nodded.

"I don't get it. Would I be purified?"

The woman shook her head. "You are not an ordinary boy, Leam Holt, and neither is the magic within you."

Leam looked at his hands, at the markings; no brightness to them, no pull. "Problem is, I think I might've missed my window. They're not glowing like before."

"Lucky for you that world is a giant house with windows on every floor."

"So what exactly would happen? When they align, or whatever?"

"Something remarkable, I would imagine."

"Yeah, but what? Would it take me away somewhere?"

"I think so." The woman's half-smile looked prideful.

"To where?"

"If it is your aim to save this particular man then the answer to that seems to be an obvious one."

Leam pictured a set of bulging, lunatic eyes. His mouth went dry.

"Leam, being courageous is not the opposite of experiencing fear. Real courage is when you are scared to do something beyond measure, but you do it anyway."

A breeze flittered onto the outcropping of grass, cool against Leam's face. "Do I have your word that fighting off Zach and going where the magic takes me gives me a better chance than letting him bring me in?"

"We're speaking of Gideon, here, Leam. He is not a man of his word. He is a man of trickery and untruths. He says what he needs to and does what he needs to in order to get whatever it is that he wants, which in this case is you. Do you honestly believe he's going to live up to his end of the deal once he has you, without your powers, in his possession? Yes, Leam, you will have a better chance to save her father with awoken magic than you would if you obey Gideon's orders. That I can promise."

"Then that's my move," Leam said. "But I'll have to... I'll go back and let her know what I'm doing and—"

"No, Leam. Zach is there. Gideon will know your plan."

"Yeah, but..." Leam's breath went short. "But right now, to her, I'm going with her and Zach. To her, I'm surrendering and her father will be spared. And what else should she think? That was my intention right before I was brought here."

"You are here, Leam, but no one has brought you here but yourself."

"But if I can't tell her why I'm doing it, she'll hate me forever. On the surface, it's nothing but a betrayal."

"I one hundred percent agree, but it's the best way to give her what she asks of you."

Leam felt his chest deflate, his shoulders suddenly heavy. "I don't want to lose her that way," he said softly.

"I doubt she wants to be lost." The woman lazily brushed a few beads of moisture off the iced tea pitcher, a clear streak keeping pace with her hand. "And you can go with her, as planned. You have that option. To use your own words, Leam, you're not an idiot. You're well aware that if you wave Zach the white flag, you'll forever be Eloa's hero, regardless of whether Gideon murders Jace or not."

A cloud slipped over the sun.

"If you go the other way, though," the woman said, "yes, you'll probably lose her. But you will get powers in return. Magic, Leam. Don't try to tell me that doesn't entice you. If you do, you'll find me one hard ducky to convince."

Leam's eyes went to the nearest glass of iced tea, the one with the mouse. His mouth was so dry.

"But there's always door number three," the woman said. "A few minutes before this kiss that you unfortunately cannot enjoy, you said, 'Could you imagine if you could just break free?'" The woman paused. "You can."

Leam looked at her. "How?" he asked.

"You can kill yourself."

The words hit Leam like a punch to the center of his chest. He couldn't pull his eyes away from the woman as her words repeated inside his head with the same cold indifference in which they were delivered. Throughout the duration of the "You can kill yourself" echo, the woman's eyes seemed to shift among primary colors—yellow, blue, yellow, red, blue—but by the time her voice had faded completely, a soft hazel brown had returned between the whites and pupils of her eyes.

Leam looked down at his hands and shook his head. "I'd rather kill as many of them as I can until they kill me."

With the resurrection of her half-smile, the woman asked, "To which 'they' do you refer?"

Leam manipulated his fingers into claws. "Anybody who tries to harm her," he answered, with the strange feeling that, while he had said it, his eyes had been changing colors, too. Swirls of blood-red vapor began to rise around the edges of the table. Leam peeked underneath. A small steel-gray cylindrical canister was spewing out crimson clouds of gas.

"What is that?" he asked, recoiling, focusing on the fluorescent-orange skull and crossbones stamped across the canister's middle.

"That is nothing of which to be afraid," the woman answered.

Leam ignored her and ignored the gas; the water, again, had his eye. After some time, he said, "I'm taking the best odds to save this freaking goddamn Jace guy." His words were soft and cold. "But she'll be lost from me forever because of it. And forever I'll go at whatever the rest of it is alone."

Leam heard the woman sigh. "Once again," she said, "I'll disagree with your last. But how you feel is up to you."

"No, it's not." He could feel a squirm in each hand, and that he was soon to be leaving. "It never is."

"Can I ask you another question, Leam?"

"If you answer one of mine."

The woman nodded and took a sip of tea, the ice cubes rattling together like shaken dice. "Are you afraid, Leam? Not here, but there. In the world with all the windows."

Leam looked out across the lake. The rowboat, or whatever he had seen out yonder, was gone. "Yes," he said.

"Then now is when you must believe in yourself the most." The woman set her glass down. Leam noticed the bird etched on the side was plunging its head under water. "Your turn," she said.

"What's the deal with the three oars?"

The woman blinked. "What do you mean?"

"You know what I mean."

"You mean oars for a boat?"

"That's right."

"Nothing," she answered.

"They're forming a triangle."

"Leam, if you don't know yet, neither do I."

"Then how do you know all these other things?"

"Because they're not related to any of your other visions."

Leam paused, his thumb over his jugular, checking his pulse. "Why'd you want to know if I was scared?"

"So you would know."

"But that doesn't make me feel any better." Again, he pictured the bulging, lunatic eyes.

"I'm afraid yours won't be a life of feeling better, Leam."

Leam's hands were gripped around the arms of the lawn chair. "Then people better stay out of my way."

The women took a sip from the mouse glass. "You're sure you aren't thirsty?" she asked, pushing the other closer to Leam. He turned his head away.

The clouds in the sky started to glow with hot light, and gleaming drops of fire rained down, illuminating the air, and then the water, and then the forest, until everything around him was shining, including the woman, and he had to shut his eyes from the all-encompassing luminescence...

As Eloa pulled her lips away from his, the particulars of the kiss were instantly lost on him. He would only remember that it was magical.

CHAPTER 53

From thirty feet away in the cramped passageway, Leam pushed his palm at the torch he had just extinguished, the black smoking wick reigniting into a pop of purplish-blue flames. The small smile for his newly-activated magic fell flat at the screeching thought that Gideon, or any of his thousands of devoted followers willing to die for the Cause, could emerge out of the deep darkness beyond the reach of the torch flames on either side of him.

He looked at his watch—maybe it had guidance to offer—but it sat on his wrist black and lifeless. He knew, though, if this was where his magic had brought him, then this was where he needed to be. He laid a hand against the stone wall on his left, and at his touch, a section, small at first, began to disappear as if an invisible giant was chomping through the widening hole, which seemed to be taking the shape of a low door as it expanded. Leam inhaled a deep breath, regretting it instantly as the scent of dead skunk raped his sense of smell. He ducked through the emerging door into a dark, damp room. Behind him, the purplish-blue light extinguished. The wall, undoubtedly, had collapsed in on itself, stealing back the door, and with it, Leam's nerves.

Leam's eyes took excruciating long seconds to adjust to the near darkness, and the weak sickly-green light lending it depth from the four corners of what was appearing to be a bare, dungeon-like room. Pinpricks of blood spiked to his skin as Leam took hesitant steps toward the sound of labored breathing, stopping just short of a row of floor-to-ceiling bars, hot against his face and emitting a soft, menacing hum.

Pressed against the wall on the opposite side of the prison bars was what looked to be a boulder, but as Leam's sight conquered the dungeon's gloom, the boulder materialized into the form of a massive body, curled up on the ground, naked, apart from a clinging loincloth. It's dirt-smudged yellowness might have once been as white as snow. From a second cell on Leam's left glinted a mouthful of gold teeth—Sebastian's missing friend—which meant that the boulder in the soiled underwear was Leam's man.

"Frost," he said. "Get up."

As the boulder lifted his head off the ground, a shower of long filthy hair fell over a face still masked in shadows. "Who's there?" the boulder muttered weakly.

"Get up," Leam said, shining soft light at the prisoner from his palm, kicking himself for not thinking of using magic to illuminate his way when he had first come through the disappearing door. In the light, the state of the boulder's face, if you could call it that, sent a chill zigzagging up the back of Leam's neck.

Leam's first thought was that the man had to be in severe pain, no way around it. Bright red veins had stung their way to tiny black dot pupils, but were in no way confined to the man's eyeballs. His entire face had been scarred with squiggly, unnaturally red lines that spread out in detailed, tree-root patterns across the forehead, nose, cheeks, chin and everything else below. A quick glance at the man revealed him to be pink all over, like a lifetime drunk, but a closer look revealed veins running jagged over the entire boulder. The sight of it was a reminder of Gideon's cruelty. A Gideon who could be so very near.

"Get up," Leam said again. A long beat of silence coated his ears until the boulder said timidly, "Don't hurt me."

"I'm here to get you out," Leam said, straining his ear at the silence for any sounds of danger. "But it's gotta be now. Gideon'll be informed any moment."

The boulder sat up against the wall, a quicker movement than the tired voice had let on to be possible. "You've come for me?" The voice registered the faintest flick of hope.

"Yes."

"How'd you break in?"

Before Leam could answer, he stiffened with fear.

Oh, no...

A soft whispery chuckle came from behind him, twisting his guts into a tight ball. Leam turned, shaking. Bulging out at him through the greenish darkness, less than two feet away, was a pair of opaque eyes in a large, clown-mask face that held them. At the end of a stick-thin arm, a powder-white hand grabbed for Leam's throat.

Leam leaped backward, smacking into the prison bars, a searing jolt attacking him from head to toe as his body was flung to the floor. He flipped onto his back, his head howling with pain, palms shaking but faced outward, ready.

But Gideon was gone. The smiling clown-mask, the soft horrible chuckle—both gone. Leam sat up bolt straight, scanning for eyes, those bulging eyes, when a voice, not a powder-white hand, reached out at him.

"The dungeon's tricked to paralyze its captives with fear." Jace's voice had strengthened. "Its walls bring forth ghosts to torture our sanity. Whatever you saw was a mirage."

Leam clamped down on his teeth, giving both cheeks a quick back-and-forth slapping. Climbing to his feet, he could still hear his heart hammering at the back of his ears. "It's not gonna be a ghost next time," he said, harnessing energy beneath the skin of his hand that felt like warm goo. "So we have to get the hell out of here."

"It won't work."

"We'll see," Leam muttered, eyeing the bars.

"Freeing me is not a necessity." Jace sounded anxious. "You can see for yourself, I'm cooked. But I can give you the formula—the codes—so you can stop it yourselves."

Leam ignored him—*What the hell was he talking about anyway?*—continuing to store mind energy in his hands.

"The bars are unbreakable!" Jace urged, sending goose bumps up Leam's back. "You have to take the codes and go!"

"Shut up! They'll *hear* you!"

"Take the codes, get back to the COO and relay them to Sebastian."

"I'm breaking you out, Frost. Get on board." Leam sized up the thirty-three wrought iron bars—he knew the exact number at one glance—that stood like rigid soldiers between him and Jace.

"I'm trapped here," Jace said, "don't you understand? Skilled men built these cells with powerful magic. The bars are unbreakable. There's no time for me, but if we're lucky—"

We, Leam thought.

"—they might still be applying the finishing touches. That would mean you'd have time to render it useless before it does what it was created to do, *if* you deliver Sebastian the codes."

"Render what useless?"

Jace's red-veined face pulsed redder. "Gujin7B! You know this already! It's why you were sent for me, weren't you?"

Leam froze, and then, "Yeah, Sebastian filled me in. But it was brief, Frost, and I've got a lot on my mind." The word *Gujin* had struck a familiar chord, and from the depths of Leam's mind surfaced the tune. "My brother overheard my father mention Gujin, too."

"So if you know the danger, *take the codes and—*"

"No, Frost." Leam extended his palm as if pushing a drawer in. "I was sent to get you out alive, not run your errands."

"But—"

Leam fired a pop of magic at the centermost of the thirty-three, where it met with a bright cracking snap of electricity, like thunder inside of lightning. When the burst of light faded, it was clear the bar remained undamaged.

"Stop for a moment and listen to me," Jace pleaded, straining to push himself up. "What's your name?"

"Leam," Leam answered, firing his palm at the same bar—CRACK—with the same result.

"Leam, whatever department you're in, whatever you know or don't know, you have to listen to me." Jace sounded like he was gaining some strength. "I'm a code breaker," he started. "Numbers, letters, signs, symbols, I know it all, I'm the best there is, and because I'm the best there is, I was able to break through their protection, to poke a small hole in their vast-stretching Blanket of Darkness. Peeking inside, I discovered a weapon in the later stages of development—a gas, a poison—and from the data I uncovered a few minutes before they got to me, I devised a formula capable of neutralizing Gujin7B. They don't know this. If they did I'd be dead, but what I *cannot* do is cure those who get infected, so if Gideon releases—"

"I don't care about any of this."

"*Don't care?*"

"Not a bit," Leam said, continuing his assault against the centermost bar, speaking loudly over the *pop-pop-popping* from his palms to make sure the boulder got it through his thick head that this wasn't his show. "I came to rescue you. That's it, nothing else. So keep your codes in your head and if I can get you outta here before Gideon comes in here *and shreds our faces off,* then you go find Sebastian and you can fix it with him."

"THAT OPTION'S FUTILE, BOY! YOU CANNOT BREAK ME OUT!"

"Shut *up!*" Leam felt his forehead, his face, his neck, get blood-pumped full of heat as he fired fiercer magic at the whole row of bars now, sending pops and bangs and cracks of light all over the dungeon. Whitish-gold sparks spit off the walls and sprayed down from the ceiling.

"Listen to me!" Jace shouted, his massive hands swiping sparks away as one would a cloud of gnats. "When these animals would slink in to torture me, Gideon came once to watch. Afterward he told me that as soon as it was perfected, he planned to release Gujin in a large area, a city or a town. If that happens... if the gas leaks, it will eat at the souls and minds of Unknowings and the number of horrors they commit against each other will rise *exponentially*."

Leam was tiring, breathing in fits, nothing now but weak graying snaps of smoke issuing from his palms, the unbreakable center bar defiant.

"Did you hear what I said?" Jace shouted.

"Yeah, so?"

"*So! So!* What do you mean *so?* What happens with this poison will severely affect the outcome of the war!"

Leam lowered his hands, inactive. Pictures clicked in his mind—flashing images of the men and women in black trench coats he had spotted earlier all over town. "Wait, Gideon said he's releasing it over a city or a town?"

"Yes."

"That'd be a big event for them, wouldn't it?"

"Very much so."

Leam felt his legs stiffen, as if the bones had been switched out for metal spears. "I saw a lot of activity tonight...trench coaters."

There was a pause, and then, "Where?"

"Where I talked with Sebastian," Leam answered. "Harbing. He was there to find the threat."

Every red vein on Jace's body had jumped at the name of the town. Leam expected Jace to say something about Eloa, about her grandparents, but instead Jace asked, "What did Harbing smell like?"

The oddness of the question startled Leam, as if something had exploded behind him. "What do you mean?"

"A smell is what I mean." Jace was on his feet now, looking strong. "Was there a smell?"

"I—I—I don't know."

"These savages, when they forced it upon me, the gas had a strong, very specific odor."

"What was it?"

"Sugar cookies."

Leam's head felt sloshy, like someone had filled it with a pitcher of water. "Yeah," he said, halfway in a daze. "I smelled those when we were on your porch." He looked down at the damp floor. "Mary and Larry's porch."

Jace stumbled toward the bars. "Then you know my daughter."

Leam nodded.

"You're her friend?"

"I was."

"But she's safe?" Jace was trembling, and through the shine of his eyes—the only part of him that wasn't covered in filth—Leam could see terror.

"She could be," Leam said. "I don't know."

"You said you were with her on the porch, though, correct? When was this?"

"Tonight."

"Then she must be alive."

Leam's eyes snapped to the wall that had birthed the door, Gideon's eyes still floating around in his head. Had he heard a noise beyond it? A voice, maybe?

"Come here, let me see you," Jace said, now only an inch from the bars, his bloodshot eyes darting over every inch of Leam's face and arms. "They must have diluted it. If they hadn't, you'd look just like me."

The dungeon, for Leam, got very warm, very quickly, as if the savages Jace spoke of were pumping hot air in through the walls. "Diluted it…"

"Yes."

Leam pictured the porch, the smell of the cookies. "So then…will it poison her? I mean eventually will she look… like you?"

"I don't know," Jace said, "I don't know, I don't know! You're both in jeopardy! You have to do what I say and stop the gas! You have to save us before we can no longer be saved! Memorize the formula, leave me here to die, and relay it to Sebastian so he can deactivate the Gujin before anyone else gets contaminated!"

"I'm not leaving you, Frost," Leam said. In swam a memory of Bram standing in the sitting room last year giving Leam the smallest of winks just before he was to be delighted.

"You're ignorant!" Jace roared. "Foolish!"

"Fool? No. No, you're the fool, Frost..." Leam shook Bram's image of kindness away, and in came one of a dead woman lying in an elaborate bath tub filled with ivy leaves, a gilded-bronze knife handle shaped like a hooded figure stuck firmly against her breastbone, a circle of dried blood scabbed into the pale skin around it.

"*Please,* Leam!"

"No."

"But—"

"Don't you know what you mean to your daughter?" Leam's face was burning up.

"We're dealing with global contamination!"

"I don't care."

"But, I'm one lousy person, I don't mat—"

"YOU MATTER TO HER, YOU UNGRATEFUL APE! SO SHUT UP AND STAND BACK!

Leam's palms became a blur and the prison bars exploded, the dungeon shaking as if falling prey to an earthquake. The explosion knocked Jace over, his head smacking the floor onto which wrought-iron pieces rattled like dropped marbles. From beyond the wall came scraping noises, panicked shuffling, men's muffled voices—all sounds Leam could no longer sweep under the rug as imaginations.

"The bars," Jace breathed, sitting up on his elbows. "Impossible..."

"Get up, Frost! They're gonna be coming right through that wall!" Leam assessed every square inch of the dungeon. "There's no way out."

"The bars. How did you break—"

"Snap out of it, it's done!" Leam pushed his palm at Jace, who rose to his feet in pace with Leam's hand as it was withdrawn. The man was enormous from so close up. "How do we get out of here?" Leam asked, panic unrolling down his body in tight strips. The muffled voices were getting clearer.

Jace threw his long hair out of his face. "Tell me how you got in."

"Right in through the wall they're coming through."

"No, Leam, how did you get into this building from wherever you were?"

Leam closed his eyes away from the greenish darkness, thinking back to the sitting room, then back to the vision at the lake. "This is where I needed to be, so then here I was."

"That's it?" Jace asked.

"That's it."

"Then do the same."

With a sound of the spinning blade of a rusted meat slicer, a razor of purplish-blue light cut through the dungeon wall, where it began to form the outline of a low door through which, Leam knew, men in black trench coats would be bursting any moment.

"Do it now, Leam."

"Do *what?*"

"The same!" Jace grabbed Leam's arms. "Think Harbing, 210 Stoneladen, and go!"

The idea was so simple it had to be right, and by knowing it was right, Leam found his calm almost instantly, a cool sensation, chilling the heat of fear. The purplish-blue outline shone brighter, a hair away from being a completed door, but as Leam harnessed Jace in close with a surge of palm-energy, he knew the owners of the voices out in the passageway would be too late. Swiping his arm over his head as a cowboy twirls a lasso, Leam conjured a translucent veil that, as it fell over him and Jace, formed into an orb. Leam pictured a section of porch floorboards scuffed up by Barry's nails and, just as he had in the Manor's sitting room not long ago, watched a devouring white flash of blinding light obliterate his surroundings.

CHAPTER 54

The light faded dark.

The fresh night air of Harbing, clear of fog in these early morning hours, swept around Leam and Jace like a thin invisible bed sheet. Both had fallen to the strip of lawn, or rather an untended garden of hard dirt pocked with a few stubborn grass tufts, between Mary and Larry's stand-alone garage and the house. Before he could completely blink away the spotty remnants of the vanished light, a cackling of excited voices sprung Leam to his feet. He grabbed Jace's ankle and flung him like a horseshoe toward cover: a clump of bushes squatting aside the three-step-elevated porch.

Ducking down next to Jace, Leam peered through the shrubbery. A group of Gideon's men—eleven, at Leam's count—walked into view, laughing and chatting in front of 210 Stoneladen. Leam muffled Jace's sharp intakes of breath with a charm of silence from his palm, wondering when the man had last tasted fresh air. Leam hoped that if these trench coaters were in such high spirits, then they probably hadn't learned of the break-in escape from DHQ. That meant Gideon might not yet know about it either.

In the small patches of silence between laughter and chatter, came a feathery whir from beneath the porch on the other side of Jace. After a glance at the street—a few stragglers were still in view beyond the property but most of the group had moved on—Leam pushed Jace aside and broke apart the barricade of lattice under the porch. Peering into the crawl space, he spotted a steel-gray cylindrical canister, identical to the one he had seen underneath the iced-tea table between himself and the half-smile woman. Faint reddish vapor rose in thin curls from a small puncture in the top. Stamped on the middle, just like in the vision, was a fluorescent-orange skull and crossbones.

Jace was apparently watching as Leam conjured the contraption into his hands.

"Be careful," Jace warned.

"It's nothing to be afraid of."

"Yes, it is. It's deformed me—stripped me of my powers. But it's the effect on Unknowings that matters. It darkens some of them, Leam, and kills off the rest."

Leam peeked at the street—no trench coaters, no movement. "What does it do to the Dark?"

"I don't know for sure, but I know Gideon. He'd rip off the head of anyone of Darkness he considered to be useless, but he wouldn't subject himself, or any of his people who are still able to aid him in his Cause, to anything damaging. My guess is the Dark will remain perfectly unharmed."

Leam kept quiet, scouring for a nearby piece of flat, suitable ground, the scent of sugar cookies tickling his nose. Finding none, he hopped leapfrog-style over the side railing onto the porch, which, with the overhanging lights switched off, was as dark as everything else out of the range of Stoneladen's streetlamps. Leam set down the canister, listening to Jace's footsteps drag across the front yard and carry his enormous bulk up the porch steps.

"I saw you, you know," Leam said, keeping his eyes on the canister. "In a dream…in a few of them actually." The floor boards stopped creaking. "You were a white horse. You were linked to red clouds of smoke."

"Gujin7B…"

"I was destined to find you," Leam said. "Destined to stop the gas."

"Leam…"

"I was. I know I was."

"There's burns and bruises all over you." There was warmth in Jace's voice like he actually cared about a total stranger. "You're covered in gashes…blood."

"I know," Leam said, dropping to his knees. He placed his hands along the top rim of the canister.

"Your shirt's torn. Who hurt you?"

"No one." Leam felt tears sting the backs of his eyes. "I brought it on myself."

"I don't believe that."

Jace's genuine concern led Leam's mind to thoughts about boundless strings of ivy.

"Did you ever know a woman named Aggie?" Leam asked, eyes on the canister, ears waiting for an answer. They waited for several moments.

"I just knew that there was an Aggie who died young."

Leam's fingers found a small circular recess just below the top of the cylinder. "Worth a shot," he muttered, flipping the lid open, his eyes quickly lost in the red wisps of rising vapor.

"Leam, what do you think you're doing? Be careful…"

Leam looked up at Jace with a half-smile. "It's nothing of which to be afraid." And he leaned in, his face directly over the canister, opening his mouth inhumanly wide as if preparing to take a monstrous bite out of the air. The tiny blood-red wisps forged into one thick plume of smoke that torpedoed into Leam's mouth with a horrid sound of suction and violent wind. His eyelids shuttered unnaturally, his legs thrown into spasms; his body, though, remained rigid. When the canister was empty, Leam keeled over, the noise falling dead. Jace grabbed Leam's hand, and with an awful grunt, lifted him to his feet.

The overhanging lights flicked on. Leam, even in a daze, knew it had only been a matter of time. The screen door flew open, smacking against the house. Larry burst out in an undershirt, tugging up the waist of his old-man pants. His eyes caught the nearest of his two trespassers first.

"Jace!" he exclaimed, halting mid-step, a mixture of fear and queasiness paralyzing the wrinkles on his face. The old man gawked at the hideous freak who was once, most likely, a healthy beautiful specimen.

"Wh-wh-what—what happened to you? Wh-where are your clothes?" Larry stuttered, grabbing at his lower back. "My god, your face, Jace! Is that you?"

"Go back inside," Jace said. Larry remained rooted, a finger pointed right at Leam.

"Dear Lord, it's you!" he roared. "You took her! He took Loey, Jace! I saw him earlier, he was right where he is now! I just finished with the police an hour ago!"

"Get inside!" Jace shouted, pushing out a magicless palm.

"They made a sketch of him only an hour ago!" Larry yelled. "An hour ago! An hour ago!"

Leam threw out his left palm—Larry's mouth snapped closed. And then the right palm—Larry slid like a snowboarder back inside the door, which banged closed behind him. Leam dropped his hands, coughing, choking down the last of the Gujin. With his tongue he could feel some of it sticking to the backsides of his teeth. As he peeked over at Jace, Larry's words still hung in the air.

"You took my daughter?" Jace asked. Leam could hear stifled tears. "Where? Where'd you go? Where is she?"

The jig was up. Leam thought to tell him everything. That it was Zach who had kidnapped Eloa. That *she*, not the Gujin, was the reason Leam had broken Jace free, to spare her the pain of that loss. It was all too complicated, though, and Leam was tired of complications. He decided on a simple, "It wasn't me."

"But she *has* been taken?"

"Yes."

"By Dark hands?"

"Yes," Leam said. "Yeah, they have her. I get you out and she goes in. It's a sick, sick world."

"And you knew all along?"

"It wasn't me, Frost." Leam could feel the muscles on his legs and arms starting to twitch; the Gujin, he guessed, setting in.

"How did I miss it?" Jace's voice had changed, as had his whole demeanor. His hands—as thick as bricks—were clenched into fists aside his hips. "Back at DHQ you said your brother heard your father speak of Gujin, but the problem there is that the only people who knew about it were the ones centrally involved in Break Lock. Anybody else with that knowledge would have to be a part of the group developing it." Jace took a step forward, nostrils flaring. "Darkness."

"I came to save you, like I said. I didn't have or want a part of anything else."

"You asked me what effect the gas has on those of Darkness. Did you think I'd miss that?" Jace took another step.

"You did miss it, Frost, until now."

The dawn of another revelation snuck out of Jace's eyes, and he said, "'Unprovoked by me, she's seeing a boy of Darkness.'"

Leam handed Jace a quizzical look as he shifted backward. The space between him and the front railing diminished as he prepared for the great beast to make his move.

"'*Unprovoked by me, she's seeing a boy of Darkness,*'" Jace repeated, now moving to Leam with unbroken steps. "Gideon said that to me weeks ago, but I didn't believe him."

"Gideon is a man of trickery and untruths."

"Even the most gifted liars can speak the truth, Leam." Jace lunged forward and snapped his hand out for Leam's throat. His advance, though, was impeded by an invisible surge of magic square to the chest.

"I'll have to stop you right there," Leam said.

"You're of Darkness, aren't you boy?" said this enormous man, standing on a porch in suburban New Jersey in nothing but a soiled loincloth. Leam almost laughed at the absurdity of it all.

"No need to say anything for breaking you out, by the way," Leam said. "Or for hopping on that grenade." He tossed his head at the steel-gray canister, lying on its side as empty as Leam's chances of being normal...of disappearing somewhere... away from people...since all he seemed to inflict on them was either anger or heartbreak. "Trying to grab my throat and choke me is thanks enough."

"You want a thank you?" Jace growled, clearly fighting against the spell that had immobilized him. His eyes were deranged.

Leam kicked the canister into the corner, where it wobbled like a tiring top.

"I just want to be left alone," he said, looking up at Jace. "I want to be alone forever."

And Leam hurdled the railing, darting across the yard, and then Stoneladen, in a flash. A month ago, the thought that he would one day cover forty yards in three steps would have sent him to the moon, which, suspended high above him, was fading away with the approach of daybreak. However in this moment, standing a few feet away from the heavy woodlands opposite Mary and Larry's house, Leam couldn't manage a smile.

He squeezed his eyes shut, fighting off itchy tears, trying to picture something, anything, to get his mind off of the toxic gas he could feel sticking to his insides.

And then it came...then *she* came...Eloa...shining in his mind...her body so close to his during those short few moments after their kiss but before his supposed betrayal, the sitting room's firelight blazing across her face as she leaned in close to whisper in his ear.

"Never doubt that you are good, Leam. You're proving it now."

Then the walls crumbled, the sitting room wiped clean from his mind, replaced by an infinite amount of greenish darkness. Eloa appeared again, this time behind thirty-three iron bars, steel-gray canisters spewing red smoke all around her, her beauty gone, her face, as sickly as the torchlight, nearly unrecognizable. She was a monster, her once perfect skin now marred by thousands of horrid, fluorescent-red veins.

Then the monster vanished, as did the bars, one by one, and the gloomy green light. Then Leam's mind—dark and blank for a moment—dropped him beneath a ceiling of fluorescent lights. He was at his desk, physics class, junior year, red smoke spewing inside the classroom through the vents in the walls. He turned to his left, to the Indian guy who always sat near the windows, the kid sniffing the air as a black trench coat slid up his legs and wrapped itself around him. Leam looked around. All his classmates were sniffing: some of them falling over, choking and red-faced; black trench coats wrapping around the rest. Leam's eyes went to the quiet girl at the end of the row, who stared at him and vomited a geyser of blood. She keeled over, her cherry-red glasses knocked askew as her lifeless face slid down a laminated poster of Sir Isaac Newton juggling apples. Then the apples and the glasses and the classroom got blurry, got fuzzy, and colorless, like television static.

How long the static took to clear Leam didn't know, but when it did, a bright image, distant and small, formed deep in the dark backdrop of his mind. A person, standing naked, like Da Vinci's Vitruvian man. Leam's heart pounded the inside of his chest like a bare-knuckled fist, his ribs rattling like dead wind chimes in their cage, because it was of himself, the image, and Leam had a good guess as to why it had appeared.

So across the darkness of his mind's eye Leam peered, trying, before his wits slipped away, to see if a red network of veins was strung all over the skin of this likeness, this small distant image. Or if a black trench coat was forming around it. Or, if Leam could just get a little closer, get a bit of a better look, if it appeared to be as dead as the quiet girl with the cherry-red glasses.

But it was too far off, too hazy through the poison that had seized his body, and was now, as Leam stood next to the tree line off Stoneladen Lane, steadily clouding his mind. He grabbed at his head—the gas was taking him, just as the bull had many times before, and Leam's last thought, before the Gujin consumed him whole, was of where he would be and what he would see if the invading blood-red fog was to ever clear.

———

Jace's eyes went to the wobbling canister, empty of the gas that had filled its belly, before flicking up at the boy of Darkness standing across the road. But without magic, what could he do to stop him?

Jace rubbed his temples, then ran his fingers over his naked stomach, coarse with protruding red veins. His thoughts drifted to Larry, to walking inside the good man's home and making an effort to explain. But instead Jace closed his eyes and let his thoughts drift further.

They had taken his powers, the evil men who had imprisoned him, but they had left something of much more value behind. His mind. For in that mind were the codes that would counteract every further breakout of Gujin7B that Gideon was sure to release. With the codes that made up Jace's formula, Counteractive Protection, a subdivision of Light's Department of Defense, would be able to create a magical lining over the earth that would instantly deactivate Gujin7B.

But still, Jace's head ached. And the ache came not from the gas that had poisoned him, although that probably had something to do with it, nor did it come for Eloa; he would stifle his emotions before they got away from him, follow protocol and create a plan to rescue her the moment the Light came for him, which he knew would be imminent. No, this headache was linked to his rescuer, the boy who called himself Leam.

The boy possessed incredible magical ability for someone his age—breaking the unbreakable prison bars and conjuring orbs for travel and escape—but Jace, the longer he thought about it, had the feeling this boy's uniqueness went far beyond mere skill. So what else was it about Leam that had struck him as odd? Was it something the boy had said?

Aggie. Aggie.

Yes, something he had said…something a little off.

"Did you ever know a woman named Aggie?"

Yes, that was it, of course.

So why would a boy of Darkness ask a man of Light about a woman named Aggie? A question spoken in longing tones; a question conveyed with the upmost importance as if the boy had been sitting on it for years; a question about a woman so obviously special to him; a question asked to a person of Light, because, evidently, no person of Darkness had ever had the answer.

And when the reason dawned on Jace, big gold calligraphic letters of a prophecy he had first read long ago, and had thought about every day since, slid across his mind, from right to left like tickertape, like football scores scudding along ESPN's bottom line, and as the last prophetic word swept past, it toed along the first of a second prophecy—Darkness's prophecy—which, in turn, streamed on by, dragging pictures into view, black and whites at first, the pictures, dating back to the beginning of Jace's hundred and ten years, terrible gruesome images he had seen stained on Unknowing newspapers and magazines and news programs, the pictures now flooding with color, on television screens, computer monitors, displaying unthinkable torture, mass shootings, animal cruelty, hate crimes, terrorist attacks—and the horrors worsened as they came, as the months and years neared the present, approaching a time when science and technology, despite the infinite opportunities for goodness their advancements were capable of inspiring, loomed dark and low over the pulse of a vulnerable planet.

But then...

...came a light.

Scrubbing his mind free of the horrific snap shots, and cleaning away the ugly thoughts they spawned, came a light. It was only a blink—it had shot onto the screen like a speed train, and had zipped off just as fast—but it had taken the darkness with it, and thankfully, mercifully, Jace saw only what was there, what was in front of his eyes and not inside his mind. A shoddy lawn, his daughter's car, a sidewalk, a street and a teenage boy at the edge of the woods who looked somewhere between sane and mad. That's what Jace could see, what was on the outside, what was visible.

Inside the boy...who knew?

ACKNOWLEDGEMENTS

My parents for their love and unceasing support. My sister for putting up with my antics all these years. Walt and Gay for their encouragement and a place to write. Melissa Johnson, my editor, for brilliant and much needed instruction and guidance. Lisa Marie Pompilio for capturing the mood through image. Dave, Ilene, and everyone at Denville Library. The row of desks at Morris County Library. Garrett, Janine, Ali, and those of you who read the work in progress. My friends for keeping me sane, or as sane as I can be, when I wasn't writing. My wife for her hard work, dedication, and beauty both external and internal. And all of you out there to ever offer encouraging words; gifts more necessary than one might think.

ABOUT THE AUTHOR

Bentz Deyo graduated from Drew University with a degree in Theater Arts. He currently lives in New Jersey with his wife and daughter. This is his first novel.

Made in the USA
San Bernardino, CA
25 February 2014